CASE CLOSED

HAUNTING AT THE HOTEL

THE CASE CLOSED SERIES

LAUREN MAGAZINER

CASE CLOSED

HAUNTING AT THE HOTEL

PICK YOUR PATH,

CRACK THE CASE

KATHERINE TEGEN BOOKS
An Imprint of HarperCollins Publishers

Katherine Tegen Books is an imprint of HarperCollins Publishers.

Case Closed #3: Haunting at the Hotel
Copyright © 2020 by Lauren Magaziner

Library of Congress Cataloging-in-Publication Data

Names: Magaziner, Lauren, author.
Title: Haunting at the hotel / Lauren Magaziner.
Description: First edition. | New York, NY : Katherine Tegen Books,
    an imprint of HarperCollinsPublishers, [2020] | Series: Case
    closed ; #3 | "Pick your path, crack the case." | Audience:
    Ages 8-12. | Audience: Grades 4-6. | Summary: "Carlos and
    his friends must help his mother solve a haunting in a remote
    hotel"-- Provided by publisher.
Identifiers: LCCN 2019045214 | ISBN 9780062676337 (hardcover)
    | ISBN 9780062676344 (paperback)
Subjects: LCSH: Plot-your-own stories. | CYAC: Mystery and
    detective stories. | Hotels, motels, etc.--Fiction. | Haunted
    places--Fiction. | Friendship--Fiction. | Plot-your-own stories.
Classification: LCC PZ7.M2713 Hau 2020 | DDC [Fic]--dc23
LC record available at https://lccn.loc.gov/2019045214

Typography by by Andrea Vandergrift
20 21 22 23 24   PC/LSCH   10 9 8 7 6 5 4 3 2 1

First Edition

To Robin Magaziner,

<u>STAND</u>
I

that you've been waiting

your your your your

```
        F      A      P
O                             P
E                             L
        S      U      A
```

Well, welcome to this page!

M U ALWAYS BELIEVE **E**

and

👁 ♥ U !

Flip **MOM** upside down, and that's the kind of parent you are.

Thank you for all your help with this series—
for buying the whiteboard, for hashing out my ideas with me,
and for distributing bookmarks to every human you've ever
talked to for exactly one second.

But mostly, thanks for being my forever best friend!
You are **MILONELION**.

DAY ONE

ELIZA IS DEAD wrong. It doesn't happen that often—because my best friend Eliza is a logical, puzzle-solving genius. But right now is one of those rare times when she's incorrect, and it feels like the Earth is tilting on its axis. As we pile out of the car, we shake our heads at each other.

"For the last time, Carlos," Eliza says, "there are no such things as ghosts."

Like I said: dead wrong.

"No such things as ghosts!" I scoff.

"That's what I said."

I pull my coat closer to me. It's not snowing at the moment, but there are a few inches of powder on the ground.

Mom had warned me about the snow and the altitude, but no one said anything about the wind-chill factor. The wind at the top of Sugarcrest Mountain is no joke. It's like being smacked in the face repeatedly with an icicle. It's especially cold now that the sun is starting to set.

"Eliza, *come on*."

1

"Prove there are ghosts," she says, her cheeks bright pink from the cold.

"Prove there aren't!"

She groans. "That's not how proof works. It's impossible to prove something doesn't exist. But very possible to prove something *does* exist."

"Well, of course there are ghosts!" I shout. "*Thousands* of people around the world have seen ghosts with their own eyes. What do you call *them*?"

"Wrong."

"Are they going to stop arguing soon?" Frank asks, tugging on my mom's sleeve.

Frank is Eliza's younger brother. He's a triple threat: loud, weird, and annoying. But after working on two mysteries together, I've actually grown fond of him. No one can crawl into small spaces or find random clues better than Frank.

Mom smiles at Frank. "Carlos and Eliza have been arguing about this for the last hour—why stop now?"

"I bet you already regret inviting us along," I tease.

Mom grabs my coat and pulls me into a side hug. "I was actually just thinking the opposite, mijo."

This isn't our first case, but this is the first case Eliza, Frank, and I have been *allowed* to be on. We've solved two cases before this, and we had to sneak our way into both of them.

Mom co-owns a detective agency with her partner, Cole. For a while, Las Pistas Detective Agency was in danger of going under. The first case we ever solved, at a millionaire's mansion, we flat-out stole from Mom to help save Las Pistas. Our second case was at a TV studio, on the set of my favorite show, and technically, we weren't allowed to be investigating. Mom caught us trying to solve her mystery. And we ended up working together.

The four of us teaming up worked so well that Mom decided to make us junior detectives for her next case . . . *this* case.

A ghost has been terrorizing the Sugarcrest Park Lodge, a small bed-and-breakfast at the top of a mountain. Nearly every night for the past six weeks, there's been some kind of haunting. Guests have been running away from the hotel screaming in the middle of the night. Nearly everyone who shows up has a harrowing ghost story. The reviews online have been terrible. The owner of the hotel, Reese Winters, hired us to save her quickly dying business and to stop this ghost before something truly horrible happens.

"So we're on a haunting case," I say to Eliza, "and you don't believe it could be a real ghost?"

"It can't be a real ghost," Eliza says, "because, again, there's no such thing as a real ghost."

I throw my hands up. "Unbelievable!"

Frank rolls a snowball in his hands and pelts it at me. It hits me in the neck, and ice slides down my back. I glare at him.

"What?" he says, blinking innocently. "A ghost did it!"

"Okay, okay, enough," Mom says, pausing at the shoveled path to the lodge's front door. "We're about to go in and make our first impression, and we have to be professional. That means no more fighting. The only way we're getting to the truth is if we gather as much information as possible and work as a team. And that means you both have to open your minds to each other's theories."

"What about ME?" Frank says.

"Empty your pockets," Mom demands.

Frank reaches into his pockets and takes a snowball out of each one.

"Again."

Frank sighs and pulls a second snowball out of each pocket.

"One last time."

Frank frowns. "But it's my snow pet! I've named her Snovember."

"Drop it!" Mom says, like she's talking to a dog with a ball.

4

Frank puts Snovember on the ground gently. Then smashes it with his foot. "I'm a yeti!"

"No snowballs, Frank," Mom scolds. "No farting in front of our client, either."

The hotel sits alone at the top of a peak. Not the highest peak in the mountain region, but we're high enough up that my ears started popping in the car. Mom has us drinking a lot of water to avoid altitude sickness.

There's almost nothing else around. No town. No supermarkets. No houses. The closest thing nearby is another hotel, a little ways down the mountain. That one is called the Super Hotel Express, and it looks about five times bigger.

But it isn't nearly as cute as the Sugarcrest Park Lodge, which has a log cabin feel to it. The outside is wood, with two chimneys made of tan stones. The fire is going right now—a cloud of smoke rises into the white sky.

"Looks like it's going to snow," Mom says, squinting up. "I'm sure it'll be a light flurry. Just a dusting."

Famous last words, I think with a gulp. Then I follow Mom as she heads inside.

The lobby of the Sugarcrest Park Lodge has a concierge desk in between two staircases that wrap around it. To the left, there's an open door to a fireplace lounge, with a rustic look. I walk closer to get a peek inside. There's a double-sided fire with couches encircling it, and a door in the back of the fire den that leads to the library, which I can tell because there's a sign that says QUIET IN THE LIBRARY . . . UNLESS YOU'RE PLAYING PIANO. THEN FORTE!

Which strikes me as *very* odd, because who puts a loud piano in a library? Unless maybe personal home libraries can break the rules.

I walk back to the lobby, where Mom, Eliza, and Frank are hovering. All around, the decorations are . . . awful, if I'm being honest. There are bearskin rugs everywhere. The walls have all sorts of stuffed animal heads—deer, moose, elk, and boars—with beads for eyes.

Eliza makes a disapproving noise as she looks at them.

"Don't worry. They're fake," says the woman at the front desk. She's younger than my mom. I'm really bad at guessing adult ages . . . but if I had to bet, I'd put her somewhere in her twenties. She's got bright blue hair, a nose ring, lots of colorful makeup on her pale face, and eyes that are two different colors: one blue and one green. She looks like a mermaid. "Welcome to the Sugarcrest Park Lodge," she says. "My name is Cricket

McCoy, your concierge. Checking in?"

"In a sense," Mom says. "We're the detectives from Las Pistas Detective Agency. Can you let Reese Winters know we're here?"

Her eyes widen. "Of course, yes." She opens a drawer and picks up a walkie-talkie. "Mrs. Winters, your detectives are in the lobby."

"Be right there," Reese Winters says through the speaker.

Cricket puts the walkie-talkie back in the drawer. "We're all so glad you're here! It's been, like, a spectacle around here lately. Like, ridiculously terrifying." She glances out the window, where the sun has gone down fast. "It's sundown. . . . I hope you're prepared."

"Prepared?" I ask.

"For the ghost," she says, nervously playing with the frayed ends of her hair.

"I am SO READY!" Frank shouts, pumping his fist in the air.

"You say that now. But it's a nightmare. We had thirteen cancellations *today* alone. Half of our guests have been ditching us in the middle of their stay. I've been asking permission to go home at sundown," Cricket says in a low voice, "so I can get out of here before the ghosts come. But sometimes Mrs. Winters makes me work well into the night, now that guests are checking out at like three in the morning. . . ."

"Is Mrs. Winters a good boss?" I ask.

"So good! Super good! Best boss ever!" Cricket says with a big smile. But her voice rises an octave.

She's lying.

I look at Eliza, who is busy staring at a piece of paper on the concierge desk. It's like she's not even paying attention to the conversation.

So I turn to Mom instead, and without even moving a muscle in her face, Mom's eyes flash. And somehow I know that she too noticed how Cricket's voice changed when she talked about Reese Winters.

There's a weird silence, which is Mom's favorite interrogation strategy. She likes to leave awkward pauses in the conversation to make people uncomfortable.

It doesn't work on Cricket, though. She clears her throat and stands up straighter behind the desk. "You can, like, wait near the fire for the Winters family. I'm sure they'll be down any moment." Then she turns back to the computer and starts typing.

Clearly, we've been dismissed.

We walk over to the fire den, only to find a round, white, middle-aged man already on a couch by the fire. Even though he's sitting, I can tell he's short. Probably not much taller than Mom. He has half-frame glasses, bags under his eyes, and a bit of stubble on his reddish face. He's definitely been up all night.

He's typing furiously into his laptop, while three books and a notebook lie open beside him.

Suddenly he looks at us. "Guests! Welcome!"

Mom holds out her hand. "I'm Cat Serrano. This is my son, Carlos. And his friends Eliza and Frank. Do you work here?"

"No," the man says. "I'm a guest too. The *only* guest brave enough to stay multiple nights, it seems. This place has been a ghost town lately." Then he chuckles at his own joke. "The name is Byron. Byron Bookbinder."

"So what are you still doing here, Mr. Bookbinder?" Mom asks.

"What does it look like I'm doing?"

Frank hums. "Blinking! No, wait, breathing! No wait, *both* at the same time. Very impressive."

"I'm writing," Byron says. "A nonfiction book. About ghost hauntings."

"So I take it it's not a coincidence that you ended up at this hotel?" Eliza says.

"No," Byron says. "This lodge has a ghostly history, and I wanted to check it out. Imagine my surprise to find my EMF reader going out of control."

"EMF reader?" I say while Eliza asks, "What ghostly history?"

Byron Bookbinder smiles, reaches into his bag, and

pulls out something that looks like a TV remote. "This is an EMF reader. EMF stands for electromagnetic field. Often you can't see a ghost, but you can *feel* it. As their spirits move through our world, there's a disruption in the electromagnetic field. When you see a red light, all is normal. But when you see a green light? A ghost is nearby!" he says excitedly.

"Does it ever go green?" I ask.

"It goes green every night I've been here. This place is flooded with ghosts."

"Let's push it now!" Frank says, reaching for the power switch.

"It's not a toy, young man," Byron says, and he tucks the EMF reader back into his bag.

"You were saying something about the history of this lodge?" Mom reminds Byron.

"Oh, yes. Very interesting story. About seventy years ago, six hikers stopped to stay in this lodge as they were climbing the summit. They broke in because the place was all boarded up. No heat, no food, no supplies. In the night, the storm got so bad that the lodge was almost completely buried under snow. By the time anyone found them . . ." He pauses. "Well, let's just say they no longer had need for oxygen. Legend has it that they've haunted this lodge ever since, still desperate to finish their climb."

"Six," I whisper. "Six people died here. Does that mean there are six ghosts?"

It seems suddenly colder in here, despite the blazing fire.

For a moment, I regret letting Mom bring me on this case. This was the first time she'd ever let me be a junior detective on one of her cases, and I wanted to be involved. I was afraid to say no, but now that I'm actually here? I'm afraid that I've said yes.

Afraid, because ghosts are terrifying. And afraid because I don't want to let Mom down. Now that she expects something of me, I feel more pressure than ever to prove that I really belong by her side as a detective.

Before we can ask Byron Bookbinder another question, three people step into the fire den. There's no doubt in my mind it's the Winters family, the owners of the hotel. We walk over to them, leaving Byron eagerly eavesdropping.

"So sorry to keep you waiting," says a woman with the most infectious smile. It's the first thing I notice about her. She is Asian, with sleek black hair that is pulled up in a ponytail, except for a swoop of bangs tucked behind her ear. She is wearing a suit and heels, and she has an air of perfection about her. Like she doesn't have to try to be so put together—she just *is*.

Naturally. "I'm Reese. This is my husband, Harris. And our daughter, January Winters."

Reese hasn't said more than four sentences, but everything about her radiates warmth. She's just one of those people who seem genuine and kind.

Her husband, Harris, is the opposite. He is a large, frowny guy in a plaid lumberjack shirt. He's white, with ginger hair tied up in a bun, an impressively thick beard, and moody gray eyes. He looks longingly out the window like he wishes he could be anywhere but here.

January Winters, their daughter, looks like she's about the same age as Eliza and me. Maybe a year older. Like her mom, January has shiny black hair. Like her dad, she has a downturned mouth. Unlike both of them, she's got big headphones on her ears.

"January, dear, don't be rude," her mom says, pulling the headphones down so that they rest on her neck. "You can listen to music later."

"I'm not listening to music," January grumbles. "I'm *making* music."

"Yes, dear, but you're in the hospitality business right now, not the deejay business." Reese turns to us with a dazzling smile. "You'll have to excuse her. She's learning."

January folds her arms.

Mom introduces us, and Reese shakes our hands—even Frank's, despite the fact that he holds out his hand like a limp noodle.

"If you all could follow me into the dining room," Reese says, "I've had Fernando prepare us a snack."

We wave goodbye to Byron Bookbinder, who looks disappointed that he's not invited to follow. The dining room is on the other side of the lobby, so we pass by Cricket McCoy again to get there. Cricket looks down at her feet as the Winters family walks by.

The dining room is just as rustic as the lobby, with snowshoes on the walls, a chandelier made of inter-twining antlers, a gnarled wood table, and a long wood bench on each side. There's someone already in here—a woman dressed in a housekeeper outfit. She's very slim, Asian, with short hair that tucks just under her ears. Her nostrils twitch as the Winters family walks in.

She doesn't like Reese and Harris. I can tell right away.

"Apologies," the woman says, in a very nonapologetic tone. "I didn't realize you needed this room. I was just dusting."

"Thank you, Sunny—if you could take the Serrano and Thompson luggage up to room 237."

"Of course," Sunny mumbles. She walks out of the

room, looking curiously behind her as she shuts the door.

Reese smiles. "We've put you in adjacent rooms— 237 and 236. But I wasn't sure how you'd want to divide up, so you can figure that out."

"Who was that?" Mom asks.

"Who? Oh, Sunny," Reese says. "She's my . . . er. Well, she's our housekeeper. She'll be changing your sheets and getting you an extra pillow—if you need it. Shall we sit?" She gestures to the benches on either side of the table. Without discussing it, the Winters family all sit on one side, while we sit on the other.

"This is a charming hotel," Mom says. "How long have you been here?"

Reese smiles. "I grew up here. My parents bought it when they immigrated, long before my sister and I were born. When they passed a few years ago, I took over. One day it will be January's."

January grunts. She doesn't look up from her phone.

All of a sudden, the doors open, and a man with a curled mustache comes in carrying a tray.

"Fried-a mozzarella, fresh-a to*mah*to salad, and espaghetti bites for you," the man says in a *very* fake Italian accent. He puts a tray in the middle of the table and bows. "Nice-a to meet you! I will be taking a-care of all your gastronomic needs."

"Huh?" Frank says.

"He'll be feeding us," Eliza translates.

The man smiles. "My name is Fernando di Cannoli, the greatest chef in all of Italy." He looks like he could be Italian, with his tan skin and dark hair. But his accent is *way* off.

"This looks delicious, Fernando, thank you," Reese says, and Fernando leaves the room. Harris, January, and Frank start eating the food.

But I'm too busy watching Mom, who opens her case notebook. If I know her, she'll skip the snacks and get straight to business. But to my surprise, she looks at me. Like she's waiting for *me* to ask a question.

Maybe I should. . . .

TO ASK ABOUT THE DETAILS OF THE RECENT HAUNTINGS, TURN TO PAGE 494.

←——→

TO ASK WHEN AND HOW THE HAUNTINGS FIRST STARTED, TURN TO PAGE 423.

"YOU MUST HAVE observed some tension between the Winters family and the hotel staff," I say. "Have you noticed any fights?"

"Indeed," Byron says. "As an outside observer to all the trouble at the Sugarcrest Park Lodge, I'm constantly surprised how often people don't care if they fight in front of me. As a transient fixture in this moment in time, I am the perfect fly on the wall."

The way Byron speaks drives me nuts. He has this snobby, self-important way about him.

"Okay," I say, trying to shake off my annoyance, "but *what* did you hear?"

"What didn't I hear?" he says with a chuckle. "An uproar between all three members of the Winters family. A phone quarrel between Cricket and a mystery person. A squabble between Reese and Luther. A spat between January and Sunny."

"A spit?" Frank says.

"A spat," Eliza corrects.

But it's too late—Frank is already dribbling a string of spit. Then he sucks it back in his mouth with a loud slurp.

I roll my eyes. "What were they all fighting about?" I ask Byron.

"I distinctly heard the words 'You don't understand me at all!' bellowed from the youngest Winters to her parents—typical adolescent behavior. I believe that Reese and Luther were having their usual dispute about selling the Sugarcrest Park Lodge. And January and Sunny were speaking in hushed tones. Much too soft to hear. But their facial expressions indicated antagonism. Yes, they were very angry with each other. And of course I only heard one side of Cricket's telephone conversation, but she sounded rather distressed."

I wonder what *that* could be about. Who could Cricket have been talking to? Would January and Sunny even have a reason to interact outside of common pleasantries? Luther and Reese's beef, we already knew about. But how far would Luther go to get the Sugarcrest Park Lodge in his clutches?

I look at Byron, who is puffing on his glasses and cleaning the lenses with a handkerchief. "Mr. Bookbinder, do you think any of them could be the ghost?"

"Absolutely not!" he says, outraged. "The ghosts are the six hikers I've been telling you about—the ones who perished in this very room. If you are *truly* after the mystery of these spectral beings, then you must follow the history! The history will lead you right!"

TO ASK BYRON ABOUT THE HISTORY
OF THE HIKERS, TURN TO PAGE 122.

←——→

TO END THE CONVERSATION, TURN TO PAGE 201.

"**WE HAVE TO** go looking for that dog," I say. "Before it attacks someone else."

January nods and cautiously opens the door. The lobby is empty and cold. The front double doors are still open, with wind flinging snow inside. Snowbanks are piled high inside the lodge. January runs across the lobby, toward the right staircase.

"Come on!" she calls to us, but Eliza and I are taking it slower, elbows linked.

The lights flicker. For an instant, I see nothing.

Then—

There.

Right behind January. The ghost has no features on its face—just a round black circle where a mouth would be, and two round black circles for eyes. Empty, soulless black pits. Its body is bent in the wrong shape. Clawed hands reach out—

"January, look behind—"

It grabs her, and she shrieks. The *thing* drags her backward, up the stairs, as January cries, "Help! Please!"

We run after her.

When we get to the top of the stairs, the monstrous ghost thing is halfway down the hall with January. It's crawling backward, arms and legs spiderlike. January reaches out to us.

Behind January, behind the ghost, the door to the

Dead Room is wide open. My blood runs cold. Kicking and struggling, January is being dragged inside.

TO FOLLOW THEM INTO THE DEAD ROOM,
TURN TO PAGE 319.

←——→

TO RUN AWAY, TURN TO PAGE 146.

I DECIDE TO confront Harris first about the glowing footprints. From our interview with the whole Winters family yesterday, it was clear to me that he was hiding something.

We check Harris's office first, but he's not there. So instead I go upstairs to his room. I can tell right away which door belongs to Reese and Harris. It's much fancier than the others, and it seems to have a special passcode system that involves symbols instead of numbers. I raise my fist to knock, but Frank steps between the door and me.

"Allow me!" Then he starts hammering the door—his fists are like mallets, and the poor door is like a whack-a-mole game.

"All right already! I beg you, please stop!" we hear from the other side of the door. Harris opens it, looking haggard. His beard is tangled, and his blue eyes are bloodshot. He's wearing lumberjack-plaid pajamas. "I was trying to take a nap," he says. "I don't do three a.m. as well as I used to in my younger years. Is this really that urgent?"

"Yes," I insist. "May we come in?"

He sighs and stands aside, and we file in.

"What's this about?" Harris demands.

"This is going to sound like a weird request," I say. "But we really need to see your shoes."

20

"My . . . shoes?" He scrunches up his face for a second. "Is this relevant to the case? Or just a weird kid thing?"

"Case relevant," Eliza and I say together while Frank says, "Weird kid thing."

"Okay," Harris says, still confused. He leads us to his closet, where he has six pairs of shoes. Eliza and I start checking the bottoms of them, while Frank hangs a pair of flip-flops on his ears.

"Is this it?" Eliza asks Harris.

"Everything but my loafers. They went missing a few weeks ago. I keep forgetting to order a new pair—*that's* what I should do today."

Could these missing shoes be the pair we're looking for? But if Harris says he lost them . . . then who has them?

"Feels like we've hit a wall," Eliza says. "It seems silly to look for a pair of shoes that went missing weeks ago when we have lots of ghost-haunting clues to examine. Especially since we don't know for certain that those shoes are the ones that made the glowing prints."

"Still, it wouldn't hurt to check on Fernando di Cannoli or Byron Bookbinder in the meantime. Just in case their shoes are the ones that made the prints."

"Fair. You pick, Carlos," Eliza says. "What does your gut tell you?"

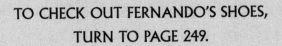

TO CHECK OUT FERNANDO'S SHOES,
TURN TO PAGE 249.

←→

TO CHECK OUT BYRON'S SHOES,
TURN TO PAGE 185.

"I'M SORRY, CRICKET," I say. "But we have to tell Reese what you and Luther were up to. She's the one who hired us, and it's our job to tell her whatever we find."

"WAIT!" Cricket says, a layer of sweat forming on her forehead. "Wait! Please! Before you do, I just want to show you something important," she says, gesturing behind her to a door under the stairwell. "A secret tunnel that twists throughout the house," she says, opening the door.

"In here?" Frank says, crawling in. "Really?"

Eliza and I stand at the entrance to the door. "Why are you showing us thi—*ahhhhh!*"

Hands have suddenly shoved me from behind. I tumble forward, with Eliza. The door locks behind us.

"Hey!" I shout. "This is just a closet!" A mothball-smelling, dust-filled closet. "Let us out of here!"

"Not until you learn to butt out of other people's business," Cricket says.

"Butt." Frank giggles.

"And learn some manners!"

THANK YOU for locking me in this closet.

Now PLEASE may I have a do-over?

CASE CLOSED.

WE MOVE TO the monitor.

"Where's the popcorn?" Frank asks.

I ignore him and lean closer to the screen. Apparently there are hidden cameras in almost every room in the lodge, all livestreaming back to this command center. The monitor is split into nine squares, and I can see Cricket in the lobby from two different angles, Byron and Harris in the fire den, Sunny in the guest hallway, and Fernando in the kitchen. I can also look into the empty library, an unoccupied dining room, a bare hallway of employee housing, and the hallway where Reese and Harris have their professional offices.

"This is the boringest movie EVER," Frank complains. "Nothing's happening!"

"Do you see Mom?" I ask, looking for any signs of her lurking just out of view.

"No . . . she's not in any of these shots."

"Come on, she has to be! Where *is* she?"

"She has to be in someone's room," Eliza says. "It's the only logical answer."

"Well, what about these spaces between the walls? Clearly there are a lot of secrets about this house we don't understand yet."

"Or," Eliza continues, like she didn't even hear me, "she could have gone down the hill to interview Luther Covington. And maybe she got trapped down there when the storm came. You heard Harris—the landlines and cell towers are out."

"I wish we could rewind these cameras. Then we could see what happened to her when she disappeared from right behind us!"

"Maybe she's sledding," Frank says.

Eliza and I look at him.

"*Sledding?* Really?"

He shrugs. "That's what I would do."

I squint at all the people moving around on the monitor. I still don't have a clue who might be behind the hauntings. Maybe I should look at the table.

TO LOOK AT THE PAPERS ON THE TABLE,
TURN TO PAGE 413.

"THIS WAY!" I say, pulling Mom over to the mud at the bottom of the slide. The ghost, I can see, is following us carefully, slipping in between the cloths quicker than a breeze.

My shoes sink in the mud, and still the ghost person follows us. I can hear the squelch of its shoes in the mud . . . just a little bit farther, and we've got 'em.

Splat.

A mudball hits me in the face. I didn't even have enough warning to close my eyes, let alone my mouth, and now I'm spitting out mud. My eyes are stinging—I can't see a thing. More mudballs come flying our way; Mom gets hit with them too. And that provides the ghost with the perfect cover to escape.

When Reese and the cops come to the basement, it is ghostless, and we are empty-handed.

Reese makes sure to tell the press all about our failure in solving her case. She's forced to sell her hotel to Luther Covington, and we are out of business. Back at square one, with Mom's agency's reputation in tatters.

When I signed up to be a detective, I thought *I'd* be doing the mudslinging at suspects . . . and not the other way around.

CASE CLOSED.

THE LODGE ISN'T *that* big—we should be able to find Byron, Cricket, and January somewhere inside.

"Thank you," I say to the group. "Stay here. We just have to . . . check something out."

Sunny raises her eyebrows, and Fernando squints at us. But they don't follow.

"What are you doing, Carlos?" Eliza whispers when we're in the hall.

"I'm thinking we should find the missing suspects. If we're quick enough, we might be able to catch our ghost."

"So," Eliza says, "you're looking for Byron and January? I must admit, Byron leaving his computer behind does seem like he left in an urgent hurry. He wouldn't leave that behind if he was headed up to his room."

"And Cricket," I say, gesturing to Cricket's empty desk. "Didn't Cricket say that Reese now makes her work nearly all night because guests have been checking out at three in the morning? Well, she's not at her post. So where is she?"

"I don't know, and I DON'T CARE!" Frank says.

Thump!

What was that? The ghost again? I look up the stairs, toward the second floor of the hotel. That's where the sound came from. "Maybe we should go see what that noise was," I say.

"No, Carlos, don't you see? We can't leave yet. This is an amazing opportunity! We can actually search Cricket's desk while she's not here. Don't you want to see if . . ." Eliza trails off. Her eyes go out of focus as she stares at Cricket's desk. That's the *second* time she's stared into space at the desk. The first was when we had just met Cricket.

"Okay, what is it?" I ask.

"Yeah!" Frank says. "You're being weird!"

"I think," Eliza says, her eyes bright, "I see a clue in plain sight on Cricket's desk."

Thump.

That sound again.

I can't be in two places at once, so I have to choose.

TO CONTINUE SNOOPING THROUGH
CRICKET'S DESK, TURN TO PAGE 125.

←——→

TO FOLLOW THE SOUND UPSTAIRS,
TURN TO PAGE 276.

I PULL THE grape lever, and I hear a click.

But it isn't the freezer door releasing. It's the sound of the levers getting locked in place. I try to tug and pull, but they're *all* frozen, right where they are.

"Bad news," I say. "It wasn't the grape lever."

Frank groans. "I gon' be tuck here fowever, awen't I?" he says, with his tongue still trapped on the pole.

I don't have the heart to answer him. Because yes, we'll be stuck here until Fernando di Cannoli needs something out of the freezer. And who knows how long that will be?

Man, I regret pulling the grape lever. Our investigation ended up being really unfruitful.

CASE CLOSED.

I TURN THE lock on Fernando's safe to thirty, and it clicks open. We can *finally* see what he was so desperate to hide when we walked in before. I'm thinking money or jewels or ghost-haunting materials, like glow-stick liquid.

Instead, there is a letter.

> DEAR MR. DI MARCO,
>
> THANK YOU FOR LETTING ME KNOW ABOUT YOUR CLAIM. I WILL GLADLY PROVIDE WITNESS TESTIMONY REGARDING THE IRRESPONSIBLE ACTIONS OF THE OWNERS OF THE SUGARCREST PARK LODGE. I UNDERSTAND YOU WANT COMPENSATION ONLY, BUT I STRONGLY URGE YOU—FOR THE WELL-BEING OF ANY FUTURE EMPLOYEES THAT MAY STRAY ACROSS REESE'S PERILOUS PATH—TO SHUT DOWN HER BUSINESS FOR GOOD. I WILL HELP YOU IN ANY WAY YOU DEEM NECESSARY.
>
> LUTHER COVINGTON

"Covington!" I say.

"Reese's perilous path?" Eliza says. "Shut down their business for good? This all sounds like a ghost-haunting plan in the hatching."

30

"I knew Luther was a snake! Who is Mr. di Marco, though?" I ask, and Eliza shrugs.

We're about to close the safe when Frank cries out. "Wait! Look at THIS!" He sticks his arm *all* the way in, reaching into the very back, a spot in the shadows I could barely see. He pulls out a driver's license. It has Fernando di Cannoli's picture, but someone else's name: Stefano di Marco.

"Mystery solved!" I say. "Kind of. Our chef has a real name and a fake identity. But which is which?"

Eliza raises her eyebrows at me. "You think Fernando di Cannoli sounds more real than Stefano di Marco?"

"You never know." Mom taught me not to assume. And if I want to impress her on this case, I need to take all her advice into account. And speaking of Mom, I want to hear what she has to say about all this.

"Mom!" I say into the walkie-talkie. "Code red. We need you to come to the kitchen ASAP. Alone. Repeat: code red. Over."

"Ten-four," she says to me. Radio speak for "Got it." She's there within minutes, out of breath.

"Did you run here?" I ask her.

"You said code red! That's an emergency code!" she says. "I was outside, digging through—"

"We don't have time," I interrupt, glancing at the

31

clock on the wall. Ten minutes have come and gone. How much longer can January delay Fernando? I hand Luther's letter and the driver's license to Mom. "We found Fernando hiding these."

Mom frowns as she looks at both our clues. "Well, this is interesting."

And she doesn't say anything more. But Eliza, I can tell, is eager to talk about this some more. "Yes, we thought it was interesting too," Eliza prods. "Why would Fernando go by a false name? And why is he corresponding with Luther?"

"Does this give Fernando motive or means?" I add, hoping I'm impressing Mom as much as Eliza no doubt is.

"Fernando already had means, just by working at the lodge," Mom says. "I do feel like this letter might contain clues to Fernando's potential motive."

Footsteps! I can hear them coming down to the kitchen.

Eliza, Frank, and I freeze in panic. But Mom, a true professional, doesn't skip a beat. She hastily shuts the painting closed to conceal the storage space behind it. "We have to hide."

"But where?" Eliza says.

We all look to Frank, who is *by far* the best at hide-and-go-seek.

"There!" he says, pointing to four industrial-sized trash cans on the other side of the kitchen. "Or there!" he says, pointing to the big metal door that leads to the walk-in freezer.

"I am *not* hiding in a trash can," Eliza gags.

"I am *not* hiding in a freezer," Mom says, wrapping her sweater tightly around her body.

"Well, we have to hide somewhere!" I snap. The doorknob to the kitchen is turning. We only have seconds!

TO HIDE IN THE TRASH CANS,
TURN TO PAGE 113.

←——→

TO HIDE IN THE WALK-IN FREEZER,
TURN TO PAGE 267.

"HAVE YOU SEEN a ghost, Cricket?"

"No, I run and hide before it gets to that point! Ghosts completely *freak me out*." She tucks a lock of blue hair behind her ear. "I've seen the effects of the ghost haunting—the fog, the broken windows, the creepy messages. And I've heard those horrible howls, so technically I've, like, *heard* the ghost. I just haven't seen any dead people floating around glowing and stuff."

"And what about other people in the house?" I ask. "Do you notice if anyone's missing during the hauntings?"

"Not really—like I said, I usually hide when something starts up. You can call me a coward," she says, "but this is, like, not a job worth dying for. I bet my coworkers feel the same way."

TO ASK CRICKET WHAT IT'S LIKE TO WORK FOR THE WINTERS FAMILY, TURN TO PAGE 107.

←——→

TO ASK WHAT SHE THINKS OF HER COWORKERS, TURN TO PAGE 325.

34

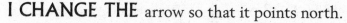

I CHANGE THE arrow so that it points north.

Instantly the room begins to shake.

"Uh . . . is it just me? Or is this room getting smaller?" Eliza says.

I look to my right and then my left—and there's no mistake. Two of the walls are closing in.

"Push on it!" Mom shouts, taking one side with Frank, while Eliza and I take the other.

No matter how hard we push and dig our heels in, the walls keep squeezing tighter and tighter until we are standing, all four of us, in a row. A wall presses in on my back, while the other wall presses in on my front. I don't even have room to shimmy sideways.

"A Frank sandwich!" Frank says, the only one of us amused by this turn of events.

"We're stuck!" Eliza says.

"Like peanut butter!"

"This isn't a sandwich, Frank!"

"Peanut butter sandwich," he says, clearly not even listening to me, "but where's the jam?"

"Don't you see?" Mom says. "The jam is exactly what we're in."

CASE CLOSED.

WE WAIT FOR Mom and Eliza to return . . . and we wait . . . and we wait . . .

We wait until the sun rises. And then we wait when the sun sets again.

"They're clearly missing," I say to Frank. "Maybe we should go look for them now?"

"Sit. Stay. Good doggie," Frank says, patting my head.

We are still sitting and waiting when we hear screams outside our door. We sit and wait as the doorknob to our room turns. We sit and wait as the lights flicker and then die. We sit and wait as a ghost comes creeping in, clawed hands outstretched.

"Wait!" I shout at the ghost.

But attacking ghosts do not wait. Ready or not, here it comes. . . .

CASE CLOSED.

I APPROACH THE coffin first. Please don't let January be in the coffin. *Please.*

I slowly lift the coffin lid—and there is *something moving inside it.*

No—a million things moving inside it!

Cockroaches. Hundreds of cockroaches crawling on top of each other, crawling to get out.

"SHUT IT!" Eliza shrieks. Bugs are her biggest fear.

I close the lid, but it's too late. Hundreds—no, thousands—have already escaped into the room. I am screaming, Eliza's screaming, Frank's screaming, Mom's screaming as cockroaches scurry up our legs, across our torsos, up our necks, and on our faces. . . .

These cockroaches are revolting, sure. But nothing bugs me more than not being able to finish my investigation.

CASE CLOSED.

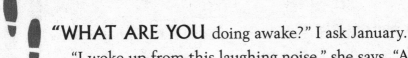

"**WHAT ARE YOU** doing awake?" I ask January.

"I woke up from this laughing noise," she says. "And then I thought I saw Fernando walking across the landing. Did you find out what he's hiding? I didn't see you again after you dismissed me from your circle."

"No, we didn't find out what he's hiding," I say.

"Maybe you should have accepted my help after all," January gloats.

Then she moves to the door of the fire den and opens it a crack. While her back is turned, I catch Eliza's eye. She smiles weakly; she's shaking off her run-in with that dog.

January turns around, tucking a lock of her black hair behind her ear. "Okay, I don't see the dog anywhere. Should we make a run for it?"

"And go where?" I ask.

"I don't know," January says, annoyed. "To find the owner of the dog, maybe? Or to figure out who's out of bed? You're the detectives—not me! Where do we go next?"

We? What *we*?

TO GO LOOKING FOR THE DOG, TURN TO PAGE 18.

←——→

TO HIDE FROM THE DOG, TURN TO PAGE 144.

I **NEED TO** know Fernando's alibi for last night, right around when the footprints appeared. If he can't account for those hours, then maybe he's guilty.

"What were you doing last night at three in the morning?"

"Sleeping?" Fernando says.

"Can anyone verify that?"

"No," he says.

"Then how do we know you're telling the truth?"

Fernando shrugs. "I'm not concerned whether you think I'm telling the truth. I was asleep. That's the truth." He looks at his watch nervously. "Is that everything? If I don't get dinner started, Mrs . . . ah . . . she'll have my head." He's still afraid to say *Mrs. Winters*.

He's getting too jumpy as a witness. I feel like, unfortunately, this is all we're going to get out of him. But Eliza jerks her head—a little gesture that I know means she wants me to dig into Fernando's alibi more. I don't know if that's a good idea. Sometimes it's best to call it quits and try again later. But Eliza makes the movement again. "Go on!" she mouths.

> **TO PRESS FERNANDO ABOUT HIS ALIBI,**
> **TURN TO PAGE 435.**
>
> ⟵⟶
>
> **TO LEAVE THE KITCHEN, TURN TO PAGE 138.**

"WE'LL HAVE A snowball fight," I say. "But first we have to talk to Reese."

I drag him to Reese's office, and he is looking severely unhappy as I knock on the door.

"Come in." Reese is sitting behind her desk, looking rather tired with dark circles under her eyes. She sighs and slouches in her chair. "Can I help you?"

"Yes," I say.

"No," Frank pouts.

"I have to know . . . why didn't you want to hire detectives?"

"But I did hire detectives," Reese says.

I'm flubbing this. "Yeah, but Harris said you didn't want to hire detectives, not even after your hotel was being haunted and your business was crashing and burning. So what was that about?"

She frowns. "Harris has a big mouth."

"I just think he has nothing to hide," I say. Unlike you, I add inside my head. I don't say it, but I think I've already pretty much implied it.

"I . . . I have done something so shameful," Reese says. "A few years ago, I—"

"Snowball fight!" Frank interrupts.

"What?"

"Snowball fight! I've waited long enough—I want a snowball fight."

40

"No, what to *Reese*, not to you. You be quiet, Frank!"

Uh-oh. That was the wrong thing to say. He puffs his cheeks out and stands up on his chair. "SNOW-BALL FIGHT SNOWBALL FIGHT SNOWBALL FIGHT!" He picks up different snowglobes and paper-weights and mugs off Reese's shelf and starts throwing them across the room. "SNOWBALL FIGHT!"

"Frank, no! Frank, stop!"

"My parents' heirlooms!" Reese cries.

"I'll have a snowball fight with you! Just stop this!"

"TOO LATE!" Frank says, and I lunge at him and put him in a headlock. "REGULAR FIGHT, REGU-LAR FIGHT!" he cries with glee.

We roll around in Reese's office.

Frank, breaking everything he can get his hands on.

Me, accidentally breaking things in an attempt to stop him.

And Reese, shrieking at the top of her lungs.

Maybe I should just have given him that snowball fight after all.

CASE CLOSED.

OKAY, I'M DONE deciphering the doorknob twist message.

"'Key is hidden behind the deer head. But antlers have a pattern. Go outside for the answer.'" I'm not sure this answer is any clearer than the numbers. "Antlers have a pattern? What's that supposed to mean?"

Eliza squints at the message. "Do you think . . . that maybe we have to press the antlers in a particular order? And something out in the grounds will give us the answer?" She frowns. "Only . . . it will be really hard to go outside, since we're totally snowed in."

"How would Mom even know this about the key?"

"It's a trap!" Frank sings.

The doorknob turns twice for no.

"Let's go," I say. Whether it's a trap or not, I can't just leave this alone. Not when there's a chance that it really is Mom behind the Dead Room door.

We lace up our boots and grab our coats, and run to the front door.

"What are you doing?" Cricket says as we pull on the doorknob. We're met with a wall of snow, six feet high. "We're snowed in!"

"Doesn't hurt to try," I say.

"Hey, how did your conversation with Reese go?" Eliza asks.

Cricket grins. "Surprisingly awesome! She was, like,

super understanding and really forgiving. But obvi I can never do anything like that again, or I'm fired."

"Well, I'm glad you worked it out," I say, trying to move the conversation along. Mom is waiting for me. "We've gotta run." Then I pull Frank and Eliza toward the kitchen, where I know there must be a delivery door for groceries.

We try the door in the kitchen. We try the door in the library. Both doors have a giant snowbank, keeping us locked in.

We catch our breath in the fire den, with Byron Bookbinder typing away on his laptop. He doesn't look up at us . . . so I guess he hasn't noticed that we stole the EMF reader.

That's when I remember the letter we never looked at—the one we took from his briefcase. I dig through Eliza's bag, but it isn't there.

"What are you looking for?" Eliza asks.

But I can't tell her in front of Byron. My heart sinks—I can't believe we lost it.

"Look!" Frank says, yanking on a window. For a second, I think it's going to be useless—totally frozen over. But then it wobbles. Maybe we *can* get out through the window. The fire den is up on a slope, so the snowbank is level with the bottom of the window. Yes, this could totally work.

"What are you doing?" Byron says, looking up from his computer. "You'll let the heat escape."

"I'm going to pass out. It's so hot—I think I'm going to faint," Eliza lies. Her cheeks turn pink, like they always do when she's lying. But it actually makes her story more believable.

"Let me help," Byron says, coming over to the window. With the four of us, we yank the window open. Frank pushes the snow aside, and there's a perfect crack, just big enough for a kid to fit through. At least we know our suspects won't follow us out here.

"I need air," Eliza says, crawling out the window and onto a bed of snow.

"I should go with her," I say, "to make sure she's okay."

Behind me, Frank pauses. "Made-up excuse," he says to Byron, and I try not to groan. Then Frank follows me out the window.

The storm last night was no joke. The snowfall has died down, but the wind is still harsh and cold, smacking snow into my face and down the front of my coat. There are pieces of tree branches everywhere— probably scattered from the wind. I had expected the snow to be powdery since it's so fresh, but the frigid temperature has frozen much of it into ice chunks.

Outside the lodge, there's a hot tub and an outdoor

firepit. There's a shed with a sign that says OUTDOOR EQUIPMENT SHED. And there's a gated area, a little bit down the slope, that looks like a creepy garden. With a fountain and some iron statues. I bet it's nice in the summer, but now that it's December, the whole place is totally blown over with snow.

"'Key is hidden behind the deer head. But antlers have a pattern. Go outside for the answer,'" Eliza recites.

"Well, we're outside," I say. "I don't see an answer."

"We have to keep looking. Maybe it's in the equipment shed. It would be a good place to hide a deer head. Or a clue to a key."

"Isn't that technically *inside*?" I say. "Mom told us to look *outside* for the answer." I keep my eyes focused on the gated garden area. From far away, those statues look almost like deer or moose or elk. That has to be important, right?

TO CHECK OUT THE EQUIPMENT SHED,
TURN TO PAGE 358.

←——→

TO CHECK OUT THE GATED GARDEN,
TURN TO PAGE 430.

45

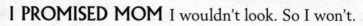

I PROMISED MOM I wouldn't look. So I won't.

"Mom!" I shout, reaching my arm behind me. "Grab my hand!"

"Get away!"

"Mom! Grab ahold!"

She shrieks.

"Mom?"

I reach my hand back as far as it can go, and something wet touches my palm . . . like someone has licked it. I shudder and pull my hand back.

"Mom? Mom!" I cry.

I don't hear her anymore.

I promised her I wouldn't turn back. But it means I had to turn my back on her.

CASE CLOSED.

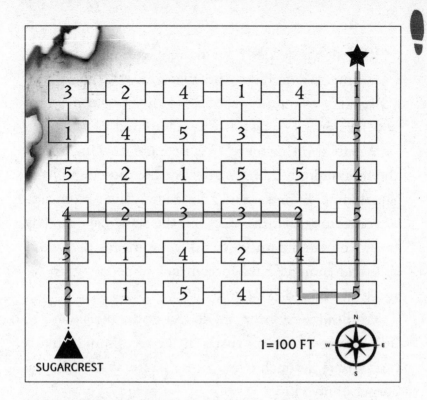

3	2	4	1	4	1
1	4	5	3	1	5
5	2	1	5	5	4
4	2	3	3	2	5
5	1	4	2	4	1
2	1	5	4	1	5

1=100 FT

SUGARCREST

"I THINK WE'VE got it!" I say. "Now let's go find . . . whatever it is we have to find!"

Outside, the storm is raging, and the windchill must be negative a thousand degrees—I've never been so cold in my life. But I tuck myself farther into my coat and walk to the back of the lodge.

That's when I see them: fresh tracks in the snow. Human ones. Starting from the firepit and disappearing over the crest of the mountain.

"Do you think someone's going where we're going?"

"I think someone *went*," I say.

"Follow the leader!" Frank says, running after the footprints. Mom takes the map and the flashlight. "Okay, let's count our paces. According to our map, we have to start by going north two hundred feet. . . ."

We follow the map, twisting and turning across the mountain, heading vaguely in the direction of the Super Hotel Express. And I don't know if it's promising or concerning that the tracks in the snow have already taken the same path we're on. That means that we're probably going to have to confront someone when we reach our final destination.

We head away from the lodge, down the slope . . . into the woods. Every rustle in the trees sounds like a bear to me. I flinch every time I see a shadow in the corner of my vision.

"You are so jumpy!" Eliza says.

"Of course I am! We're following a ghost trail."

"A human trail."

"Does it really matter right now?" I snap. My voice echoes in the cold, dark night. "I'm sorry," I say to Eliza. "I'm just really . . ." Afraid.

But I don't want to say it out loud. I *can't* say it. Because I don't want Mom to know how scared I really am. I don't want her to think I'm a bad detective—or that it was a mistake to bring me here.

Mom puts her arm on my back. "I feel a little jumpy

too, hijo. I don't love being out in the wilderness at night. In a snowstorm. Where there's no cell service. With a cornered criminal on the loose."

"How do you not let it affect you, Mom?"

"I guess I try to focus on one task at a time and push through my fear. On this case specifically, I've reminded myself that we're here together."

I nod.

At last we reach the final direction: north one hundred feet.

It puts us right in front of a cave. It's wholly dark inside—like a little black hole in the middle of a mountain.

"D-do we go in?" Eliza shivers.

"Aye!" Frank says.

"We have to warm up somewhere," Mom says. "If we stay out in the wind too long, we'll freeze."

One task at a time. Push through fear. Remember we're here together. "Yes," I whisper.

"That's three yes votes," Eliza says. "And for the record: one no."

And even though Eliza is the only no vote, she steps into the cave first. Smart and brave. You do *not* want to mess with my bestie.

I click on my flashlight and follow.

The cave walls are craggy, lined with shelves of paint

(both spray paint and brush paint), masks, bodysuits, and all sorts of horror costume pieces. Eliza shudders as we pass a shelf of creepy broken dolls. I shudder as we pass a shelf of ventriloquist dummies.

"This is awesome!" Frank says. And as we get farther into the cave, there is a desk with sound-mixing equipment, which I recognize from our last case at a TV studio.

"The cave is getting smaller," Eliza whispers, and I realize she's right. The ceiling is sloping down.

At last we reach a wall . . . the end of the cave. And I'm confused. We followed footprints in the snow to this very spot—I really thought we would be confronting our ghost.

"Carlos?" Eliza says nervously. She points her flashlight to the mouth of the cave, where a figure stands in shadow.

I feel Mom tense beside me.

"Ghost! Ghost! Ghost!" Frank says, like a blaring alarm. But we don't need his warning: we all see it. Gliding toward us. In my flashlight beam, all I can see is one yellow eye peeking out from behind long, tangled hair.

I shudder.

Frank nudges me gently, and I look down. He's shining his flashlight on his pockets, which are *packed* with snowballs. Should I throw one at the ghost?

Or should I take away the ghost's source of light? If I turn off the flashlights, the ghost can't see us . . . and then it can't hurt us.

TO THROW A SNOWBALL AT THE GHOST,
TURN TO PAGE 337.

←——→

TO TURN OFF THE FLASHLIGHTS,
TURN TO PAGE 266.

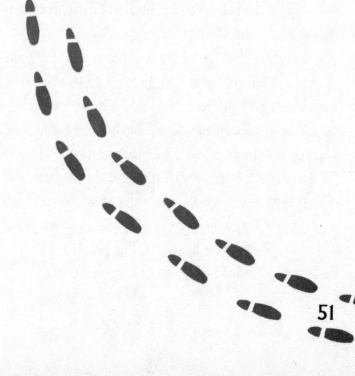

51

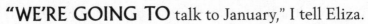

"WE'RE GOING TO talk to January," I tell Eliza.

We walk into the dining room. January has her thick headphones on and doesn't seem to notice us until we're right next to her. She hits pause on her music and looks up at us with an expression of pure boredom. "Can I help you?"

"What are you listening to?" Eliza asks.

"A mix I made."

"I thought you wanted to learn video editing, not sound editing?"

"Where did you hear that?" she says, kicking her feet up on the table.

"Your dad."

"Yeah, I'm into *both*. Which Dad would know if he ever paid attention to my interests instead of this dumb hotel."

Dumb hotel? It's not news that she's pretty unhappy. But is January actively bringing about the hotel's demise, or is she just practicing a normal level of disrespect? I remember suddenly what Harris said about January going through her tween angst, fighting with her mom. Maybe I should ask about that. Or I can skip right to an accusation, just to see how she'll react.

TO ASK JANUARY WHY SHE'S FIGHTING WITH HER MOM, TURN TO PAGE 165.

←——→

TO ACCUSE JANUARY OF HAUNTING THE LODGE, TURN TO PAGE 353.

I ENTER MOON, leaf, house, star, sun, lightning, flower, heart, snowflake into Reese's alarm pad. It blinks so brightly that it looks like a bolt of lightning is going through the screen. And then it goes dead.

I try the door, but it's locked. "What happened?" I ask as I jiggle the door handle with more force.

"It's not opening?" Eliza says.

"OPEN SESAME!" Frank yells.

I slam my shoulder against the door, but it doesn't budge. "I think that was the wrong code—should we try again?"

Eliza taps the screen pad. "The power's shut off to the lock. I wonder if it's an emergency fail-safe—"

"*What* are you doing?" cries a voice from down the hallway. We look over, and Harris is storming toward us, his face as red as his ginger hair. "Is this what I'm paying for—to have you break and enter while we're preoccupied with the haunting?"

"We're not breaking and entering!" I say.

"We broke the lock, and we *are* trying to enter," Eliza whispers.

"When a false passcode is put in, it triggers the police automatically. They are on their way," Harris says.

"The police!" I say. "Call them off!"

"No way," Harris says firmly. "I caught you red-handed. Now stay here until—"

54

"RUN!" Frank cries, and we make a break for it. We sprint down the hall, slide down the banister, and run out the door into the cold, blustery storm. In a shed outside, we find a sled; we grab it and go before the police arrive.

But as we speed down the mountain slope—on the lam, with the case behind us, and Mom still missing—I can't help but think it's all downhill from here.

CASE CLOSED.

I POINT TO the letter addressed to Byron. "Let's see what our resident author is hiding."

Eliza nods and pulls a paper out of the envelope.

October 15

Dear Byron,

You promised me a draft of your book six months ago. We are now running behind schedule.

I know you are rather meticulous about your research. But seeing as we cannot push your book to a later season or delay the production schedule any longer, we don't mind if you bend the truth a little. If that's what it takes to get this book done.

Like, say, six hikers were climbing the mountain. And they stopped in an abandoned house there. They got trapped, they died. Yada yada, and voilà! Six ghosts with a compelling origin story. (Feel free to use that, if it speaks to you.)

If you don't get this draft to me by the start of the new year, we're going to have to talk about canceling your book contract, and you will be obligated to pay back the entire advance we gave you two years ago for this book.

Cordially,
Rita Tome
Publisher

I look up. "He *lied?*" I know it's silly for someone used to detective work to be so shocked by this. But Byron is a nonfiction author.

"Liar liar, pants on fire!" Frank says. "Hey—let's throw his pants in the fire!"

"Hold on there, Mr. Good Ideas," Eliza says. "We're definitely not going to do that."

"Aw," Frank says. "Then what's even the point?"

I can't get over this letter. "So he's going to print false information in his nonfiction book . . . and his editor is cool with it."

Eliza grabs my hand, and her gray eyes are bright. "But what if Byron is creating the hauntings he's writing about? He can make up a history for the hauntings and make up hauntings themselves, but then he'd carry out hauntings in a place of his choosing, so they would still be 'real,' in a sense. He'd have witnesses to the hauntings. Other guests of the hotel to validate his story when the book gets published."

"Yeah. It might explain why the hauntings only started six weeks ago. Especially when those fake hikers were supposed to have died, like, seventy years ago."

"Look at all this motive," Eliza says. "If he doesn't finish a draft of the book by the beginning of the year, he has to give *all* the money back."

"It's December. He doesn't have much time to finish his book, does he?"

"Maybe Santa will give him a time machine!" Frank says.

"Or a winning lottery ticket," I say.

"Or a publisher with integrity," Eliza says.

"We should talk to Byron," I say. "Or should we read the other letter?"

"Hey, where *is* the other letter?" Eliza says. She frantically pulls the sheets off the bed, and Frank crawls under the bed for good measure.

"Not here!" Frank says. "But look! A toenail clipping!"

"It's gone!" Eliza says. "I can't believe we lost such an important clue! It was just here!"

"It's okay," I say. "We already have a lead to go on. We can look for the other letter later."

We find Byron in the fire den with his computer, typing away on a book we now know is a lie. My blood is boiling, just looking at him.

I have to tell him I know he's faking his facts. But with Mom missing and the threatening mirror message, I'm so *angry* that he jerked us around. I am tempted to smash his computer—and all his stupid lies—to smithereens. And I wouldn't even feel bad about it.

TO ACCUSE BYRON OF MAKING UP THE GHOST STORY, TURN TO PAGE 171.

←→

TO SMASH BYRON'S COMPUTER, TURN TO PAGE 391.

58

BY THE TIME Eliza and I get back to our room, Mom and Frank are there waiting for us.

"We just had the *weirdest* conversation with Ree—" But I stop short at the excited look on Mom's face.

"We found something!" she says breathlessly.

"Found what?"

"A clue! Frank was amazing!"

"YOU HEAR THAT? I'm amazing!"

"What did we hear in the Dead Room, Frank?"

"*Tick, tick, tick, tick.*"

"Exactly! There is some sort of clock beneath the floor. And twice while I was trapped there, I heard it go off."

"At midnight?" I ask.

"No, I'm certain it wasn't, because I heard lots of noises in the halls. And right before it went off, it sounded like someone was winding the clock. So . . ."

"So you think the grandfather clock downstairs could be a way into the walls of the house?"

Mom nods. "So Frank and I went to the library and found a book on restoring old clocks. Inside was this." She pulls out a piece of paper with a handwritten message.

At midday, you said you had five hours to go until the party, but your guest was going to be one hour early. The zipper of her dress broke, which tied you up for three hours, but you still arrived

two hours before the cake, which was there six
hours after the floral arrangement.

"What is this?" Eliza says. "Who is the message for?"

"I don't know, but let's set the clock," I say. I'm certain that *something* is about to happen.

The lobby is empty—with Cricket mysteriously missing. But that's good. Now we don't have to make up an excuse for why we're playing around with the grandfather clock.

"You read the clue again, Eliza, and I'll move the clock hands."

ADD FOUR HUNDRED TO THE HOUR
THE FLORAL ARRANGEMENT ARRIVED,
AND TURN TO THAT PAGE.

←→

TO ASK ELIZA FOR A HINT, TURN TO PAGE 288.

"ELIZA, I CAN'T figure this phone code out."

"Sure you can!" Eliza says, pulling the paper closer to her.

---

968   46   843 56229,   63   46   843 4255.

9428 8463?

84733. 36 668 438 228448.

4 63837 36.

"Just start with the easy ones first, Carlos. Like the last row. There's a lone four. It can be G, H, or I. Which of those stands alone?"

"I, obviously."

"Okay, now let's look for two-letter words. We have a lot of forty-sixes, thirty-sixes, and one sixty-three. What could they be?"

"Four six could be *go*," I say.

"It could also be *in*," Eliza says. And she's right.

"Ugh, this is impossible!"

"Well, let's move on to thirty-six."

"Do," I say. "That's the only possible word. And sixty-three is *me* or *of*."

"And eight four three? It appears twice."

"T-H-E."

"Excellent," Eliza says. "I think for the longer words, the trick is to think about the vowels. Since the vowels are all on different numbers, it really limits your word options."

"You're starting to lose me."

"Yeah!" Frank shouts from across the room. "You guys sound like NERDS."

"We *are* nerds," Eliza says proudly. Then she turns back to me. "What if I filled in some more words I see?"

"Eliza, you are a lifesaver!"

YOU GO/IN THE LOBBY, ME/OF GO/IN THE HALL.
968   46   843 56229,   63   46   843 4255.

_____ TIME?
9428 8463?

_____. DO ___ ___ CAUGHT.
84733. 36 668 438 228448.

I _____ DO.
4 63837 36.

She hands the pen back to me. "Can you help me with the last few words, Carlos? I'm having a brain fart."

"Ha! Fart," Frank giggles.

ADD THE TIME TO MEET TO 300,
AND TURN TO THAT PAGE.

"IS THERE SOMEONE who would want you to abandon the hotel?" I ask Reese.

"Abandon . . . what do you mean?"

"Maybe someone is faking the ghost hauntings to get you to leave. Do you have any enemies we should know about?"

Eliza is gloating beside me, with a huge grin. It gets me a little annoyed, but I have to shake it off. It's important, in detective work, to explore all possible theories. And *yes*, I believe in ghosts. But I also believe that people can, possibly, fake a haunting too. So I have to explore all the options and keep an open mind, as Mom said outside.

Reese hums. "Well, Luther Covington is a natural enemy."

"Who's Luther Covington?" Eliza asks.

Reese sighs. "Luther owns the hotel down the hill. The Super Hotel Express."

"Oh!" I say. "We passed that hotel on our way here!"

"Yes. Even though Luther has three times more guest rooms than we have, he's been trying to buy the Sugarcrest Park Lodge for two years."

"Is this lodge for sale?" Mom asks.

"No. It is not. That's why he's such a thorn in my side. He's even worse now that the hauntings have started. When guests flee my hotel in the middle of the night, they go to his hotel. My lodge is sinking, while his hotel is booming."

"Motive," Eliza says softly, and I have to agree.

"Anyone else who's mad at you?" I ask. "Anyone we should investigate?"

"I wouldn't presume to tell you how to do your job," Harris says, in the tone of someone who absolutely is about to tell us how to do our job. "But I think you should investigate *everyone* at and around the hotel."

"Except us," Reese says.

"Including us," Harris corrects. "We have nothing to hide."

"WE'LL SEE ABOUT THAT!" Frank shouts.

Reese shifts uncomfortably, and January looks at her with a sideways glance.

I make a mental note to discuss *that* with Mom, Eliza, and Frank later.

"So," I say. "Besides Luther Covington, you can't think of any reason why someone might want you gone?"

Reese Winters looks away. "No."

A lie.

"Mr. Winters? Any reason why someone might want Reese to leave the hotel?"

Harris Winters looks away. "No."

Another lie.

"January? Can *you* think of anything?"

January looks straight into my eyes. "No," she says firmly. And even though she keeps eye contact, I have this gut feeling that she's lying too.

We have a *lot* of uncovering to do.

Suddenly we hear loud footsteps, and the door to the dining room swings open.

"No, Mr. Covington! You can't go in there!" Cricket cries weakly behind him.

"You've rejected my offer!" the man shouts, slamming his hands on the table.

"It's very rude to interrupt a meeting, Luther," Reese says.

Luther Covington towers over Reese. He is nearly twice her height, with a bald head, dark brown skin, and eyes that flash dangerously. Reese has this warm energy about her, and this guy just radiates an icy chill. "Look, my offer is the best one you're going to get. Now that you've run your property into the ground with all this ghost stuff, it's not worth as much as it was six months ago."

"We have nothing more to say to you!" Reese says furiously. "Go back to your own hotel. Leave us be."

"I *will* be the owner of the Sugarcrest one day soon."

"Don't you have your own hotel to run?" Reese snaps as she escorts Luther out. Harris and January quickly follow. The door closes behind them, leaving just us Las Pistas detectives in the dining room.

"Hey!" I say. "What if we wanted to talk to Luther?"

"We can always find him later," Mom says. "We have a lot to start with."

66

"It seems like they lied to us . . . a lot," I say. "They're all hiding something. Did you notice how they wouldn't meet our eyes?"

"Sometimes," Mom says, "the biggest ghosts are secrets."

"No," Frank says. "The biggest ghosts are bigger ghosts."

"What do you mean by that?" Eliza asks Mom.

"Just that . . . a secret can haunt you and plague you even more than a ghost might."

"A ghost mite?" Frank says. "What's a ghost mite?"

Mom ignores him as she peeks out the door to make sure that the Winters family isn't coming back. Then she turns to face us, her dark eyes twinkling. "So where do we start?"

"You're asking us?"

Mom grins. "I thought three *expert junior detectives* who've gone sneaking around behind my back twice would have a lot more opinions!"

I smile, but my stomach also does a jump at the words *junior detective*. I hope I'm worthy of the title. "I think," I say, "Reese has enemies she's not telling us about."

"And why wouldn't she tell us about them?"

"She's hiding something."

"Possibly. Or?"

I hesitate, and Eliza comes to my aid with an answer. "Or she's protecting someone." Eliza consults her notebook. "We can interview Sunny, the housekeeper, or

Chef Fernando di Cannoli, since we didn't get to talk to them at all yet."

"Good. Do you have your backpack?" Mom says.

I point to Eliza's bag. "Three flashlights, loaded with batteries. And one fully charged walkie-talkie."

"I expect you to keep that with you."

"You're not coming with us?"

Mom shakes her head. "While you are interrogating, I will check our rooms for any bugs."

"Cool!" Frank says. "I love bugs!"

"Bugs?" Eliza squeaks, a sickened expression on her face. "Isn't this a reputable hotel?"

Mom laughs. "Not *those* kinds of bugs. I want to see if anyone has left recording or listening devices in our room. If so, I want to disable them before anyone hears too much about our findings. Meet me back in the room when you're done?"

Without waiting for our response, she leaves through the dining-room doors.

Eliza sighs in relief, then turns to me. "What do you think, Carlos? Should we start with Sunny or Fernando?"

TO INTERROGATE SUNNY, TURN TO PAGE 291.

←——→

TO INTERROGATE FERNANDO, TURN TO PAGE 180.

AS I STARE at the door to the outdoor equipment shed, I can feel the cold getting deeper and deeper into my bones. If we don't crack the code to the combination lock, then we'll surely freeze out here.

"Eliza—help!"

OUTDOOR EQUIPMENT SHED

Q – 3
M + 2
R + 1
S + 1
Q + 1
S – 2
H + 2
P – 5
I – 3
N + 5

"Okay, so find the Q in the first line, Outdoor Equipment Shed," Eliza says. "Now count three letters back from the Q."

"It's O," I say. "And then next one is M + 2, so I would . . ."

"Find the M in the line," Eliza says. "And count two letters after the M." I look at the word *equipment*.

M + 2 would be two letters after the M in equipment. N. "The letter N."

"Exactly," Eliza says. "Carlos, let's split up the work! You get the five in the middle—I'll get the two at the beginning and the three at the end."

OUTDOOR EQUIPMENT SHED

Q – 3   O

M + 2   N

R + 1

S + 1

Q + 1

S – 2

H + 2

P – 5   R

I – 3   E

N + 5   D

"You can get the rest, right, Carlos?"

"Got it," I say.

THE SOLUTION TO THE PUZZLE
IS YOUR NEXT PAGE.

WHAT A MESS! Thanks a lot, Frank. The only way out of this is to shut down the whole computer system.

I reach forward, only the desk is super tall. I jump high, grab the plug, and yank. I pull the plug out, but the desk clerk hugs the computer to his chest.

"What are you doing?" he says. "You know we have an external hard drive!" Oh no. That means all the guest records are backed up and saved somewhere. "SECURITY!" The desk clerk snaps his fingers, and three security guards swarm us. "You're trying to crash our system!"

Time to come clean. "No, we're not. We just needed to meet Mr. Covington. Can we talk to him?"

"No."

"Well, can you at least give us a lift up the mountain?" I ask.

"Up the mountain? But the only thing up there is the . . . Sugarcrest." The clerk's eyes widen. "I get it! You're spies for our competitors! You're helping them gather intel on our business!"

"We're not, we swear!"

"Like we'd trust the word of a spy!"

"I spy with my little eye," Frank says, "something ginormous!"

"The security guards?" Eliza says as they stomp closer to us, their muscles rippling.

"Yup!" Frank says.

The security guards drive us even farther down the mountain—and miles farther—until we reach an airport. They drag us out of the car and leave us at the departure curb. "See a spy, make 'em fly. Bye!"

"Nice poem!" Frank says, waving cheerfully as they drive off.

This outcome is just plane awful.

CASE CLOSED.

WE PUT THE code 7341 into the keypad. Here goes nothing. . . .

Click.

The door opens.

"Open sesame!" Frank cries.

"We have to get out of here—and fast!" Mom says.

Mom leads us through the halls, back the way we came. We are retracing our steps until we get to the grandfather clock again. We push the back, and it swings open like a door. We scramble out into the lobby.

"We have to get to the client before they do!" Mom says, running up the staircase.

I take two steps at a time. I don't pause until I reach Reese's hallway.

It's disturbingly silent as we move toward her door. Mom turns the doorknob, and the door swings open. I wonder if the spy on the inside left it unlocked for Sunny.

Either way, Mom opens it, and we follow her in.

The suite is dark, but I can see the shadows of fifty tall and menacing people standing in her apartment.

No, not people—mannequins. I can see it, finally, in the moonlight. Stretching all across the suite, in every room. They have glossy, painted faces—bulging eyes and grinning mouths that stretch far wider than the average mouth.

Well, this is creepy.

"Hello, Creeper McCreeperson," Frank says, shaking

the hand of the nearest dummy. No, wait—he's wiggling its arm until it unscrews completely. Frank swings the arm like a baseball bat. "Now I can fight the others."

"Shhhh!" Eliza whispers. "Do you hear that?"

The mannequins are whispering. I mean . . . they're dolls, so their mouths aren't moving. But there are voices coming from them.

"This hotel does not belong to you."

"Last chance."

"Get out."

We slowly walk through the rows of mannequins as they chant. Eliza's hand finds mine, and she squeezes tight.

Suddenly I hear sobs from the other room—the living room. We turn the corner, and Reese is on the floor in a puddle of tears. Surrounded by ten different looming mannequins.

"H-help me."

"Mrs. Winters," Mom says. "It's Sunny. And someone in your house. Where are Harris and January?"

"I don't know," she hiccups.

"Get out," the mannequin whispers menacingly.

"Last chance."

"We know what you did, Reese."

I stop dead. What did Reese do? Is this haunting vengeance for something? My mind goes back to the conversation Eliza and I had with Reese in her office.

74

She said she had stabbed her sister in the back. She'd betrayed her. She'd stolen the lodge right out from under her, and her sister always suspected but never knew. . . .

"Sunny is Reese's sister," I say.

"What?" Eliza says.

"Sunny—she's Reese's sister. That's why she's doing this! Sunny was supposed to inherit the hotel, but Reese convinced their parents to give it to her. And—"

"*Ahhhhhhhh!*" Reese screams, looking at something behind us.

Two figures in long flowy cloaks, holding scythes, are standing at the edge of the room. They look like Grim Reapers.

One points at Reese.

The other says, *"We've come to collect."*

There's *no way* we're giving Reese over to these monsters! Frank holds his mannequin arm out in front of him threateningly as the two fake reapers weave between the dummies.

TO USE THE MANNEQUIN ARM LIKE A BASEBALL BAT, TURN TO PAGE 86.

←——→

TO KNOCK OVER THE MANNEQUINS LIKE DOMINOES, TURN TO PAGE 159.

"WHAT HAPPENED WITH the mice?"

Reese stares at her shoes as she talks. "Last week we called you for help, finally. And that's because . . . well . . . the straw that broke the camel's back . . . was that we woke up to dead mice."

"AWESOME!" Frank says.

"No, *not* awesome, Frank," I say.

"Gross," Eliza whispers.

"Where were the mice, Reese?" Mom asks, putting her pencil down. Leave it to the professional detective to ask the pointed question.

Reese gulps. "A path of them, leading from my bedroom, all the way out the front door. The end of the path had a message in the snow. GET OUT." She shivers. "Mice are my greatest fear. I . . . all their little bodies . . ."

Harris squeezes Reese's shoulder.

So . . . either someone who knows Reese's fears planted the mice and is using ghosts to get her to leave the hotel. Or there are some seriously scary supernatural forces at work here.

TO ASK WHO MIGHT WANT REESE TO FLEE THE HOTEL, TURN TO PAGE 64.

←——→

TO ASK WHETHER THEY THINK THE GHOST IS REAL, TURN TO PAGE 389.

WE CAN ALL talk later. Right now, we need to find a way out of the Dead Room before we all turn into human icicles!

"We have to get out of here . . . now!" I say. "Everyone, take a flashlight. I know we can't see well, but we have to find some exit."

"There might not *be* an exit," Mom says, which alarms me because it's so not like her to be so negative. "I've been here for a day, and I haven't found anything."

"Th-there has to be," Eliza says. This temperature is really affecting her. "The c-c-cold air has to blow in from s-somewhere. A vent or a passageway. M-maybe this connects to the secret p-passage in the walls we found yesterday."

"Eliza, you have to keep moving. Get your blood pumping, or you're going to freeze!"

Eliza is examining the walls, Mom's shining her beam on the ceiling, and Frank is wiggling on the floor. I turn to focus on a different wall, made of thick, wooden planks with peeling black paint. I can barely see anything in my flashlight's dim beam.

"BLOODY MARY BLOODY MARY BLOODY MARY!" Frank suddenly chants.

"What are you doing?" I say.

"Trying to summon Bloody Mary!"

"Well, *don't*!" The last thing we need around here is *another* violent ghost.

"You c-can't, Frank," Eliza says with a shiver. "You need a mirror."

"Here's a mirror!"

"Where's a mirror?"

"HERE."

I make my way over to Frank, who is looking between two floorboards. I put my face on the floor and my eye to the crack in the planks.

A big brown eye is staring back at me.

My brown eye.

"Watch out," Mom says, pushing me out of the way. She knocks on a few floorboards until she finds a loose one, then spends fifteen minutes trying to coax it up. It's like wiggling a loose tooth, but finally she yanks it out. For the two floorboards around it, she uses one of the flashlights to hammer beneath them until they pop up from the nails.

Sure enough, there's a pretty large mirror under the boards. Without hesitation, Mom slams her shoe through the mirror. It shatters into a bunch of pieces, revealing a long pipe leading down—almost like a slide. A very steep slide. We can't see the bottom. "I'll go first, just in case," Mom says, easing her legs into the pipe. "Here goes nothing!"

She is totally silent the whole way down. That's a professional for you.

"You next, Eliza," I say, because she is shivering violently.

"D-don't let Frank g-go last," she says, and she disappears down the slide.

"You heard your sister, Frank," I say. "Frank?"

I turn around. A six-foot-tall woman is standing behind Frank, her fingers outstretched. Her mouth in an eternal scream.

I drop the flashlight in panic. "FRANK! RUN!"

He turns around—spots the lady behind him. For the first time in his life, I think he's speechless. Then he dives headfirst into the slide. Behind me, the ghost is coming closer, her skin like a raisin, rattling breath filling the room.

I jump into the tube and plunge straight down.

I land in something soft and squishy—a puddle of mud. The space down here is creepy. I'm assuming we're in some sort of unfinished basement, but it's hard to tell in the darkness. I wish I hadn't dropped my flashlight. "Hello?" I call, and my voice echoes around and around. It must be huge down here.

On the plus side, it's like twenty degrees warmer than the Dead Room, and a pink flush has returned to Eliza's cheeks. She's stopped shivering altogether.

"Where are we?" I ask.

"Under the lodge," Mom says. "Everyone okay?"

I don't want Mom to know about the ghost Frank and I saw upstairs. "We're great. Right, Frank?"

"But Carlos! What about—"

"What next, Mom?" I interrupt.

"We have to keep going," Mom says urgently. "Come on. This way."

I silently follow her across the basement. There are lots of cloths dangling from the ceiling. They're nearly invisible to see, but somehow I keep running right into them.

Suddenly, something from the EMF reader makes all sorts of noises. I reach into Eliza's backpack and fish it out. The needle is jumping wildly, and the light is flashing red—a ghost is present.

Bang!

The noise echoes from the pipe we'd all slid down. Maniacal laughter fills the basement and echoes around. I've never fainted before, but I might now. I edge closer to Eliza and stare at the EMF reader.

"It detects changes in the electromagnetic field, Carlos," Eliza says. "Can I?" I hand it to her, and she waves it near the wall. "There's a door here. Powered by electricity. It's making the meter go wild!"

"But how do we get in?" Mom says, turning to stare at the door with us as the laughter behind us gets closer. I don't want to be a coward, but I don't dare turn around. Frank, though, is the only one watching the basement behind us with wide, horrified eyes.

Eliza runs her fingers across the wall. "I think there might be . . . yes! There's a mechanism here. If we can just figure it out."

"Eliza, can you do it?" Mom says. She turns around, and her eyes get just as wide as Frank's. "Carlos, help her. Do not turn around."

My stomach leaps into my throat. I am curious, but I do know what they say about curiosity and cats. So I don't turn around.

I kneel down and help Eliza. And leave the ghost fighting to Mom and Frank.

"What do we do?" I ask.

"We have to make sure all the batteries are facing the right way. Each battery has a plus end and a minus end. When they're placed in their rectangle slots, no plus can be next to another plus, and no minus can be next to another minus."

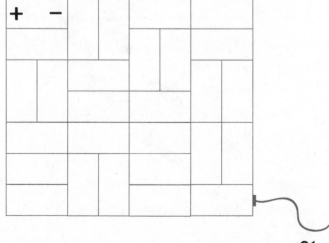

IF THE FINAL CHARGE IS POSITIVE, ADD TEN TO THREE HUNDRED, AND TURN TO THAT PAGE.

←——→

IF THE FINAL CHARGE IS NEGATIVE, SUBTRACT TEN FROM THREE HUNDRED, AND TURN TO THAT PAGE.

←——→

TO ASK ELIZA FOR A HINT, TURN TO PAGE 274.

REESE, HARRIS, AND January won't be jazzed about a broken window. We have to get away from the scene of the crime—*now*! We'll tell them the truth later, once the shock of it wears off. Because it's no good trying to reason with angry people.

Very carefully, I reach through the hole in the window and unlock the latch. Then I gently push the first-floor window open.

We crawl in. Then I shut the window and blinds behind me.

"That was fun!" Frank says. "Let's do it again!"

"Has anyone ever told you how much trouble you are?"

"Every day!" Frank says proudly, leaning on a cabinet. It pops open . . . and I see something interesting.

"Hold on—move aside, Frank!"

The inside right door of the cabinet has a bunch of letters carved into the wood. I open the left door, and that whole half of the cabinet is locked with a three-digit lock.

"What do you think this is?"

"Letters," Frank says.

"I know, but do you think it has anything to do with the lock on the cabinet?"

Frank shrugs. "Don't know, don't care."

"You're impossible," I sigh.

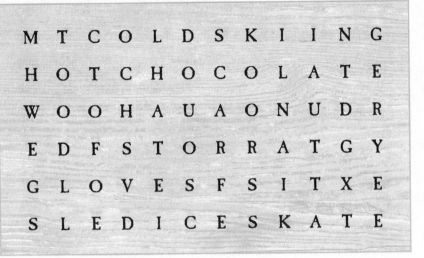

```
M T C O L D S K I I N G
H O T C H O C O L A T E
W O O H A U A O N U D R
E D F S T O R R A T G Y
G L O V E S F S I T X E
S L E D I C E S K A T E
```

"Oh, I wish Eliza were here."

"But you have FRANK," Frank says. "Frank is way more fun."

"We don't need fun," I mumble. "We need puzzle brilliance." I guess if I treat it like a word search, maybe something will reveal itself to me. I just hope I can find all the words!

"I see *rat* . . . and *sit* . . . but I don't think those are right," I say to Frank. "Knowing the Winters family, they'd probably have all winter-themed words. Like *sled* or *luge*."

"What's a luge?" Frank says. "Sounds huge."

"It's an Olympic sport. Now *shhhhhh*! Let me concentrate on finding more winter words."

THE LETTERS NOT USED IN THE WORD SEARCH
WILL LEAD YOU TO YOUR NEXT PAGE.
READ THEM IN ORDER TO FIND YOUR NUMBER.

←——→

TO ASK FRANK FOR A HINT, TURN TO PAGE 351.

85

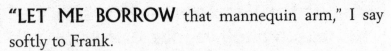

"LET ME BORROW that mannequin arm," I say softly to Frank.

"It's mine!" he whispers.

"I'll rip you off two more to make up for it."

Frank passes the arm to me.

The culprits move closer. I pull the mannequin arm back behind my shoulder. I have a decent batting average. Let's hope it comes in handy.

I swing the arm with all my might.

The second it connects with one of the ghosts, the arm cracks in half and falls to the floor. Unlike a baseball bat, it's hollow. So it did absolutely nothing.

Meanwhile, the ghost pushes me, and I trip into Eliza, who falls into Mom, who knocks Frank down. And all of us tumble into an open closet.

The door slams.

They must stick a chair under the doorknob or something, because we can't get out no matter how much we bang and rattle the door.

"Ahhhhhhhhhh!" Reese screams.

"Reese!" Mom shouts. "REESE!"

I can't believe I thought that a mannequin arm would be a good substitute for a baseball bat. Boy, was I a dummy!

CASE CLOSED.

"WE SHOULD TELL Reese," I say. "She's in danger!"

"Carlos, wait!" Eliza cries after me, but it's too late. I run into the fire den, where eight pairs of eyes swivel in my direction.

"We've just decoded the message on the ground," I say. "And Reese, the ghost is coming for you tonight."

"What?"

"The ghost is coming—"

"No, I heard you!"

"Then why did you say *what*?" Frank says from behind me.

Reese mutters to herself as she paces back and forth across the fire den. And I'm starting to think we shouldn't have said anything. She is clearly freaked out and losing her grip. "What do I do? What do I do?" Reese whispers. "Where do I go? What do I do? WHAT DO I DO? Run, of course . . . I have to run right now!"

Without a pause, she sprints out the front doors of the hotel, into the dark night, waist-deep in snow. And that's the last we ever hear from Reese Winters.

CASE CLOSED.

JANUARY CAUGHT US snooping through the mail—maybe if we tell her what we know, we can convince her not to tell anyone.

I nod at Eliza. "It's okay. Tell her."

Eliza pulls the letter out from behind her back. "We got this letter from Cricket's box."

January's eyes go wide. "What does it say?"

"We don't know," I say. "We haven't read it yet."

"So you're investigating Cricket?"

"No," I say, while Eliza says, "Yes."

"Yes, no, maybe so!" Frank adds.

There's an awkward pause.

"We're investigating everyone," I clarify.

"So what have you found—about everyone?" she asks. "Have you found anything about me? My parents? Sunny? Fernando? Mr. Covington? Mr. Bookbinder? Tell me what you've got!" January demands.

She's halfway between eager and aggressive. Is she worried about what we've found? Is she trying to protect someone else's secret? Does she have one of her own? Or—having just spent six weeks living in a haunted house—is she just curious to get to the answer?

I don't respond to her questions. I counter with one of my own. "Why are you awake right now?" I ask her.

"Same reason everyone's up. The ghost, yeah?"

"But why weren't you down in the fire den with everyone else?"

"How am I supposed to know where everyone else is?" January says. "I was in my room, trying and failing to go back to sleep. But when Mom and Dad didn't come back to bed, I left to go find them. Is that a crime now?"

"YES! ARREST HER!" Frank shouts as he points at January.

"Now show me the letter," she demands.

"Sorry, January," I say. "This information is classified."

"If you tell me what's in it," she says, "I promise not to tell my parents exactly *how* you seem to gather information. Otherwise . . . well, I can't guarantee that my loose lips won't sink your ship."

Oooh, January is good.

"Or," Eliza says, folding her arms, "we can tell your parents that we found *you* here, rifling through the mail."

"But that's a lie."

"I have two witnesses to back up my story." Eliza gestures to Frank and me. "What do you have?"

January looks mad. "My parents will believe anything I say."

"Why don't we test out that theory?" Eliza says, and January hesitates. Eliza has called her bluff. January may be good, but Eliza is even better.

January steps aside to let us by. But when we're half-way up the stairs, she calls out to us. "Be careful."

And I'm not sure if that was a warning . . . or a threat.

When I get back to the room, I lock the door behind us.

"So," I say. "How much do you want to bet she'll tell Harris and Reese, even though she promised us she wouldn't?"

"A hundred dollars," Eliza says.

"A hundred dollars," Frank says, "AND ONE PENNY."

I sigh. "We'll probably be in a lot of trouble really soon, then."

Eliza nods. "And so will your mom."

"Mom? Why?"

"Because I'm sure Reese and Harris will yell at her for not supervising us."

I pull the walkie-talkie out of my pocket. Mom hasn't been answering all night, and I'm starting to worry that a ghost really did take her. What possibly could have separated us? Why wouldn't she be answering her walkie-talkie? I don't even know where to begin to look for her.

"Come in, Mom. Over!"

Silence.

A dread fills my chest.

Eliza puts her arm around my shoulders. "Your mom is a brilliant professional investigator," Eliza says. "I'm sure she's fine."

"What if she's not?"

"She is," Eliza says.

"Ghosts are angry and vengeful. If she was taken by one—" I see Eliza opening her mouth. "And don't you dare say ghosts don't exist!" I snap.

Eliza closes her mouth, looking at me with concern and shock.

I crawl under the covers, just miserable. Mom has been so worried about the dangers for Eliza, Frank, and me—but why have I never realized the dangers for her? Being a detective *is* a risky job, and she always investigates a case alone. For the first time ever, I'm scared for her.

Eliza and Frank get ready for bed. Frank falls asleep in his big sister's arms, and Eliza nods off soon after.

I don't sleep, though. For hours, I stare into the dark, thinking about Mom.

I DON'T REMEMBER when I drifted off. But I wake up in a pool of sweat. Our room is so steamy, so foggy—I can barely breathe.

"Eliza!" I gasp. "Frank!"

She wakes up with a jolt, and Frank yelps.

There's a sound like running water. And our bathroom door is shut, even though I *distinctly* remember leaving the bathroom door open last night.

Frank stares intensely at the bathroom door. "Concentration." He claps twice. "Sixty-four." *Clap, clap.* "Do not open—the bathroom door. If you do—you will die. Concentration, sixty-five."

His hand-game chant definitely gives me a queasy feeling.

Especially when he punches me from behind and says, "Knife in your back, let the blood drip down!"

"Frank!" Eliza says. "That's enough. We're not playing Concentration!"

"Light as a feather, stiff as a board?" he says.

"No."

"Then what are we playing?"

92

"We're not playing at all," I say. "This is very serious."

"Oh," Frank says. "Then let me find my VERY SERIOUS FACE." He frowns deeply and furrows his eyebrows.

He clearly doesn't understand the gravity of our situation. A ghost might be facing us on the other side of the door. Or worse.

I take a deep breath to steel my courage. Then I turn the doorknob to the bathroom. Steam floods out. Eliza tries to fan it with her hands, so it won't set off the fire alarm. Inside the bathroom, we find the source of the steam: all the faucets are on, and boiling-hot water is gushing out of the sink and tub.

But it's the mirror that catches my eye. In the steam, someone's drawn four stick figures, one big one, two small ones, and one even smaller one. They all have Xs for eyes and tongues sticking out. Dead stick figures. Fun.

Eliza points into the steamy mirror and gasps. "Turn around!"

A message in red lipstick is on the tile in the shower. The lipstick is dripping from the steam, which makes it look even creepier.

desert the spirit and run far away
get out while you can in the light of day,
be gone from this place by three forty-five,
be gone from here if you want to survive.
this is your warning, for if you do stay,
then i'm the hunter, and you are my prey.

"Shut off the sink!" I shout as I touch the bathtub faucet. "YOWCH! It's burning hot!"

"Be careful!" Eliza shouts, too late to be helpful.

How long has the faucet been running, that it's so hot? Were we all so tired we slept right through the sound of running water? I use a towel to twist the metal handle until the water stops.

Our four stick figures start to drip and fade away in the mirror, but the red message in the shower still remains. We have to figure it out.

FIND THE TIME YOU MUST LEAVE,
AND TURN TO THAT PAGE.

←→

TO ASK ELIZA FOR A HINT, TURN TO PAGE 281.

I HAVE TO untie January . . . I can't just let her sit here, trapped!

I wrench my arm away from Eliza's grip and go over to January.

I untie her arms, and she rubs her wrists. "Rope burn," she mumbles. "Come on, we have to get out of here before that ghost materializes again! Follow me!"

"Aye aye, captain!" Frank says.

She hops over the low beam and ducks under the higher ones, and we follow her, weaving through tight spaces. We're not headed back to the Dead Room— I don't know *where* we're headed.

"Do you know where you're going?" Mom asks January.

January gives her a noncommittal shrug. And we trudge forward.

"Did you know this existed?" Eliza whispers. "Passages in the walls—that's a very interesting architectural feature!"

"No," January says. "I had no idea! I'm going to have to tell my mom about this."

We turn right, then left, then right again. January is seriously booking it. I don't blame her for wanting to get out of here as speedily as possible.

Man, it's quiet. Must be the insulation in the walls, because I can barely hear our footsteps anymore.

"We have to get out of here quickly," January says. "This way!"

"January, for someone who has never been inside the walls before, you really seem to know your way around."

January stops cold. "Are you accusing me of something?" Her voice is sharp.

I turn around. No one is behind me. What the heck! "Where's Mom? Eliza! Frank!" I haven't been looking over my shoulder—I was hurrying to keep up with January. When was the last time I heard them? Frank . . . not since we untied January. I haven't heard Mom since she asked January if she knew where she was going. Eliza . . . not since she made the comment about architecture. No wonder it seemed too quiet as we were walking!

I look at January. She is grinning.

TO ACCUSE JANUARY OF BEING THE GHOST, TURN TO PAGE 500.

⟵——⟶

TO RUN AWAY, TURN TO PAGE 257.

96

"ELIZA, CAN YOU help me with this magic circle thing?"

"Sure!" she says cheerfully. She is *always* cheerful when it comes to puzzles. Particularly math ones. "Well, first things first, we can only use the numbers one through seven once. We know seven isn't in the middle—"

"We know that?"

"Absolutely," Eliza says. "If all the numbers add up to the same sum, the number that goes in the middle is probably going to be close to your middle number, so that the numbers around it can fluctuate around it."

"Huh?"

"Here," Eliza says.

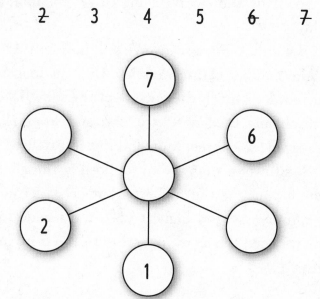

"Okay, why did you do that, Eliza?" I ask her. Math is not my strength (just like understanding suspects isn't Eliza's strength), but I'm *determined* to understand this problem.

"I put seven and one on the same line, and six and two on the same line," Eliza says, "because we're going to have to add up along the line. What's seven plus one?"

"A thousand," Frank says.

"Eight."

"And what's six plus two?"

"A thousand!" Frank says again.

"Eight!" I say.

"Excellent," Eliza says.

"So is the sum we're trying to get to the number eight?"

"Not quite," Eliza says. "We still have to fill in that middle number before we know the true magic sum. But first let's finish the outside of the snowflake. We have already used one, two, six, and seven. Which means we have three, four, and five left to use."

"So if we're doing your opposites thing," I say, "where you put the highest number with the lowest number, second highest with the second lowest, now we need the third highest with the third lowest, right?"

98

Eliza beams. "I can't believe you say you're bad at math!"

"If three and five are the remaining circles on the outside of the snowflake, that means there's only one number left for the middle. And then?"

"We add up each line, and we know the true sum. One plus seven plus the middle number, two plus six plus the middle number, and three plus five plus the middle number—they should all be the same sum."

ADD TWO HUNDRED TO THE SUM OF EACH LINE, AND TURN TO THAT PAGE.

ONE HUNDRED. ALL this work for such an easy number.

"That's a t-terrible code!" Eliza says. "Combinations like one two three or one one one or one hundred are the first things people guess! V-very unsafe."

The lock to the shed clicks open. Inside, it's full of gear. Cross-country skis, downhill skis, snowshoes, sleds. There's a desk where guests of the lodge would sign in and sign out whatever they were borrowing.

We crouch down by the desk and try to warm up. It's actually cold inside the shed. But at least we're safe from the wind.

"When we ran out of the hotel," Eliza says, her voice a little higher than usual, "we left the front door open behind us, didn't we?"

"We did."

"Then this was a setup!" she says. "Someone lured us out here with footprints that stop in the middle of nowhere, all in an attempt to lock us outside."

"Someone? Don't you think maybe it was the ghost?" I ask Eliza, and she rolls her eyes at me. "Fine, but my theory makes a lot more sense than yours."

"What makes you say that?" she says.

"We *barely* got to investigate yesterday. Why would anyone try to freeze us to death? We definitely haven't found any incriminating information yet. Or *have* we?"

100

"Maybe it's more about driving us out of the lodge. Maybe they want us to get scared and leave."

"I'm not scared of *anything*!" Frank cries. He roars like a lion and then jumps onto the desk. "'Specially not ghosts!"

"It was very suspicious about Luther, wasn't it?" Eliza says as I stand up and examine the downhill skis. "Why was he lurking around a rival hotel in the middle of the night?"

I grab a pair of skis off the wall. From a cubby, I take ski boots.

"What are you doing, Carlos?"

I grin. "You don't think Reese or Harris will mind if we borrow this, do you?"

"And where are you going with those skis?"

"*We* are going to Luther's property. He's got some explaining to do."

"YAY!" Frank says. "Adventure!"

"Are you sure that's a good idea? I mean, we have safe shelter here to wait out the night. Besides, have you ever skied before?" Eliza says, her eyebrows raised.

"Of course not," I say.

"Me neither!" says Frank.

"But Eliza, we're just going downhill. How hard can it be?"

TO STAY IN THE SHELTER AND WAIT OUT THE
NIGHT, TURN TO PAGE 120.

←——→

TO SKI DOWN TO LUTHER'S PROPERTY,
TURN TO PAGE 251.

102

"WHAT DO YOU think of the Winters family?" I ask Sunny.

She stiffens. Her lips are in such a tight line, they practically disappear. I can't tell if she secretly hates the Winters family, or if she's just a miserable person. Finally she sniffs and says, "I think my opinion doesn't matter here."

"What do you mean?" Eliza says. "Of course it matters."

"I do my job, I do it well, and my feelings are irrelevant."

Eliza will not let this go. "But if you hate your employer, and suddenly there is a reported ghost haunting at this hotel, then your feelings *are* relevant. They give you a potential motive."

"Plus, you should always share your feelings," Frank says. "Sharing is caring!"

Sunny's nostrils flare. Clearly this line of questioning isn't giving us any answers. I have to try something else. . . .

"How long have you been working here?"

"Four years."

"And where did you work before here?"

Sunny sighs tiredly. "I really have to finish my work. I have a lot of beds to turn down, laundry to do, and towels to fold."

"Really?" Eliza says. "In a vacant hotel?"

Sunny crosses her arms. "I . . . we . . . well . . . we don't want the beds to get dusty!"

Beds to get dusty? If the sheets are already clean, why would she rewash them? Is this an order from the Winters family, or is this suspicious behavior?

"If I don't get back to my work, I'll get in trouble!" Sunny says, tucking a lock of hair behind her ear. She looks around the corner, like she's afraid Reese and Harris are going to tell her off at any moment.

I can tell we've lost her. Time to cut her loose and circle back again later.

TO END THE CONVERSATION, TURN TO PAGE 422.

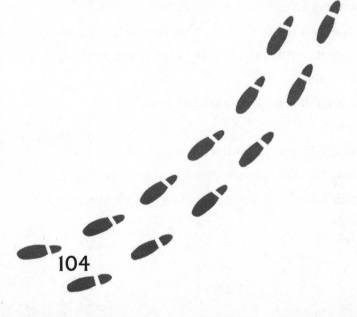

"WE HAVE TO find Sunny," I say. "I just know it in my bones."

We leave the kitchen, go down the hall, and find ourselves in the hotel's lobby. Cricket isn't at her post, and the door is open to the fire den, which is empty too.

"Sunny?" I shout. "Where are you?"

My voice echoes around the lobby.

"Let's go to her room."

She's not there. We jiggle the doorknob. Locked.

"Is this what you do?" Reese says sharply from the other side of the hallway. "Just try to break into rooms when no one is around?"

"Why didn't you tell us Sunny is your sister?" I say. I don't mean to say it—it just comes out.

"Who told you?" Reese says quietly.

"It doesn't matter!" I say, as Eliza says, "Fernando." She winces. "Oops."

"Why wouldn't you tell us that important piece of information?" Mom says.

"What are you hiding?" I say.

Reese's nostrils flare dangerously. "I have nothing to hide!" she snaps. It sounds like a lie to me. But I would never say that to her.

"LIAR LIAR PANTS ON FIRE!" Frank shouts.

I groan.

"I will not stand here and be accused of . . . of . . ."

"Withholding important information?" Eliza suggests.

"I don't like the direction this case is taking, and I certainly don't like your conduct. Breaking into rooms and such! I'll be having a word with the Better Business Bureau. Several words!"

Mom blanches. "But we're so close to solving your case!"

"But by what means?" Reese says. "At what cost? No . . . you're done here!"

Because of Reese's formal ethics complaint, Mom loses her private investigator license. I can't help but feel like this is my fault, even when Mom assures me it's not. I wanted to prove that I could be an equal partner, and now we're both equally out of the detective game.

CASE CLOSED.

"DO YOU LIKE working for the Winters family?" I ask.

"Sure," she says.

"Do they treat you fairly?"

"Sure," Cricket says.

"Do you have any complaints?" Eliza asks.

"I . . ." She drops her voice to a whisper. "You know, it's really bad etiquette to talk ill about your employers."

"So there's something bad you *could* say," I say.

Cricket looks angry with herself.

"What about January?" Frank asks. "January has September, April, June, and November. What were we talking about again?"

"January is not my boss, but I like her well enough. She *does* fight with her mom an awful lot, though. Typical young-teenager angst. My mom and I totally fought like that when I was January's age. But it always falls on me to cover it up for the guests, and it's, like, mortifying, you know? But maybe you should talk to Sunny or Fernando—they've got a lot to say about the Winters family."

They do? Because Sunny was tight-lipped. I suppose we could try Fernando . . . or we could press Cricket for more employee gossip.

> TO ASK CRICKET WHAT SHE THINKS OF HER COWORKERS, TURN TO PAGE 325.
>
> ←——→
>
> TO INTERVIEW FERNANDO, TURN TO PAGE 180.

ELIZA HOLDS THE mirror up to the other mirror, and finally we can see all the letters completely. I stare at the message.

WITH YOUR MOM NOW LEAVE AT 1:08 AND SHE COMES HOME

"Well . . . that's a problem," I say. "We're not leaving without Mom, and it sounds like the ghost isn't giving up Mom until we leave."

"Catch-22," Eliza whispers. "A classic oxymoron."

"Hey!" Frank shouts. "*You're* the oxymoron!"

Knock, knock.

It's coming from our hotel-room door. Reese is standing there, and for some reason, she won't look any of us in the eye. Her gaze is firmly on her feet.

"I'm sorry to disturb you this morning," she says, tucking a lock of her smooth black hair behind her ear. "I—I have some regrettable news."

My stomach jumps. Is it about Mom? Suddenly I feel like I can barely stand. I reach for Eliza, and she holds on tight to my arm.

"Is your mother around?" Reese says. "I have to tell her too."

I breathe a *huge* sigh and feel like a two-ton weight has been lifted off me. Eliza lets out a shaky laugh, which prompts Frank to shout, "What's so funny? Hello?"

But I'm too relieved to answer him. So whatever bad news Reese has to deliver—it has nothing to do with Mom, which means it can't be that bad after all.

"Detective Serrano is not available at the moment," Eliza says, her cheeks rosy from the lie. "We'll pass along your message. What is your, uh, regrettable news?"

"We are snowed in. The storm got very rough last night—the snow is higher than all the downstairs windows. The doors are lodged shut. The phones are down. And . . ." She trails off and blushes even redder than Eliza just did. "Sunny has lost the master key."

There's silence in the room as the information bomb lands.

"What?" Eliza and I say.

"She . . . she says it was stolen from her. Right out of her room. We have no idea who has it. I caution you not to leave any valuables in your room, and I deeply apologize—"

"Are you sorry?" Frank says, poking Reese in the stomach. "Or are you sorry YOU GOT CAUGHT?"

"Both?" Reese says meekly.

"Do you and Harris have a master key?" Eliza asks.

Reese shakes her head. "No, unfortunately. Sunny has the only one. After the locksmith changes all the locks, though, I may have to rethink that plan." She looks down again. "If you could leave this little incident out of your online reviews of the lodge, we would be very grateful. Our reviews are already abysmal. . . ."

So *that's* why she is so nervous. "Don't worry, Mrs. Winters," I say. "We won't be leaving a review for the hotel—we're not guests. We're working."

"Oh, thank you!" she says with a watery smile. "If you'll excuse me, I have to go tell Byron Bookbinder. Please pass this information on to your mother."

She leaves, and we close the door behind her.

"Well, that's a problem," Eliza says. "The most important key in the whole hotel? Missing?"

"And my mom's missing." A much bigger problem than a stupid missing key.

"And we're snowed in," Eliza adds.

"And snow snakes are on the loose!" Frank says.

Eliza and I both look at him.

I snort. "Snow snakes? What in the world are *snow snakes*?"

"Snakes that live in snow!" Frank says. "I saw one yesterday!"

Eliza laughs. "Snakes are cold-blooded, so they need warm-weather temperatures. Reptiles can't live in the cold."

"Snow snakes can!" Frank shouts.

"But snakes hibernate in the wint—"

"*Sssssssssssss!*" he hisses. "SNOW. SNAKE."

He stands up on the bed looking almost angry.

I shake my head. I almost forgot—we're talking to someone who believes unicorns are real . . . and that they have rainbow poop. "Oh, of course, Frank," I say. "I forgot about snow snakes!"

"Well," Frank huffs, sitting back down on the bed again. "I'll forgive you this one time only. But NEVER. FORGET. AGAIN."

I turn to Eliza. "So we never actually looked at our clues from last night."

"Oh, you're right!" Eliza says, digging into her backpack. "Between tackling January and the mirror threat and Reese's news, I got distracted."

I'm glad she didn't mention the fact that I snapped at her last night. I'm so ashamed I can barely look at her. After all, it's not Eliza's fault that Mom is missing. I'm not mad at Eliza—just at the situation. And the ghost. "Eliza, I'm sorr—"

"I know, Carlos. You don't have to apologize," she interrupts. Her gray eyes find mine, and she looks solemn. "I understand completely. I'm worried about her too, you know. . . . Oh—found them!" She pulls out two envelopes and lays them down on the bed.

One is the letter we stole from Byron's briefcase. It

says FORMAL WARNING on the envelope. Pretty threatening.

The other is the letter we stole from Cricket's lockbox. It has Cricket's name on it . . . and it's from the Super Hotel Express. Pretty suspicious.

Both letters seem promising. But which is going to get us to the truth of the haunting?

TO READ THE LETTER TO BYRON BOOKBINDER,
TURN TO PAGE 56.

⟵⟶

TO READ THE LETTER TO CRICKET McCOY,
TURN TO PAGE 481.

"QUICK! GET INTO the trash cans!" I whisper.

We each climb into our own can. I close the lid above me and immediately regret my choice.

The smell is *foul*. Beyond foul—absolutely putrid. It's a mix of bananas, tuna, onions, and some sort of soft cheese . . . but everything's rotten.

After a minute, I start to wonder when we'll know the coast is clear. How long do we have to stay in here? Another five minutes, I can handle. But five hours? I'll *die*.

Suddenly my can starts to move. Like it's being rolled away. And then lifted up . . . we're getting thrown out! "Hey! Wait!" I shout, trying to push up my lid, but it's stuck. The can turns upside down, and I go tumbling into a garbage truck.

"HEY!" I shout, but no garbage collector hears me. Frank, Mom, and Eliza follow—in that order. And the truck starts driving away.

"Where are we headed?" Eliza says, between choking breaths.

"Probably a dump," Mom says.

"HEAVEN! We're headed to heaven!" Frank says, throwing trash into the air like confetti. "Hey, Eliza, look at this!"

"Frank, that's just a piece of broken plastic."

"I will treasure it forever!" he says.

I look around at the mountains of trash in the truck and feel like crying. I refuse to believe that our case has ended with refuse.

CASE CLOSED.

"WHERE WERE YOU during the haunting last night, Byron? And why did you leave all your stuff behind?"

"To start, I was fiddling around with my EMF reader, and the needles started to jump toward the green. The temperature dropped in this room, despite the fire. I suddenly found myself quite cold. So I put the EMF reader in my bag, put my bag on my chair, and stood up to see if I could adjust the temperature in the room. That's when I saw it."

"It?" Eliza squeaks, her eyes wide.

"In the reflection of the window, I saw it behind me. A figure gliding by."

"A ghost?" I say.

"I don't know for sure—it floated by so fast," he says, looking away. "But I suspected, so I scurried after it. I needed to find it and catalog it for my book." He's examining his shoes so intently.

"Where did it go?"

"I . . . I don't know."

"Look at me," I say, and Byron meets my gaze. But only for a nanosecond. He breaks away again and looks at the floor as a flush creeps into his face.

"You're lying," I say. "You didn't follow it."

"No," he admits. "I did not."

"I thought you weren't going to lie to us! And you *just* did!" I search his face—his watery-looking eyes, his flat nose, his reddish round cheeks. For some reason, I don't think he's blushing because he was lying, like what happens when Eliza lies. I think he's blushing because he's embarrassed. Then it hits me. "You were afraid," I say. "You freaked out—so much that you left your precious computer and all your research behind. And then did you run from the ghost?"

"I hid," Byron Bookbinder says, his voice no louder than a peep.

"SCAREDY-CAT!" Frank shouts, pointing at him accusatorily.

"A ghost writer, cowering from a ghost. That is reprehensible." His lip wobbles. "I have to tell you—I wasn't just scared. I was *petrified*. You can't imagine the sheer terror of being alone, the ghost at your back, the stillness, the darkness. I ran for my life." He shudders.

Goose bumps prickle up my arms. The way he's talking really freaks me out.

Suddenly the door to the fire den opens, and Harris Winters comes in carrying some firewood. I nearly jump out of my own skin. He takes one confused look at this unlikely gathering of hotel guests and says, "Don't mind me. Just want to keep the fires going."

It's hard not to mind him, though, since he literally interrupted our conversation. I have to wait for him

116

to leave. I don't like conducting our work in front of prying ears.

We stop the conversation. From the next room over, someone is playing the piano . . . if by "playing the piano" I mean "poking a yowling cat."

We all cringe, and Frank covers his ears with his hands.

"MAKE IT STOP!"

"Oh, my poor ears!" Harris groans.

Suddenly the music stops. Just like that.

Is it a haunting? Is it possible to have a daytime haunting? Maybe I should go check it out.

"Excuse us," I say to Byron and Harris, and I pull Eliza and Frank toward the library door. Byron looks alarmed at our abrupt departure, but Harris couldn't care less. He's continuing to feed the fire; he doesn't even look our way.

When we're in the library, I close the door. And *this* is where things get really weird.

There's no one in here.

Eliza immediately frowns—her puzzle-solving expression.

Frank does the opposite: he lights up into a wide smile. "Cool! The ghost plays piano!"

Huddled together, we slowly approach the piano. There doesn't seem to be anything extraordinary about it. Other than the fact that it *just played itself.*

I reach into Eliza's backpack and pull out Byron's EMF reader. But the reading on the room seems normal—the needle is pointing right at red. No jumps or spikes in ghostly activity whatsoever. Honestly, I don't know if I'm disappointed or relieved about that.

Frank moves closer to the piano and sits down at the bench. And I wince because I know what's going to happen next. It's inevitable with Frank.

He starts banging on the piano. Hard. I think my ears might be bleeding.

I take a closer look at the sheet music on the piano . . .

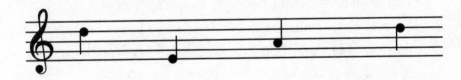

"I wish I took music lessons," I say. "I don't know how to begin reading that."

"I can help," Eliza says cheerily. She turns the sheet music over, draws one of these music line things, and writes letters on them.

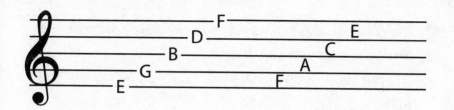

"Since when do you play an instrument?" I ask her.

"I don't. But anyone can learn to read music. It's just like another language! If you tell me what notes to play, I can find the corresponding key on the piano, and we'll see if this sheet music has anything to do with our disappearing pianist."

TO PLAY D E A D, TURN TO PAGE 372.

←——→

TO PLAY F A D E, TURN TO PAGE 227.

MAYBE ELIZA'S RIGHT. Maybe it's just too risky to leave the safety of our shelter.

I put the skis down. "Okay," I say. "Let's wait out the night."

The three of us cuddle up close for warmth. We have no blankets, and this shed is colder than it looks, but we drift off eventually.

There are no windows, so we can't tell if it's morning when we wake up. But I feel like we've slept a long time. Too long.

"Come on," I say, going to the door. "Time to get back to the case—" The door is locked. I look back at Eliza in panic. "We're locked in!"

"How is that possible?" Eliza says. "And don't you dare say it was the ghost!" she snaps as I open my mouth. I can see the wheels turning in her brain as she paces. "Obviously whoever lured us out of the house came to check on us . . . and then when they realized we were in here, they locked us in."

"Well, the door is the only way out—there aren't any windows!" I bang on the doors, and Eliza joins me. "Help! Help!" we shout.

I turn to Frank. "We need your lungs."

He takes a deep breath. "HEEELLLLPPP! LET US OUT OF HERE!"

We scream, and we scream, but it's no use. We're all alone out here.

"Out of the frying pan into the fire," Eliza mumbles.

"I'm hungry," Frank says.

Eliza just *had* to mention a frying pan at breakfast time.

"I'm hungry," Frank says again. "I want bacon."

"Well, you won't get bacon unless we get out of here," I say.

"BACON!" Frank shouts, pounding on the door. "BACON! BACON! BACON!"

Well, we're definitely not bringing home the bacon on this case.

CASE CLOSED.

"SO WHAT IS the history of the hikers?" I ask. "You said they died in this room seventy years ago?"

"That they did," Byron says.

"So how did you come to find out about the hiker story?" Eliza asks.

"Excuse me?"

"How did you hear about the story? Who told you?"

Byron hugs his computer closer to his chest. "Everyone knows that story! It's . . . it's practically legend."

"Like the abdominal snowman," Frank says.

"Abominable," I say.

"A bomb in a bull?" Frank snickers. "That's silly!"

I turn back to Byron Bookbinder. "Answer the question. When did you first hear about the hikers?"

"I . . . I don't know. A while ago. Yes, yes . . . it was about three years ago."

"But if the hikers died seventy years ago, then why didn't the hauntings begin until six weeks ago?"

"Who knows? They don't operate on our mortal timelines, do they? But when I heard there was recent activity, I had to come see."

"Is there a reason Reese says this history is fake?" Eliza asks.

Byron straightens his crooked glasses and huffs. "What does she know? Is she a historian? Is she a

122

published author? I am the authority on ghosts—are you questioning my scholarly knowledge? Or perhaps my authorial intent?"

My head is spinning from his twenty-cent words, but Eliza knows what he's talking about.

"Neither," she says. "I'm just doing my due diligence as an investigator—"

"Get out!" Byron howls, his face glistening like a honey-glazed ham. "Get out, get out, get out!"

I don't think Eliza's question was out of line, but Byron seems particularly touchy about his writing. Note to self: remember that later.

GO TO SLEEP ON PAGE 439.

"LET'S TALK TO Cricket," I say. "Since she's right here."

As we approach her desk, I can see her playing some candy game on her phone. I'm guessing, from the way she jumps and hides her phone as we approach, that she probably *shouldn't* be doing that at work.

Then again, it's not like her job is super busy, with only one guest and four detectives roaming the hotel.

"Can I help you?" she says in a friendly voice.

"We wanted to ask you more questions," I say.

"Ask away," she says with a wide smile. Her front two teeth have a gap in between them. "It's, like, literally my job to answer questions!"

TO ASK CRICKET WHAT IT'S LIKE TO WORK FOR THE WINTERS FAMILY, TURN TO PAGE 107.

←——→

TO ASK CRICKET WHETHER SHE'S SEEN A GHOST, TURN TO PAGE 34.

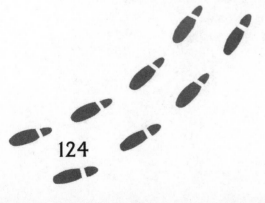

I WANT TO examine the clue Eliza sees on Cricket's desk. Having a solid clue in our hands would be worth two ghosts in the bush. Or something like that.

"Okay, Eliza, what did you find?"

She points to a piece of paper—one of the many scattered across Cricket's messy desk. "That piece of paper on Cricket's desk. What does it look like to you?"

I pick it up and examine it. It looks like nothing. Random scribbles. Absolute gibberish.

"I think it's just scrap paper, Eliza."

She hums thoughtfully. And she goes on the other side of the concierge desk. She starts pulling out drawers—the top two are normal drawers with typical office supplies: pens, paper clips, tape, scissors, Sugar-crest Park Lodge stationery. The second one is full of guest keys. The third one opens, but it has a solid top that requires a three-digit code in order to get to the contents of the drawer.

"That scrap paper," Eliza finally says, "isn't so scrap. It's how we're going to get into Cricket's bottom drawer."

"How?" I say.

She grins, her eyes lighting up like they always do when she encounters a good puzzle. "Open your mind, Carlos. Look at the problem . . . from a different angle," she says, and then she laughs to herself.

THE PASSWORD IS YOUR NEXT PAGE.

TO ASK ELIZA FOR A HINT, TURN TO PAGE 264.

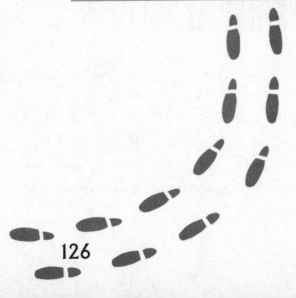

126

"TELL US ABOUT this driver's license," I say, laying it on the countertop in front of Fernando. "Is it yours?"

Fernando—or Stefano, I guess—looks down at his feet. Usually when people look down at their feet during a conversation, it tells me they're trying to avoid the topic, or even thinking up a lie. But this time, the gesture just seems . . . full of sadness.

"It's mine," Fernando says. "I'm undercover."

Undercover?

"Are you a SPY?" Frank says in awe. "I wanna be a spy when I grow up. A SUPER SECRET AGENT SPY."

"Are you a detective? A federal agent?" Mom asks.

"No . . . I . . . I'm my own spy." We all look at him, confused expressions on our faces, until he continues. "A long time ago I had an accident that ruined my life. I slipped on ice, hit my head, and got amnesia."

"Amnesia?" I say blankly.

"It's a loss of memory, due to some sort of traumatic brain injury," Eliza explains.

"When did this happen?" I ask.

"Years ago."

"*Where?*" Mom says shrewdly, like she already knows the answer.

Fernando looks up at her defiantly. "At the Sugarcrest Park Lodge."

My brain is spinning. *Why* would he come back to the Sugarcrest Park Lodge, the site of the accident that ruined his life? There would be no reason to come back here, except for . . .

"Revenge," I say out loud. "So you *are* the ghost!"

"No! For the millionth time, I'm not! I came back here, undercover, to gather evidence for my negligence claim. I need to document the ways in which the Sugarcrest staff practices unsafe standards, so I can sue the hotel for intentionally putting my health and safety at risk. Years ago, on the night in question, there was a raging storm, and the Parks sent me out for firewood on unsalted pathways frozen over with ice—they knew it was dangerous. I didn't even have insurance, working for them. I went bankrupt paying for my own medical care. My memories came back little by little, but I could never get back the time or income I lost. So I'm ruining them the best way I know how: legally, through the court system," he finishes grandly.

"And the letter from Luther—it was about Luther being your court witness, right?" I say, finally understanding. "He's going to help you try to win your claim against the Winters family."

"Not the Winters family, the Park family. It's Reese's maiden name. Her parents owned the hotel at the time of my accident. But I still think I deserve compensation from the hotel for all my suffering. I hope a judge will agree."

"Okay," I say, "but if you're not the ghost, then who is?"

Fernando shrugs. "I don't care at all about the ghost. I've barely been paying any attention to it. I suppose Luther Covington has mentioned to me once or twice how much he wants to buy this property for cheap."

"He's mentioned that to us too," I say.

"He might have a scheme. I'm not part of it, but I wouldn't put it past him. He seems like the kind of person who always gets what he wants, one way or another."

I nod. Luther *is* very much like that.

"Anyone else?" Mom says.

"Reese and her daughter have fought quite a lot lately—"

"We knew that already," I say.

"January doesn't want to be homeschooled anymore, but Reese won't let her go to public school."

"It's a moot point," Eliza says. "January's been helping us with our case. She helped us distract you yesterday."

Fernando nods. "Well, the only other person I can think of is Sunny Park, who has a good reason to be bitter."

A weight drops in my stomach.

"Sunny Park?" I turn to Eliza.

"Park?" she croaks. "As in the Sugarcrest *Park* Lodge? As in the former owners of the hotel?"

Fernando scrunches his brow. "Yes, Reese and Sunny, the Park sisters. Surely you must have . . ." He looks at all four of our dumbstruck faces, and knows instantly that we surely did *not* know.

My thoughts are on a racetrack. For some reason, Reese left out a *very* convenient piece of information: that her housekeeper, Sunny, is also her sister. No wonder Sunny always seems so miserable! Her sister gets to manage the hotel, while she's stripping bedsheets.

But why didn't anyone tell us about Reese and Sunny's relationship? I could understand why Sunny wouldn't want to say anything, but why didn't *Reese* tell us? That seems like a huge oversight! Especially when her sister might have a *ton* of motive, in the form of resentment and anger!

"We have to go," I say, dragging Mom, Eliza, and Frank out of the kitchen. When we're alone in the hall, I add, "We have to find Sunny." More and more, I think I'll see her behind the mask of the ghost.

"If Sunny's the ghost," Eliza says thoughtfully, "then she's always been a step ahead of us. We have to get ahead of her. I know we wanted to wait until daylight to follow the map your mom found in the firepit, but we have to pursue it now. Maybe Sunny was burning it for a reason."

We look to Mom, who smiles. "I'm letting my junior detectives take the lead on this one."

TO FIND SUNNY, TURN TO PAGE 105.

←——→

TO FIGURE OUT THE MAP CLUE, TURN TO PAGE 348.

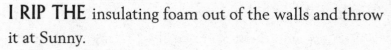

I RIP THE insulating foam out of the walls and throw it at Sunny.

She laughs.

And laughs.

And laughs.

"What were you planning to do with that—keep me warm?"

She holds it in her hands and closes in on me. I scream, but it's muffled by the soft, springy insulation.

"Huh," Sunny says as she wraps me like a burrito. "This actually comes in handy."

They fetch Mom, Eliza, and Frank—and wrap them in the insulation too. Our cries and shouts are muted as they load us one by one into a pickup truck.

We drive for hours, or possibly days. At last the truck stops, and when I look up and out the top of my foam roll, I can see we're at a dock near the ocean.

"What are you doing?" Mom asks.

"This foam is about to become *sea*-foam," Sunny says, rolling us over the edge.

We float away, to a far-off island, and there's not one ghost of a chance we'll get back to save the Sugarcrest Park Lodge in time.

CASE CLOSED.

"WHY ARE YOU doing this?"

"Because you don't scare easily. I thought that putting Detective Serrano in the Dead Room for a spell would freak her out enough to leave this place for good."

Mom and I look at each other. Neither one of us will admit it to Sunny, but it almost *did* make her flee.

"No, I mean . . . why are you terrorizing the hotel?" I ask.

Sunny doesn't answer. "You know, we ran those guests out of the hotel with a single scream, but we pull out all the stops for you, and it still doesn't work."

"We?" I say.

"Wee wee." Frank snickers.

We. Does that mean what I think it means? All this time we've been looking for the culprit. But we don't have just one culprit . . . we have *two.*

"Who's your partner in crime?" Mom says.

"Like I would tell you!" Sunny snorts.

"A spy on the inside," Eliza says. "Only three people are on the inside of the Winters family suite."

Harris. Reese. Or January.

I think back to the conversation we had with Harris. He seemed so innocent. And even more than that: *he* was the one who hired us, against Reese's wishes.

Could Reese be working with Sunny to haunt her own hotel? That's a wild theory . . . it couldn't possibly

132

be true! Or did Sunny convince January to team up with her against her own mom? Or was Harris lying to us all along? And *why* would one of them team up with Sunny—for what purpose? My brain is on a merry-go-round, and I can't get it to stop.

"I need this to go my way. Tonight's haunting is going to be . . . killer." Then, after a pause, Sunny says, "I never expected you to catch on to my little secret. The ghost *or* my partner. Too bad you won't be able to know about the latter."

"Pity," Mom says, as she gestures to Eliza to start examining our only exit.

"Yes, yes, a deep shame. You're just too good at your jobs. Let that be some comfort to you as you dehydrate to death beneath the Sugarcrest Park Lodge." Sunny chuckles. "Maybe the Sugarcrest will *really* be haunted now. Or maybe not."

"YOU BIG MEANIE!" Frank shouts into the speaker. But he gets no response. I have a bad feeling we're already cut off.

TURN TO PAGE 369.

WE HAVE TO move closer to the ghost. It's the only way we're going to get to the truth. And as dangerous as our rooftop situation is, I didn't come here *not* to solve the mystery!

Frank and I tiptoe across the roof like we're acrobats on a wire.

I can't see the ghost, though. Not through its mask. If I want any information, I'm going to have to ask the ghost a question.

"Who are you?"

"Your worst nightmare," the ghost replies, from underneath the mask.

Something about ghosts talking makes them much less scary. And besides, I recognize the voice. It's just who I thought it would be.

"Sunny," I say.

She doesn't take the mask off.

"You caught us," I say with a shrug. "So . . . six weeks ago you must have found out somehow that you're the true owner of the Sugarcrest Park Lodge."

She pauses and cocks her head to the side. It seems like that's information that maybe she *didn't* know.

"If you stop all this ghost-haunting business, if you stop trying to murder Frank and me, then maybe you can walk away with the hotel and everything you want."

134

She cradles one wrist. "How do you know?" she replies, her voice muffled.

"Take off the mask, and we'll talk about it."

She reaches up and pulls off the mask. It drops next to her, in the snow on the roof. "Tell me more," she demands.

"Frank and I found a will with your name in it. In Reese's office. It looks like she was trying to hide it."

Sunny snorts. "You tricked me into removing my mask! That's an old will." She laughs, but she sounds miserable. "Nothing has changed for me after all," she says sadly. "I was supposed to be the owner of the lodge—all my life, our parents were preparing me for the role. But then, a month before they both died, they secretly changed the will to make Reese the owner."

"And you think Reese had something to do with that?"

"Of course I do," Sunny says. "She's always wanted the lodge, ever since we were girls. But I was the one who was groomed for the position. It was a shock to me when they read the will, but Reese . . . my sister didn't react at all. It was like she knew it was coming."

"Okay, but what I don't understand," I say, "is that Reese's—I mean, *your* parents—died a few years ago. Were you just biding your time, waiting to drive her out at the first opportunity? What changed six weeks ago?"

Sunny smiles. "I got a teammate."

"*Boo!*" says a voice in my ear, and I jump a mile.

Behind me is the creepy "come play" pigtailed ghost. Or, as I call her when she's not wearing the wig, January Winters.

"See?" Frank says. "I told you she wasn't Sunny! I TOLD YOU SO."

Like a bolt of lightning, everything clicks together for me. January was lonely on the mountain . . . she wanted to go to a real school . . . she told her mom she was interested in video editing and music, but her mom wouldn't listen. She probably has all the equipment she needs to make ghost sounds—and the ability to play those recordings with speakers placed inside the walls. And she definitely made that sound bite of my mom screaming. She could torture Reese and Harris from *inside* their suite.

"You really are an unpredictable team," Sunny says. "My niece told me to watch out for you two, but I am surprised you got there first. . . ."

I have to find an escape—fast! January is blocking the window, so that's out. We could go down the chimney. There's no smoke, so we should be all right. Or . . . we could jump off the roof into a snowbank. There does seem to be a spot where the snow blew higher . . . the fall might not kill us.

"The detective and the smarty-pants haven't caught up to you yet," Sunny continues. "I was very glad to see you all split up. Taking on two of you isn't nearly as challenging as taking on all four of you."

"Taking on?" I say, stalling for time.

"My aunt misspoke," January says in my ear. "She said *taking on*. She meant *taking out*." Then she grabs Frank by the hair.

I have to help Frank. . . . I must pry him away from January. But after that, where do I go? What do I do? I need an endgame plan—and fast!

TO CRAWL DOWN THE CHIMNEY,
TURN TO PAGE 412.

←——→

TO JUMP OFF THE ROOF, TURN TO PAGE 461.

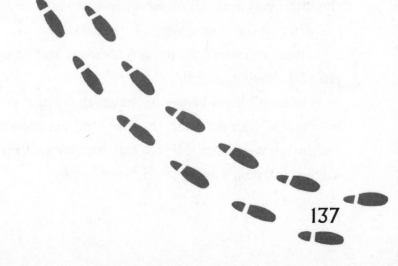

"THANK YOU, FERNANDO. I think that's every-thing."

"Very well," he says, clearly relieved. "Come a-back soon!"

We exit the kitchen, and Eliza takes me aside, under the stairwell. "Why did you pull us out of there?"

"Because," I say, "there's something more important than questioning him. We have to lure him away. So we can get a peek at whatever he hid in the wall."

Eliza thinks. "What would drive him away?"

"An emergency," Frank says.

"But what kind of emergency?"

"A foodmergency!"

I snort. "What in the world is a foodmergency?"

"Like when you need a pizza, and you need it NOW. That is a foodmergency!"

"Okay, well," I say, after I've gotten my snickers under control, "if the three of us called him away from the kitchen, I don't think he'd come."

"What about your mom?" Eliza asks.

Somehow I don't think he'd obey my mom's orders either. I shake my head.

"I'll help!" says someone from above us. January Winters is leaning over the banister, eavesdropping on our conversation. "I can call him away from the kitchen," January says. "He'll listen to me."

I look up at her—from the neon headphones in her hair to her bomber jacket, from her ripped jeans to her doodled-on sneakers. "Why would you help us?"

She shrugs and slides down the banister. She joins our huddle.

January didn't seem like she cared about the hauntings—or us—yesterday, but now her eyes glint with mischief. "I'm bored. There's nothing to do around here. And now I want to know what Mr. di Cannoli's got hidden in the wall."

I look at Eliza. Should we trust January?

TO TRUST JANUARY, TURN TO PAGE 386.

←——→

TO REFUSE JANUARY'S HELP, TURN TO PAGE 425.

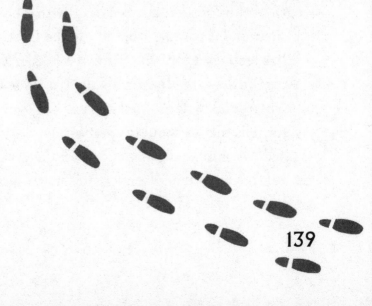

139

OKAY, I CAN do this. I'm not scared of a little maniacal laughter, right?

"Hahahahahahahahahahahahahahahahaha." It comes again—a throaty, sinister cackle.

I grab Eliza's hand. "This way!"

We run down the hallway of guest rooms, to the top of the stairs. But the noise isn't coming from downstairs—it's coming from the staff side. We turn the corner to the staff housing.

The laughing gets louder. It echoes. Shivers go down my spine. Why isn't anyone else in the house awake to witness these horrible sounds? Where are Reese, Harris, and January? Where is Byron Bookbinder? Where are Sunny and Cricket and Fernando di Cannoli?

We are alone. All alone with the laughter.

The hallway feels, suddenly, so very small, and my breath catches. Because I'm staring straight down the length of the corridor, at a red door with a brass knob.

The sound is coming from inside the Dead Room.

Eliza realizes it too. She stiffens. We take baby steps toward the door, holding hands tightly. It's not too late to turn around. I don't want to run, but something in my gut tells me we shouldn't stay either.

Shadows shift under the door, and the cackling gets louder and louder and louder. It sounds almost like screams. . . .

140

TO TURN BACK AND FIND THE HOWLING,
TURN TO PAGE 254.

←——→

TO TRY TO ENTER THE DEAD ROOM,
TURN TO PAGE 323.

WE'RE TAKING TOO long to crack Fernando's wall safe, and who knows how much longer January can keep him distracted? I need Eliza's help.

Eliza points to the top right slice. "Look at this one: B-A-A-M-E-L-L. It's missing the letter T. When you add T back into the word and unscramble the letters, it makes *meatball*."

"Oh!" I say. I feel like this puzzle is finally clicking for me.

I point at the slice at two o'clock. "C-K-C-I-N-E. It looks a lot like *chicken*."

"So it was missing the H," Eliza says. "I think we should keep track of the missing letters, and so far we have TH."

"O-N-S-O-N?"

"It makes you cry when you cut it."

"The cheese?" Frank says.

I groan. Why is everything farts with him? "Frank, it's onions. So our missing letters are THI."

"I think you can get the next one. With that many Ps, it should be obvious. *And* it's the most popular pizza topping ever."

"Anchovy?" Frank suggests.

"We said *most* popular, not least popular, Frank."

"Moving on," Eliza says. "The second-to-last wedge is hard. Because the missing letter appears in the word twice. But just try to think about what kind of sauce goes on pizza."

142

"Red!" Frank shouts.

"But what's another name for red sauce? It's also a main ingredient of ketchup," Eliza says, trying to draw the answer out of us. "After this slice, I think we're done!"

"Wait, what about the last wedge?"

Eliza grins. "Well, here's a hint: we already mentioned that topping in this conversation. Got our missing letters? Then let's get in this safe!"

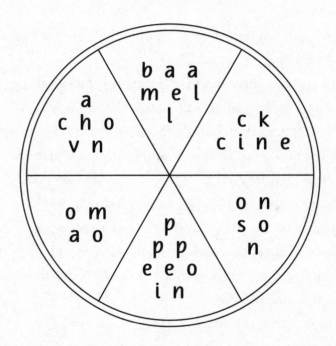

THE SOLUTION TO THE PUZZLE
WILL LEAD YOU TO YOUR NEXT PAGE.

"WE CAN'T POSSIBLY go looking for that dog!" I say. "It's three times the size of each of us!"

"Yeah, but if you put us all together, we're the size of that dog!" January says.

"No . . . we have the perfect hiding place here, so let's not leave."

Eliza nods in support.

"I thought you were detectives. Don't you want to detect?"

"We can't detect if we're mauled by literally the biggest dog I've ever seen," Eliza says.

"Come on, you cowards!" January growls, taking my hand and pulling on it. "We can't stay in here!"

"That's exactly what we're going to do!" I say, pulling my hand away from her and folding my arms.

"Fine," January says. "If that's how you want it!" She plops on a couch across the way, glaring at me.

I don't know why January is so eager to risk her neck, but I feel good about my decision to hide. I fiddle around with my walkie-talkie and wipe my forehead. Man, it is hot in here.

I look across the room at January, on her phone. And Eliza, sitting on the floor with her knees to her chest. They're both glistening with sweat.

"Does the room seem warm to you?" I try to ask. But the words don't come out. My tongue is so dry. I stand

144

up. The thermostat reads one hundred five degrees and steadily climbing. One hundred six . . . one hundred seven . . . one hundred eight . . . one hundred nine. Someone messed with the temperature in this room— we have to get out of here!

"Eliza! January!" I croak, but they've both totally passed out.

My vision swims, and then I lay my head down on the couch. Just a quick catnap. Then I swear I'll tackle the dog problem. . . .

CASE CLOSED.

THIS IS TOO much! We can't follow a murderous-looking ghost into a room called the *Dead Room* without any plan or reinforcements. I have no choice but to run!

I back away, and Eliza goes with me. We head toward room 237. We are screaming and screaming—it's hard to hear where my screams end and Eliza's screams begin.

I get to our door when I hear it—a light growl.

"Eliza," I say quietly. "Where's our room key?"

"I . . . I have it somewhere."

Grrrrrrrrr.

"Eliza?" I say more urgently. "I'm going to need the key now."

"I'm looking!" she cries. "I'm looking! I don't know where—"

"Eliza!" I shout. She looks up. At the end of the hallway is a big, ferocious, bearlike dog.

We shriek so loud, my throat is raw. *"AHHHHHH-HHH!"*

The dog comes thundering toward us. It leaps—I close my eyes.

It smacks straight into a couch cushion. One of the ones from the fire den. Mom is there, holding it like a shield.

"BAD DOG!" Frank scolds.

"Let's go!" Mom says. "Back this way!"

146

I'm so happy to see them, I could cry.

We run to the stairs, the dog on our tail. Only, downstairs in the lobby, there are four more dogs, just as big, just as ferocious. We can't go down there.

The original dog is behind us—blocking our way to our guest rooms.

It seems like there's only one place we *can* go. The ghost and the dogs are forcing us all to the same place. . . .

The Dead Room.

It's the one place I don't want to go.

I look down. Could we outrun the dogs? Or outsmart the dogs? Is it worth a chance?

"Carlos," Mom says, her voice a warning. "Don't—"

How much am I willing to risk to avoid the Dead Room?

TO GO TO THE DEAD ROOM, TURN TO PAGE 477.

$\longleftrightarrow$

TO GO DOWNSTAIRS AND FACE THE DOGS,
TURN TO PAGE 352.

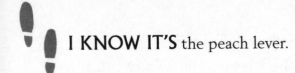

I KNOW IT'S the peach lever.

First letter is in SHARP but never in DULL.
Second letter in EYES but not in a SKULL.
Third letter is in ALWAYS but never FOREVER.
Fourth letter you can find in any WHICHEVER.
Last letter is in FINISHED, but not in an END.
Together you'll know which lever to bend.

P is in sharp, *but not in the word* dull.
E is in eyes, *but not in the word* skull.
A is in always, *but not in* forever.
C *is in the word* whichever.
H *is in the word* finish, *but not in* end.

It's peach!

I pull the lever, and the door clicks open. We tumble into the kitchen. Except for Frank, of course, who is still stuck to the pole. The kitchen is empty but for the hum of appliances—and there is a trail of green ghost slime that snakes across the floor and leads into the old dumbwaiter.

"A ghost!" I whisper, as Mom goes to the sink and fills a bowl with warm water.

"Carlos, there's no such thing," Eliza says, "and I'll prove it!" My best friend bends down and feels the

148

ghost slime. She sniffs it. Then, delicately, she tastes it.

"Eliza!" I gasp. "Gross! That's something Frank would do!"

She grins. "It's not ghost slime."

"Then what is it?"

"It's jelly! Jelly with green food coloring."

Mom brings the bowl of warm water over to Frank. "I have to raise the temperature of the pole without burning your tongue. So Frank? Stay still." She pours the warm water all over the pole and his tongue. She has to fill up twice, and by the third pour, Frank's tongue starts to come loose.

The fourth pour does the trick, and Frank's tongue lolls out of his mouth like a dog's. "Don't do that," he says to Eliza and me. "Not fun."

"Like we'd ever do that, Frank!" I say. "Only you."

Mom grabs some slices of turkey out of the fridge, a loaf of bread from the pantry, and two different condiments. "After that, I think we deserve dinner. And until we figure out who locked us in that freezer, maybe we better eat it alone."

"So what did you find, Mom?"

"Huh?" she says, squirting more mayo on her turkey sandwich. We're all sitting cross-legged on Eliza's bed, sharing the food and talking about our progress in the case. Frank is eating very slowly, occasionally letting his sore tongue take a rest between bites.

"You talked to Sunny earlier, right?"

"Oh yeah." Mom takes a big bite of sandwich. "What a bust!"

"You didn't get anything out of her?"

"On the contrary," Mom says putting her sandwich down. "She had lots to say about how this hotel is going to the dogs. Kept talking about how Reese was ruining the hotel. She used the word *disgrace* a lot. Come to think of it, Sunny didn't seem to think highly of Harris either."

"And what led you outside?" Eliza asks.

"Outside, I was looking for any sort of mechanism that would explain the hauntings," Mom says. "Some special-effects equipment, something like that."

"And did you find anything?"

"A speaker," Mom says. "And . . . this."

She lays out a paper in front of us. It looks a little charred along the edges.

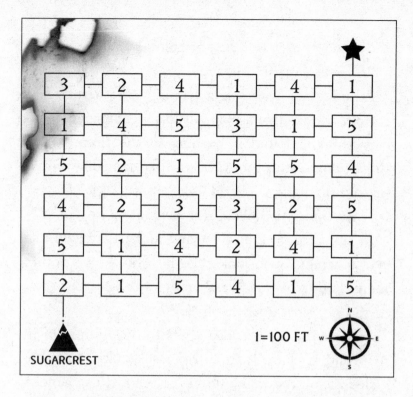

Eliza swallows her bite. "What's that? Looks like a map. Pass the ketchup, Frank."

"What's the magic word?"

"Please," Eliza says.

"Nope!"

"Pretty please."

"Nope!"

"Here," I say, snatching it out of his hands and throwing it to Eliza.

"Hey, no fair!" Frank says. "*I* was the ketchup king!"

"Here, be the lord of mayonnaise."

"It's never as good," he grumbles.

"So, is it a map?" Eliza says.

"Could be," Mom says through another bite. "It certainly looks like a map—it has a compass rose and everything. I found it burning in the firepit. Good thing I dove for it, hmm? Seems like someone was trying awfully hard to get rid of it."

"You *what?*" I choke. "You dove into a fire for it?"

"I used tongs. Don't get any ideas, daredevil," she says to Frank, who looks like he would love nothing more than to dive recklessly into a fire.

"So . . . what does this mean?"

"I have no earthly idea," Mom says, rolling up the map and sticking it in Eliza's backpack. "You three called me on the walkie-talkie before I had a chance to follow it, and now it's too late for today. It's not a good idea to explore the woods alone at night. Luckily I have three genius sidekicks I can drag with me first thing in the morning."

"Uh, Mom," I say. "Hate to break it to you . . . but I think you're *our* sidekick."

She laughs and ruffles my hair.

NIGHT TWO

"AHHHHHHHHHHHHHHH!"

I jolt out of bed. The clock blinks 2:29 a.m.

"Is it a ghost?" I say, turning the light on.

"There is no ghost, Carlos!"

"Oh yes there is!"

Eliza shakes her head and gets out of bed. "There's no reasoning with you!"

"Me?" I say. "At least I open my brain to other possibilities. At least I don't shoot down every theory that comes my way."

"*You're* shooting down *my* theory!" Eliza says.

"Yeah, because it's wrong."

"Then explain the green jelly—"

There's a knock on our door. "Carlos," Mom says. "It's me."

I open the door to find Mom and Frank standing in their pajamas, determined looks on both their faces. "Let's go."

Unlike the haunting yesterday, there are no noises in the walls or flickering lights or glowing footprints. The atmosphere doesn't feel charged. And there is hustle and bustle across the lodge—all our suspects running to the source of the scream.

In the middle of the lobby, I see the reason for the shriek. On the floor are these weird symbols . . .

ᚲ ⼂ ^   ⼝ ⼂ ^   ᚲ ⼂ ⼂ ᚲ ⼂

⼝ ⼂ ⼂ ⼟   ⼂ ⼝ ⼟ ᚲ ᚲ   ⼂ ⼝ ⼂

⼂ ⼝ ⼂ ⼂   ⼂ ⼂ ᚲ ⼟ ⼂ ⼂ ⼂

^ ⼝ ⼂ ⼟ ᚲ ⼂ ^

They're written in fake ectoplasm. Also known as green jelly, as Eliza figured out yesterday. She gives me a snobbish look, but I will *prove* that ghosts exist, by the end of this.

Everyone—Harris, January, Fernando, Cricket, Sunny, and Byron—is standing at the top of the stairwell, looking down at the symbols with a bird's-eye view. The only person on the floor of the lobby is Reese, who is shaking.

"It just . . . I saw it glide across the floor. I swear—it was just here! It's out to get me! It left this message!"

"Where did it go?" Mom asks.

"I—I don't know! It just disappeared."

"See? Sounds like a ghost," I whisper in Eliza's ear.

154

"Sounds like Luther Covington," she replies in a low murmur. "The only one who's not accounted for right now."

Mom quietly says, "You three—see if you can decode the ectoplasm message while I deal with Reese and the others." Then she faces the group. "If you all could follow me into the fire den."

"Now?" Sunny groans. "I want to go back to bed!"

"Precisely!" Byron says pompously. "Writing a book is a toil, even with the best of slumbers. But now my REM cycle has been agitated . . . tomorrow will be an agonizing workday! I must return to my torpor!"

"Not yet," Mom says. "Now follow me."

Everyone obeys. It's amazing how Mom can command a whole group of people to do something they don't want to do, just because she tells them to do it. I want to take notes from the master . . . but Mom has left me with a job to do. Now that the lobby is empty, we have a very short time to figure out what this message means.

I look at the message again.

⟨wingdings cipher symbols⟩

"What is this?" I mutter.

Eliza frowns. "This looks familiar. . . ."

"Is it an old cipher you read about in a book?"

"Nope!" Frank says, sliding down the banister. "It's wingdings!"

We follow him down the stairs.

"What's a wingding?" I say.

But it's Eliza who explains. "It's a computer font . . . it turns words into symbols."

"How do you know that, Frank?"

But Eliza answers again. "Frank likes to turn all my homework into wingdings before I print it out—luckily Mom, Dad, or I catch it before I hand it in like that. Except one time . . ."

"Ha! That was funny!"

"It was *not*!" Eliza says.

I walk over to Cricket's front-desk computer. Let's get the key to the code, then.

IF THE MESSAGE SAYS THE GHOST IS COMING FOR REESE, TURN TO PAGE 87.

⟷

IF THE MESSAGE SAYS THE GHOST IS COMING FOR HARRIS, TURN TO PAGE 416.

"EAST," I SAY, as I turn the arrow to the east.

Suddenly the floor begins to rumble. At first it's a tiny tremor—but it grows into a giant earthquake.

The four of us huddle together, arms wrapped around each other, as the room continues to shudder and quiver and wobble. All we can do is brace ourselves and hold on for dear life. But how long can the structure of the building withstand this earthquake? How long before this room—or the whole lodge—collapses?

There's no sign that the shaking will stop any time soon. This is a disaster . . . a natural disaster.

CASE CLOSED.

I RUN FORWARD and push the nearest manne-
quin. It knocks into two behind it . . . and soon they're
all falling like dominoes.

"AUGH!" shouts our one culprit as she topples, and
the other one gets trapped under three of the bodies.

Eliza shines her flashlight in our culprits' faces. One
we already know: the betrayed sister. The other is a
complete shock.

"J-January?" Reese sobs. "But *why?*"

January snarls. "Because it's the only way to get our
family off this stupid mountain!"

Suddenly I remember the conversation we had with
Harris in the hallway—about January being lonely on
the mountaintop. About needing some friends. But to
go this far is just *crazy.*

But she really *could* do it. Now that I think about it,
January was practicing her sound-mixing skills. I bet
putting together a haunted soundtrack of howls and
shrieks was a breeze for her.

"You don't scare as easily as I thought you would,
Mom," January says. "So we had to switch our plans."

"If something happens to you, the hotel goes to your
daughter," Sunny says.

"And then I could sign it over to Aunt Sunny. And
then we can all have what we want."

"Um . . . except for Reese," I say.

"What do you mean by *if something happens?*" Eliza

says, but neither Sunny nor January answers.

"Aren't you going to say SORRY?" Frank says.

Sunny and January look at the floor. I'll take that as a no.

"We would have gotten away with it too," Sunny snarls. "If it weren't for you kids!"

"Well," I say, standing over Sunny, "I guess you're just unlucky."

Three months later.

Eliza and I are sitting at my kitchen table.

"Okay, see how you multiply the fraction here, Carlos?" Eliza says.

"No."

"You have to flip the nominator and denominator—"

"Eliza." I slam my notebook closed. "This is boring."

"You solve math puzzles harder than this *all* the time. Homework should be a breeze!"

I snort. "It's different. It's easier to do math in life-or-death situations."

"That's literally the *opposite* of what anyone would ever say."

Ding!

Saved by the doorbell!

Mom goes to get it, and it's Frank. "Elizaaaaaa," he says. "Dad says you have to come home now."

Eliza starts packing up her homework, and Mom ushers Frank inside. "Actually," she says, "I've been waiting until we all got together to give you this." She pulls out a letter from her purse. "I got it on Tuesday."

Eliza and I lean over the letter, and Eliza reads it out loud.

Dear Las Pistas Team,

Thank you so much for everything—I don't know what I would have done without you. I've been meaning to write, but things got so hectic here.

I've realized how important it is for January to grow up with peers her own age, so she, Harris, and I have moved to the town of Bear Ridge, just an hour away from the lodge. January is doing much better, and it's been great to see her so happy in her new environment.

As for the hotel, I've left it in Sunny's capable hands. She was right—in a way. She went about it terribly, but I think I understand now how hurt she was that our parents picked between us. So . . . we've decided together to split the hotel shares. She owns 49 percent, and I own

51 percent. We are near-equal partners. And
she will have it for the next five years—until
January goes to college.

I know what you must be thinking—that
I must miss the hotel. It's true. I do love the
hotel, but I love my daughter and sister more.

Hopefully I will never need a detective again,
but if I do, I know where to turn.

Best, Reese

"It stinks that she had to leave the hotel, though,"
I say. "Just because January threw a tantrum. Doesn't
seem fair."

"Yeah," Frank agrees. "No fair. My temper tantrums
get me NOTHING."

"Hmm. I don't look at it like that," Mom says. "It's
clear that January wasn't being her best self in that
environment, and they did everything they could to
help their daughter. You know, there isn't anything I
wouldn't do for you, hijo."

"Including bringing me in on another case?"

"Para siempre." She laughs. "Always, always, always."

CASE CLOSED.

I HAVE TO go with my best friend. "I pick Eliza."

She sighs in relief. "I was nervous for a second."

I don't say anything—to spare Frank's feelings—but she didn't have anything to be worried about.

"Frank," I say. "I chose you to go back to the Dead Room, because I think you're braver than me, Eliza, and my mom. Don't you agree? Aren't you the bravest person in this room?"

"Bravest person on the planet!" he boasts. "Maybe even the universe."

"You're not scared of a little old Dead Room, right?"

"I AM SCARED OF NOTHING." He tugs on my mom's sleeve. "Let's go!"

Mom gathers up four flashlights in her hands as Frank tries to pull her out the door. But before she leaves, she says my name. Very softly. "Carlos."

She's going into the belly of the beast . . . again. That's what I admire about my mom—she risks it all to find the truth, to help people in danger.

So I push my fear away. Because that's what my mom does.

"Be careful," I tell her.

She nods once, and then she's gone.

"Let's go, Carlos," Eliza says, not two seconds after Mom closes the door. We leave the room and run down the curved staircase, into the lobby. The door to the fire den is open, and I can see Byron typing away. He squints at us, then shuts the door. Weird.

Cricket is missing from her desk, which does seem odd, considering she told us that she and Reese had worked things out.

Fernando di Cannoli comes out of the kitchen with a tray of food, sees us, yelps, and does a complete about-face. Bizarre.

Harris is in his office, talking to Sunny, who is scowling quite intensely. No surprise there. I'm sure she's getting scolded for losing the master key.

Reese Winters is in her office alone. January has her homework spread out in front of her on the dining-room table, also alone.

"Reese," I say. "Or January. They're alone. And we have questions for them."

"We do?" Eliza says.

I know I do.

TO QUESTION JANUARY, TURN TO PAGE 52.

←——→

TO QUESTION REESE, TURN TO PAGE 355.

164

"JANUARY, WHY ARE you fighting with your mom?"

"None of your business!" January snaps. "Anyone ever tell you how nosy you are?"

"Every case," I say.

"Now answer the question," Eliza demands.

"Wow, you two are super rude."

"Just trying to solve the ghost haunting," I say. "It's impossible to do that without prying for more information."

"If you don't tell us why you're fighting with your mom, we're going to assume you have something to hide," Eliza says.

January's nose twitches. "If you *must* know," she says, chipping away at her black nail polish, "my parents don't get me. Sometimes I feel like they treat me like a puppet. They expect blind obedience, always wanting me to do exactly what they say, the moment they say it. Have they ever taken the time to get to know *me*? Maybe if they understood me at all, we wouldn't argue so much." She folds her arms. "But from my side, Mom starts all the fights. I just finish them. So go talk to her about why she stirs up drama."

January opens her textbook again and starts reading. It feels like we've gotten all we can out of her, so Eliza and I retreat from the dining room. Without even

165

discussing it, we walk toward the door of Reese's office. It feels like the key to the mystery, like all the answers to all the secrets are behind this door.

I knock.

"Come in," Reese says. She looks tired. She rubs her eyes slowly. "I was just . . ."

She doesn't finish her sentence.

"Can we ask you a question or two?" I ask.

She nods.

TO ASK ABOUT HER FIGHTS WITH JANUARY,
TURN TO PAGE 437.

←——→

TO ASK WHY SHE DIDN'T WANT TO
HIRE DETECTIVES, TURN TO PAGE 394.

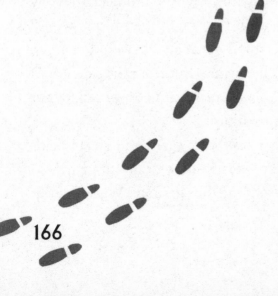

166

ELIZA AND MOM are crouched near the door, trying everything they can to get us out of this cramped underground room. And I hate to disturb them, but I need help cracking this code.

"Help?" I say simply.

Eliza takes the paper from me. "Hmm . . . I think we have to start with what we know. We know that there are no repeated digits."

"Funnily enough, I worked that one out by myself," I say sarcastically.

"Just thinking aloud here," Eliza says.

"Carry on!"

She turns her pigtail braid between her fingers. "The first digit will probably be a large one, since it's the sum of the second and third digits."

"Is that where we start?"

"No," Eliza says. "I think we start with the second clue and the fourth clue."

"Okay?" I look at the paper again.

Four digits . . . and no repeated digits.

The first digit is the sum of the second and third digits.

> The second digit is two more than the last digit.
>
> The third digit is one more than the second digit.
>
> The fourth digit is an odd number.

"The second clue says that the second digit is two more than the last digit."

"And," Eliza says, "the last digit is an odd number. Which means . . ."

"The second digit also has to be an odd number!"

Eliza writes down some possibilities.

? 3 ? 1
? 5 ? 3
? 7 ? 5
? 9 ? 7

"These are the only things that can make clue two and clue four true," Eliza says.

"The third digit is one more than the second digit," I say. I grab the paper from her and write.

? 3 4 1
? 5 6 3
? 7 8 5
? 9 8 7

"And the last clue," Eliza says. "The first digit is the sum of the second and third digits. And if this is only a four-digit code, then only *one* of these options can be true."

"Oh! I think I see what you mean!"

"See how fun math can be?"

"Okay, *fun* is taking it a bit far," I tease.

> THE FIRST TWO DIGITS OF THE PASSCODE
> WILL LEAD YOU TO YOUR NEXT PAGE.

THE BEST WAY to stop the ghost is to knock the boxes over. They're ten feet high and full of stuff. If we crush the ghost in a knickknack avalanche, we can easily escape.

"Frank," I say, my voice real low, "follow my lead."

"Follow the leader? I LOVE THAT GAME!"

The ghost comes flying—no, running—toward us.

"Now!" I shout, toppling a pile of boxes. Like a house of cards, they all come tumbling down.

The only problem is . . . they're burying *us*, too!

Frank and I cover our heads with our arms as the dusty boxes and loose trinkets trap us in a tiny corner of the attic. There's a mountain of stuff now between the escape route and us. We're at the mercy of the ghost, and completely boxed in.

CASE CLOSED.

"YOU!" I SAY to Byron Bookbinder, and he jumps.

"Apologies," he says. "I didn't realize anyone was in here with me. Sometimes I get so absorbed in the cadence of my own writing that I'm able to block out all sounds! I'm working on a particularly riveting chapter in which the lead hiker—"

"Cut it out," I snap. "We know the hikers aren't true."

"Of course they—"

"No," I say firmly. "They're *not*."

I pull out his letter from his publisher, and Byron's round face gets redder than a tomato. "You went through my briefcase?"

"And we'd do it *again*!" Frank yells. Then he adds an evil laugh for emphasis. "Mwahahahahahahaha!"

Byron is part flustered, part angry. "How dare you . . . what gives you the right to . . . when did you . . . this is highly immoral!"

We stare at him in disbelief. Like *he* can lecture us about being immoral?

"We're just trying to get to the truth," I say. "You're the ghost, aren't you? You made up this phony story about the six hikers, and then you started haunting the Sugarcrest Park Lodge."

His brown eyes narrow behind his thick glasses. "Now why would I do that?"

"So that when your book came out, the story would

seem true," Eliza says. "Hundreds of people could verify that hauntings had happened here, and no one would question the truth of the book."

"It explains a lot," I say. "Like how you told us you were going to stay in this room all night, but when the haunting happened, you were gone."

"I . . . I had to. It was only a momentary absence. I . . ." He wipes his sweaty forehead with his sleeve. "I know you're suspicious of me. And *yes*, I have done wrong. But I am not this ghostly apparition. Ask me what you want, and I'll be unflinchingly frank."

"Frank?" Frank says, perking up. "You're going to be Frank? YOU CAN'T HANDLE BEING FRANK."

"Calm down, Frank," Eliza says. "He means he's going to be honest."

I squint at Byron, and he seems to shrink under my gaze. Can we really trust a known liar to tell the truth?

TO ASK WHERE HE WAS DURING THE HAUNTING, TURN TO PAGE 115.

←——→

TO ASK FOR MORE DETAILS ABOUT THE LETTER FROM HIS EDITOR, TURN TO PAGE 392.

WE HAVE TO follow the glowing footprints. "Come on!"

The footprints head out the front door and into the snow.

"Carlos! We don't have our winter coats!" Eliza shouts behind me.

"We'll only be outside for a minute! Come on!" It's freezing in this snow flurry, but I run after the footprints. They belong to some extraordinarily big feet. Definitely a man's feet. Harris Winters, Fernando di Cannoli, Byron Bookbinder, and Luther Covington pop into my head.

The footprints stop, suddenly, about a hundred feet from the front door.

"Carlos, look!" Frank says, pointing to our left. A car's lights go on and the engine revs. In the front seat is Luther Covington.

But how did he get over there, when the footprints stop right *here*? Did he cover up his own tracks? Or are these someone else's footprints?

The car starts driving down the mountain.

"HEY, WAIT!" I call after Luther, but he's gone.

"What's he doing here at three in the morning?" Eliza says.

"Ghosting," Frank says.

I look around. "Hey, where's my mom?" I had

173

thought she was right behind us . . . but did she not follow us outside? I shiver. "Let's go back inside."

"Brrrrrrrrrr," Frank agrees.

We trudge back to the front door of the lodge, but when I tug on the handle, my stomach plunges.

The door is locked.

I pull on the doors frantically—I knock on the wood.

"Eliza, pass me the walkie-talkie!"

She opens the bag and digs through it, but a few moments later, she whimpers, "Oh no, no, *no*! It's not in here."

"What do you mean? It has to be!"

"I took it out and put it on my nightstand," she says in a small voice. "Just in case we needed to call your mom in the middle of the night. I forgot to grab it again."

The wind blows right through our pajamas, and we look at each other in horror.

The knocking clearly isn't working. The howl of the wind is so loud, and the ghost was wailing and thumping around inside. For all we know, the ghost is *still* wailing and thumping around. We can't stay here and keep knocking—it's *freezing* outside, and starting to snow.

"Around the house! Maybe there's another way in!"

It's hard to see in the dark and with the icy wind, but there's an iron garden a little ways down the hill.

The lodge's backyard also has a hot tub and a firepit with no fire right now. And then there's a shed. Shelter! That's where we have to go!

We fight the wind and the cold to get there. I can see my breath in front of me, and my nose hairs are freezing from the inside. Frank is coughing behind me—and the icy air is tickling my lungs too.

"Almost there!"

Eliza starts rubbing her hands together to create friction.

At last we reach the door, where the sign says:

OUTDOOR EQUIPMENT SHED

M TO F 9 A.M. TO 4 P.M.

SAT AND SUN 9 A.M. TO 6 P.M.

GUESTS, PLEASE FEEL FREE TO BORROW EQUIPMENT.

RETURN BEFORE CLOSING HOURS.

It's way, way, *way* past closing hours, and my stomach sinks when I notice a three-digit lock. There's just no way we're going to figure it out with so many combinations.

"This is bad," I say, suddenly feeling even colder than before. The weather was unpleasant but bearable when I could see the light at the end of the tunnel, but now that there's no end to our freezing, I want to collapse.

"Hey!" Frank says. "Look at this!" He points to a note taped near the doorframe.

HARRIS,

I CHANGED THE PASSWORD. LINE ONE.

Q − 3
M + 2
R + 1
S + 1
Q + 1
S − 2
H + 2
P − 5
I − 3
N + 5

SORRY FOR ANY INCONVENIENCE,

CRICKET

"Line one." Eliza shivers. She squints the sign on the door. Then she points to the first line of the sign. "I think that refers to this."

"Look," she says. "The first clue is Q minus three. And there's a Q in 'Outdoor Equipment Shed,' in the word *equipment*. So Q minus three . . . would be three letters before Q on that line. We have to keep going like that. Find a letter in the line; add and subtract until we get our new letter."

"You just saved our butts, Frank," I say, shivering.

Frank kisses his muscles. "YOU'RE WELCOME."

THE SOLUTION TO THE PUZZLE
IS YOUR NEXT PAGE NUMBER.

TO ASK ELIZA FOR HELP, TURN TO PAGE 69.

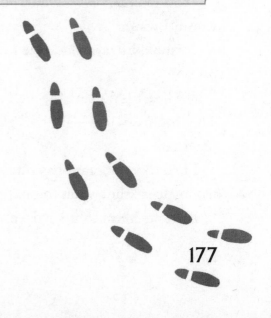

177

MOM SCREAMS AGAIN, and *that's it*! I have to turn around to help her.

I swivel to see what's behind me—what could possibly make fearless Frank scream, or Mom's eyes bug out, or Eliza cover her face.

And it makes my stomach drop to the floor.

There's not just one ghost. There are hundreds. Glowing blue, with sunken eyes and wispy limbs and mouths curved in a sinister smile. And they're all kids.

Screaming, hollow, skeletal kids.

I gasp as I lean against the steel door. My chest is on fire; my hands are shaking. I can't breathe—I can't breathe!

"Carlos? Carlos! They're fake! It's not real!" Eliza shouts, and even though she's next to me, her voice sounds miles away. "Calm down! Just breathe!"

"You look *terrible*," Frank points out to me. "If you vomit, I wanna see."

"Frank!" Eliza scolds. She puts a gentle hand on my back.

My heart is pulsing through every nerve in my body. The room swims—all the ghost children blending together.

I feel like my brain has totally shut down. But luckily, my legs know what to do. . . .

I run to Mom. She's frozen, mesmerized, staring at

178

a ghost close to her, whose round face is sinking into itself, becoming hollow and bony until at last it's just a skull with eyeballs and a black hole for a mouth.

Then it screams—a horrifying, guttural sound. A noise so disturbing that Mom steps back and trips into me.

Seeing me snaps her out of her trance. "Carlos, I told you not to look!"

"Too late for that now!" I snap as the ghosts dance in front of us.

"They're holograms!" Eliza cries from the doorway. "Run to us! Quickly! They're not real!"

"Phony baloney!" Frank echoes.

A shadow moves behind one of the thin cloths hanging down from the ceiling, and *sure*, these blue ghosts are holograms. But there's a *real* culprit—or maybe both of them—slinking around in the basement with us. This is our chance to catch them.

TO RUN THROUGH THE DOOR TO SAFETY,
TURN TO PAGE 222.

←——→

TO STAY AND BATTLE THE GHOST,
TURN TO PAGE 407.

I **WANT TO** interview Fernando now.

After a little trial and error of peeking into closet doors, Reese's office, and a laundry room, we finally find the kitchen. It is shockingly silver—the fridge, the freezer door, the counter, the stove, the oven. All of it is stainless steel. The vibe is modern and sleek, the opposite of the rest of the lodge. The lighting is so harsh, it hurts my eyes.

And standing with his back to us is Fernando di Cannoli.

He turns around. "What are you doing here?" he asks in his fake accent.

"We're here for ice cream," Frank says. "A sundae. With hot sauce. Cherry on top."

"What?" I say. "No, we're not—"

Eliza clears her throat loudly. "We're not here for one sundae . . . we're here for three," she says.

Fernando frowns. "Well, the customer is always right, I suppose," he says, walking to the freezer.

When he's gone, I turn to Eliza. "What are you doing?"

"I'm hungry," she says. "And this is a kitchen. Frank had a good idea."

"I am *always* full of good ideas!" Frank says. "And don't you forget it."

I sigh. Outnumbered by Thompsons.

180

But it's hard to stay annoyed about the investigative delay once Fernando comes back with a tray of three sundaes, so tall that they're dripping over the edge of the glasses.

"Where's the whipped cream?" Frank demands.

"I think he means *thank you*," I say.

"No, I don't! I mean where's the whipped cream?"

Fernando gets a can from the fridge and squirts a bit of cream onto Frank's sundae. "Happy now?"

Frank replies by face planting into his sundae. No spoon—just face. He gets it all over and grins through the chocolate.

"You're really not supposed to be down here," Fernando says nervously. "If Mr. or Mrs. Winters finds out . . . I don't want to get in trouble." He looks around, like he seems afraid of the wrath of the Winters family. It's weird; they seemed pleasant when we talked to them. So I don't understand why Fernando is so worried.

"Reese and Harris won't mind us down here," I say to him. "We're detectives."

"You? You're just kids!"

Frank emerges from his sundae to stick out his tongue.

"The truth is, Mr. . . . uh . . . Cannoli, we're trying to get to the bottom of these ghost hauntings," I say. "We heard there was a haunting in the kitchen two nights ago."

His eyes go wide.

"Did you see it?"

"Sì, signore!" he says with a nod.

TO ASK FERNANDO ABOUT THE GHOST
SIGHTING, TURN TO PAGE 485.

←——→

TO ASK FERNANDO ABOUT THE WINTERS
FAMILY, TURN TO PAGE 317.

"WE JUST SAW you," I say to Luther, "at the Sugarcrest Park Lodge. Why were you there?"

"Well, if you must know, I was going to give Reese Winters a little *persuasion* to sign the hotel over to me."

"What do you mean by *persuasion*?" Eliza asks. "That sounds like a threat."

"You know what else sounds like a threat?" I say.

"A threat!" Frank says.

"No, a ghost haunting. Reese told us the ghost had been leaving these cryptic and threatening messages."

Luther's nostrils flare for a second. And then he laughs. "I don't know much about the hauntings there, but I assure you, I don't need a ghost to do my threatening for me. I carry out all the threats myself."

"At three in the morning?" I say.

"At all hours of the day and night. Business never sleeps." And then he presses his fingers together like a supervillain on the verge of accomplishing his evil plan.

I shake my head at Luther. Something isn't sitting right with his story. There's no way that he would make a business deal at three in the morning. It doesn't even make sense—Reese would be sleeping.

"I don't believe you," I say. "Reese is sleeping at three in the morning."

"Is she? Seeing as I just saw her, I'd have to say you're

wrong. She has been having trouble sleeping ever since the ghost appeared. She looks *awful*," he gloats. "So occasionally I make nighttime visits, because I am much too busy to go all the way up the mountain during regular work hours."

"Doesn't anybody sleep anymore? I'm so sleepy," Frank whines. Then he wilts like a flower, resting his head in his sister's lap.

If Luther's telling the truth, then maybe he saw the ghost or some clue, even if he doesn't understand what he saw. Then again, I don't really trust him. Those footprints, him leaving . . . the timing was too convenient. I look down at his shoe. Maybe, if I ask, he'll let me examine his shoes. Then I could tell if the footprints were his.

TO ASK LUTHER WHAT HE KNOWS ABOUT
THE HAUNTINGS, TURN TO PAGE 445.

←——→

TO ASK LUTHER TO SEE HIS SHOE,
TURN TO PAGE 253.

WE HAVE TO talk to Byron about the glowing footprints.

We find him in the fire den, hunched over his laptop. He's typing feverishly, and I stand on my tiptoes to read over his shoulder.

> The tragedy of a haunting such as this one is not in the spectral spirits themselves, but rather in the fervent denial of any supernatural occurrences. The current proprietors of the hotel—whether out of ignorance or imprudence—steadfastly repudiate the evidence before their eyes.

Byron whips around.

"*What* sort of deed are you undertaking?"

"Uh . . . we just came to talk to you."

"How much did you see?"

"Nothing," I lie. "I swear we only came to ask you something."

He snaps his laptop shut.

"But now that you mention it, what were you writing?" Eliza says, her eyes narrow. "This doesn't sound like a particularly flattering chapter on the Winters family."

"AHA!" Byron says, getting to his feet and pointing at us. "I suspected as much! You came here to steal my work—to plagiarize!"

"We're not writers," I say. "We're detectives."

Byron laughs hysterically. "Oh, *I* see what this is. You were so affable yesterday, cuddling right up to my computer. And before I know it, you're going to snatch my work for yourselves! Well, I won't let that happen. REESE!"

Byron calls Reese into the room and says we're trying to steal his manuscript. She, of course, takes the side of her only guest.

We're booted from the case. Mom too.

I think that's the end of it, but nine months later, Byron's work of fiction comes out, featuring three nosy characters that ruin the main character's life. Named Carlos Santiago, Eliza Thomas, and Frank Thomas.

"Yay! I'm in a book!" Frank says.

"Yeah, but he made us all look horrible. You're a villain!" I gripe.

"Mwahahahahahahaha!"

Frank may think it's novel, but I'm furious.

CASE CLOSED.

"WHY DO YOU have a letter from Luther?" I ask Fernando. "Are you two conspiring to haunt the hotel?"

"Nothing like that," Fernando says. "But I'm not at liberty to discuss—"

"Unfortunately," Mom says, "you aren't at liberty *not* to. We need to know what's going on with you, and we need to know now."

Fernando nods slowly.

"The letter talks about shutting down the business for good," Eliza says. "Using . . . ghosts?"

"Ghosts were Luther's suggestion. Not mine. I only reached out to Mr. Covington because I needed help . . ."

"Ghost help!" Frank says.

"No, not ghost help!" Fernando barks. "I don't care one whit about this ghost! I am here for compensation only."

"Compensation?" I say. "Like, you want money for doing your job? Or . . . something else?"

Fernando hangs his head low. Okay, definitely something else.

"Are you stealing?"

"No."

"Are you doing something illegal?"

"No."

"Does it have something to do with your other

name?" Eliza asks. "Stefano di Marco?"

He doesn't say no.

TO ASK ABOUT THE DRIVER'S LICENSE,
TURN TO PAGE 127.

"THIS IS CHALLENGING," I say, staring at the map.

"Tell me about it," Eliza groans.

"Oh no, not you too! You were supposed to help *me*!"

Eliza and Mom both laugh.

"Why don't you start backward?" Mom suggests.

Frank starts walking backward—and promptly runs into a decorative table.

"Let's keep the backward in our brains," Mom says, beckoning Frank back over to us.

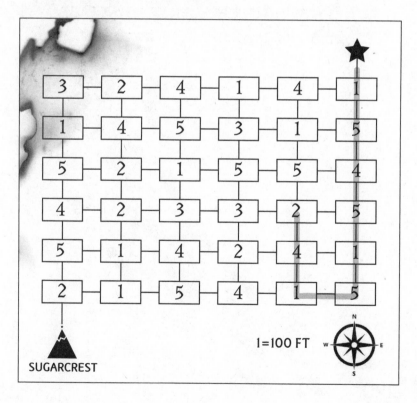

"Well, we know we have to land on the final one square in the top right corner . . . that will lead us to the star."

"What will get you to the one square?" Mom asks.

"The five—all the way on the bottom right?"

"Sure," Eliza says. "A puzzle like this just requires some trial and error, doesn't it? We can't be afraid to mess up. If we keep trying, we'll get it."

ADD UP ALL THE NUMBERS FROM THE SQUARES YOU PASS THROUGH. TURN TO THAT PAGE.

THE LETTERS IN the inner circle are definitely white. I place the tiles. The briefcase shakes violently. So violently, in fact, that I drop it right onto the wood floor.

Ca-thunk.

"Carlos," Eliza says quietly, "did you just drop Byron's computer?"

"BUTTERFINGERS, BUTTERFINGERS!" Frank yells, pointing at me.

"I—I'm sure it's okay," I say.

Spoiler alert: it was *not* okay. When Byron came back, we had to tell him what happened. He opened the briefcase to find his computer in shambles and all his hard work gone. He had only printed out the first fifty pages of the book, and he lost more than two hundred pages of work. (What writer doesn't back up their work?)

We were escorted from the Sugarcrest Park Lodge for causing their one and only guest emotional distress. And a month later, Byron Bookbinder sued us for damage to his property and livelihood. This was a costly error.

I can only hope that, one day, we can lay the ghost of this failed case to rest.

CASE CLOSED.

I KEEP STARING at the inscription beneath the deer, and I still can't find any numbers in the poem.

"Eliza, can you help me? How many numbers do you see?"

"I see three total in the whole poem. I guess that means we don't have to pull all eight antlers. Just the three, in the order we see them."

"But what if I don't see them? Is *forth* one?"

"No . . . that's spelled wrong to be fourth. I don't mean synonyms. I mean there are actual numbers, spelled correctly, embedded in the poem."

"Show me," I demand.

A buck and a doe went forth down the slope
On a day that would seem unappealing.
The snow cascaded, and soon an avalanche
Left our poor deer both reeling.
All tangled in knots, they grumbled and griped
At their poor, unwise venture with feeling.

"See? Look there, Carlos!" Eliza says, pointing at the second line. "Straddled between *that* and *would* on the second line is the number two!"

On a day thaT WOuld seem unappealing.

192

"Oh, Eliza! I get it. The numbers are hidden in plain sight, between two words like that."

She grins. "As far as I can see, that *two* is the only number in the first three lines. But I see the next one in the fourth line."

"Can't you just do it for me?" I gripe.

"Where's the fun in that?" she says cheerfully.

Left our poor deer both reeling.

"Did you find it?" she asks me.

"A hundred!" Frank shouts.

"Frank, there are only eight antlers!" Eliza says.

I think I've found the number, actually . . . sitting between the last two words on that line. "Got it," I say to Eliza.

"Now," she says. "Skip the next line—there's nothing there. But the final line of the poem will give us one last number."

All tangled in knots, they grumbled and griped
At their poor, unwise venture with feeling.

"It will?" I say.

"Take a closer look at *unwise venture*," she says. "You ready with our three numbers?"

"READY OR NOT, HERE WE COME!" Frank shouts, his voice nearly drowned out by the howling wind.

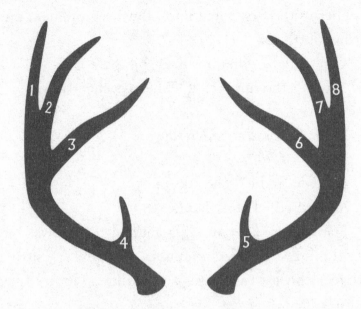

THE ORDER IN WHICH YOU PULL
THE ANTLERS IS YOUR NEXT PAGE.

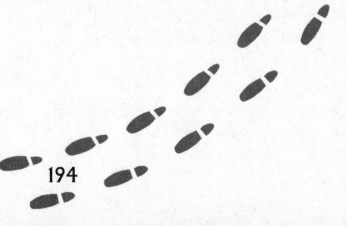

WE HAVE TO go to the attic. It's the only way to help Mom get out of the Dead Room.

With Frank on my shoulders, I pull down the string to the attic hatch, and an awful stench wafts down. It smells like something's rotting up there.

I climb up, and the smell gets worse. My eyes are watering.

"Ugh! What's that smell?"

"Whoever smelt it, dealt it!" Frank shouts.

Eliza hops up into the attic, and she coughs into her sleeve. "This is *unbearable*," she coughs, but she follows me through the attic anyway.

The odor is making me dizzy. I wobble on my feet. Suddenly my head is on the wood floor, and Eliza and Frank are lying next to me. This is no ordinary smell I'm breathing in . . . this is sleeping powder!

"What do I do with you?" says a voice from behind us. "Sticking your nose where it doesn't belong . . ." I try to see who's talking, but I can't turn around. My head is too heavy.

I wake up with a jolt.

"Carlos!" Eliza whispers. "I'm glad you're awake—I think we were dropped off here."

"Where is here?" I say.

"An olfactory factory."

"Old factory factory!" Frank says.

"*Olfactory* factory," Eliza corrects. "*Olfactory* means related to your nose."

I guess this is the perfect place for one ghost to ditch three nosy detectives.

CASE CLOSED.

"WHAT IS THE hair incident?" I ask.

"Two weeks ago . . . Harris and I woke up to . . . well, a haircut."

We all stare at Reese.

"What do you mean, a haircut?" Eliza asks.

"Up until two weeks ago, I had hair down to here." Reese gestures halfway down her chest. "But in the middle of the night, the ghost snipped off the left side of my hair. I had to get it chopped up to my shoulders to even it out. And the ghost cut off two inches off Harris's beard."

"And you both slept through that?" Mom says, surprised.

"Like a rock," Reese says.

"That's not *that* scary," Frank says. "I get haircuts all the time. They don't even hurt!"

Reese frowns. "The scary thing was that the ghost was *in* our room. With scissors. Sure, it was only a haircut this time . . . but who knows what it will do with those scissors next time?"

"Don't forget the message on the wall," Harris says.

"Oh, yes. It said CUT AND RUN."

"So . . . the ghost described what it did?" I say. "That's weird."

"Or," Eliza says, "maybe it's a warning to you two. Telling you to cut and run. It's an expression that means 'flee.'"

"Or," Mom says, "maybe it's not a warning at all. Maybe it's a command . . . a threat."

We all sit in silence. All except Frank, who hums to himself as he merrily scarfs down another spaghetti bite. Oh, Frank!

TO ASK WHO MIGHT WANT REESE TO FLEE THE HOTEL, TURN TO PAGE 64.

←——→

TO ASK WHETHER THEY THINK THE GHOST IS REAL, TURN TO PAGE 389.

CHOOSING BETWEEN MY best friend and my best friend's little brother is a very dangerous game . . . I feel like I'm picking kickball teams, and I'm bound to hurt someone's feelings. But my gut is telling me to take Frank. He is unpredictable—I just know he'll unearth clues with me. We need to dig up clues right now, more than we need Eliza's puzzle-solving skills.

Besides, when he isn't being a huge pest, Frank is pretty fun.

"I'll take Frank," I say.

"WINNER WINNER CHICKEN DINNER!" Frank shouts in Eliza's face.

Eliza looks wounded.

"You're the smartest person I know," I tell her, trying to soften the blow I just delivered. "Eliza, if you and Mom get stuck in the Dead Room, I'm counting on Mom's experience and your logic to get you two out."

She nods seriously and starts gathering up the flashlights. She tries to hand me one, but I shake my head.

"No, you keep it. Frank and I aren't going anywhere dark. You'll need all four flashlights . . . just in case."

Mom puts a reassuring hand on my shoulder. "It's going to be okay, Carlos."

It's a bad sign when I don't know who she's reassuring—me, or herself.

I nod once, and then Mom and Eliza leave the room.

Now it's just Frank and me. "Okay, Frank, who should we investigate? Remember our suspects?"

"No."

"Reese didn't want to hire detectives, even though her whole hotel business was being ruined by ghosts. Don't you want to talk to her?"

"No."

I sigh, frustrated. "Then what *do* you want?"

"I want to have a snowball fight!"

Maybe keeping Frank on task is going to be harder than I thought. I better decide for us.

TO TALK TO REESE, TURN TO PAGE 40.

←——→

TO HAVE A SNOWBALL FIGHT, TURN TO PAGE 285.

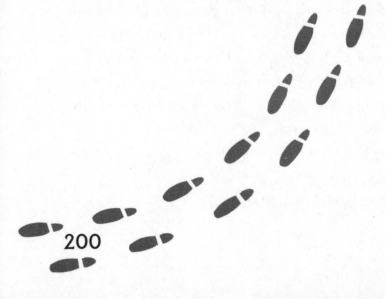

200

"THANK YOU, MR. Bookbinder, that's all we need for now."

Byron, honestly, looks relieved to see the back of us.

"Yes, you three best be off," he says. He looks back at us intensely, his eyes magnified behind his glasses. "The ghosts don't emerge until the whole lodge is still. Quiet like death."

My stomach swoops.

"The sun is down, so the time is nearly upon us. The faster you go to bed, the faster you'll meet them." He grins, and the hair on my neck stands up.

GO TO SLEEP ON PAGE 439.

"SORRY, JANUARY," I say. "We have to keep our work a secret."

"I know something you don't know!" Frank taunts.

January huffs, and her eyebrows converge into an angry V on her forehead. "MOM! DAD!" she shouts.

"Run!" I head for the stairs, but Frank scuffs his foot on the floor like a bull about to head-butt a red cloth.

"CHAAAAARGE!" he cries, running into January and tackling her around the middle. They both fall backward, and January shrieks.

"Go, go, go!" I shout as I hop up the stairs. Eliza runs after me, and Frank gets to his feet, narrowly avoiding January's fingers clawing at him.

"You'll pay for this!" she says. "I'm going to tell on you!"

But we keep running, and we don't stop until we get to my room. We collapse on the bed, panting.

"How much trouble do you think we'll be in with Reese and Harris?" I ask.

"WHO CARES!" Frank says. "I wanna do that again!" Then he hops toward his sister and tackles her.

"*Frank!* Get off me!"

Frank pops up and starts jumping on the bed; Eliza looks furious.

Knock. Knock.

We all freeze. The room is so silent that I can

practically hear my heart beating.

"Mom?" I say.

But when I go to open the door, no one is there.

"Probably someone playing a prank," Eliza says.

"When are you going to admit that this place is haunted?" I say. "Ghosts exist, Eliza, and they're here! How else do you explain Mom's disappearance?"

She presses her lips together. "I'm sure there's a logical explanation why—"

"Why my mom would vanish into thin air on the first night of the case? Yeah, the logical explanation is a *ghost*. Just admit it already! You can be wrong every once in a while, Eliza—it won't kill you!"

She looks like I slapped her in the face. "Carlos, I . . ."

But whatever she's going to say, whatever words of false comfort she's going to give, I don't want to hear it. Until I find Mom again, nothing will loosen the tightness I feel in my chest. I bury my face under the pillow and stay there until I fall asleep.

CRASH.

It's a sound to make us all jerk out of bed.

"What is it?" Eliza says, clutching the covers.

"It came from the bathroom." I roll out of bed and almost forget I was upset with Eliza last night. But our safety—and protecting my friends from a ghost that Eliza doesn't even believe in—is more important than any residual anger I feel. I edge closer to the bathroom door, which is just a little bit ajar. Then I kick the door until it swings wide open. Broken mirror shards are *all* over the floor, and I pull Frank back before he hops into danger.

"Be careful, Frank!" Eliza says. "You could cut your feet!"

Frank ignores his sister. He leans forward, picks up a shard off the floor, and stares into it. "Mirror, mirror, on the wall, who's the fairest one of all?" Frank says. "What's that? It's ME? You are *too kind*!"

I roll my eyes.

"Mirrors don't just spontaneously combust," Eliza says, scanning the room for who knows what.

204

"Ghost," I whisper.

She shakes her head and points at something on the wall by the tub. It's a mechanical device that looks almost like a slingshot. "I'm sure this thing was on a timer," she says. "When it went off, it threw something hard at the mirror, with incredible force. Probably that," she says, pointing at a small metal ball on the ground by the toilet.

"Yeah, but this slingshot thing wasn't in the bathroom last night. I would have noticed it *for sure* when I was brushing my teeth."

"Which means . . . ," Eliza says quietly, giving me a dark look.

She doesn't finish her sentence, but I know exactly what she's thinking. Someone—or *something*—was in our room while we were sleeping. Planting the device, setting it up to go off.

"But *how* would someone be able to get into our room, unless they had a . . ." She stares off into space.

"Unless they had a what?"

"EARTH TO ELIZA!" Frank shouts in her ear.

"A master key!" she says. "The only people who would be able to get in here would be ones with a master key. Definitely Sunny . . . and probably Reese and Harris."

I look down as I stare at the glass shards. And that's

205

WITH YOUR RACK NOW LEAVE AT 11:08 AND SHE COMES HOME

when I notice red lines on some of the mirror shards.

"Um . . . Eliza? Do you think that's a message for us?"

She tiptoes into the bathroom, extra carefully, and begins to sort through the pieces. At last she stands back and examines her work. The mirror looks almost like a jigsaw puzzle now, with just a few pieces missing. The message is visible enough . . . only I don't understand what exactly it's supposed to say. I step beside Eliza and look at the mirror.

"What do you think?" she asks me.

"It looks unfinished," I say.

"SO FINISH IT!" Frank calls from the doorway.

FIND THE TIME YOU MUST LEAVE.
TURN TO THAT PAGE.

←——→

TO ASK ELIZA FOR A HINT,
TURN TO PAGE 296.

I PUSH PAST Frank to open the bedroom door. Before we get Harris even angrier.

I only open it a small sliver—I don't want anyone to see the nightmare happening in the bathroom. Even so, the steam rolls out into the hall.

"Someone taking a shower?" Harris says.

"Something like that. How can we help you?" Then suddenly I notice Sunny, lurking quietly behind Harris. "You!" I shout, pointing at her. "You have the master key to everyone's room." It hits me like an avalanche that Sunny could have sneaked into our rooms, set up this "haunting," and then left.

Sunny turns whiter than an eggshell.

"That's what we came to talk to you about," Harris says bashfully. "Sunny's key was stolen last night."

Eliza and I look at each other.

"Stolen!" I say.

Sunny nods. "I always keep the master key in the same place—on a hook in my room. When I left my room in the middle of the night because of the banging in the walls, the key was there. When I came back, it was gone."

"Did you lock your room?" I say.

"Absolutely," Sunny says. "I am very paranoid about that. I always lock my room."

I look at Harris, whose beard twitches. He looks both

angry and worried—but I can't tell, from his expression, whether or not he knows we snooped through the mail yesterday. "We're going to have to call a locksmith," he finally says. "This is what happens when you run a lodge with skeleton keys, instead of a hotel with swipe cards."

"But how long will it take the locksmith to get here?" Eliza asks quietly. "The snowstorm was raging last night. Are the roads drivable?"

Harris clears his throat uncomfortably. "No," he says. "They're not. We're . . . um . . . locked in here."

His words seem to echo around in my brain. Locked in—*locked in*?

I wonder if the ghost knew about the snowstorm when it asked us to leave at three forty-five. Not that it matters: I'm not taking one step out of this lodge until I find my mom.

"And there's more," he says, like he's about to kick us while we're down. "The phones aren't working. None of them."

"So," I say, "to get this straight: we are all trapped in the lodge together, with no means of communication, no way of getting out, and the ghost or whatever might have the key to every room?"

Harris winces. "It sounds bad when you say it like that."

"It sounds bad *any* way you say it," Eliza says.

Harris looks to the door next to ours. "I was actually hoping to catch a word with your mother. . . ."

"She's following a lead," I say. "We'll let her know when she comes back."

He nods, and Sunny follows him, tail between her legs. I actually feel bad for her—I'm sure the locksmith and key replacements are going to come out of her paycheck, since the master key was her responsibility.

But the big question is . . . who took the key? And why? Just to torment us? Or for something else too?

"Well," Eliza says, "this is bad news all around." She slips a sweater on over her pajamas, then does some sort of magical maneuver to somehow take her pajamas off under her sweater. "We have to get moving."

Frank takes that as his cue to run around the hotel room. He flits from one side of the room to the other, jumping between the beds, shouting, "LAVA!" as he avoids the floor.

"Carlos, we picked up two important clues last night, and we haven't looked at either of them!"

"What clues?"

Eliza reaches into her backpack and pulls out two letters.

The first is the letter we stole at the beginning of

the night: the one addressed to Byron with the words FORMAL WARNING on the envelope. I nearly forgot about the letter we took from Byron's briefcase when we nicked his EMF reader. Wow, we had a really long night last night.

The second is the letter we stole at the end of the night. The one we took from Cricket's mailbox.

"Which one are you more interested in?" Eliza says, holding both letters out to me, one on each palm. "Which envelope should we open first?"

TO READ THE LETTER TO BYRON,
TURN TO PAGE 56.

←——→

TO READ THE LETTER TO CRICKET,
TURN TO PAGE 481.

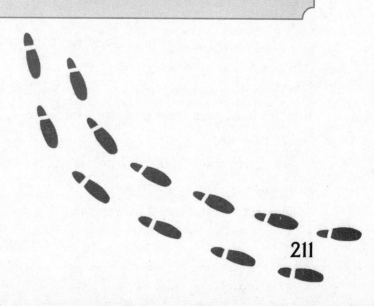

I THINK I'VE got this magic circle in the bag. The sum of each line is twelve, and once I put in all the numbers correctly . . .

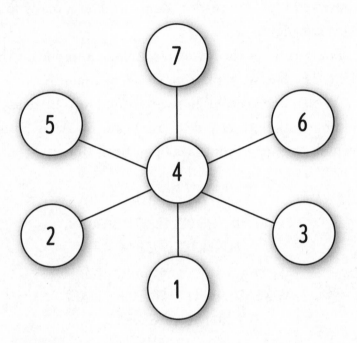

. . . There's a clicking sound, and the top of mailboxes tilts open. I'm in.

The only mailbox with any mail inside is Cricket's. Just a single letter. This must be what we're looking for.

"Let's read—"

Eliza freezes as footsteps creak on the stairs. Painfully. Slowly. We turn around . . .

January Winters is standing on the steps with her

arms crossed. No ghost, thank goodness! I let out a sigh of relief, but the relief turns sour when I realize January's expression is angry. "What are you doing over there?"

"None of your beeswax!" Frank shouts.

January's eyes narrow on Eliza. She approaches us, and even though she's only one person against our three, I feel very much backed into a corner. "What's that you're hiding behind your back?"

"Nothing," Eliza lies, turning pink in the process.

"Tell me what you're hiding, or I'll call my parents here right now!"

TO TELL JANUARY WHAT YOU'RE HIDING,
TURN TO PAGE 88.

←——→

TO KEEP THE LETTER A SECRET, TURN TO PAGE 202.

"SPY ON THE inside?" I say. "What does that mean?"

Eliza groans. "Of course, *of course*! I get it now. To set up all those ghost hauntings inside Reese's apartment, you needed someone in the Winters family—someone who lived in the suite—to do some of the legwork. So did you enlist Harris's help? Or January's?"

"You are a clever one. I like this little trick you three have going here. You make people think that Cat Serrano is the only detective on the case. I admit she was the target I went after. But you kids are industrious. I didn't start paying attention to you until it was far too late."

"So you're going to kill us?" Mom says, very calmly. She looks almost bored at the thought. "Rather unoriginal."

"I'm not going to kill you. No need to get my hands dirty. You'll die of dehydration . . . eventually. I doubt anyone will ever find you, but if they do, it will look like an accident. You got yourself stuck. Oopsie!" she says cheerfully. "In the meantime, you'll have to excuse me. I have a rather pressing event to orchestrate: the haunting to end all hauntings." There's a long pause, and then she says, "These are my last words to you. You should have left the hotel while you could. I imagine that will be your last regret."

Her words echo around the lair.

TURN TO PAGE 369.

I THINK I'VE figured out the walkie-talkie message:

CHASE THEM TO LIBRARY IN FIFTEEN
MINUTES
DON'T LET THEM FIND KEY UNDER PIANO
LID

"What key?"

"Okay, Frank, if you don't get your shoes on—"

"I'll wear my socks then!"

"Stop fighting!" I shout. "What key aren't we supposed to fi—"

The lights flicker. The door rattles on its hinges. Someone is trying to get into our room.

Frank throws off his covers and quickly puts on his shoes, and Eliza leans up against the wall, hiding from sight of the door. The overhead light flashes again.

Then the door stops shaking. The doorknob turns . . . slowly. And just as the door opens, the lights go off. Even though I can't see, I know—*I know*—someone has slipped into our room.

"Eliza?"

"Carlos!"

"Frank!" Frank says.

Suddenly something brushes my ankle.

I know by now that someone is *behind* the ghost— but all the same, my blood runs cold. And my dread only gets worse when I feel something sticky and hot on the back of my neck. It is *breathing on me.*

"Eliza," I say, forcing my voice to sound as calm as possible, despite the *thing* behind me, despite the hot breath on my neck. "Stand up. Frank—take her hand. Slowly head to the door. . . ."

I can hear the rustling of the bed and footsteps.

"Carlos, do you want your flashli—"

"*Don't* turn on the flashlight, Eliza!" But it's too late. She clicks it on, and right behind me is a monster. A bloody face—a raw red mouth from ear to ear, with sharp fangs and an unnerving grin. And even though I know it's costume makeup, even though I know it's not real—that there's somebody we know beneath the paint—I can't help but shriek. And so does Eliza. And Frank.

"RUUUUUUUUNNNNN!" I roar.

We sprint out of the room. I trip on the hallway carpet, and Eliza turns to help me up, screaming as the monster comes out of the room. The beast is behind us, snarling and snapping at our heels. It chases us to the stairs—

Chase them to library.

Of course! That's the message we decoded. That's where the culprits *want* us to go, but we don't have to obey! What if I ran somewhere else? What if, instead,

I ran out of the hotel? Would it follow us out into the snow?

On the one hand, it might be smart to get as far away from the ghost as possible. They *clearly* planned a haunting for us in the library that we don't want to fall into. On the other hand, maybe we should get that key—maybe it will help us find Mom.

TO RUN OUTSIDE, TURN TO PAGE 280.

←——→

TO RUN TO THE LIBRARY, TURN TO PAGE 380.

"QUICK!" I SAY, dashing into the fire den. Burning fireplaces illuminate the room. Does the fire run all night?

I flick on the lights, but they won't turn on. "The lights are dead!" I say. Between the burning fires and our flashlights, we don't need the overhead lights to see, but there's something comforting about being able to turn on the lights. With the darkness behind me, any old ghost could sneak up on me and—

Something grabs my shoulder.

"GOT YOU!" Frank says gleefully.

"Frank, you little—"

Screeeeeeech.

It's definitely coming from inside the walls. I go over to the wall and knock. "There's got to be a way in!"

"Hey—where's your mom?" Frank says.

We point our flashlights all around, but she's gone. Did she not follow us in here? Where did she go? "Mom? Mom! We have to go back!" I open the door to the lobby, but Mom is gone.

Vanished.

Into thin air.

There is fog rolling through the lobby, so thick I can no longer see the glowing footprints. . . .

THUD.

I jump. Then I close the door behind me—shut out the swirling fog before a ghost can appear. I lean against the door. My heart skips wildly.

"Carlos," Eliza says breathlessly. "Look."

She points her flashlight at a chair. Byron Bookbinder's chair. He's not in it . . . but his briefcase is. The one with the EMF reader. This could be our only shot at taking it. Unless he's already wandering around the lodge, using it himself. It's a gamble to break into his bag; we could get caught.

Oooooooooooooo!

Then again, we really could use the EMF reader.

I nod at Eliza in the dark. Then realize she can't see me. "Go for it," I say. "Do it quickly."

She jiggles the briefcase. "It's locked," Eliza groans. "Come here, Carlos. Frank, you have to cover us—ouch! Not literally! Warn us if Byron is coming."

When I stumble over to her, we aim both our flashlights at the lock.

It's a weird symbol with a bunch of blank spaces.

?	?			?	?
?	?			?	?
?	?	**E**	**A**	?	?
?	?			?	?
?	?			?	?
?	?			?	?

"Hmm . . . it's missing something," Eliza says, digging into the side pocket of the briefcase. She pulls out a bag, dumps it out on the couch, and spreads out—

"Scrabble tiles?" I groan.

But looking closer at them, they aren't exactly Scrabble tiles. They're tiles attached together in pairs.

I look at Eliza. "So, what do we do with these?"

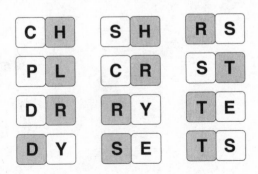

She frowns. "I think," she says, so softly that she could be talking to herself, "we have to make six-letter words, using these tiles, with EA always in the middle. And"—she presses a blank space on blank tile close to the middle—"if we have the right letters on the inside spots, and we press them only, I wonder if the box would open."

Ugh. Only a writer would lock his briefcase with a word puzzle!

IF THE LETTERS ON THE INSIDE ARE GRAY,
TURN TO PAGE 313.

←——→

IF THE LETTERS ON THE INSIDE ARE WHITE,
TURN TO PAGE 191.

"MOM, WE HAVE to run!" I shout, grabbing her by the hand.

The ghosts shriek behind us, but I don't have time to look over my shoulder. I yank Mom, then pull her through the door.

Eliza and Frank are there, arms outstretched, to help us in. And then Eliza pushes the door shut behind us.

Safe!

We run away successfully, but we never get that close to the ghost again. We spent two more weeks on the case, spinning in circles, hitting dead end after dead end, before it's clear that we're getting nowhere, and Eliza, Frank, and I have to get back to school. We end the case in disgrace.

This choice is definitely going to haunt me forevermore.

CASE CLOSED.

LOOK, I AM *not* voluntarily walking into the Dead Room. So if that means facing this monster behind us, so be it.

"Stay close to me," I whisper, my voice low enough for only Eliza and Frank to hear. They both stir next to me.

Suddenly I sprint to the left. Eliza follows, and Frank brings up the rear. I think the beast is caught off guard since we sprinted straight at it. It flinches, and I don't even have to slide—I soar.

We make it past the beast—and we're safe! Me, Eliza, and . . .

"Frank?" I say, suddenly realizing he's *not* next to me.

"HELP!" he cries.

The beast has Frank by the ankle. It drags him back, and we run forward—but not fast enough. It pulls Frank into one of the guest rooms and locks the door.

"ELIZA! CARLOS!"

"LET US IN!" I shout, knocking on the door.

"FRANK! FRANK!" Eliza shrieks.

I slam my body into the door until it splinters on its hinges, and we force our way inside. But the room is empty. No ghost, and no Frank.

CASE CLOSED.

"MOM, WE HAVE to know—how did you end up here?"

"I got attacked from behind when I was running after you," she says. "I'm so sorry I let my guard down. But better me than you."

"Well," Eliza says with a shudder, "now it's *all* of us."

"Why would someone do this?" I ask. "It was the first night—before you even did any investigating! I thought the culprit never attacks until you get close to the truth."

Mom laughs. "Carlos, there *are* no rules for how a culprit will or won't act." Then she says thoughtfully, "I have a feeling this is a scare tactic."

"Scare tactic? What does that mean, Mom?"

"Whoever is behind the hauntings doesn't want us to get within a hundred feet of the truth. They would never wait for us to get truly close. So if they scare us before we can investigate, maybe—in their mind—we'd quit the case and go home. Remember, they were able to drive away *all* the lodge's guests with these hauntings. But we're not so easily scared," Mom says, squeezing my hand.

I don't know *what* she's talking about—I've been terrified this whole investigation. But it makes me feel good to hear her say she thinks I'm brave.

224

"I am very hard to scare," Frank says. "Very, very, very, very, very, very, very—"

"We get it," I say.

"—very, very, very, very, very, *very* hard to scare."

"Th-that's because you're always the one doing the s-s-scaring," Eliza says.

I don't think my hug is helping her get warm. I take her hands in mine—they're ice-cold. We have to find a way out of here before she freezes. But there are still things I need to know.

Like . . . why did they lure Eliza, Frank, and me here now? Why not earlier, when they brought Mom here? And why not later?

TO ASK MOM WHY THEY LURED US HERE, TURN TO PAGE 361.

⟵⟶

TO SEARCH FOR A WAY OUT, TURN TO PAGE 77.

IT'S IMPORTANT FOR Mom to get all the information I have. So I tell her about the lair. The coded notes we found. The cameras.

"So someone could be watching right now?"

I think back to the camera monitors we found in that underground room—within the walls. We didn't see Mom on the monitor, but it really wouldn't surprise me if one of the cameras *is* in the Dead Room. Maybe it was just too dark to see.

"I don't know," I say. "I can't think straight right now. What do you think, Eliza?"

Silence.

"Eliza?"

She's asleep on the floor.

"C-C-Carlos," Frank whispers. "Too c-cold." And then he nestles under Eliza's arm and closes his eyes. Come to think of it, my eyelids feel heavy too. My brain is slow. Did we stay in here too long? Is this what freezing feels like?

I'll think about it later . . . for now, I'm just going to close my eyes for a second. . . .

CASE CLOSED.

I HAVE ELIZA play F A D E. But nothing happens.

She plays it again. Still nothing.

And again.

"WILL YOU STOP THAT!" bellows Harris, storming into the room. "What are you doing?"

"Playing piano!" Frank says brightly.

"No you're not!" Harris says, gesturing us away from the piano keys. "*This* is how you play piano." He begins to play a very beautiful song, and I go to leave, but Harris stops me.

"Where are you going? This music lesson is for *you*, you know."

"We don't need it."

"Oh yes you do! Now sit and listen, or you're fired."

I sit and listen. How long can one song last, anyway?

"Er . . . how long is this going to last?" I ask Harris.

"Well, this particular concerto is only seven hours long . . . but after that I have a sonata, a fugue, and a symphony! You should probably prepare yourself to be here for quite a while."

"But—"

"Shhhhh!" he says. "No speaking during a concert." He plays. And plays. And plays.

I have to face the music—this one ended on a sour note.

CASE CLOSED.

WE HAVE TO save the bank slips before Cricket destroys the incriminating evidence. I open her drawer, take all the papers I can find, and shut it again.

"We have to show Reese this evidence right away," I say.

We find Reese in the fire den with Harris and Sunny. "I have something to show you."

I hold out the papers.

The doorway to the library opens, and Cricket lunges out. Like a ballerina, she leaps across the room, grabs the deposit slips from my hands, and tosses them directly into the fire.

The papers crumble to ash. "HEY! What did you do that for?"

"That was our evidence!" Eliza cries.

"What evidence?" Reese asks.

"That Cricket was depositing lots of money into her bank account, ever since the hauntings started."

"Is this true, Cricket?" Reese asks.

"No, ma'am."

"It *is* true!" I shout.

"Where's your evidence?" Cricket demands.

I point to the fire. "There! *There* is my evidence!"

"That's no evidence at all," Reese says with a frown. "You know . . . I don't feel comfortable with you going around accusing people of wrongdoings without evidence. Perhaps I made a mistake in hiring Las Pistas Detective Agency. Harris, get me the number of a new detective agency. Let's try this again from the top."

CASE CLOSED.

WE FOLLOW THE poem on the tapestry, pressing the corresponding symbol each time it comes up in the poem. The passcode is long, but we got it: sun, snowflake, house, heart, flower, sun, leaf, snowflake, snowflake, snowflake. Funny how many snowflakes are in the poem, but I guess they *are* the Winters family!

The door clicks open, and we hurry inside.

The electricity isn't working in Reese's suite either, so I shine my flashlight around. There's a small staircase that goes up ten steps, a landing, another ten steps, another landing, and one last one. The first landing has a mini kitchen. The second landing has a lounge area with couches and a television. The last landing has another lounging area, with a door that must lead to Reese and Harris's bedroom and bathroom.

"Let's go," I whisper. I'm not sure *why* I'm whispering. It just seems like an appropriate thing to do.

My heart is beating insanely fast. Partly because I know we're doing something we shouldn't be doing. And partly because I keep seeing shadows dance at the corner of my vision—but every time I whip the flashlight around, nothing is there.

There's a dark presence in this room. I feel it. An evil spirit.

"Eliza," I whisper. "Something's in here with us."

230

"You're just paranoid," she says softly, like she's not convinced. "Frank?"

"Present!" he says cheerfully, like Eliza's taking attendance.

As we creep up the stairs, footsteps patter behind us. I shine the light, but there's nothing there. I shudder. "Do you see anything strange?"

"Yup," Frank says. "Eliza!"

"Anything strange that's not me?" Eliza says.

"Yup! Carlos!"

I sigh and look around for the source of the thumping sound, but since we've entered the apartment, it's been completely silent. So . . . did the ghost move on? Or did it stop because we're in here? Or—the most terrifying prospect of all—did it lure us here on purpose?

Frank jumps on the couch, while Eliza and I sweep the upper living room. Eliza's looking behind the television and in the cabinets, and I'm going through the mail on the table. Bills for Harris. A brochure for a film editing camp, addressed to January. And a letter from the Super Hotel Express for Reese.

I turn the envelope around and—

"Wait!" Eliza says before I can open the letter. "You can't open someone else's mail! It's a felony."

"It's already been opened," I say, showing her the

rip at the top. "So technically I'm just reading already opened mail."

Eliza considers that for a minute before she says, "Proceed."

As suspected, the letter is from Luther Covington, the owner of the hotel halfway down the mountain. I read it out loud.

DEAR LOSER,

YOU SHOULD HAVE SOLD ME YOUR STUPID HOTEL SIX MONTHS AGO WHEN I FIRST ASKED. YOU COULD HAVE GOTTEN TWICE AS MUCH OUT OF ME AS IT'S WORTH NOW. IT IS VERY GRATIFYING TO SEE YOUR VALUE PLUMMET; I RELISH YOUR BLUNDER. BET YOU WISH YOU HADN'T REJECTED MY OFFER NOW. NAH NAH NAH NAH BOO BOO.

"He actually wrote *nah nah nah nah boo boo*?" Eliza interrupts, moving closer to peek over my shoulder. "He really did!"

"Neener-neener!" Frank sings.

"Is this just a letter to taunt Reese? Seems a little rude."

"A lot rude," Frank says gleefully.

"Can I finish now?" I grumble.

> YOU'RE TOO DENSE TO EVEN REALIZE THAT ONE
> OF YOUR STAFF MEMBERS IS DOUBLE-CROSSING YOU
> AND WORKING FOR ME. NOW THAT I HAVE SOWN
> THE SEEDS OF DOUBT, I HOPE YOUR HOUSE OF CARDS
> COMES TUMBLING DOWN. I WILL PURCHASE THE
> WRECKAGE.
>
> > CORDIALLY,
> > LUTHER COVINGTON

"Ouch," Eliza says. "That last line is cold."

She's missing the forest for the trees, focusing on a mildly insulting last line when the biggest clue so far is staring us right in the face. "Eliza, that's not nearly as important as a double-crossing staff member!"

"Yes, that's troublesome," she says, rolling her braid between her fingers thoughtfully. "But are you sure that's real? This whole letter seems to be a taunt. Have you considered that maybe Luther just said that to torture Reese?"

It seems a little far-fetched to me, but Mom did tell me to keep a more open mind to other theories. I wonder what Mom would say about this letter if she hadn't

233

upped and disappeared on us. I don't know whether to be worried or angry. I think I'm somewhere in between.

"Seriously, Carlos," Eliza continues. "If Luther provokes Reese into thinking that someone she trusts betrayed her, then she might truly crack."

"Step on a crack, and you break your mother's back!" Frank chants.

Screeeeeeeee.

The sound of metal scratching metal. We all look up from the letter. The sound *definitely* came from inside the suite. The kitchen, it sounds like. I don't even have to ask Eliza and Frank if they heard it too. Judging from the way Eliza sharply intakes her breath and the way that Frank stiffens beside me, I know they heard it.

Slowly, carefully, Eliza folds the letter and slips it into her pocket. My heart is fluttering. Between the three of us, our flashlights are shining everywhere. But nothing is on the stairs.

Hands down, the worst thing about ghosts is their invisibility.

"Go, go, go!" I say, and the three of us thunder down the suite stairs. We open the door, run into the hall, and slam the door behind us again.

There was something *dark* in Reese's suite, and I don't just mean the power outage. In the hallway, I can breathe easier. We're all panting and holding our hearts.

"That was *awesome!*" Frank says. "It's fun to be scared!"

I do *not* share that feeling.

"So now what?" Eliza says, her voice shaking. "Do we tell anyone what happened in there?"

"We can't tell *anyone* what happened in there. No one can know we did that. Except for Mom." I put my hand on my walkie-talkie. Then pull it up to my mouth. "Come in, Mom! Hello?"

A noise comes from the Dead Room door. I look over, but there's nothing to see.

Tap. Tap.

The sound is coming from the *inside*. We have to get out of here before the ghost slips under the door crack and materializes in the hallway.

"Let's go!" I pull Eliza and Frank down the hall, and we don't stop until we whip around the corner—to the landing of the foyer staircase.

"Where are you taking us?" Eliza says.

"Away from there," I say with a shudder. "But I guess we should talk to Reese or Luther."

"The recipient of the letter, or the sender of the letter," Eliza says thoughtfully. "Well, if we talk to Reese, we have to be very careful not to tell her we got this information by snooping in her room and reading her mail."

We both look at Frank, who is notoriously bad at keeping secrets.

"What?" he says innocently.

TO TALK TO REESE, TURN TO PAGE 376.

←——→

TO TALK TO LUTHER, TURN TO PAGE 396.

A buck and a doe went forth down the slope
On a day thaT WOuld seem unappealing.
The snow cascaded, and soon an avalanche
Left our poor deer boTH REEling.
All tangled in knots, they grumbled and griped
At their poor, unwiSE VENture with feeling.

TWO. THREE. SEVEN. Got it!

The second I pull, the deer's head opens up like a mailbox flap, and there's a secret compartment inside the statue's neck. I reach in and pull out—

"A skeleton key," Eliza says.

She isn't joking. It's even shaped like a skeleton. "You think this is the key to the Dead Room?" I ask.

"It's a key to a TRAP!" Frank sings.

Eliza twists her hair between her fingers—her nervous habit. "There's only one way to find out."

I nod and start marching back toward the lodge. Hopefully Byron is still in the fire den and can give us a hand back through the window. We pass the hot tub and the firepit. I'm nearly at the window when I hear Frank cry out behind me.

"Wait! I found something!"

"If it's fox scat, I'm *not* coming to look!" I shout.

He hops into a bush near the firepit and emerges with something in his hands. "It's a rock!" he says happily. "With holes in the top. And a wire!"

Eliza turns back and examines the object. "Frank, this isn't a rock—it's a speaker. A speaker that's designed to look like a rock. To blend in . . ." She trails off, then looks up at me, and I know exactly what she's thinking.

That maybe a camouflage speaker could play howling noises.

"We can examine this later," I say impatiently, looking up at the lodge. Getting Mom out is my first priority.

Byron is gone from the fire den, but we're able to shimmy through the window with a boost from the extra-tall snowbank. Key in hand, I head to the Dead Room door. A green light is shining from the other side . . . and a creepy howling seems like it's coming from above.

"Speakers," Eliza reminds me. And in this moment, it actually feels good to think like her—to have a logical explanation behind the hauntings. Because sometimes I'm still not sure.

"Here goes nothing," I say, putting the skeleton key in the keyhole.

"Trap!" Frank says.

"Speaking of traps, please shut yours," Eliza says.

Frank sticks out his tongue at his sister.

238

"It's okay, Carlos," Eliza says. "We're right here with you."

I turn the key, and the lock clicks. Then I turn the knob slowly. Fog rolls out of the Dead Room . . . Is it a ghost?

Fingers curl around the doorframe. . . .

"Carlos! *Help!*" Mom gasps, stumbling forward.

"Mom!" I run to her, and her knees buckle. And suddenly she's on all fours on the carpet, trying to catch her breath. "I can't believe it! How did you . . . how long were you . . ."

She cups my face in her hands and inspects me all over, while I'm examining her. She is pale and sweating . . . and a little shaky. She nods at Eliza and Frank.

I don't know whether to be angry or relieved at Mom. "What happened to you? How did you get in there without a key? Why didn't you call for help on the walkie-talkie?"

"The ghost took it," Mom says. When she stands up, her legs are trembling—I give her my arm to hold on to. It takes me a moment to recognize the expression on her face, because in my whole life I've never seen her look like that before. . . .

She is petrified.

"What happened?" Eliza asks.

Mom shakes her head. She drops her voice to a

whisper. "We shouldn't discuss this here."

I agree. In the hallway, any one of our suspects could be listening in . . . including our ghost.

When we get back to the room, Mom curls up on the bed. My mom is usually fearless, but now she looks small. What did the ghost do to her? What did she see?

I sit down next to her, and she pulls me into a hug so tight that for a second I think she's part boa constrictor. "I'm so, so sorry," Mom whispers into my hair. "I'm sorry I brought you to this case. It's more dangerous than I thought. I never imagined I'd be held hostage in a room like that."

I swallow the lump in my throat. I don't want to cry, but my eyes are prickling. All the pressure of this case is getting to me: needing to impress Mom, needing to save Mom, and needing to hide how scared I've been. It all comes bubbling out in hot tears.

"What *did* you expect, Mom?" I say, wiping my face on my sleeve.

"I thought it was going to be some minor howlings. Nothing serious. I clearly underestimated the ghost." She hesitates. "Now I see why the guests all fled. I have half a mind to pack up and go myself."

"We can't," Eliza says. "Even if we wanted to. We're snowed in. Walls of snow are blocking the exits, and the car is buried. Even the telephone lines and cell towers are out. We're stuck until the weather clears."

"Well, that is unfortunate," Mom says.

This is *so* not like her. She never gives up on a case, and she never runs. Not even when things get really hairy. So what in the world happened to make her this afraid?

"What happened in the Dead Room, Mom?" I ask. "Tell us everything."

Mom shudders. I grab her hand and give it a squeeze. I actually think that helps. Her shoulders relax. "I was right behind you three. And something—the ghost—grabbed me from behind. I don't know exactly what happened, but I woke up inside the Dead Room. All alone. No flashlight . . ."

"What's in there?" Eliza whispers.

"I don't know . . . my eyes never adjusted to the dark. It was pitch-black the whole time. I could feel around, though. There was no exit, no matter how much I explored. And I heard . . ."

"What did you hear?"

"Breathing," Mom says with a shudder.

"That's nothing!" Frank says. "Everyone breathes!"

"Ironically . . . except ghosts," Eliza points out. "Since they're supposed to be dead."

Good point, Eliza. Mom nods, and she looks impressed. But I'm not surprised. Eliza is brilliant.

"But hearing . . . that's what saved me. Because—it must have been hours later—I heard someone outside the Dead Room door mention hiding the key in the deer head and something about antlers."

"And you don't know who said it?"

"The voice was a whisper. It's hard to tell whose voice it is when it's a whisper. But I was encouraged, because if I could hear people on the outside, maybe they could hear me on the inside. So I started furiously knocking and rattling the door. Every time I heard you in the hallway, I shook the door with all my might, hoping you'd come investigate."

"We thought it was part of the hauntings," Eliza mumbles.

"Well, eventually you found me and broke me out." Mom smiles weakly. "The thing is, though . . . I have to go back in."

Am I hearing her correctly? *"What?"*

"Properly prepared this time . . . with a flashlight. Now that I have the key, I can take a look around. Maybe there's a clue to find."

"I don't like this idea," I say.

"This is the job, Carlos. This is what being a detective is."

I shake my head. "No, Mom. Being a detective means relying on your team. From now on, we should use the buddy system. You and a buddy go investigate the Dead Room. Me and a buddy carry on the fieldwork. The four of us can meet back here in exactly an hour."

"That's an excellent plan," Mom says. "And I'll let you choose your companion, Carlos. Who do you want by your side—Eliza or Frank?"

TO PICK ELIZA, TURN TO PAGE 163.

←——→

TO PICK FRANK, TURN TO PAGE 199.

"YOU PLAN ON buying the Sugarcrest, right?" I ask Luther.

"Yes."

"And the fact that it's not for sale means nothing to you?" Eliza adds.

"Why should I care?"

"Because it's against the rules," Frank says.

Luther snorts. "There are no rules when it comes to business. Business is war. Kill or be killed. Some businesses—like the Sugarcrest—are fresh, juicy warthogs, just waiting for a lion to come along and eat it. I am that lion."

Yikes. This guy is *intense*.

"Let me give you some business advice—no, *life* advice. If you want to be successful, you're going to have to make some enemies."

Eliza and I look at each other and roll our eyes. "No offense, but that's horrible advice," I say.

"Are you making an enemy out of Reese?" Eliza asks.

Luther smirks. "Naturally."

"And that's why you're haunting her hotel?"

Luther arches his eyebrows. "Who, me?"

"YES, YOU!" Frank shouts.

"Couldn't be."

"THEN WHO?"

244

TO ASK LUTHER WHY HE WAS AT THE SUGARCREST JUST NOW, TURN TO PAGE 183.

←→

TO ASK LUTHER WHAT HE KNOWS ABOUT THE SUGARCREST HAUNTINGS, TURN TO PAGE 445.

THE LEFTOVER LETTERS spell out *two hundred forty-six*. I enter that number into the lock. It clicks open—we're in!

And good thing too, because I don't think we have much time before Reese, Harris, and January get back. Especially now that the sun has gone down.

I reach into the cabinet and grab the papers inside. Then Frank and I slip out Reese's door before she knows we invaded her private space. I try to hide the papers in my shirt, but I don't think it's doing the trick, because Cricket is staring at me as I cross the hallway. And that's when I notice the clock behind her.

Thirteen minutes *past* the time I was supposed to meet Mom and Eliza. They probably think something happened to us.

"Quick, Frank!" I say, grabbing him by the hand and sprinting up the stairs. We head to room 237, and I let myself in with my key.

Mom and Eliza aren't there.

"Okay, don't panic," I tell myself. "Think logically. Like Eliza."

"Logic is for squares," Frank says, jumping on the bed.

As far as I can see, there are only two reasons why they wouldn't be here:

1. They thought we got into trouble, so they went searching for us.

or

246

2. They got into trouble themselves.

I kick the bed in frustration. I have *no idea* what to do next. I don't want to wait here if they're in trouble—they might need our help. But what if they do manage to get back here, and we've gone looking for them?

Curse the ghost for stealing our second walkie-talkie!

"Hey, aren't you going to look at the thing you stole?" Frank says, still jumping on the bed.

Oh, right—I forgot. I reach into my shirt and pull out the papers I was hiding. There aren't that many pages, but they're all stapled together.

We, Young-soo and Hana Park, give our hotel, the Sugarcrest Park Lodge, to our eldest daughter, Sunny Park.

I look up.

Sunny Park . . . is that the same Sunny who's the housekeeper here? It *has* to be, right? How many Sunnys could there be associated with the Sugarcrest Park Lodge?

Now I'm *really* confused. What does Sunny have to do with any of this? I mean . . . Reese was hiding this will. Does that mean this will proves that Sunny is the real owner of the hotel?

My head is spinning. So . . . is Reese trying to drive

247

Sunny out? Or is Sunny trying to drive Reese out?

"Frank!" I say. "Do you know what this means?"

"What what means?" he says. "I can't read, remember?"

"Sunny is Reese's sister . . . she's a Park too. . . ."

"Okay!" Frank says, and he goes back to humming.

Clearly this means more to me than him. I have to find Eliza and Mom. They'd know what to do with an important clue like this! But I still don't know whether I should wait here for them like we'd promised, or I should go looking for them.

TO STAY PUT AND WAIT FOR MOM AND ELIZA, TURN TO PAGE 36.

←——→

TO GO LOOKING FOR MOM AND ELIZA, TURN TO PAGE 408.

I'M CURIOUS WHETHER our glowing footprint belongs to Fernando di Cannoli. He was really shady when we talked to him yesterday.

We walk into the kitchen, where Fernando is shoving something into a compartment in the wall. The second he hears us, he jumps and slams a picture frame closed, so that a still-life painting of fruit in a basket covers the area of the wall that was just open.

Is that a wall safe? I thought only billionaires had those! We *have* to take a look behind that picture.

"You a-scared me!" Fernando di Cannoli says, his accent *so* ridiculously over-the-top again. "Um . . . how a-much of that did you see?"

"How much of what did we see?" Eliza says.

Perfect answer, Eliza! Fernando starts to relax; I can tell from his posture.

"How can I—the greatest chef in all of Italia—help you?"

"Food, glorious food!" Frank sings. "We need it now, and we need it FAST."

"Please," Eliza reminds him.

Frank opens his mouth wide. "Ahhhhhhh," he says, like he's at a doctor's office.

Fernando sets some cheese in a can on the table. Which seems beneath the greatest chef in all of Italy, but it satisfies Frank.

249

"We need to talk to you," I say to Fernando.

Fernando's face is glistening with sweat. "I don't have time to talk."

"It'll be quick," Eliza promises.

This is the second time Fernando hasn't wanted to talk to us. When he's not performing his over-the-top chef persona, Fernando seems to be really . . . squirrely.

If I only have a limited time, do I want to ask Fernando about his alibi? Or do I want to find an excuse to bend down, so I can look at his shoe?

TO BEND DOWN AND EXAMINE
FERNANDO'S SHOE, TURN TO PAGE 293.

$\longleftrightarrow$

TO ASK FERNANDO ABOUT HIS ALIBI LAST NIGHT,
TURN TO PAGE 39.

TURNS OUT, DOWNHILL skiing is *very hard*.

My skis keep crossing over themselves, which makes me crash into the snow. Eliza is going down the mountain by stepping down sideways, ski by ski. Frank cannot control his speed.

"*Wheeeeeeeeeeeeeeeee!*" he cries, just narrowly avoiding a tree.

"Eliza, you must have read something about skiing!" I shout across the hill, after my fifth fall.

"I think you're supposed to go down pizza pie!"

"I'm more in the mood for apple pie," Frank says. "Or pumpkin pie."

"We're not eating pie, Frank," I say.

Eliza makes her skis into a wedge and slowly starts gliding down. "Actually, this is a lot easier!"

We all follow her lead and slide toward Luther's property, which we can see from a mile away because it's got neon glowing lights.

At last we reach the front entrance to Luther's hotel. The Super Hotel Express is tacky, run-down, and charmless. I'm starting to understand why he wants to own the Sugarcrest so badly. If his business is doing well, looking like this, I imagine he'd make a ton more money off a place that's as classy and comfortable as the Sugarcrest.

My boots clack on the floor of their lobby, and I'm dragging my skis behind me, leaving a trail of snow

251

that's making the front-desk clerk wince.

"I . . . what are you doing?"

"We just came in from nighttime skiing," Eliza says. Usually Eliza turns pink when she lies, but luckily, her cheeks are still red-raw from the cold outside.

The desk clerk gives us a very snooty look. "Are you guests here? Because I'm afraid I can't permit you to go any farther if you aren't guests."

"We have a room," I say.

"A fancy room!" Frank says. "With chocolate on my pillow!"

The clerk frowns. "I need to verify that."

Uh-oh.

"What is your name?"

Eliza and I look at each other in panic.

Confidently, Frank says, "Mickey."

The desk clerk types it in. "And your surname?"

"Mouse!"

I hold in a groan.

"Well, I'm afraid we don't have a Mr. Mouse staying with us. . . ."

TO UNPLUG THE COMPUTER AND ERASE THE
GUEST RECORDS, TURN TO PAGE 71.

←——→

TO BOOK A ROOM AT THE SUPER HOTEL EXPRESS,
TURN TO PAGE 501.

I KNOW THIS is going to be the *weirdest* question I ever ask a suspect, but my gut says, "Go for it!"

"Mr. Covington, can I examine your shoe for a second?"

He blinks, confused. We definitely caught him off guard with that one. "My shoe?"

"You know," Frank says, "they're like hats for your feet. You tie 'em in a knot, tie 'em in a bow. One, two, buckle my shoe?"

Luther stares blankly.

"You know, for a business guy, he's not very smart," Frank whispers, loudly enough for Luther to hear. "He doesn't even know what a *shoe* is."

"Please," Eliza says. "It's important."

Luther nods once and slips off his left shoe. We turn it over, and I can tell right away it's not the correct shoe. It's too small. Luther is tall enough to graze a tree, but his feet are surprisingly tiny. Not to mention that the rubber of his shoe has a straight-line pattern. We're looking for squigglies.

"The glowing footprint isn't yours."

"What glowing footprint?" Luther frowns. "Don't tell me you *really* think there's a ghost up there!"

"Isn't there?" I say.

"No."

TO ASK LUTHER WHAT HE KNOWS ABOUT THE HAUNTINGS, TURN TO PAGE 445.

"AAOOOOOOOOOOOOOOO!"

The howling echoes throughout the lodge. I'm going to find its source.

Eliza and I make our way down the stairs. The front doors to the lodge are wide open again. Only, in the storm, snow is flying into the lobby, and light from the lobby is spilling out onto the fresh powder.

The sound comes again, and it is clearly from outside.

Then, there—a long shadow appears in the snow. One with a huge mass. Furry and monstrous.

"B-b-bear!" I shout.

It turns and looks at me—with a long snout, dripping drool, fangs bared. It's not a bear. It's a *dog*. The biggest dog I've ever seen.

It snarls at us.

"SHUT IT!" I shout, trying to close the double doors before the monster gets loose in the lodge. But they are not budging. There's a sizable snowbank in the lobby now that's blocking the doors from shutting.

The shadow moves into the hotel. I can hear the low-pitched growl so close to me that it's practically rumbling in my ear.

"Run!" I mouth at Eliza.

But our run is a tiptoe. A slow, quiet retreat into darkness so that the bear-dog doesn't hear us. We can't make it up the stairs. Our only chance is the fire den.

"Quick, this way!" says a voice behind us. January—thank goodness.

At the sound of her voice, the dog charges toward us. But we slip inside the den and shut the doors . . . just in time to hear the dog collide with the wood.

Its barks are deep and guttural, and it scratches the door, eager to get in. Then, suddenly, it stops. No more howls, no more snarls, no more scratching, no more maniacal laughing from some distant corner of the house. Just . . . silence.

The quiet might be even creepier than the growling.

"What was *that?*" January says, holding her heart and panting. "What's it doing in my family's hotel?"

TO ASK JANUARY WHAT SHE'S DOING AWAKE, TURN TO PAGE 38.

←——→

TO STOP THE DOG FROM ATTACKING SOMEONE ELSE, TURN TO PAGE 18.

I TURN THE arrow until it faces south.

The floor shakes.

And tilts.

Above us is the door, and below is darkness.

"HOLD ON!" I shout, trying desperately to grab on to a rope—but there is none. Or dig my fingers into the ground—but there is nothing to hold on to. The slick floor is like a slide.

And so down we go, into a deep, dark pit.

I can't believe how quickly this case went south.

CASE CLOSED.

I HAVE TO get out of here! I have to run!

I turn my back on January and *bolt*. Like my life depends on it. Which it does.

I'm halfway down the tight hall when something steps into the path, blocking my way: the ghost that kidnapped January earlier. Standing there with clawed hands and a clean mask of two black holes for eyes, and one for a mouth.

I feel wobbly on my legs. I'm surrounded. I've got nothing to fight back with except for the foam insulation in the walls. And nowhere to go. The ghost is in front of me, January behind. Trapped.

"I don't understand," I say. "You're the ghost."

January nods.

"Then who is this?"

"Also the ghost."

"Two ghosts," I groan. "No wonder you were able to pull off so many hauntings. So your kidnapping was—"

"All staged," January says. "We planned it together."

"You're haunting your own mom," I say, my head spinning. "Why?"

"I'm trying to get her to leave. Well, *we're* trying to get her to leave, together. Aunt Sunny and I."

"Aunt?" I choke as Sunny pulls off the ghost mask. "You're Reese's sister?"

"See, family helps each other out," January says.

"Aunt Sunny has been dying to take over the lodge, while I'm dying to leave. I want to go to real school, with kids my age. I want to live in a town, not all alone at the top of a mountain."

"Byron said you and Sunny were fighting."

Sunny frowns. "We had disagreements on the severity of the hauntings."

"Dead rats leading out of the hotel is a bit too far," January says.

"Well, clearly it wasn't far *enough*, since my sister is still here. We need to make things more severe. When we're finished with these detectives, Reese will finally see that it's too dangerous to stay here."

Oh no. I need to keep them talking while I think of a way out. . . .

"And the dogs were part of that plan to go bigger with the hauntings?" I ask.

"Yes. We've had to get more and more creative, since nothing seems to be scaring my sister away. I found a feral pack, roaming the woods. I led them here."

"And the glowing footprints? That was a man's shoe!"

"My dad's," January says. "I stole his shoe right out of his closet."

"We're in the walls now, so that's how you were able to make banging and howling noises where no one could see you. Oh, and the first night, when my mom saw your mask and you disappeared, you went into a secret passage in the wall, didn't you?"

"Aunt Sunny and I grew up here. We know the layout of the hotel. Add in my sound-mixing skills," January says, tapping her neon headphones, "and it was very easy."

They're inching closer to me. They're done talking.

I look around. But all I can see is foam insulation, used to keep the house warm. Can I do something with that?

January has nearly reached me, and I think I see a ventilation shaft behind her. I know it's definitely big enough for Frank to fit into—if only Frank were here. I don't know if it will be big enough for me . . . but I think it will be?

I just have to figure out what my best mode of escape is: using insulating foam as a distraction so I can run? Or hopping down a ventilation shaft?

TO THROW THE FOAM, TURN TO PAGE 131.

$\longleftrightarrow$

TO JUMP DOWN THE SHAFT, TURN TO PAGE 364.

"WHERE'S THE GHOST, January?" I ask. "Did you see where it went?"

"I don't know," she says. "Can you untie me?"

"Why would the ghost just leave you here?" I ask.

"I don't know! Here—I think you can cut through the rope."

"Did you get a good look at the ghost?"

"No, I didn't really. I was too busy *being kidnapped,*" she snaps at me. "Untie me."

"Well, was it a human or a ghost?"

"I don't know."

"Did it evaporate? Or did it go somewhere? What did you see?"

January's eyes narrow. "You ask a lot of questions."

"I just don't want the ghost to surprise us . . . or trap us in here."

"Well, it's a little late for that," January says.

"Boo," says a voice in my ear just as hands grab my shoulders. I'm yanked backward, quickly.

"Carlos!" Mom shouts.

But Mom, Eliza, and Frank become distant figures in the distance as I'm half dragged, half carried away. Near the Dead Room, I try to kick my ghost captor. But I end up ripping my pant leg and scraping my knee on a jagged wood plank in the process. It's bleeding and painful, and I'm sure I just picked up four different splinters.

But at the moment, this boo-boo is the least of my ghost problems.

CASE CLOSED.

"HELLO?" TYLER FROM the Super Hotel Express says in my ear. "Anyone there?"

I put the phone on speaker so Eliza and Frank can hear too. "Um, yes," I say in a higher voice. "This is Reese from the Sugarcrest. I need to speak with Luther immediately."

"Ma'am, are you feeling okay?" Tyler says. "Your voice sounds funny."

"I'm getting over a cold. Frog in my throat."

"Cough cough!" Frank says, and Eliza elbows him.

"Oh . . . okay. I'll transfer you right over to Mr. Covington."

I point at Eliza, my way of telling her to take over.

"Me?" she mouths.

"Reese," Luther says coldly.

"I, um, got your correspondence," Eliza says in her best Reese voice. It's not quite right, though. Eliza's no actress.

"Who is this?" Luther says sharply.

"Reese."

"Liar," Luther says. "This isn't Reese's voice, and this isn't Reese's cell."

Eliza winces, and Frank puts his hand on his forehead.

"I'm calling about our correspondence," Eliza continues stubbornly. "Your most recent letter."

There is a long pause. So long that I start to wonder

if Luther has hung up on us. "Is . . . is that you?" he finally says.

You who? None of us answer.

"Look, I sent you the most recent check. Is that what you're calling about? Have you looked in your mailbox yet? It's got to be there today—or worst case, tomorrow. Sorry I was delayed, but I upheld my end. What about your end—are you slowing down lately? I want more results!"

Frank coughs.

"That's all you have to say for yourself?" Luther makes an angry noise, like a whinny. "I am a very busy, important man with things to do! So if you have anything to say, *say it*."

We say nothing. I wouldn't even know where to start.

"Then do not waste my time anymore." He hangs up with great force.

"That was a bust," Eliza says to me.

"Was it?" I look toward the mail slot in the lobby by the door. "He seemed to think he was talking to a partner or informant. He said he sent the check in the mail. We have to follow this lead."

TO LOOK IN THE MAILBOXES FOR A LETTER FROM LUTHER, TURN TO PAGE 400.

263

I SQUINT AT the scrap of paper from Cricket's desk. "Eliza, this is seriously hurting my eyes," I say.

"Let me try!" Frank shouts, snatching the paper out of my hands. He holds it on his face like a blindfold. "Ah . . . I see, I see," he says sagely.

"What do you see?" I take it back from him and put the paper so close to my eyeballs that it's practically a contact lens.

"Made you look!" Frank giggles.

I should have *known* Frank was pulling my leg. He never solves puzzles like Eliza can.

"Carlos, think about the angle, the way I was looking at it. The paper was practically horizontal to my eyes."

"So . . . you want me to hold the paper sideways?"

She nods. "Close one eye, hold the paper just under your line of sight, and tilt the page. If you tilt it at the right angle, I know you'll see the secret message very clearly."

THE PASSWORD IS YOUR NEXT PAGE.

"QUICK! EVERYONE TURN off your flashlights!"
I shout.

Everyone clicks off their lights, and the darkness covers us. I can't see a thing—not even moonlight can make it this deep into the cave. All I can hear is Frank's, Eliza's, and Mom's heavy breathing.

"Shhhh," I whisper, and sure enough, all three of them quiet down.

We've done it! I can't see even a millimeter in front of my face. There's no way the ghost can find us in here—

Something yanks my ankle, and I trip to the ground with a yelp. Around my ankle—I realize in horror—is a rope. It pulls me upward until I am dangling upside down. I thrash around, but it's hopeless. I'm a rabbit in a snare.

"Here's a little secret," comes a whisper in my ear. "Ghosts can see in the dark."

CASE CLOSED.

266

"INTO THE FREEZER!" I whisper. "Go, go, go!"

We all file into the big industrial-size freezer, and we are careful *not* to shut the door behind us. We leave it open a crack.

In the fluorescent lights, we're crouching by a big shelf of vegetables. Mom's reading Luther Covington's letter *again*. Eliza's holding Frank's mouth closed.

I try to listen to the person in the kitchen, and I can't tell if it's Fernando or January or someone else. Is it a friend? Or an enemy? I edge closer to the door to get a peek. . . .

The freezer door slams shut. We're lurched into darkness.

"Carlos!" Mom whispers.

"I'm okay, Mom!" I say quietly, even though I'm shivering. Did the person in the kitchen lock us in purposely? Or was it an accident? Or was it a ghost?

"No, no, no, no, no, no, no," Eliza mutters. "*Please* tell me we're not locked in the freezer."

"Okay," Frank says. "We're not locked in the freezer. Feel better now?"

"No," Eliza says.

I fumble my way to a wall. Everything in here is ice-cold, of course. I wish I knew how much time we have before we become human popsicles. I wish I could see. I wish I had a phone or a torch or a flashlight—

267

"Eliza! Where's your backpack?"

"Here, why?"

"Flashlights!" I say. "You still have one with you, right?" The battery won't be frozen yet. Maybe we can find a way out of here.

She digs into her backpack and flicks on a flashlight. It's dim, but it works.

"Excellent preparation, Eliza," Mom says. "And quick thinking, Carlos." I can see her breath in the air. "Look around, kids. There should be some sort of emergency lever or fail-safe that will open this door from the inside."

Eliza flashes the light around and—there! Three levers to pull. One clearly marked with a grape symbol. One with a peach symbol. One with an apple.

Good luck getting out of this one, Fernando!
—January
First letter is in SHARP but never in DULL.
Second letter in EYES but not in a SKULL.
Third letter is in ALWAYS but never FOREVER.
Fourth letter you can find in any WHICHEVER.
Last letter is in FINISHED, but not in an END.
Together you'll know which lever to bend.

"What is that?" I ask.

"It looks like January made a riddle for Fernando . . . ,"

Mom says with a frown.

"She must be *really* bored," Eliza says.

"Well, she is the only kid here," I say. "I'd be bored too, if I were her."

"No wonder she was eavesdropping on us."

"So what do we do with this?" I say to Eliza and Mom.

Eliza leans closer to the riddle. "Each line refers to a different letter in whatever word we're finding. The final answer will tell us which lever will get us out of here. But one clue at a time. First we have to look for a letter that's in *sharp* but not in *dull*."

"You mean . . . all of them?" I say.

"Yes, but that means the first letter of our final answer can only be S, H, A, R, or P. We've already eliminated one lever. Keep going, and I bet we'll eliminate another lever soon too."

"Uh-oh," says Frank. His voice sounds weird.

"Uh-oh what?" I say.

"I lucked da pull."

"What?"

"I *lucked* da *pull*."

Eliza swivels her flashlight, and Frank's tongue is on a pole in the freezer, stuck there. He is frantically trying to rip his tongue away, but it won't budge.

He tries one more time. "I lucked da pull!" And it dawns on me what he's trying to say: *I licked the pole.*

"You didn't!" Eliza says, horrified. "Frank, you *know* that tongues stick to cold objects!"

"Thun!" he says.

"No, *not* fun!"

"I hope you like being attached to this freezer," I say. "Because that's where you're going to stay . . . forever."

The flashlight flickers out for a second, then comes back on. It's enough to make my heart race. Are we running out of light? Are we running out of time?

"Hurry," Mom says. "There's no time to waste."

"Geh me ouhha hea!" Frank shouts. *Get me out of here!*

"We're working on it, Frank!" I turn back to the riddle. It's our only hope.

TO PULL THE GRAPE LEVER, TURN TO PAGE 29.

TO PULL THE PEACH LEVER, TURN TO PAGE 148.

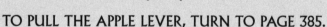

TO PULL THE APPLE LEVER, TURN TO PAGE 385.

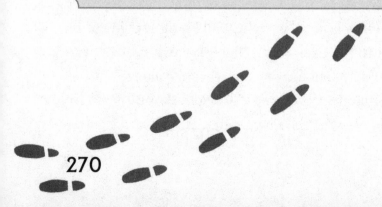

270

I HAVE TO check out the dumbwaiter. If Fernando saw a ghost in there, then maybe there's a clue. I walk over and look inside. It's small—only big enough for one of us.

"I wouldn't do that if I were you," Eliza says, as my torso is halfway into the dumbwaiter.

But I crawl in anyway.

"Carlos, be careful!"

The doors close behind me, and the little elevator goes down, down, down. Eliza and Frank disappear as the contraption slowly but steadily descends into darkness. I can hear them, but they sound terribly far away.

"How do we get this to come up?" Eliza shouts at Fernando.

"You can't!" he replies. "It's broken."

"What do you mean, *broken?*"

"Broken means it does not work."

"I know what broken means! But how do we get Carlos out?"

"We don't," Fernando says. "At least not without a firefighter. But with the storm coming, it might be many moons."

My legs, all curled up in the dumbwaiter, are starting to cramp. If I sit here for many moons, I won't be able to investigate! But what choice do I have? The dumbwaiter is stuck!

Speaking of *dumb*waiters, this was a dumb move.

CASE CLOSED.

"ELIZA, CAN YOU help me with this phone alphabet thing?"

"Phonetic alphabet," she says, over my shoulder. "And sure!"

A = alpha	N = november
B = bravo	O = oscar
C = charlie	P = papa
D = delta	Q = quebec
E = echo	R = romeo
F = foxtrot	S = sierra
G = golf	T = tango
H = hotel	U = uniform
I = india	V = victor
J = juliet	W = whiskey
K = kilo	X = x-ray
L = lima	Y = yankee
M = mike	Z = zulu

CHARLIE HOTEL ALPHA SIERRA ECHO TANGO HOTEL ECHO MIKE TANGO OSCAR LIMA INDIA BRAVO ROMEO ALPHA ROMEO YANKEE INDIA NOVEMBER FOXTROT INDIA FOXTROT TANGO ECHO ECHO NOVEMBER MIKE INDIA NOVEMBER UNIFORM TANGO ECHO SIERRA.

DELTA OSCAR NOVEMBER TANGO LIMA ECHO TANGO TANGO HOTEL ECHO MIKE FOXTROT INDIA NOVEMBER

DELTA KILO ECHO YANKEE UNIFORM NOVEMBER DELTA
ECHO ROMEO PAPA INDIA ALPHA NOVEMBER OSCAR
LIMA INDIA DELTA.

"The first letter of each word is the *only* letter we need. So if we ignore the weird words and just focus on the first letter only, that will give us our message. Frank—I told you to get your shoes on!"

"I don't *wanna*!"

"I got it from here," I say, as Eliza rolls toward Frank and begins to bicker with him. When I finish writing down the first letter of every word, I have:

CHASETHEMTOLIBRARYINFIFTEENMINUTES

DONTLETTHEMFINDKEYUNDERPIANOLID

Now all I have to do is figure out where the spaces go and read the message!

ADD TWO HUNDRED TO
THE NUMBER IN THE DECODED MESSAGE,
AND TURN TO THAT PAGE.

MOM IS SCREAMING, and the pressure is too much—I can't solve this puzzle!

"Eliza! Help! Where do I even start?"

"With the first battery in the top left corner. Everything should unfold from there! I'll get some of the others for you."

"Eliza!" Frank calls.

"Carlos—my brother! I need you to do the rest! Remember, you have to switch back and forth between pluses and minuses. A plus can't be next to another plus, and a minus can't be next to another minus. Call me when you figure out the charge in the bottom right corner!"

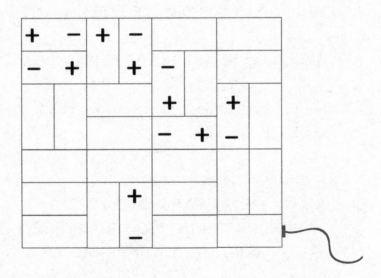

IF THE FINAL CHARGE IS POSITIVE, ADD TEN TO THREE HUNDRED, AND TURN TO THAT PAGE.

←→

IF THE FINAL CHARGE IS NEGATIVE, SUBTRACT TEN FROM THREE HUNDRED, AND TURN TO THAT PAGE.

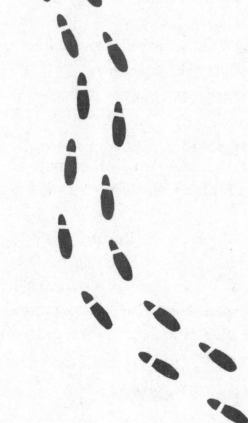

275

AS MUCH AS I want to keep poking around Cricket's desk, we have to follow the noise.

Thump.

That's *got* to be the ghost, right? More banging in the walls? Or maybe it's Mom. My heart leaps at the thought.

We bound up the stairs and veer to the right. I'm staring at the door of the Dead Room, wishing, hoping, praying that the sound isn't coming from there.

Thump.

I run halfway down the hallway and stop in front of the door where I *definitely* heard the sound.

"Carlos, this is Reese and Harris's bedroom. We can't go in there!"

"We have to," I say grimly.

"If we get caught, your mom will be fired for sure!"

I put my hand on Eliza's shoulder. "Let's not get caught."

When we get to Reese's door, I realize that we're going to have a really hard time getting in. Reese doesn't have a lock with a skeleton key, like the guests do. She doesn't have a card slot or a normal alarm pad. What she *does* have is a bizarre, unique alarm pad with shapes and symbols on it.

"Now what?" I groan. "Why can't she have a lock and key like everyone else in the lodge?"

"Maybe she thinks a keypad is safer," Eliza says. "After all, there's no way to pick the lock, and there are hundreds and thousands of combinations to choose from. We probably shouldn't test it until we understand it."

"Maybe it has something to do with *this*!" Frank shouts from across the hallway. I shine my flashlight at him, and he's wrapped up in a blanket. No, not a blanket—a wall tapestry.

"Frank!" Eliza hisses. "Where did you get that?"

"Put it back now!" I scold him.

"No!"

"Frank!" Eliza scolds.

"But Elizaaaaaa," he whines. "I'm cold!"

"Still," she says, "you shouldn't pull rugs off the wall, no matter how soft they look."

"But this one's important," Frank says, laying it down on the floor. "All the symbols are on it! Starting with moon, and ending with snowflake!"

He's right. There's a crest in the center of the tapestry, with all the symbols around it. At the edges of the fabric are words.

In sun and in snow,
This household stands tall.
Our love for it grows
Spring, summer, and fall.
But winter is what we cherish the best,
For Winters we are, and Winters are blessed.

Eliza grins. "Carlos! Frank is right—this tapestry *is* useful. I'm pretty sure we know what we have to press."

TO PRESS MOON, LEAF, HOUSE, STAR, SUN,
LIGHTNING, FLOWER, HEART, SNOWFLAKE,
TURN TO PAGE 54.

←——→

TO PRESS SUN, SNOWFLAKE, HOUSE, HEART,
FLOWER, SUN, LEAF, SNOWFLAKE, SNOWFLAKE,
SNOWFLAKE, TURN TO PAGE 230.

←——→

TO ASK ELIZA FOR A HINT,
TURN TO PAGE 398.

THERE'S NO WAY I'm letting the ghost chase me to the library, so I make a sharp turn and run outside.

"Carlos! Where are we going?"

"Away from the ghosts!"

The wind hurls fistfuls of snow at us. Over and over again. It's like being spit on by Mother Nature. I never knew how loud a storm could be. I can barely hear Eliza, begging us to turn back.

After a few minutes in the storm, I realize I've made a huge mistake by leaving the lodge. My clothes are soaked through, and all three of us are shivering. I pull Eliza and Frank back to the hotel, but the doors are locked.

We shiver as we hopelessly stare at the double doors. We're dangerously close to turning into snowmen. Whose smart idea was it to run out in the middle of a storm?

Oh right. Mine.

We knock on the doors with all our might, but no matter how much or how hard we knock, the doors don't budge. There's snow way in.

CASE CLOSED.

280

"ELIZA, WHAT DOES this even mean?" I squint at the message. It looks like a different language, almost!

desert the spirit and run far away
get out while you can in the light of day.
be gone from this place by three forty-five,
be gone from here if you want to survive.
this is your warning, for if you do stay,
then i'm the hunter, and you are my prey.

Eliza grins.

"What are you so happy about?" I say suspiciously.

"Cheese," Frank says sincerely. "Candy. Farts. Ghosts. Snowmen. Handstands. Dandelions. Sea lions. Regular lions. There's a lot to be happy abou—"

"Not you!" I say. "I meant Eliza!"

"I'm happy," she says, "because I know what to do with this message."

"Yes?"

"Hold a mirror in front of it, and everything will be crystal clear."

THE TIME TO LEAVE IS YOUR NEXT PAGE.

281

I THINK OUR only escape from this monster is to go into the Dead Room. I pull the key out of my pocket, and the beast snarls. In the dark of the hall-way, the fang-toothed smile is the only thing I can see. And it gets even wider as it points to the key in my hands.

"It *wants* us to go in," I say.

"NO WAY, JOSÉ!" Frank shouts.

"Carlos," Eliza says quietly. "It's a trap. They knew we took their walkie-talkie, and so they gave us that secret coded message on purpose. They *wanted* us to go for the key under the piano lid. So that they could force us into the Dead Room. Whatever we do, we *can't* go in there."

Thud, thud, thud, comes the knocking from inside the Dead Room.

"In," says a sharp voice from behind the beast mask. A female voice. But I just can't place it.

I put the key in the keyhole, and it turns. Sure enough, this *is* the key to the Dead Room. I'm glad we were able to solve that mystery before, ya know, dying in the Dead Room.

"In," she repeats.

"DON'T DO IT, CARLOS!" Frank cries.

I open the door. I open it wide, but there is only darkness inside. Then, from behind, the beast charges and shoves us in. The door closes behind us, and the lock clicks.

We're locked in.

A hand grabs my shoulder.

"*AHHHHHHHHHHHHH!*" I shriek.

"*AHHHHHHHHHHHHH!*" Eliza shrieks.

"*WHY ARE WE SCREAMING?*" Frank yells.

The hand slides off my shoulder, and as I click on my flashlight, I finally understand who was knocking on the door from the inside.

"Mom?"

She grabs my face and starts kissing my cheeks rapidly, over and over again.

"Mom, you were in here this whole time? Why didn't you walkie-talkie us?"

"He took my walkie-talkie!" Her voice is scratchy, probably since she hasn't used it in a while.

"He?"

"Or she . . . I didn't get a look at their face." Her face turns serious. "But what are *you* doing here? You shouldn't be here! Carlos, it's a trap!"

"What do you mean, trap?" Eliza asks.

"They lured you here on purpose—this is some kind of scare tactic!" She looks around frantically. "Let us out!" she shouts hoarsely.

"OR YOU'LL BE SORRY!" Frank adds.

Of course no one comes to let us out, and the room is eerily silent. And cold. It's like ten degrees colder than the hallway. Poor Eliza's teeth are already chattering.

I reach into Eliza's backpack to hand Mom some water. Then I wrap my arms around Eliza to keep her warm.

"T-t-thanks." Eliza shivers.

Mom drinks so fast that she ends up choking on the water. "Wrong pipe!" she coughs. Mom puts the cap back on the water bottle and wipes her mouth with her sleeve. "Thank you," she says. "I've been so thirsty. I think this room is soundproof. I was screaming all day yesterday, and no one came. And if all four of us are in here, we have to assume that no one is coming to rescue us."

"Are you okay, Mom? Did they hurt you?"

"I'm fine," she says.

TO ASK MOM HOW SHE ENDED UP IN HERE, TURN TO PAGE 224.

TO SEARCH FOR A WAY OUT, TURN TO PAGE 77.

FRANK IS SUPER prone to temper tantrums, and who knows what will happen if I don't get him his snowball fight.

"Okay, Frank. You win. One snowball fight."

"Yayyyyyyyyyyy!"

I grab our coats off the foyer's hideous antler-sculpture coat hook. The front doors are still blocked by the snow, so we crawl out the fire-den window again.

The grounds look like the sand dunes of the desert . . . only it's all snow. The wind nips at my face, and I sink even farther into my coat.

I take Frank around the side of the lodge—in view of the sunset. Down the mountain, I can barely make out Luther Covington's Super Hotel Express. I nearly forgot about him, since I haven't seen him since yesterday. But just because I don't see him doesn't mean he's not around. And he's still a suspect. Everyone is a suspect until we figure out the truth.

I stand by the wall of the lodge, and Frank runs across the mountaintop, nearly sinking into snow up to his waist. He starts making his snowballs, and just as I'm reaching my hand down to do the same, I hear voices coming from the window above me.

"Come on, Mom," says a voice I recognize as January. "This is too much. It's not even safe here anymore. Why won't you leave?"

"Because this place is my family legacy! It will be yours one day."

"I don't want it," January grumbles.

"I agree with our daughter," says a deep voice. "Honey, how many hauntings is it going to take before you realize that it's dangerous here? You're putting January in danger. Don't you care about that?"

"Of course I do! But I also care about her future."

"I don't need Sugarcrest, Mom. I have a future in a lot of things!"

"Yes, like the hospitality industry."

"No, like video editing and music production," January says.

"Now's not the time for this fight again," Harris says. "Reese, these attacks are getting increasingly worse. I know for a fact that the ghost trapped Detective Serrano in the Dead Room."

"How?" Reese says. "That place is perpetually locked! I've lived here since I was a girl, and even *I've* never been able to get inside!"

"I don't know," Harris says. "All I know is that we have to leave."

"Carlos—ONE TWO THREE FIGHT!" Frank says, suddenly beside me. He pelts a snowball at me. I turn around just in time to see a huge chunk of ice flying overhead, headed right for the window—

CRASH.

A direct hit on Reese's office window. Oh no!

The conversation above me immediately stops.

"What was *that*?" Reese says. I can hear her high heels clicking as she runs to the window to look out; I grab Frank, and the two of us sink into the snow right beneath her window. She won't see us unless she leans out the window and curls her torso over the edge.

"A haunting or a vandal?" Harris says.

"I don't know. I'm putting my boots on!"

All three of them leave the office and shut the door.

"What did you *do*, Frank?" I groan.

"Ice ball!"

It doesn't seem like we have any choice but to own our mistake. Unless . . .

I look up at the window, and we've shattered the glass just enough for me to reach my hand inside and unlatch the window. If we crawled through the window, maybe we could escape the wrath of the Winters family. . . at least until they cool down a little.

TO RUN AWAY BY CRAWLING INTO THE LODGE
THROUGH THE WINDOW, TURN TO PAGE 83.

$\longleftrightarrow$

TO FESS UP TO THE WINTERS FAMILY,
TURN TO PAGE 344.

THIS GRANDFATHER CLOCK puzzle is too confusing. "You're going too fast, Eliza!" I say. "Slow it down."

"It might be easier if we break it down," she says. "'At midday.' So start it at twelve o'clock. Yes, perfect. 'At midday, you said you had five hours to go until the party.' So five hours after twelve o'clock is . . ."

"Five o'clock," I say turning the hands.

"'But your guest was going to be one hour early,'" Eliza recites. "Which means the guest arrives at—"

"Four o'clock," I say, setting the clock back an hour.

"'The zipper of her dress broke, which tied you up for three hours.'" Eliza looks up. "Three hours after the time she arrives—four o'clock. That puts us at seven o'clock."

I nod and put the hands at seven.

"'But you still arrived two hours before the cake.' So if we get to the party at seven, and the cake arrives two hours later . . ."

"Nine o'clock," I say.

Eliza nods. "The cake . . ." She looks down at the paper again. "'Was there six hours after the floral arrangement.' So six hours *before* the cake arrived is our final number."

ADD FOUR HUNDRED TO THE HOUR
THE FLORAL ARRANGEMENT ARRIVED,
AND TURN TO THAT PAGE.

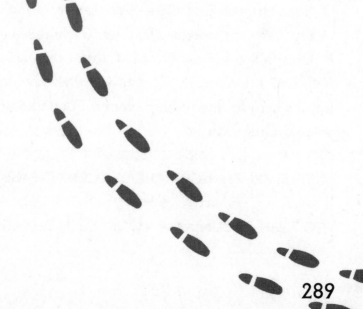

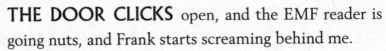

THE DOOR CLICKS open, and the EMF reader is going nuts, and Frank starts screaming behind me.

"GET AWAY!" Mom shouts. And she grunts, like she's punching or kicking or I don't know. I promised her I wouldn't turn around, and so I don't. I push Eliza through the door and blindly reach behind me for Frank.

"Frank! Come grab my hand! Eliza, where is he?"

But Eliza is now looking at whatever's behind me. Her mouth is in the shape of an O. And then, as if she can't look anymore, she closes her eyes tight. "Frankie!" she shrieks.

"Frank!" I yell again.

A small hand reaches mine, and I yank him forward—through the door.

"Mom!"

She gives a huge tennis grunt. "GET. AWAY."

"Mom!"

"Don't turn around, Carlos!" she says, even more frantically. Then she screams like she's attacking something.

Do I follow her directions? Or do I turn around to help her? I don't really want to see what's behind me, but it's hard for me to help Mom if I don't know what we're dealing with.

TO STARE STRAIGHT AHEAD, TURN TO PAGE 46.

←——→

TO TURN AROUND AND LOOK, TURN TO PAGE 178.

WE WALK AROUND the hotel looking for Sunny, but she's like a ghost herself: nowhere to be found. Eventually we head back to the top of the stairs. Eliza and I lean over the banister while Frank runs around the floor to let out his excess energy.

"Where could she possibly be?" I ask. "You don't think she went outside, do you?"

"In this cold?" Eliza says, just as the wind rattles the windows.

"Wheeeeeeeeeeee!" Frank yells as he whips by us again.

"Are there . . . secret passageways and rooms to find?"

"I don't know, Carlos. I know just as much about this lodge as you do!"

"So . . . where is she?"

"Wheeeee—" Frank stops running, halfway down the hall, and he grins at us. "Found her!"

I run toward him, and he points at a door. Room 237.

"Hey," I say, "isn't that—"

"Our room," Eliza confirms.

The door swings open, and someone comes out of our room backward, pulling a cleaning supply cart . . . and it isn't Mom.

Sunny turns around and recoils, like we startled her. We haven't said anything to each other yet, but I can already tell she's going to be a difficult suspect. She has that way about her—the way she presses her mouth together tightly. And the way she glares.

"Where's my mom?" I ask, gesturing toward the hotel room.

"Am I your mother's keeper?"

I try to edge around her to look for Mom, but she pushes the cart into me.

"Calm down," Sunny says. "She's in your room. She kicked me out before I was done."

"Done what?"

"What do you think?" Sunny snaps, gesturing at her cart. "Next time I *won't* turn down your sheets, if this is the thanks I get."

"Sorry," I say. She turns to leave, and Eliza nudges me.

TO ASK SUNNY WHAT SHE THINKS OF
THE WINTERS FAMILY, TURN TO PAGE 103.

←——→

TO ASK SUNNY WHETHER SHE'S SEEN
A GHOST HERE, TURN TO PAGE 300.

 292

I'M PROBABLY ONLY going to get one solid chance to examine his shoe. "I wanted to ask you . . . ," I say to Fernando. "Ooops! I think I dropped my contact!"

I don't actually *wear* contacts. It's something my Mom does sometimes. But I bend to the floor and pretend to search around with my hands. I grab Fernando's shoe.

"Hey!" he shouts. "That's my shoe!"

"Sorry! I can barely see without my contacts."

Fernando takes a step back, and Eliza holds up her hands. "Wait! You can't move, Mr. di Cannoli. What if you accidentally step on Carlos's contact?"

I examine the length of his shoes . . . they're definitely long enough to be the footprints from last night, but I won't know for sure until I get a good look at the rubber underneath.

"I think you *did* step on my contact," I say. "Can you lift your foot, so I can make sure you didn't squish it? Mom'll *kill* me if I don't find it."

Fernando sighs and lifts his foot. I take a peek at the pattern on the sole. . . .

It's not the ghost shoe.

"Found it," I say, pretending to put the contact back in my eye.

Fernando cringes. "Aren't you going to wash that first? It's been on the ground."

Ooooops.

I can see the wheels in Eliza's head turning, trying to think of a good explanation of why I'd risk an eye infection. But surprisingly, Frank rushes to my aid, his mouth full of spray-can cheese. "Five-second rule," he says.

Fernando nods. "Ah, sì, certo!"

TO ASK FERNANDO ABOUT HIS ALIBI,
TURN TO PAGE 39.

←——→

TO LEAVE THE KITCHEN,
TURN TO PAGE 138.

WE CAN'T DO any more investigating until we find Mom. She was right behind us during the haunting. And now she's missing.

"We have to go find Detective Serrano now," I say. "We'll be back later."

"What do you mean, find her?" Harris says. "Where is she?"

"We don't know," I admit. "She was right behind us . . . and then she was gone."

"GONE!" Reese sobs. "Taken by the ghost! Dragged to the other side!"

She stands up. "That's it—that's the final straw. I'm shutting down the hotel."

"What?"

"You're selling?" Harris says incredulously.

"I can't sell. If I sell, more people will be victims of the ghost, and I can't have that responsibility on my shoulders. No, I'm closing it down. We're all getting the heck out of here!"

"But wait, Mrs. Winters! First we have to find my m—"

"Too late for that! Let's go, go, *go*!" Reese cries as she drags Eliza and me out of the house. "I'm getting rid of the deed right away, and no one will *ever* come back to this old haunt."

CASE CLOSED.

NO MATTER HOW hard I stare at the reassembled mirror fragments, I can't figure out what the message is supposed to say. "Eliza, can you help?"

She hums and kneels over the mirror pieces. "It's got to be mirror related," she mumbles under her breath.

That seems obvious to me. Of course it's mirror related—the message is *on* the mirror!

Eliza leans forward, grabs a mirror fragment to the right of all the letters, and tilts it up. Then she laughs.

"WHAT?" Frank says from the doorway.

"Take a look, Carlos," she says, switching places with me. "Now put the mirror at a ninety-degree angle with the letters. Right down the line—yes, like that! Now what do you see?"

The first mark, which I thought was a V, is actually a W when duplicated in the mirror. The second letter looks like an I. Then a T. Then an H. "With," I say. "The first word is *with*."

Eliza nods.

"What about this?" I ask, pointing to the next word. An R is just chilling out in no-man's-land. In the mirror it looks like there's an R, and then a backward R.

"I think," Eliza says, "that when a letter can't be mirrored, the culprit just put it off the line. We should only count the R once . . . and ignore the backward one in the mirror. Do you think you can get the rest of the message? Since you're already sitting in front of it?"

WITH YOUR MOM NOW LEAVE AT 1:08 AND SHE COMES HOME

FIND THE TIME YOU MUST LEAVE,
AND TURN TO THAT PAGE.

THERE'S NO WAY I'm opening the door for *anyone*. Not after we found this threatening mirror message!

"I'm sorry, Mr. Winters, but we're not at liberty to open the door for anyone."

"What do you mean?" he says. "I've come to deliver a message!"

"We won't come out!"

"NOT BY THE HAIRS ON OUR CHINNY CHIN CHIN!" Frank cries.

"What hairs?" Harris says. "You're prepubescent!"

"I'm so sorry, Mr. Winters," Eliza says. "But we're not coming out."

"And what about Detective Serrano?"

I cringe. I can't tell him that Mom's gone missing, because I don't want him to think she can't do her job. "She's, uh, not coming out either," I say.

There's a tense pause. Then Harris pounds the door so loudly that it shakes on its hinges. *"Fine!"* he bellows. "You can starve in there for all I care!"

Out of spite, he barricades the door to our room. After hour and hours—or maybe days and days—we're practically *begging* to be let out of our room. But Harris doesn't care.

"I'll teach *you* not to open the door for your employer."

CASE CLOSED.

"HAVE YOU SEEN a ghost in the lodge?" I ask Sunny. "You do live on the premises, right?"

Sunny runs a hand through her silky black hair and leans on her cleaning cart. "Yes, I live here. And no, I haven't seen a ghost."

"Do you think ghosts are real?" I ask.

"I really couldn't say."

"COULDN'T? OR WOULDN'T!" Frank shouts, sticking a finger in her face.

"Couldn't," she says. "How do I know if ghosts are real? You might as well ask me if there are aliens, or if you can ever truly know someone, or if it's possible to time travel."

Frank's eyes grow wide. "Are there? Can you? Is it?" He pulls on Eliza's sleeve. "Can I time travel, Eliza?"

"Sure. You're time traveling right now . . . going forward, second by second. But what we want to know," she says, turning to Sunny, "is what you think is haunting this place. Do you think it's a person or a ghost?"

Sunny's lips press together. She is irritated with us. "I haven't the foggiest, and you're preventing me from doing my job."

TO ASK SUNNY WHAT SHE THINKS OF THE WINTERS FAMILY, TURN TO PAGE 103.

←——→

TO END THE CONVERSATION, TURN TO PAGE 422.

"HAVE YOU SEEN the ghosts in this hotel, Mr. Bookbinder?"

"Of course I have," he says. "There are six of them. They look just like the hikers. Can't you feel their presence all around us, even at this early evening hour?"

I shrug.

"No?" Byron says. "Sit down on the couch there—yes, just like that. Now close your eyes. Really *feel* the power of the ethereal world, reaching out to you through the veil of death. Concentrate! Now . . . can you feel the spirits?"

My hair brushes to the side, and my heart starts pounding. "I feel them! They touched my hair—"

I open my eyes to find Frank's fingers on my head.

"There's an egg on your head, and the yolk is running down!" he whispers.

I shake my head, and Eliza tries to suppress a laugh.

Byron doesn't seem to notice. He's too busy digging into his bag for his EMF reader. "Every night, the needle on my ghost detector goes wild. And this is the place to look for them. The hikers, guess where they died? Right here! In this very room."

"Hey!" Frank says. "I wanted to guess! You ruined it!"

"My posterior will not leave this chair until I see the ghosts again."

"You're not going to sleep in your room?" Eliza says, surprised.

"I'm a ghost writer! Well, I'm not a ghostwriter, I'm a writer of ghosts. But still! I didn't come to this lodge to sleep. My editor is counting on me to get a good account of the paranormal activity that's happening here. And I've had my eyes open."

I wonder if he's had his eyes open about *all* the comings and goings in this hotel, or just about the ghost things. I guess it can't hurt to ask.

TO ASK BYRON IF HE'S OBSERVED ANY TENSION BETWEEN THE WINTERS AND THE HOTEL STAFF, TURN TO PAGE 16.

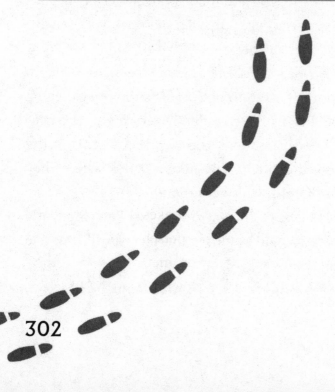

I'VE CRACKED THE cipher, and I shine my flashlight over the decoded message:

> You in the lobby, me in the hall.

> What time?

> Three. Do not get caught.

> I never do.

> Go team kind

> Minus the D, you mean

It's a conversation. I look up at Eliza, and her eyes are wide too.

"There are two culprits," I whisper to Eliza. "Two people working together." I guess my ghost theory has been blown right out of the water.

"It explains so much, logistically!" Eliza says, barely able to contain her excitement. "I mean, there was just so much going on last night. It only makes sense that someone wasn't doing it alone! If one person was in the walls banging and scratching metal on metal, and the other person was taking care of the glowing footprints . . ."

"But who?" I say. "Who could possibly be working together?"

"Cricket and Luther," Eliza says, and then she curses. "If only we hadn't lost the letter between them!"

"Harris and Reese could be plotting," I say. "Or Harris and January. Harris and Luther."

"It doesn't just have to be Harris, Carlos."

"Then who do you think? And what is team kind? Is that what they call themselves?"

Eliza frowns at the paper. "What does that last line mean? Go team kind . . . minus the D?" She looks up at me, an urgent expression on her face. "Kind minus the D."

"Er . . . does that mean something to you, Eliza? Because it means nothing to me."

"Kind minus the D is kin. Go team kin."

I stare at her blankly.

"Kin is another word for relative," she explains. "If that *is* what our two ghosts mean by that, it means that two relatives are working together."

"But . . ." I pace back and forth, trying to think. "Who's related to each other besides Harris, January, and Ree—"

Screech!

I don't even have to pivot to know the sound is coming from Frank. He's holding a walkie-talkie—and for a second my heart stops. But then I realize it's not the same model as the ones Mom and I have. It's a different walkie-talkie.

"Testing, testing, one two!" Frank says into the button. "Red leather, yellow leather, red leather, yellow leather, red leather, yellow leather."

"Stop that!" I say, snatching the walkie-talkie out of his hands. It belongs to the ghost team. We shouldn't play around with it. Still, I slip it into my pocket. Who knows when it could come in handy? I mean, we'll have a direct line to listen to the bad guys, whoever they are.

Frank pouts and stomps his foot. Just when I thought he had grown out of the tantrums.

"What's that leather thing you were saying, Frank?" Eliza says. Clearly an effort to distract him, but he falls for it hook, line, and sinker.

"A tongue twister!" he says. "Unique New York. Say it! Three times!"

"Unique New York, unique You Nork, unique You Nork," Eliza and I end up saying. Frank nods once, satisfied with our failure.

"What now?" Eliza says.

"Try 'a proper cup of coffee in a copper coffee cup'!" Frank says.

"I meant with the investigation."

"It's time to wait for the ghosts," I say. "Now that we

know there are two, we are better prepared to catch them in the act. And to get Mom back."

We retrace our steps through the walls, exit out of the bookcase in the library, and head back to room 237. The mirror threat is still there, and our sheets are still crumpled up—probably since Sunny couldn't get into the room, now that her key was stolen.

I don't want her in here anyway. Just being in here reminds me that when we were sleeping, *someone* was setting up the bathroom threat. The ghost was here. In the room. With us.

It makes me not want to sleep. I stare ahead with my eyes open. I am the guard dog, and I won't let anybody get inside undetected again. Not while I'm on watch!

"CHARLIE HOTEL ALPHA sierra echo," says a crackling voice.

"Eliza?" I say groggily. I don't remember falling asleep, but I must have.

"Tango hotel echo mike."

I roll over and flick on the lamplight. Eliza and Frank are curled up together, fast asleep.

"Tango oscar."

I roll out of bed, looking for the source of the sound.

"Lima india bravo romeo alpha romeo yankee."

It's coming from the pocket of my jacket. Out of it, I retrieve the walkie-talkie that I got from the ghost's lair yesterday. Someone is talking into it! But I don't recognize the voice.

"Eliza!" I say, shaking her bed. "Frank!"

"Ghost?" Frank asks.

"No," I say. "A code."

Frank groans and plops back down on the bed. He pulls the covers on top of himself and attempts to go back to sleep.

But a secret code is enough to get Eliza up. "What's the code?"

I hand her the walkie-talkie. "Uniform november delta echo romeo—"

"Carlos, get me a piece of paper!"

I grab her the hotel notepad and a pen as fast as I can. She is sitting on the edge of the bed with the walkie-talkie next to her ear. And even when I get her the notepad, she continues to sit there, eyes closed, without writing anything down.

"Uh . . . Eliza? Did you fall asleep sitting up?"

"Shhh!"

"Lima india delta. You got it? Over."

Eliza presses the button to talk, and I start waving my hands frantically. *What* is she doing? She can't talk to them! She'll give away everything!

But she doesn't listen to me. "No," she says into the walkie-talkie. "Please repeat. Over."

"Really? Okay. Pay attention and listen *closely*." Eliza throws the walkie-talkie at me and picks up the pen and paper as the voice says, "Charlie hotel alpha sierra echo tango hotel echo mike tango oscar lima india bravo romeo alpha romeo yankee india november foxtrot india foxtrot tango echo echo november mike india november uniform tango echo sierra."

Eliza scribbles frantically.

"You got that? Here's part two: delta oscar november tango lima echo tango tango hotel echo mike foxtrot india november delta kilo echo yankee uniform november delta echo romeo papa india alpha november oscar lima india delta. You got it? Over."

"Ten-four," Eliza says into the walkie-talkie, and she collapses on the bed, massaging her hand.

"Okay," I say. "So . . . we have the full message. But what does it mean? Tango hotel oscar delta? This is gibberish!"

Frank softly snores from across the bed, and Eliza smiles. "Haven't you heard of the NATO phonetic alphabet?"

"The what?"

Eliza flips the pad of paper to a new page and starts drawing. This time, it's a chart.

"It's a code people use for over the radio. Because so many letters sound alike when said aloud. D, B, E. F and S. M and N. Each word corresponds with a letter, so that whoever's listening can be sure of what letter was actually said."

I tear off the chart, so I can look at it side by side with the message Eliza transcribed.

309

A = ALPHA	N = NOVEMBER
B = BRAVO	O = OSCAR
C = CHARLIE	P = PAPA
D = DELTA	Q = QUEBEC
E = ECHO	R = ROMEO
F = FOXTROT	S = SIERRA
G = GOLF	T = TANGO
H = HOTEL	U = UNIFORM
I = INDIA	V = VICTOR
J = JULIET	W = WHISKEY
K = KILO	X = X-RAY
L = LIMA	Y = YANKEE
M = MIKE	Z = ZULU

CHARLIE HOTEL ALPHA SIERRA ECHO TANGO HOTEL ECHO MIKE TANGO OSCAR LIMA INDIA BRAVO ROMEO ALPHA ROMEO YANKEE INDIA NOVEMBER FOXTROT INDIA FOXTROT TANGO ECHO ECHO NOVEMBER MIKE INDIA NOVEMBER UNIFORM TANGO ECHO SIERRA.

DELTA OSCAR NOVEMBER TANGO LIMA ECHO TANGO TANGO HOTEL ECHO MIKE FOXTROT INDIA NOVEMBER DELTA KILO ECHO YANKEE UNIFORM NOVEMBER DELTA ECHO ROMEO PAPA INDIA ALPHA NOVEMBER OSCAR LIMA INDIA DELTA.

310

"I'm going to try to wake Frank again," Eliza says. "Why don't you take a crack at this?"

I nod. Let's see what message we've intercepted!

ADD TWO HUNDRED TO THE NUMBER IN THE DECODED MESSAGE, AND TURN TO THAT PAGE.

←——→

TO ASK ELIZA FOR A HINT, TURN TO PAGE 272.

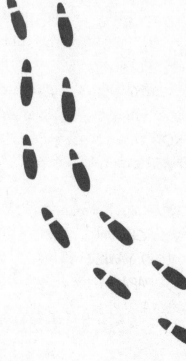

311

"HELLO, THIS IS the realtor for Reese Winters. She is finally hoping to sell the hotel to your boss. Can you put him on the line to discuss our counteroffer?"

A quick pause. "Yes, this is Luther Covington."

"My name is Carl . . . Carl Ser . . . mano. A realtor for the Sugarcrest Park Lodge. Mrs. Winters wants to make you a counteroffer, but first we have some questions—"

"Whatever it costs, I'll take it!" Luther shouts, and he immediately hangs up the phone.

Uh-oh.

It takes Luther all of one hour to drive up the hill with a giant bulldozer. He razes the property to the ground, while we're still in it.

"What in the *world* do you think you're doing?" Reese cries, crawling out of the rubble. "This is millions of dollars in damages!"

"I am the new owner of the Sugarcrest Park Lodge, and I'll do what I please with my own property."

"You are not!"

"Am too! A realtor sold it to me."

"Who?"

"Carl . . . Mr. Carl Sermano."

All eyes turn to me.

Millions of dollars in damages.

Uh-oh.

CASE CLOSED.

THE LETTERS ON the inside of the circle on Byron's briefcase lock are definitely gray. I put them in place, and the briefcase clicks open. I breathe a sigh of relief.

The printed pages of Byron's manuscript take up most of the room in the briefcase. It has an awful title: *The Ghostly Nightmare on Sugarcrest Mountain, The Hotel of Fear and Sorrow: Check In Now, Check Out Never* by Byron Bookbinder. There's also his computer and his charger, and as much as I would like to take his computer to examine later, I have a feeling that an author would know *instantly* if their computer was stolen. Like a sixth sense.

I'm hoping Byron doesn't have the same type of attachment to his EMF reader, which I put in my pocket. Just to borrow—I'll return it later. But it may help me find Mom.

I'm just about to close the briefcase when I see a letter addressed to Byron. With the words FORMAL WARNING on the envelope.

"Someone's coming!" Frank says gleefully. "Maybe a ghost!"

I grab the letter and stuff it in my pocket. Eliza slams the briefcase shut.

Just in time!

The door opens, and there's a figure in shadow. Eliza shrieks.

Then it steps into the fire den, and I release a breath.

It's no ghost—it's just Reese. She's holding a robe around herself and shivering violently. "D-did you hear that? That voice?"

"The howling?" Eliza says.

"No—*no!*" Her eyes are wide. She shakes Eliza by the shoulders. "It was my father. My *father's* voice."

I was not expecting *that*. I want to ask Reese more questions, but she's shaking terribly. Suddenly she has a blank look on her face—she stops trembling. Her mouth goes slack, and somehow that's even more terrifying than the shaking.

Is she just in shock, or is she being possessed?

I grab her hand and lead her to the couch in front of the fire. "Just sit down, Mrs. Winters. It's okay, we're here for you."

Footsteps thunder, and Harris, Fernando di Cannoli, and Sunny appear in the archway.

"Sweets?" Harris says, running over to his wife. He touches her face gently, but she still stares blankly ahead, at nothing. "Reese!" He turns to us. "What's wrong with her?"

"She's dead. RIP," Frank says.

"No she isn't!" Eliza says. "She's just shocked, I think. She says she heard her father."

"Her father has been dead for four years," Harris says.

My chest feels tight. I know that ghosts means *people*

314

coming back from the dead, but I'm just not ready for that.

Harris wraps his arms around his wife. Then he turns to look at Sunny and Fernando.

The two of them are wearing the weirdest expressions. Like they're half smiling but trying to hide it. The question is: Are these guilty smiles? Or the smiles of disgruntled employees who are simply happy to see their boss suffer?

"What did you see and hear?" I ask.

"And smell and touch?" Eliza adds.

"And taste!" Frank says, licking Eliza's pajama sleeve. "Yum. Flannel!"

She shakes him off.

"Nothing! I observed nothing!" Fernando says in his fake accent. "I . . . uh . . . wanted to get a start on tomorrow's breakfast."

"At three in the morning?" Eliza says skeptically.

While Frank says, "Can I have pancakes for breakfast? No wait, waffles! No wait, *pizza!*"

I turn to Sunny. "What about you? Did you see anything suspicious?"

Sunny yawns dramatically. Then she says, "I heard a banging noise and a few howls, same as everyone else."

"Where *is* everybody else?" Harris says, frowning.

It's true: it's a little suspicious that they're not here. I mean . . . there's no way Byron, Cricket, and January didn't hear all the howling and banging, right? Maybe I should search for them.

Then again, what in the world happened to Mom? Where did she go? And does she need our help?

> TO SEARCH FOR THE MISSING SUSPECTS,
> TURN TO PAGE 27.
>
> ←——→
>
> TO SEARCH FOR MOM,
> TURN TO PAGE 295.

I **DECIDE TO** ask Fernando about Reese, Harris, and January. He seems too nervous about them, and I can't let that go. "What do you think of the Winters?"

"Winter is a very cold and lonely season. Nothing like we have in Italy! Sun and happiness every day in Italy!"

"No, what do you think of the Winters *family*?"

"Oh," he says.

And that's *all* he says.

"And?" Eliza prompts. "Any more details?"

Fernando di Cannoli twists his mustache. "No."

Okay, new approach.

"Have you ever been in trouble with them before?"

"I . . . I think you should go now," Fernando says, scooping up our sundae glasses.

"Hey!" Frank says.

"You just had snacks *and* a sundae. You can't possibly still be hungry," I say.

"I don't have to be hungry to eat ice cream!" Frank says. "I can eat it anytime, anywhere, anywhy, with anywho. I have a stomach, and then I have an ice-cream stomach. TWO STOMACHS."

Fernando di Cannoli wipes his forehead with a rag. "Go. I have cooking to do."

We leave the kitchen.

"Well, that was a bust," I say.

"Was it?" Eliza says. "He got really weird when we

mentioned the Winters family. Almost like he's hiding something."

But what?

It's getting late, and I think it's time we call it a night, but as we pass through the lobby, I see Byron Bookbinder typing away on his typewriter in front of the fireplace, in the room next door. Without really thinking, I drag Eliza and Frank over to him.

Byron is curled up on the comfy chair he's claimed as his writing space. He adjusts his half-moon glasses and blinks up at us with tired, beady eyes.

"We have questions for you, old man," Frank says. Byron isn't even that old!

Byron laughs in surprise. "You do? Well, I admire anyone who is trying to quench their thirst for knowledge. Curiosity is the mark of a good writer."

"It's also the mark of a good detective," Eliza says. "Which is what we are."

Byron nods seriously. "Yes, I suppose that's true. How can I help you? I am at your service."

TO ASK BYRON IF HE'S SEEN THE GHOSTS,
TURN TO PAGE 301.

←→

TO ASK BYRON IF HE'S OBSERVED ANY TENSION BETWEEN THE WINTERS AND THE HOTEL STAFF, TURN TO PAGE 16.

WE CAN'T DITCH January—we have to follow her in.

"Let's go!" I shout to Eliza, and we dash down the hall. As we run into the room, the door shuts behind us. It clicks tight. The room is pitch-black, and there are scratching, scuttling noises on the floor. January is choking out, "Help me!" But I can't do anything without the flashlight.

I find it. I flick it on. And . . .

No one else is in the room with Eliza and me.

A shiver goes through me. I shine the light around.

Where could the ghost have gone? Where did it take January?

In the corner of the room is a coffin. A real one. For humans. And two of the walls are smeared with red . . . *something.* I'm just praying it's not blood.

The floors are creaky, the ceiling is low. Everything about this place screams *GET OUT.*

"What do we do now?" I say.

"We have to think of a way out," Eliza says.

Everything happened so fast. And I just don't understand what happened to January. She was here one second and *gone* the next.

"It's all my fault," I say.

"What? Carlos, of course it isn't!"

"It is, though. If only I had let January help us yesterday—then maybe we wouldn't have gotten

319

ourselves into this situation at all. I've been making bad calls this whole time—I've been letting this ghost get into my head."

"It's okay to be afraid," Eliza says gently.

I moan. "I just wanted *so badly* to impress my mom. *Now* what's she going to think?"

"That you're doing the best you can."

"And what if my best isn't good enough? You know how much I want to be a detective one day."

"One day? Carlos, you're already a detective. A great one. And if your mom didn't think so, then she wouldn't have invited you on this case. She believes in you, and so do Frank and I. So believe in yourself, and nothing—not even fear—can stop you."

A minute goes by, or two, or ten. My heart is hammering in my ears, and it's hard to tell how much time is passing when I feel like the Dead Room is outside of space and time.

The doorknob jiggles. I grab Eliza's hand tightly. This is it—the monster-ghost creature is coming for us. I take a deep breath—

Two people are pushed inside the Dead Room.

"Mom?"

"Carlos?"

"Frank?"

"FRANK!"

"What are you doing here?" Eliza says. "And where have you been?"

"Down at the Super Hotel Express. Luther's place," Mom says. "Long story short—we got a fake tip that you two were down at his place. We went down there to get you, discovered immediately that we'd been lured out of the lodge under false pretenses, and battled the elements to get back uphill."

"Did the ghost get you too?" Frank asks. "We got chased in."

"No, we followed it in."

"Voluntarily?" Mom says, somewhere between incredulous and angry.

"We had to, Mom! It had January in its clutches! But we couldn't get to her in time—who knows where she is now? We have to save her!"

Eliza hums. I know that sound. She's thinking about something. After a moment she lets us into her genius thoughts. "About that," she says. "If we think our ghost is paranormal, then January could really be anywhere. But if we think our ghost is a human, then they can't have just vanished into thin air. Which means there must be a way in and a way out of this room, other than the front door—and that other way is where the culprit took January. I wonder if we can find a secret escape by poking around."

321

"I love secrets!" Frank says. "And escapes! And poking!"

I look around with the flashlight. The room is bare . . . there seem to be only two things to really look at. Which one will get us closer to saving January?

TO LOOK IN THE COFFIN,
TURN TO PAGE 37.

←——→

TO EXAMINE THE BLOOD MARKS,
TURN TO PAGE 419.

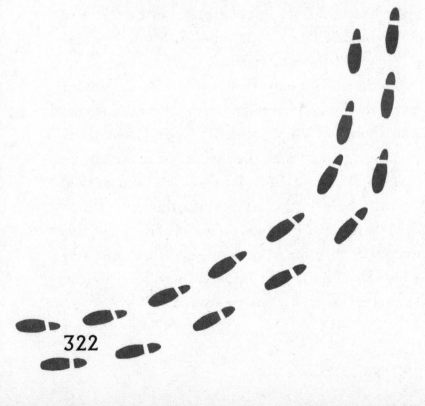

OKAY. THIS IS it. I'm going to go into the Dead Room.

With all the laughter.

The crazy, hysterical laughter.

Are we sure we want to do this?

Because it's not too late to turn back now.

The laughter is getting louder and louder and LOUDER.

My hand is on the doorknob. . . .

And then suddenly I'm on my back, looking up at the antler sconces.

"What happened?"

Eliza leans over me. "You fainted, Carlos. I think you got so scared you just . . . passed out," she says.

"I did?" I cover my face. "What happened to the ghost? Did the laughter stop?"

"What laughter?" Eliza says.

"You're kidding, right?"

But she doesn't look like she's kidding. "I don't know what you're talking about, Carlos. There was laughter earlier, but once we got to the door, there was . . . nothing. You just fainted. Reese called the paramedics. They're on their way, fighting the snowstorm to get to you. I don't know what you saw or heard . . . but you're the only one who did."

"No, you heard it too—I know you did!" I say.

"Of course," she says. "Shhhhh . . . just take it easy . . . the paramedics will be here any second. . . ."

"I don't *need* paramedics! I need to catch the ghost."

"Shhhhhhh," Eliza says soothingly. "Calm down . . . that's it . . ."

CASE CLOSED.

"WHAT DO YOU think of your coworkers?" I ask Cricket. "The ones that aren't part of the Winters family?"

"What is there to say?" Cricket says. "We don't really interact. We all have different jobs."

"I know," Eliza says, "but what is your impression of Sunny? We just talked to her."

"She's fine. It takes her a while to warm up to people. . . . I think she's shy." Cricket thinks for a second. "I also think she's unhappy here."

"How do you know?"

"Just the little things she says. I told her that she should look for a new job, but she got mad at me. I don't know why she's so attached to this place, but I think she's been here a super long time, so like, maybe she's holding on to old, fond memories? Personally, I think everyone should let go of the past and be present in the *now*."

"I'm getting a present now?!" Frank says excitedly. I swear, he only hears every third word of what someone says.

"So you and Sunny get along?" I say.

Cricket lowers her voice. "Well, I like her better than Fernando di Cannoli."

"Why? What's wrong with Fernando?" I say.

She wrinkles her nose. "I don't want to throw anyone under the bus."

325

"The wheels on the bus go round and round," Frank sings.

"What does that mean?" Eliza says.

"Maybe you should just go talk to him. I'm not one to judge—"

"Yeah right!" Frank says, and Eliza nudges him.

"—but I think Fernando is a total phony. I don't know what his deal is, but he's a weird guy. Always skulking around. I caught him eavesdropping on conversations . . . more than once. I'm telling you, he's bad news."

TO TALK TO FERNANDO, TURN TO PAGE 180.

WHEN I TILT Cricket's paper, I can see exactly what Eliza was talking about. There's a message that can only be read at a certain angle, and the message says: The password is three two seven.

"That's why you were zoning out during the conversation!" I say. "I thought it wasn't like you to lose focus like that."

"Well, I saw the message from a good angle, and I saw what it said clearly. I was confused . . . and impressed by how tricky it was. Cricket could hide the password in plain sight because anyone looking at the paper straight-on—or even at most angles—would think nothing of it."

"Yeah, but if someone reads it at the right angle, then they know her password. That's stupid of her to keep it out like that."

Eliza gestures to the cluttered desk—the papers in messy stacks, the pens without caps, the caps without pens, three empty granola-bar wrappers, and a bunch of paper clips attached like a snake. "It doesn't really seem like Cricket is all that organized, Carlos."

Fair point.

We open the drawer, and Frank gets on his knees and leans over the drawer. "Let me press the buttons! Please please please! Pretty please with sugar on top!"

I sigh and hand him the paper, and he types three

two seven into the digital pad.

The lock clicks open, and now we can lift off the top of the drawer. Inside, there are boring-looking slips of paper. My eyes glaze over, but Eliza seems to be interested. Her mouth drops open.

"What does it say?" Frank says.

"They're bank deposit slips," Eliza says. "Cricket has put a few thousand dollars into her personal bank account, all in the last six weeks."

"And is that wrong?" I say.

"Yes, if you're the concierge at a boutique hotel like this one! There's no way Cricket is making this much money. And besides, six weeks ago is when the haunting started."

"The haunting begins, and so does Cricket's sudden flood of cash," I say. "So is she stealing from the hotel while Reese and Harris are distracted by ghosts?"

"I don't know," Eliza says, "but this is really suspicious."

"It's bananas!" Frank says.

I nod.

"No, I mean, it's *bananas*!" Frank reaches into the bottom of Cricket's drawer and pulls out a rotten banana in a sealed plastic baggie. Eliza starts to gag, and I grab it from Frank and put it in the trash can.

"Cricket is *disgusting*," Eliza says from inside her

shirt, where she'd retreated, like a turtle. "Do you think we should talk to her about this?"

"I guess. But I'm not sure anything we say is going to convince her to throw out her old bananas."

"Not about the banana!" Eliza says. "About the bank statements!"

"Oh, right!" I say. "Let's wait for her to come back."

We wait for her at the concierge desk, and after twenty minutes, she finally shows up.

"Where have you been?" Frank asks.

"When the ghosts show up, I leave. They're not paying me enough to stick around for that," Cricket says as she slips back into her concierge chair.

Funny she brought up her pay. "We have something to admit," I tell her. "We saw your bank deposit slips."

The smile slides off her face. Her eyes dart over to some metal mail slots by the door, a mailbox for each employee. Why would she be looking there when the deposit slips are in her desk drawer? "So not only have you been, like, peeking at my desk . . . you've also unlocked my drawer's safe?"

Eliza and I hang our heads in shame, but Frank nods. "Yup, that's exactly what we did. By the way . . . TOSS YOUR BANANAS, YOU BANANA."

"This is a major violation of my privacy—you had no right to do that!"

"Can you just tell us where the money is coming from?" Eliza asks.

"You have no right to ask that!"

Her eyes dart again to the mail slots.

"Maybe you should look at us," I suggest.

. Her green eye and her blue eye swivel back to me, and from the daggers she's glaring, I know I'm definitely *not* in her good graces right now.

"Did you get the money legally?" Eliza asks.

"I'm not doing anything wrong!" Cricket says. "How dare you . . . you little brat!"

"Takes one to know one!" Frank says. Then he turns on his heels and walks away toward the kitchen. Either he's bored or he's hungry. But as long as he doesn't stop Eliza and me from doing the real investigative work . . .

I lean on Cricket's desk. "You have to admit, it looks a little suspicious."

"It looks a little *nothing*," she says, "because I don't know what you're talking about. What deposit slips?"

Eliza and I look at each other, confused. "The ones in your drawer! We saw them!" Eliza says.

"You never saw them. Because they don't exist."

The implication is clear: Cricket is going to destroy the deposit slips.

I look at Eliza urgently. We have to drive Cricket away from here . . . but how?

330

"I can tell what you're thinking," Cricket says. "But I'm not leaving my desk all night. And there's nothing you can do about it."

Suddenly the lights flicker, and the expression on Cricket's face changes. She pulls her sweatshirt up around her ears and cowers in fear. A howl echoes through the lobby. She looks determined to stay but is clearly sick about it.

Ooooooooooooo!

She turns totally ashen, almost feverish. Her white skin is clammy with sweat. She looks over at the mail slot again. "I can't leave. I can't . . . !"

"*Cricket*," growls the ghost.

"Eeeeeeeep!" she yelps, and she runs. She's more afraid of ghosts than I am.

"'When the ghosts show up, I leave,'" I say, echoing Cricket's words. "Lucky a ghost showed up."

"At the exact moment we needed it to?" Eliza says skeptically. "Yes . . . very lucky."

"Luck is for suckers!" Frank shouts. He leans against the stair railing, a big smile on his face. "You're welcome, by the way."

"For what?"

He stands next to the light switch and flicks it on and off rapidly. Then he covers his mouth and lets out a muffled howl. Then he growls, "*Cricket!*"

"That was *you?*"

"Easy peasy lemon squeezy!"

"Yes, that was very clever, Frank!" Eliza says, trying to hide the shock in her voice.

I feel bad . . . I completely underestimated Frank. "Thanks, buddy."

"I like playing ghost. Let's go haunt more people!"

"That's literally the *opposite* of what this case requires," Eliza says.

"Cricket might come back at any moment," I say. "So do we collect the bank deposit slips and save our evidence before Cricket destroys it? Or do we look in the mailboxes?"

"Huh? The mailboxes?"

"Didn't you see? Cricket's eyes kept drifting over there. She was looking more panicked about the mail slot than about her desk drawer. I wonder if there's another clue in there."

TO LOOK IN THE MAILBOXES, TURN TO PAGE 400.

←——→

TO COLLECT THE BANK DEPOSIT SLIPS,
TURN TO PAGE 228.

"WAIT, MR. WINTERS! Before you go, we hear you constantly wander the halls in the middle of the night."

Harris frowns. "Who said that?"

Cricket, but I'm not telling him that. "It doesn't matter who said it—is it true?"

His big beard twitches. "I don't know what you're doing, or what kind of case you're trying to make against me. But you have no idea what it's like to be under this kind of stress and mortal peril for so long, all while trying to keep it together for your wife so that she doesn't crack under the pressure. So *of course* I'm up in the middle of the night. I'm up at all hours lately—can't you see my bloodshot eyes? I can barely sleep a wink."

Frank starts winking at Harris repeatedly, to the point where Harris looks concerned. "Is he okay?"

"Ignore him," I say. "We all do."

"HEY!"

"And with all that time wandering the halls in the middle of the night," I say, "you haven't seen *anything* suspicious?"

"I wish I could be of more help," he says with a shrug. He checks his watch. "I really do have to run. With everything on Reese's plate right now, I have to pick up the slack. . . ."

TO ASK WHAT IS ON REESE'S PLATE,
TURN TO PAGE 454.

I POINT THE arrow west.

The wall slides open, revealing a cold, dark, web-filled hallway.

"Cool!" Frank says, hopping into the hall. "Let's do that again!"

"The only thing worse than the Dead Room," Eliza whispers, "is an *extended* Dead Room."

A cold breeze blows our way, and we all shiver. Is this where the thing that grabbed January went? Could we be getting close to a lair?

"January?" I call. My voice echoes back to me repeatedly. *January, January, January . . .*

"Let me go first," Mom says, stepping in front of Frank. "If we meet trouble, I want you all to run back."

It's not like we'd be very safe, trapped inside a locked Dead Room. But I decide not to mention that to Mom. I still want to help her on the next case . . . if we survive this one.

We inch forward.

Ahead, all the way down the hall, something is glowing. A ghost?

Something drops onto my head. *"Ahhhh!"*

"What?" Eliza shouts.

"Spider! In my hair!"

"Jealous." Frank pouts as Eliza frantically smacks my head to get the spider out.

334

"Shhhhhh!" Mom says. "Quiet." She's squinting at the glowing figure at the end of the hallway, which is flickering. "I don't like that," she says, stepping forward anyway. We have to—there's no way we're going to sit and wait around in the Dead Room!

I can't see Mom's face in the dark, but I know her well enough to know something's off. "What's wrong?" I ask.

"I thought we were finding a way out," she says. "But with that glowing ghost in the distance, I wonder if the ghost *wanted* us to open the wall in the Dead Room."

"I don't know, but it doesn't matter," I say. "We don't have a choice. We can't just sit around in the Dead Room, so we have to keep going."

We walk forward, and the ghost flickers out. That *should* make me feel good, but it makes me feel a lot worse.

"HELP ME!"

"That's January!" I whisper. "Let's go!"

I lead the charge, twisting through the passageway. It's narrow—and gets even narrower the more I walk. There are support beams everywhere. Some are so low Mom has to duck under them, which makes me think we must be somewhere within the walls of the lodge.

At last I turn a corner, duck under two beams, hop over a third, and there is January, tied to a beam.

"Oh, thank goodness!" she cries. "Help me!"

I move forward to untie her, but Eliza puts her hand on my arm. "Wait! Where is the ghost?"

"What?"

"Ask her where the ghost is!"

What is Eliza doing? Free January first—ask questions later! Who knows how long it will be before the ghost comes back?

TO UNTIE JANUARY, TURN TO PAGE 95.

$\longleftrightarrow$

TO ASK JANUARY WHERE THE GHOST WENT,
TURN TO PAGE 260.

I DIG INTO Frank's pocket, grab a snowball, and pelt it across the cave. It's a direct hit with its face—that's definitely going to smart. I throw another, and Frank throws a third. My second misses, but Frank's connects.

"CHAAAAARGE!" Frank yells, leaping across the cave and tackling the ghost around the middle.

Bam! The ghost goes down. The mask slides off and flies across the cave. At first I only see her back. She has long black hair. Which is weird, because I am pretty sure Sunny has chin-length hair.

Then she turns around, a ferocious expression on her young face.

Eliza gasps. "January?"

She crawls toward us.

"You're the ghost?" I say. "But . . . but it's your mom's hotel! I don't understand!"

Frank hugs January's legs so tight that she can't move out of his grip. She just thrashes back and forth like a fish on a line.

"Let me go!" January snaps.

"NO!" Frank says. "NOT UNTIL YOU SAY THE MAGIC WORD."

Not *again* with Frank's magic word nonsense!

"Please," says January, annoyed.

"Nope! Try again!"

"Abracadabra!"

"Nice try!"

"I hate you!"

"Oh yeah? Well, I hate you times infinity!" Frank says. "No, I hate you times infinity plus one!"

I can't believe Frank is doing this shtick to someone who isn't his sister. But even more, I can't believe January is the ghost. "But January—you were helping us!"

"Helping you down the wrong trail," she says between gritted teeth. "Helping you look *away* from me. Can you get off?" she shouts, giving Frank another kick.

"No!" Frank says. His favorite word.

"HELP!" she cries, looking to the mouth of the cave.

A ghost is standing in the mouth of the cave—in shadow, but I can definitely detect clawed hands and a bloodstained dress.

What's going on? I thought January was the ghost!

"Did I forget to mention my partner?" January says.

The second ghost pulls off the mask. Now that I know she's related, I can't help but see the family resemblance. I feel so stupid for missing it before.

"Sunny Park and January Winters," Mom says with a low whistle. "What a team!"

"So whose idea was it?" I say.

They look at each other and frown. I don't peg

either one of them as the evil-villain-who-loves-to-monologue-about-their-diabolical-plan type . . . but I have to try.

"Come on," I plead. "We deserve to know!"

"It was my idea," Sunny says.

"You were jealous that Reese got to run your parents' hotel," I say. "So you invented this ghost for revenge on your sister."

"But why would you go along with this, January?" Eliza says.

"I hate this place. I don't want to own it today, tomorrow, someday, any day. I would give it to Aunt Sunny if I could. I want to move away from here . . . go to regular school."

"So you got together and invented a ghost. But . . . how?"

"I found a speaker outside, remember?" Mom says. "So they were pumping scary sound effects into the hotel. And they were using props, like green jelly. Neon glow-stick liquid for the footprints."

"The footprints!" I say with a groan. "That must have been your dad's shoes, January."

"You didn't *really* think the ghost was a man just because of the shoes, right? Anyone can have access to men's shoes!"

"The jelly—you stole it from the kitchen and added

food coloring," I say. "You knew we were in the kitchen because we enlisted your help to keep Fernando away. Would have been pretty easy for you to sneak back in by yourself and lock us in the freezer."

"But," Eliza says, "you left a clue inside the freezer that helped us get out."

"I mean, I knew it was in there," January says. "I'm not mad you got out—I just needed to scare you away from the property."

"The sounds in the walls, the howling, the ghost that disappeared after I saw its face," Mom says. "That was all done from inside the walls, wasn't it? There must be a secret passage, just like Eliza said."

"Enough of this," Sunny says. "Can you wriggle out of this child's grip, January?"

"No," she says, trying once more to throw Frank off her.

"Then I'm sorry, but—" Sunny slams her hand on the wall and hits a button. In front of Sunny, the top of the cave opens up. Giant icicles come flying down, like prison bars, trapping us inside the cave.

"You can't just leave me!" January says.

"Oh yes, I can," Sunny says, turning and running.

"Hey! HEY!" January shouts. Then she turns furiously to us. "I can't believe she left me!"

Mom is wearing her best disappointed face—the one

that always makes me crumble. Only, thank goodness, it's not directed at me. "January, with these haunting stunts, you got your mom's attention, but this is no way to earn her trust or respect," Mom says. "Surely you know that . . ."

"Shame! Shame!" Frank says, still squeezing her feet, acting like the world's best parasite.

January looks away.

Meanwhile Eliza has walked over to the other side of the cave to examine the icicle prison bars. She tries to pull one up out of the ground, but the point has dug in too deep. It's wedged tight. "Is this the only exit?" she asks January.

"Yeah. We're stuck."

"We'll see about *that*!" Frank says, getting off January and marching over to the row of icicles.

Frank leans over, puts his mouth right on one, and begins to suck.

"Haven't you learned your lesson after licking that pole?" I ask.

"Nope!" Frank says cheerily. "I never learn anything!" Then he puts his mouth back on the ice. At least his tongue isn't getting stuck again.

Mom frowns. "There's no way—"

But Eliza copies him with the icicle right next to it.

"Mom, did you know Frank can eat a freezy pop in

seven seconds without getting a brain freeze? We've timed him."

"I . . . I didn't know that," she says, watching Frank lick the icicle.

It takes a few minutes, but he finally breaks through. Then he moves to a spot lower to the ground. Soon enough there's a hole just big enough for a kid-sized person to crawl through.

I look back at Mom.

"There's no time! Go!"

"But Mom—"

"Don't worry about me. January is going to stay with me . . . and we'll be talking about responsibility and respect."

January looks like she'd rather die than hear a mom lecture, but she doesn't argue.

"GO!"

We crawl through the hole. "I'll be back for you, Mom!" I say, and we slip out of the cave and into the blizzard.

There are footprints on the ground to follow, and I start to run after them while Frank hops into a nearby bush.

"Batmobile!" he shouts. He pulls the bush aside to reveal a snowmobile. It looks like it's been here for a while, since there are no snowmobile tracks on the ground. I bet Sunny didn't even know it was here, or she would have used it herself.

How does Frank *always* find things like this? It's like he has a talent for knowing just where a clue or useful item will be.

"Frank, we can't take this," Eliza says. "We're not old enough to drive!"

"Ohhhhh, jingle bells, Batman smells, Robin laid an egg, Batmobile lost its wheel, and Joker got away!"

I look at the snowmobile. It *would* be a lot faster to follow Sunny in this. Since she has such a long head start on us.

Eliza seems to know what I'm thinking, because she shakes her head no. "Carlos, we can't! It's dangerous!"

TO TAKE THE SNOWMOBILE, TURN TO PAGE 473.

←→

TO FOLLOW ON FOOT, TURN TO PAGE 433.

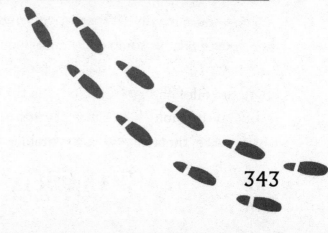

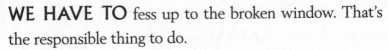

WE HAVE TO fess up to the broken window. That's the responsible thing to do.

We wait in the snow while Reese, Harris, and January come running around the house. It takes them a while to get to us.

But when they do finally come toward us, I try to wear my most apologetic face.

"What happened out here?" Reese says. "Did you see who broke this window?"

"I'm so sorry," I say. "It was an accident."

Reese frowns. "This was an antique window."

"It was an accident," I repeat.

"Even so, we're going to have to take this out of whatever earnings you'd be making. Which means . . . *you* actually owe us a few thousand dollars."

"But it was an *accident*!" I say.

"Is he broken?" January asks her parents. "He's repeating himself."

"You can't punish Las Pistas Detective Agency over an accident!" I say.

Reese smiles kindly. "It's not a punishment. This is taking responsibility for your actions. Welcome to adulthood."

"I take it back!" I say quickly. Mom's business can't afford to take a hit like this.

But it's Frank who answers me. "NO TAKE-BACKSIES!" he says, pelting me with another snowball.

CASE CLOSED.

344

I CLEAN THE steam off the bathroom mirror until we can read the message fully in the reflection:

desert the spirit and run far away
get out while you can in the light of day.
be gone from this place by three forty-five,
be gone from here if you want to survive.
this is your warning, for if you do stay,
then i'm the hunter, and you are my prey.

Frank tents his hands, palm facing palm.

"Not *that* kind of pray, Frank. The other kind." I gulp. "We're supposed to be hunting the ghost. Not the other way around!"

"Clearly we've touched a nerve," Eliza says. "But *which* nerve?"

"This one!" Frank says, poking her in the arm.

"What about Mom?" I ask. "We can't leave here without her!" My stomach twists. Where could she be? Is she in danger? And then a thought so terrible comes into my head, I can barely even think it . . . but what if Mom already *was* the prey for the ghost?

"Don't worry, Carlos," Eliza says. "Your mom is a professional."

"Professional detective," I say. "Not ghostbuster."

"We'll find her soon," Eliza says.

I look at the letter. I feel as helpless as I've ever felt. I wanted so hard to prove to Mom that I deserve to be here. But do I deserve to be here if I can't find Mom?

"Threats and danger follow us around, don't they?" Eliza says with a frown. "Why can't we ever have a nice, quiet case where we solve the mystery with no problems whatsoev—"

Knock, knock!

Eliza and I freeze.

"Who is it?" Frank says in a singsongy voice.

Please be Mom, please be Mom!

"It's me, Harris Winters."

"Mmmm . . . sorry, we're not home right now. Please leave a message after the beep. BEEEEEEEP!"

"Open up!"

"What's the magic word?" Frank demands.

"Please," Harris says reluctantly.

"Nope! Try again. You only have nine hundred ninety-nine tries left before I tell you the answer!"

Harris growls in frustration, and I should probably open the door, especially since he's one of the people running the hotel. Then again, we don't know who left this mirror message or why. What if he's the one behind this threat? Maybe it's not safe to open the door for him.

Or even if he didn't write this message, maybe January told Harris that we were snooping through the mailbox last night. It's possible that he could be angry or argumentative.

TO OPEN THE DOOR, TURN TO PAGE 208.

←——→

TO IGNORE THE DOOR, TURN TO PAGE 299.

347

ELIZA'S RIGHT—WE should look at the map again. If we figure out where it leads, we can figure out why someone would try to burn it. And while I want to talk to Sunny, this feels more important somehow. Like it will get us physical evidence.

"Okay," I say. "Let's figure out this map."

It doesn't make any more sense the second time I look at it. Clearly it's a map because of the directional compass in the corner . . . but what are these numbers? I'm assuming we're starting at the bottom left, but how do we get to the star?

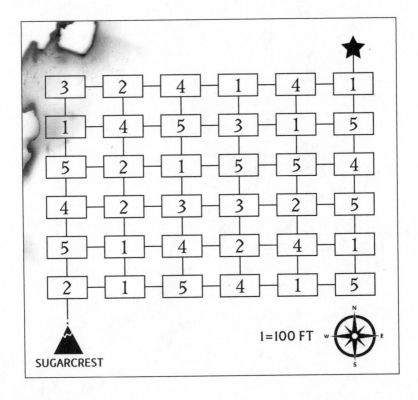

A crease forms on Eliza's forehead as she studies the map.

"What do you think?" Mom says after a solid five minutes of silence.

"I think these are measurements of distance," Eliza says, pointing at the numbers. "We start in the left corner, and we have to go two hundred feet in one direction. Then the next square will tell us how many paces to go in another direction. And so on until we reach the destination."

"But . . . how do we know which direction to go in?"

"I think that's what we have to figure out," she says.

"So we start with the two," I say. "We can't go diagonally."

"Right."

"And we have to stay in the same direction for two spaces."

"You got it," Eliza says.

I pull the parchment closer to me and get to work.

ADD UP ALL THE NUMBERS FROM THE SQUARES YOU PASS THROUGH, AND TURN TO THAT PAGE.

←——→

TO ASK ELIZA FOR A HINT, TURN TO PAGE 189.

"OKAY, FRANK. LET'S see if you're as good at puzzles as Eliza! What do I do with these letters?"

"Read them. Duh!"

"Okay . . . well, I already said that I think the words will have to do with winter and mountainous areas. Do you think that's right?"

"I think it's left," he says, just to be difficult.

I sigh. "Okay . . . here are the words I've found." I grab a paper off Reese's desk and write them down:

coat

luge

cold

moose

gloves

scarf

hat

skiing

hot chocolate

sled

ice skate

"What now?" I ask Frank, who is spinning in circles.

"CIRCLE!" he cries. "CIRCLE!"

That's not actually bad advice. Maybe if I circle the words I find, I'll see some clue, either with the words or the leftover letters.

> THE LETTERS NOT USED IN THE WORD SEARCH
> WILL LEAD YOU TO YOUR NEXT PAGE.
> READ THEM IN ORDER TO FIND YOUR NUMBER.

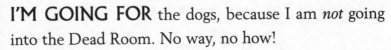

I'M GOING FOR the dogs, because I am *not* going into the Dead Room. No way, no how!

I slide down the banister, into the lobby with four dogs baring their fangs at me.

"Carlos! No!" Mom shouts. She runs after me, and while my eyes are on her, one of the dogs lunges at me.

Its teeth sink into the fabric of my jeans, narrowly missing my leg. But the dog still drags me across the floor. I kick and thrash, but it's no use. The dog is too strong. Another one bites into my jacket, and now the two of them are pulling me out the door.

"Mom!" I shout. A dog is blocking her way to me. "Mom! Help!"

"Carlos! I'm coming!"

And then I'm out in the snow, being pulled across the mountaintop and into the forest. We go so deep into the woods that I'm lost. Every day I try to escape, but the dogs find me before I reach the edge of the woods and they drag me back to their shelter.

Once I stop trying to escape, the dogs make me part of their pack. Soon I'm howling at the moon, scratching fleas, and biting bones. Life used to be ruff, but now it's so much easier living as a dog. *Aoooooooo!*

CASE CLOSED.

352

I HAVE TO accuse January.

"You're the ghost."

"Don't be ridiculous," January snaps. "Haven't you heard? The lodge will belong to me one day. Why would I want to *devalue* my future inheritance?"

"Maybe you don't want your inheritance," Eliza says.

"Who doesn't want free money?"

It's tough to argue with that one.

"You really think I have time to be the ghost, when I'm so busy with homework? My private tutor isn't satisfied unless I have no fun whatsoever. Besides, what kind of cruel, heartless person does this to their parents? And I'm just one kid. I wouldn't know the first thing about haunting a hotel. Plus, what makes you think it's a human, and not a real ghost? Because that's a real possibility."

She's giving a million excuses, and I don't know if that makes me more or less suspicious of her.

"All I know," she concludes, "is I'm not the one behind this."

"Okay, then who do you think is?" I ask.

January shrugs. "Sounds like a lot of not my problem. Buh-bye."

I roll my eyes. "Thanks a lot for your help," I say sarcastically as I exit the dining room. I drag Eliza to the right—to an office near the kitchen. Through the glass

353

door, I can see Reese with her head bent over her desk. I think she might even be napping.

I knock, and she pops up suddenly.

"I wasn't sleeping!" she says as we walk in.

Oh, she was definitely sleeping.

"Can we ask you some questions?" I ask.

"Of course. Sit."

We grab the chairs in front of her desk, and I wonder which question to ask first. . . .

TO ASK ABOUT HER FIGHTS WITH JANUARY, TURN TO PAGE 437.

←→

TO ASK WHY SHE DIDN'T WANT TO HIRE DETECTIVES, TURN TO PAGE 394.

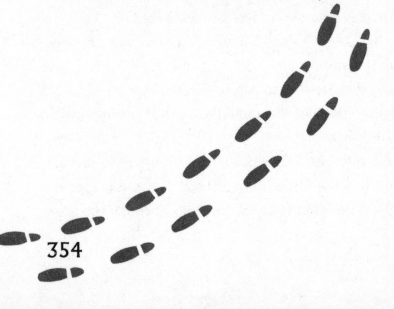

I WANT TO know what Reese is hiding. It might be the key to the entire mystery, since all the hauntings have been focused on her. If she has a secret, it's got to come out.

We find her in her office, looking wearily at her desk.

"Come in," she says, rubbing her eyes. She looks really tired. There are big puffy dark spots under her dark eyes, and she looks like she's having trouble staying awake. "How's the case going?"

"Why didn't you want to hire detectives?" I ask her. I'm cutting right to the chase. We don't have any more time to play around. The sun is setting, and another ghost haunting will be here before we know it.

Reese cocks her head and smiles, but Eliza interrupts her before Reese can get a word out.

"Please don't pretend like you wanted detectives. Harris told us that *he* was the one who hired us. You made us believe it was a mutual decision. So what are you hiding that you don't want us to find?"

"Nothing," she says. It's a terribly unconvincing lie. She's shaking and terrified, though I can't tell whether she's scared about the thing she's hiding or the ghosts.

"If you don't help us, we can't help you," I say.

"I know," she whispers. "But no one can help me now. This is my penance."

"What do you mean by penance?" I ask Reese.

But it's Eliza who answers. "A penance is a way to make amends for a wrongdoing. So . . . Mrs. Winters," Eliza says, giving her a dark look. "What did you do wrong? What are you punishing yourself for?"

Reese stares at us, her fingers pressed together in a tent. The clock ticks loudly from the wall.

"Answer the question," I say.

"They take on the voices of my parents, sometimes. The ghosts. They say . . ." She pauses and sighs deeply. "The ghosts remind me of what I did to my sister. Not in any words . . . just the sound of my parents' voices reminds me."

"Your sister?" I say. I am totally confused now. "What does that have anything to do with the ghosts?"

"I stabbed her in the back, and now these ghosts are coming to remind me of my greatest shame. The secret I swore would never get out. The knife I put in my sister's back."

She is *really* freaking me out now. Her eyes have this glassy sheen to them—eyes that are almost deadened. She didn't actually put a knife in her sister's back, right? That's just an expression. . . .

"Mrs. Winters," Eliza says tentatively. "What happened to your sister?"

"She never forgave me, and yet she never knew the full story of my betrayal. How I took the lodge right

356

out from under her. How I forced our parents to give it to me. I wanted her to leave, but she is always here, always watching me. I pay the price every day, every time I see her face."

Just when I'm going to ask her another question, the clock starts chiming from the foyer. That's our signal to go meet Mom and Frank. Which we have to do, on time, or they'll think something bad happened to us.

I stand up. "Sorry . . . we have to go."

Reese doesn't even look at us. She clutches her stomach like she is in pain. "This gnawing hasn't left me for years. It's eating me alive. I was haunted long before a ghost ever appeared."

She turns her chair around to face the setting sun. And I'm left with only the echo of her troubling words.

MEET MOM AND FRANK ON PAGE 59.

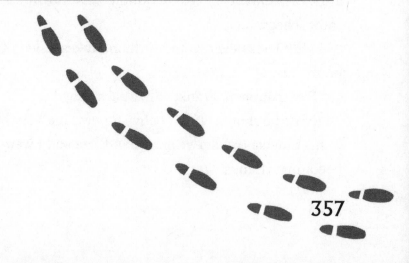

357

"LET'S GO LOOK at the equipment shed," I say.

Up close, I can see some fine print under the OUT-DOOR EQUIPMENT SHED sign that posts the hours of operation.

M TO F 9 A.M. TO 4 P.M.
SAT AND SUN 9 A.M. TO 6 P.M.
GUESTS, PLEASE FEEL FREE TO BORROW EQUIPMENT.
RETURN BEFORE CLOSING HOURS.

Eliza turns the doorknob. "It's open!" she says, surprised.

"It's only three o'clock," I say. "Of course it's open!"

It's dark inside, with lots of sports equipment hanging on the walls. If we weren't solving a mystery and were just staying at the hotel as guests, this would all be very tempting. "Do you see any deer heads?" I ask, walking the length of the wall. So far it's looking like a lot of snowshoes, cross-country skis, downhill skis, snowboards. . . .

Frank walks over to the wall and takes a sled off the hook.

"Put that back, Frank," Eliza says.

"No!" he shouts with a babyish pout. It's a flashback to his terrible toddler years, when Eliza and I were first becoming friends.

358

"Frank," I say warningly.

"Carlos!" he replies.

"You can't go sledding."

"Yes, I can!"

"No, you can't."

"No, I can't."

Does he *really* expect me to retort with "Yes, you can?"

"Frank. That trick is *not* going to work on me."

He grins. "IT ALREADY DID!"

And that's when I realize that while we were arguing, he's slowly edged closer to the door. He makes a break for it, and Eliza and I are too far away to grab him.

He runs out into the snowy tundra with his sled.

"FRANK, NO! FRANK, STOP!"

But it's too late.

Frank runs and jumps onto the sled—away he goes!

"After him!" Eliza shrieks.

"We can't—"

"We have to!"

She grabs a sled off the wall, and though I *hate* it, I know Eliza's right—we have to go after her brother. So the two of us follow Frank all the way down the mountain, screaming our heads off the whole way.

We catch up to him at the very bottom.

"That was fun! Let's do it again!" Frank says.

But we can't do it again. Looking up the mountain now, I can't even see the top. The roads are closed, and poor weather conditions make it too dangerous to hike up. There's just no way we can get back to the Sugarcrest Park Lodge. We're done.

I wanted to slay this case . . . not *sleigh* it.

CASE CLOSED.

"WHY DID THEY bring us to the Dead Room now?" I ask. "Why didn't they lure us here when they brought you here?"

"Because I'm the detective," Mom says.

"Hey!"

"Sorry . . . let me clarify," Mom says. "I'm the *hired* detective. I'm sure whoever is behind these ghost attacks didn't think that you three would be an integral part of my detective team."

"Th-they underes . . . underestimated us." Eliza is shaking from the cold, and even Frank's teeth have started to chatter. "I-is it just me, or is it getting c-c-colder in here?"

"It's not just you," I say. The temperature is dropping, and fast. I turn to Mom. "So they ignored us for a while. But why lure us here tonight? Why now? What changed?"

Mom blows warm breath into her hands. "Did you find an important clue? Get too close to the heart of the mystery?"

The ghost's headquarters! In the tunnels in the walls. We found those coded notes—we discovered that there are multiple culprits. And we took the walkie-talkie. The moment we stole that was the moment we put targets on our backs.

I groan. "We took the walkie-talkie out of the lair.

We should have known they'd notice that it was gone! We were going to use it to spy on them, but they turned it around on us and tricked us in here." I feel so, so stupid.

Mom shudders. "It's okay, hijo. But . . . wait. You said you found a lair?"

Eliza whimpers, and Frank presses his nose against my hand. It's like an ice cube.

"Hey, can your nose fall off?" Frank says between shivers. Then he grabs my nose and yanks. "GOT YOUR NOSE!"

"Ow! Frank! You're supposed to pretend your thumb is my nose—not *actually* pull my nose off!"

"Eww, awesome! Your nose is all runny. Eliza, look! I'm a human tissue."

She doesn't respond.

"Eliza?" I say, squeezing her hand.

"Y-yes?" Her voice is very faint.

"The lair, Carlos!" Mom reminds me.

Right, I nearly forgot. I feel sluggish. I think I'm having a brain freeze. The cold is clearly affecting Eliza. And even Frank seems less peppy than normal. I feel like we're spending too long in this room. Maybe it's time to get out.

"Carlos, quickly," Mom says. "This is important. Tell me about the lair."

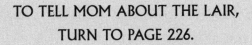

TO TELL MOM ABOUT THE LAIR,
TURN TO PAGE 226.

←→

TO SEARCH FOR A WAY OUT,
TURN TO PAGE 77.

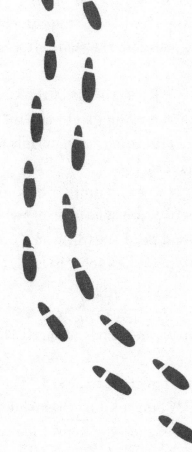

363

I HAVE TO get down that ventilation shaft. It's my best way out of here.

"Hey," I say to Sunny and January. "Can you just explain one thing for me? How did you—"

I cut off midsentence and *charge* at January. Head tucked in, like a football player about to tackle. January yelps and hops out of the way instinctively, and I dive headfirst down the ventilation shaft.

"FOLLOW HIM! He knows too much!" yells Sunny, and January goes into the shaft after me, feet-first.

The shaft lands me in the middle of the kitchen—I drop straight out of the ceiling and onto the floor. I have so much momentum that I somersault forward, knocking into Fernando's legs.

"Watch out!" he cries as he drops a bowl of pasta. Noodles and spaghetti sauce splatter everywhere.

I have a five-second head start in front of January, and I know exactly where she's going to land. I quickly grab the trash can and put it in place.

Squish.

January falls out of the vent and lands right in a heaping pile of garbage.

She gags. "Oh god, I'm going to be sick. The smell!"

"You don't like it?" I say, pulling the string tight on the garbage bag so that she's trapped inside with just

364

her head sticking out. "Because to me, it's the sweet smell of success!"

Fernando fetches Reese, who bursts into the kitchen like a hurricane.

"Fernando said you needed . . ." She takes in the scene: her daughter tied up in a trash bag, me keeping watch. "I don't understand. January? What's going on? Why are you . . ."

Suddenly it hits Reese. She gasps, eyes wide as she stares at her daughter. And she turns as white as a . . . well . . . you know. "It can't be. January, you wouldn't!"

Tears pour down January's cheeks. Either her mom's reaction has activated her conscience, or the smell of the garbage is really getting to her.

"I'm sorry, I'm sorry, I'm really sorry," January cries. "It was me, Mom! I was the ghost!"

"But how? Why?"

"It all started eight weeks ago, when I told you about that summer program for video editing and sound mixing, and you said I had to stay here and learn the family business because you want me to take over the hotel. But Mom, I don't want to take over—"

"Nonsense! Of course you'd want to—"

"Mrs. Winters," I say quietly. "Listen." Then I nod at January.

"I don't want to take over the hotel."

Reese nods slowly, like she's finally hearing her daughter for the first time.

"But . . . I found someone who *does* want to run it. Aunt Sunny. So we started haunting this place—so I could go to a real school and take real sound mixing classes."

"The ghost sounds . . . you made them on your computer?"

January nods. "I understand if you hate me forever—I'm so, so sorry, Mom. I really am."

"Don't cry," Reese says, walking over to her daughter and untying the garbage bag. "We'll figure this whole thing out." She gives her daughter a hug, even though she smells like old fish and rotten eggs, and even though a banana peel is stuck to her shirt. "I have unconditional love for you, January. Don't you know that?"

That makes January sob even harder.

When the hug eventually ends, Reese wrinkles her nose. "All right, sweetheart. Go take a shower, and then we'll talk about it—"

"Not. So. Fast." I step in front of her. "You and Sunny have kidnapped my team, and I need them back."

Sunny and January returned my mom, Eliza, and Frank. They were unscathed, but understandably shaken.

January's change of conscience was a bit unnerving, but even weirder was that Sunny also apologized to her sister. They've already decided to schedule a counseling meeting to possibly work on their issues without Reese having to press charges.

The only thing Reese is pressing at the moment is a box of cookies into my hands. "Here," she says. "I've had Fernando make you cookies for the road, and here's a week of free hotel stays, whenever you want to come back. In addition to the compensation we've agreed upon."

"That's very generous, thank you," Mom says, picking up two of our suitcases.

"You seem very happy," I say to Reese.

"TOO HAPPY," Frank says. "You're the ghost, aren't you?"

"Frank, we already found the ghost."

"We did?"

Eliza and I sigh, and Reese laughs. "I *am* happy. Happy not to be going to bed afraid every night. Happy to have a bit of transparency."

If there's one thing I know about ghosts, it's that they're transparent. I wonder if that applies to detectives on ghost cases. There is something on my mind . . . and I wait until we're in the car to get it off my chest.

"Mom," I say as she slowly drives down Sugarcrest

Mountain, "that was the scariest case I've ever been on. I was terrified the whole time. I've never screamed so much in my life. I thought I was going to pass out. And . . ."

She raises an eyebrow at me.

I hesitate. "Is it crazy to want another case like that?"

"I've created a mystery monster," Mom mumbles.

That she did.

CASE CLOSED.

"HELLO? HELLO!" I shout, but Sunny has shut off the speaker.

I turn to Mom. "How were you so calm talking to her? Aren't you scared?"

"Terrified, actually," she says with a smile. "Welcome to detective work . . . where a ghost is the least scary thing that haunts you. But no use fretting when we have work to do."

Work? What is she talking about?

"Eliza, how is that door looking?" Mom asks.

I was so focused on Sunny that I was barely paying attention to Eliza. And here she is, crouched by the iron door, playing around with the lock—a typical keypad with nine digits.

"Nothing yet," she says between gritted teeth. "I'm afraid to press any buttons in case a fail-safe turns on and locks us in. But there has to be some way. . . ."

Mom goes over to Eliza, and I stand back and let them work. But soon I'm distracted by Frank, who finds a stack of papers on the only table and starts folding them.

"What are you doing, Frank?"

"Paper airplanes," he says. "Want to race?"

"You know we're in danger here, right?"

He shrugs.

I grab a piece of paper. It has a message between our

two culprits. I feel like Sunny left a stack of clues down here to torture us while we slowly dehydrate to death.

"Ready, Carlos?" Frank says, and he doesn't even wait for my response before he launches his airplane across the room. It soars straight into Eliza's head. She turns and glares at us.

"Again! Again!" Frank cries, picking up another paper. Only . . . under that paper is a third paper that catches my eye.

Four digits . . . and no repeated digits.

The first digit is the sum of the second and third digits.
The second digit is two more than the last digit.
The third digit is one more than the second digit.
The fourth digit is an odd number.

Could this be the code to the lock?

"Eliza!" I run the paper over to her. She reads it hungrily, then looks up at me. "There's no way Sunny would be stupid enough to leave the passcode to the door in the *same* room she was planning to lock us into, right?"

"Hijo, in my line of work, you learn that the more complicated the crime, the clumsier the culprit. These six weeks of near-constant ghost haunting must have taken lots of effort and planning. Our culprit was sure to slip up somewhere."

"Culprit*s*," Eliza says. "Plural. Maybe Sunny wasn't the one who messed up. Maybe it was her bungling accomplice."

"In any case, I think we should take a risk on this code," Mom says. "We have nothing to lose. So Carlos— can you and Frank take the lead on cracking the code while Eliza and I try one last thing with the door?"

"We're on it!" I say.

Frank responds with an enormous fart.

Well, *I'm* on it, at least.

THE FIRST TWO DIGITS OF THE PASSCODE
WILL LEAD YOU TO YOUR NEXT PAGE.

←——→

TO ASK ELIZA FOR A HINT,
TURN TO PAGE 167.

371

ELIZA SCOOTS NEXT to Frank on the piano bench, and I tell her to play the D E A D notes that we need. Then, suddenly, the piano stops vibrating—it just goes dead silent. Like someone put a muffler on the strings. And across the room, a bookshelf swivels open to reveal . . .

A secret passageway in the walls.

"Well, that explains a lot," Eliza says.

"It does?"

"We heard those thuds in the walls during last night's haunting. I'll bet you anything that whoever is behind these hauntings was in the walls, banging."

"Who would know about a secret passageway in the walls?" I ask.

"Anyone with X-ray vision," Frank says, like he's given me an actual lead and not nonsense.

"Whoever owns the Sugarcrest would probably know," Eliza says. "The Winters family. And possibly anyone who works here, like Cricket, Sunny, and Fernando di Cannoli." Eliza pauses. "But . . . well, we found this secret passageway, and it's only our second day here. So I wouldn't cross anyone off our suspect list yet."

"Well, should we go in?" I peer into the dark hallway. It seems to be claustrophobically tight, and full of spiderwebs. The perfect place for a ghost to lurk. I'm head to toe full of dread.

But I have to find Mom . . . I have to go forward.

The moment we step inside the hall, the bookshelf slides back into place behind us. It's pitch-black.

"Eliza?"

"Here," she says, clicking on a flashlight. She uses it to dig into her backpack and fish out one for each of us. "You have to be quiet, Frank."

"Quiet as a mouse!" he shouts.

We shuffle through the hallway. I can hear Eliza's heavy breathing behind me. And Frank's creaky foot-steps. The rest is silence. And darkness.

I don't know where in the house we are, or where we're going, or what we'll find at the end of it. I only know that the hairs on the back of my neck are sticking straight up, and I have this paranoid feeling like we're being watched.

I stop, and Eliza bumps into me.

"Ow! Carlos, what's the holdup?"

I point my flashlight. Ahead, there's a rotting wood staircase that leads *down*. It's so dark that I can't even see what's at the bottom.

"Should we?" Eliza says.

"Should we . . . *go in there*? That's sure to be a ghost trap!"

Two cockroaches scurry down from the wall, crawl across my shoe, and disappear down the stairs. I'm certain we *all* saw that in the flashlight beam. I am definitely panicking.

"Don't you want to find your mom?"

"I do, but . . ."

But the ghost. It's haunting me, even when it's *not* haunting me.

"You stay here," Eliza says. "Frank and I will look for your mom and be back soon. You ready, Freddy?"

"The name is *Frank*. And don't you forget it!"

"Wait, Eliza." I swallow the lump in my throat. "Don't leave me behind. I'll go."

Is it possible that Mom is down here? I really hope not—because it would be freaky to be down here alone. And at the same time, I hope she *is* here because I need to find her.

The steps wobble under my feet. We hold onto the railing as we go down and down—so far belowground that we've left the heating of the lodge. The air is cold.

Or maybe that's the ghost. . . .

I put my foot on solid earth and flash my light around. We're in a little dirt room—tree roots poke out of the ceiling. It's a wonder this thing hasn't collapsed. There's nothing here but a small wooden door, like the entrance to a cupboard or something.

I open it.

And I gasp.

It's like a security guard's workspace, with a computer displaying cameras all around the lodge. There are also papers scattered everywhere across a collapsible

374

table, a wardrobe, a sound mixer, and candles with the wax still wet.

"Eliza," I say. "The wax is still melted! Someone blew out the candles . . . recently."

"Probably whoever was playing that piano," Eliza says. She and I fan out, searching every area of the room, under the table, in the corner. But I don't see anyone hiding here.

"Ooooh!" Frank says in delight. "Oooooooooooo!" We turn our lights to him. He's wearing a scary pale-faced ghost mask. "There are fifteen different kinds in here—oooh! This one is bloody!"

We sift through the ghost masks with him, and I can feel my heart racing. "It's a lair," I say, finally understanding. "It's an evil lair. We found it."

"But who does it belong to?" Eliza asks.

"I don't know. But maybe if we poke around, we can get some clues. We could look at the monitor to see what they're taping in the lodge with hidden cameras. Or maybe we could look through papers on the table."

TO LOOK AT THE MONITOR, TURN TO PAGE 24.

←——→

TO LOOK AT THE PAPERS ON THE TABLE,
TURN TO PAGE 413.

375

WE HAVE TO talk to Reese about the letter from Luther we found in her room.

We find her in the fire den, face buried in her hands. Harris sits beside her, rubbing her back gently. Hopefully our evidence will make her feel better.

"Mrs. Winters," I say. "We have to ask you about your staff. Do you think there's a possibility that someone would double-cross you?"

"Double-cross? What makes you use that word?" Reese says, and my stomach sinks. She recognizes Luther's word. I shouldn't have used it.

Eliza and I look at each other. I have no idea what to say, and I can tell Eliza doesn't want to put her foot in her mouth like she sometimes does.

"If you could answer the question," I say. "Do you think—"

"You went through my mail," Reese says. "But that's a felony!"

"It's only a felony to open, intercept, or hide someone else's mail," Eliza explains.

"And technically the mail was already opened," I add.

"And was the door to my room *technically already opened*?" Reese asks pointedly.

I gulp. And when Reese's furious eyes meet my terrified ones, I feel like she's X-raying my brain. We both know that I trespassed (at best) and committed breaking and entering (at worst). In other words: mail tampering isn't the only crime I got caught at today.

"SECURITY!" Reese cries.

"You don't have to do that!" Eliza says.

"SECURITY! SECURITY!"

Harris looks at her. "Er . . . honeybunches, we don't have security."

"Cinnamon toast, *you're* the security," she says.

"Oh. Right."

With his lumberjack muscles, he picks us up as easily as a pile of logs. He carries us to the door, opens it, and tosses us out into the cold.

"You kids like breaking and entering, yes?" Harris asks from the door.

"Yes!" Frank says.

"Well, if you enter this hotel again, I will break you." And with that, he slams the door.

CASE CLOSED.

"CAN YOU STOP fighting with Frank for *one second* and help me with this message?" I say to Eliza. I try to hide the annoyance from my voice, but I don't think I'm successful at it.

"Of course," Eliza says. "Sorry."

"I'm not sorry!" Frank says. Big surprise—he *never* apologizes for anything.

11-5-25-9-19-8-9-4-4-5-14-2-5-8-9-14-4-20-8-5-4-5-5-

18-8-5-1-4-2-21-20-1-14-20-12-5-18-19-8-1-22-5-1-16-1-

20-20-5-18-14-7-15-15-21-20-19-9-4-5-6-15-18-20-8-5-1-

14-19-23-5-18

"It has to be a code so obvious that we'd know how to solve it instantly," she mumbles to herself. "If only these numbers were letters . . ." She looks up and gasps. "That's it! These numbers correspond with letters of the alphabet!"

"Oh! So eleven is the eleventh letter of the alphabet . . ." I have to sing the alphabet to myself as I count on my fingers. "It's K."

"Okay," Frank says.

"No O. Just K. The letter K," Eliza confirms.

378

"And the second letter is E. And the third . . ." I sing the alphabet and count again. "Y. The first three letters are KEY."

"We can't sing the alphabet for every number. That's way too time-consuming." Eliza takes the notebook from my lap and starts writing in it. "Here—I bet it will be a lot easier if we write down the key to the code ourselves."

1	2	3	4	5	6	7	8	9	10	11	12	13
A	B	C	D	E	F	G	H	I	J	K	L	M

14	15	16	17	18	19	20	21	22	23	24	25	26
N	O	P	Q	R	S	T	U	V	W	X	Y	Z

Excellent. With the key in front of me, I know I can decode the mystery Dead Room person's message.

TO GO OUTSIDE, TURN TO PAGE 42.

←——→

TO GO THE ATTIC, TURN TO PAGE 195.

I WANT THAT key, and that means I will let this ghost chase me to the library.

"This way!" I shout, turning right at the bottom of the stairs. I open the door to the fire den, usher Eliza and Frank in, and close the door behind me, just before the beast gets in.

The fire is glowing blue. Bright blue in every single fireplace. Not a lick of orange fire to be found. It makes the room feel sinister. Which is not helped by the *thing* behind us, scratching and clawing at the door.

"Why did we go this way?" Eliza cries. "We're trapped in here now! The only way out is through the library and into the secret bookcase passage!"

"I know," I say. "That's the point. We have to get that key."

"Carlos, you don't even know what the key is for!"

"I know they don't want us to have it. That makes me want it."

"That's something Frank would say!" Eliza groans.

"Frank wouldn't say it because Frank didn't say it!" Frank says. "Or *did he*? Mwahahahahahahahahahaha!"

"Okay, that's enough," I say. "There's probably some scary haunting in the library waiting for us, but we just have to get under the piano lid, get the key, and go."

We tiptoe into the library and shut the door. The temperature in here is about zero degrees. I think I can feel my nose freezing from the inside out.

"GHOST!" Frank shouts, pointing his flashlight at a rocking chair in the corner of the library. I just noticed a quiet creaking sound that fills the room. The chair is rocking back and forth. Back and forth. Back and forth.

But there is no one in the chair.

Eliza and I grab on to each other, our arms encircling Frank. I close my eyes. I'm following the old, trusted principle of "If I can't see it, it can't see me."

Frank wriggles to get out of our hug. "Get off me! I want to poke it!"

The rocking chair stops. There is silence in the air, and I can see my breath in the flashlight beam.

"Piano lid," I whisper, peeling the lid up. Tucked into the wires is a skeleton key, big and brass, and I think I know exactly where this key goes.

"I bet this is the key someone stole from Sunny," I say. "The one that opens all the rooms!"

Eliza frowns. "Why would they leave it under the lid of a piano, where anyone could find it?"

"I don't know—how often do you usually look under the lids of pianos?"

"ALL THE TIME," Frank says.

"Fair enough," Eliza says.

"We can test it out, and if it's the master key, then we can return it to Harris!"

We slowly back into the fire den, where the flames have switched back to a normal comforting color. There is no more clawing or scratching at the door, and I open it very slowly to find . . . nothing. The lobby is empty, and the lights are back on.

We walk up the stairs, and everything is *so normal* that it's freaking me out. I swear I can feel the mounted animal heads looking at me, following me as I walk up the stairs, but when I turn around again, everything is where it should be.

Paranoid. I am just being *paranoid*.

"Okay," I say, stopping in front of room 237. "Let's open the door to our room." I put the key in, but it doesn't turn. "Is it jammed?"

"Let me try!" Frank says, pushing me out of the way. He takes the key out and spits in the keyhole.

"Okay, *what* are you doing?"

"Loosening it up!" Frank says. "Now try!"

I try again, but the door still won't unlock. This is *not* the master key. I turn the key over in my hands until I find two letters carved into it: DR.

"DR . . . doctor?" I say.

"Drew?" Frank says.

"Dead Room," Eliza whispers. The moment she says it, something yowls downstairs.

"*Oooooooooooooooooooo!*"

382

"I ain't afraid of no ghosts!" Frank shouts down the hall.

I don't want to admit it, but I think Eliza is right. I walk down the hall, careful not to look downstairs, where the howling is only getting louder and closer. . . . And I round the corner to the hallway of staff rooms, where the Dead Room is waiting.

I get about halfway to the Dead Room when I see a shadow in front of me. From something *big* standing behind me—behind us. I don't want to turn around. . . . Eliza grabs my wrist.

It's the beast.

The lights flicker—and then die. With my back facing the Dead Room now, I slowly step away from the beast, but it keeps trying to close the gap between us. Its fangs glow in the darkness.

Then, from behind us—

Thud. Thud. Thud.

Something is knocking from the *inside* of the Dead Room.

What do I do—*what do I do?* We either have to run past the beast in front of us . . . or use our key to go into the Dead Room behind us.

Thud. Thud. Thud.

A bead of sweat trickles down my face. There's no guarantee we'd all be able to run past this monster.

But if we do go into the Dead Room, we'd be running straight into whatever's knocking on the door . . . is the monster we know better than the monster we don't?

TO RUN PAST THE BEAST, TURN TO PAGE 223.

⟵⟶

TO GO INTO THE DEAD ROOM, TURN TO PAGE 282.

I **PULL THE** apple lever.

Suddenly a shelf from the freezer tips over, and a whole barrel of apples drops from the highest ledge.

"DUCK AND COVER!" I shout as the apples come raining down on us like hail. Just when I think the barrage is over, more come flooding. They bury me up to my eyes.

"An apple a day keep da doctah away!" Frank says, with his tongue still stuck on the pole. And, as the shortest one, with his head submerged under the apples.

Eliza groans. "I think I'm bruised all over."

"The only way out is through," Mom says grimly. "Start eating!"

We've hard-core ended our case with some hard cores.

CASE CLOSED.

I DECIDE TO trust January. But mostly out of convenience . . . because we need her help.

"Okay, January. You can help us."

"*Yes!*" she says, and she high-fives Frank.

"You have to distract and delay Fernando as much as possible," I say. "Whatever you do, keep him away from the kitchen."

"Got it," she says. "This is fun already!" She walks over to Cricket's concierge desk, and we peek around the wall. From our angle, we can see January clearly, but not Cricket.

January rings the concierge bell. "I need Fernando di Cannoli, and I need him *now*."

Cricket is so flustered by January's tone that she picks up the phone and drops it.

"Give me that!" January snaps. She dials four numbers. "Fernando? This is January, and I need a selection of your finest cheeses, breads, and grapes for a party I'm throwing for my parents ASAP. This is your top priority. If you're not in the dining hall in two minutes, I will *end* you." She slams the phone down before she even hears a response. Then she winks at us and waves goodbye.

You know . . . it's kind of fun to have an ally.

Fernando comes running out of the kitchen with a tray of breads, fruits, and cheeses. He is frantic and

386

nearly trips over his own feet as he races to please January.

"Let's go!" I say when he passes by us.

Back in the kitchen, I know we don't have much time. I pull the picture frame out from the wall, and it swings open, like a door on a hinge.

And *of course* there's some sort of lock that needs to be cracked before we can get to Fernando's big secret.

I groan.

"I mean, if he's going through all this trouble to hide something, you knew it wouldn't be unlocked, Carlos."

"Hey, a kid can dream."

"We got this!" Eliza says. "You, me, and Frank—Frank? Where are you?"

Frank is face-first in a cookie jar.

"Leave him!" I say. "We don't have time to get him to cooperate—we have a code to crack." I squint at the lock . . . which is *of course* in the shape of a pizza.

"Seems like something's missing out of each pie slice," Eliza says, more to herself than me.

"What do you mean, something's missing?"

"It looks like each slice is supposed to spell a different pizza topping. But each wedge has just one letter missing."

"So I have to figure out what the missing letter is in each wedge?"

Eliza nods. "We should keep track of all the missing letters. I bet they will tell us what number to enter on the lock behind the picture."

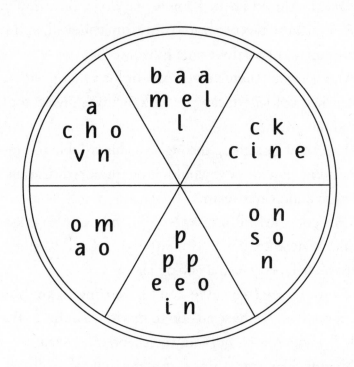

THE SOLUTION TO THE PUZZLE
WILL LEAD YOU TO YOUR NEXT PAGE.

←——→

TO ASK ELIZA FOR HELP, TURN TO PAGE 142.

 388

"SO, DO YOU think the ghost is real?" I ask the Winters family.

Eliza tries not to roll her eyes at my question, which results in a rapid blink spasm.

Reese doesn't notice. She's looking at her husband, who puts a thick, protective arm around her. "These hauntings have been scaring me silly."

"That's not the question, though," Eliza says. And even though she doesn't like this line of questioning, I'm thankful she always has my back.

"I don't know if it's real or not. . . . It seems so real." Reese shudders. "It can't be real, though. Can it?"

Eliza and I look at each other. We both have a different answer for Reese . . . but neither of us says anything.

To my surprise, Frank pops in with a question. "But have you *seen* it? Up close? With your eyeballs? You can't see it till you believe it!"

Reese and Harris both mumble, "No."

But January nods.

"You have?" Eliza says, astonished.

"There was one in my room one night. It was freaky. I saw one in the hall once too."

"What did it look like?"

"Um . . . like a ghost?"

Reese reaches for her daughter. "You never told me this, honey."

"Well, it's true." January glares at us, as though daring us to call her a liar. "It was hovering above my bed! It was all white and wispy and drooling. The one in the hallway was headed toward our suite, Mom."

Reese yelps and nearly jumps out of her chair.

TO ASK WHO MIGHT WANT REESE GONE, TURN TO PAGE 64.

I'M SO MAD, I can't even take it. I pick up Byron's computer off his lap and smash it down to the ground.

The screen shatters into a spiderweb of broken glass. Instantly my temper dissolves, but I can't undo what I just did.

Byron Bookbinder's mouth opens and closes like a fish. For the first time, this writer is totally speechless.

But then his face turns purple and a vein pops out of his forehead. He grabs a decorative sword off the fireplace mantel.

"They say the pen is mightier than the sword. BUT LET'S SEE, SHALL WE?"

I bolt, and Byron chases me out of the hotel, down the mountain, into the town in the valley. He chases me across state lines until he can't run anymore. I get away—but I am miles from the case.

Unlike Byron, I'm not a writer . . . I don't get writer's block. But in that moment, I definitely was a blockhead.

CASE CLOSED.

"WHAT'S THE DEAL with your book?" I ask Byron. "Why would your editor ask you to put fictional stories in a nonfiction book?"

"That's not right," Eliza says, with serious disapproval in her voice.

"And if you're not right, you're left!" Frank says.

"No, you're wrong!" I correct.

"*You're* wrong!"

I look at Byron. "Sorry about that. Continue."

"My manuscript was due six months ago," Byron says meekly. "If I don't have a draft of it by the end of this month, I'll have to pay back my publisher. And the thing is . . . I already spent the money. I can't afford to pay it back. So you see, it was out of desperation—not deceitfulness—that I went forward with my editor's suggestion."

"It was desperate *and* deceitful," Eliza says. "Those aren't mutually exclusive terms."

My head is spinning. Eliza and Byron having a conversation is like listening to a thesaurus battle a dictionary. I don't know half the words they're using, but I get the general point: Byron thinks he has an excuse, because he wasn't able to afford to pay his publisher back. Eliza thinks it's just dishonest and nothing can justify it.

I'm with Eliza on this one. "I can't believe your

editor would ask you to lie," I say.

"I don't think she expects to get caught. Frankly, they're looking for a return on their investment, and they don't care how they get it."

"But what I don't understand," I say, "is why you didn't have your book ready to go six months ago. Why didn't you write it last year?"

"After my first book was released four years ago, I found it nearly impossible to put pen to paper. The fear has paralyzed me."

"What fear?" Eliza asks.

"I can't write a single sentence without doubting every syllable. Perhaps you won't understand this, but I feel this immense pressure to be perfect."

Weirdly enough, I understand it a lot. I think that's what I feel whenever I'm trying to impress Mom on a case. It's what I've felt since coming to the Sugarcrest—and it also makes me overthink every decision.

TO ASK WHERE HE WAS DURING THE HAUNTING, TURN TO PAGE 115.

←——→

TO ASK IF HE HAS ANY IDEAS ON WHERE MOM COULD BE, TURN TO PAGE 429.

"YOU MADE IT sound like you and Harris hired Las Pistas Detective Agency together," I say to Reese. "But Harris told us that you weren't the one to hire us. In fact, you actively opposed hiring a detective, right?"

She nods. Just once.

"Why wouldn't you want us helping you?" I ask. "I don't understand."

"The ghosts aren't going to go away, no matter what you do."

Eliza scrunches her eyebrows together. "Why not? If we find the culprit—"

"There is no culprit," Reese whispers. "They're very real. And they are with me for as long as I stay at the Sugarcrest Park Lodge. They are the punishment for all my failings, and no one can help me."

Someone has clearly done a number on Reese. She's haunted by ghosts. And clearly by a secret that she fears will get out. I don't understand what she's hiding yet, but I am going to find out.

"What are you so afraid of?" I ask.

"Rats, heights, ghosts, I suppose . . ."

"No," I say. "I mean . . . what are you so afraid we'd find? So scared that you didn't even want to hire us?"

Reese shakes her head. "I can't. *She* doesn't even know."

She? But I don't ask. I stay silent and wait for Reese to fill in the blanks.

"I . . . I am a horrible sister," she says.

"Okay?"

"I can't tell you what I did. She can't ever know."

"But Mrs. Winters. We don't even *know* your sister," I say. "So we couldn't tell her even if we wanted to."

Reese covers her mouth and shakes her head. "The lodge should have been hers. I took it away. She never knew, but she suspected. I stabbed her in the back, and I fear she is so angry, and it's my fault. It's all my fault."

"Don't worry," I say. "We'll get the ghost—we promise."

Reese doesn't even seem to hear me. "Our parents. I wonder if they have regrets about me, the daughter they chose to carry out their legacy."

The grandfather clock in the lobby starts chiming. We have to meet Mom and Frank.

"We'll be back," I say. "Are you going to be all right, Mrs. Winters?"

She doesn't answer. Her face is in shadow, and I can tell her mind is clouded by darkness. Whatever the ghosts are doing to Reese doesn't seem nearly as bad as the guilt that's eating her up.

It feels like ages ago when Mom told us that sometimes the biggest ghosts are secrets. Looking at Reese's gaunt, haunted face, I finally think I know what she means.

MEET MOM AND FRANK ON PAGE 59.

"WE HAVE TO talk to Luther about this letter to Reese," I say, walking back toward the hotel lobby. "We can go right to the source."

Eliza shakes her head. "Let's say you're right, and Luther really *is* working with someone else in the hotel. You think he'll just tell us? No chance he'd let that slip!"

The lobby is still empty; Cricket is nowhere to be found. I head to the double doors, open them wide, and stop dead in my tracks. The blizzard is raging outside—the wind howls violently, and the snow is coming down so thick it looks like someone took an eraser and scrubbed out the landscape.

"Wow, that's worse than I realized," Eliza says.

"New plan," I say, going to the landline phone on Cricket's desk. I breathe a sigh of relief when I hear the dial tone. We have an operator connect us to the Super Hotel Express.

"Hello, this is Tyler at the Super Hotel Express. How may I help you?"

I pause. Eliza and Frank nudge me to talk, but something is stopping me. Something Eliza said, actually: "You think he'll just tell us? No chance he'd let that slip!"

Getting information out of Luther won't be easy or straightforward. We have to trick it out of him. But how?

TO PRETEND TO BE REESE CALLING ABOUT
THE LETTER, TURN TO PAGE 262.

←→

TO PRETEND TO BE A REALTOR MAKING HIM
A COUNTEROFFER ON THE SUGARCREST PARK
LODGE, TURN TO PAGE 312.

397

I'M STARING BETWEEN the tapestry poem and the tapestry symbols, and all I can think is, We're running out of time to sneak into Reese's quarters.

"Eliza, do we go in order of the symbols, or in order of the poem?"

She hums thoughtfully. "That's a good question," she says. Because she's my best friend, I know she's about to do what she *always* does when she encounters a particularly difficult problem: talk it out. "I wonder if one of them is a decoy."

"A decoy!"

"Well," she says, shining a flashlight across the tapestry, "if it were me, I wouldn't want people knowing the passcode to my suite. So I'd maybe make a big flashy decoy and a smaller, more forgettable real clue."

"The poem must be the real clue, then!" I pause. "But how do we know what order to press things?"

"I think, as we read the poem, whenever we hear a word that corresponds with the symbol, we press it immediately. Ready, Frank?"

He stands at attention. "Yes, ma'am!"

Eliza flashes her light on me. "I'll read the poem out loud. Whenever you hear a word that has a symbol that goes with it, you tell Frank. And Frank, you press the buttons."

"Wooooooo!"

Eliza clears her throat and reads.

In sun and in snow,
This household stands tall.
Our love for it grows
Spring, summer, and fall.
But winter is what we cherish the best,
For Winters we are, and Winters are blessed.

TO PRESS MOON, LEAF, HOUSE, STAR, SUN, LIGHTNING, FLOWER, HEART, SNOWFLAKE, TURN TO PAGE 54.

←→

TO PRESS SUN, SNOWFLAKE, HOUSE, HEART, FLOWER, SUN, LEAF, SNOWFLAKE, SNOWFLAKE, SNOWFLAKE, TURN TO PAGE 230.

WE WALK ACROSS the lobby to the mailboxes. They're behind the door, near a window that overlooks Sugarcrest Mountain—in the distance, we can see the lights from Luther's hotel, the Super Hotel Express.

There are five silver boxes mounted to the wall, protruding out quite a bit, one for each member of the Sugarcrest Park Lodge staff: Reese, Harris, Fernando, Cricket, and Sunny. The only problem is that we need a key to get into each person's box.

"Rats," I say.

"Where?" Frank says excitedly.

"There has to be a way to put the mail in the mailboxes," Eliza says. "See how there's no slot to slip the envelopes in? I bet there's a way to open all the boxes at once, so whoever's delivering the mail can slide letters into their correct spaces without having to open each box individually." Eliza takes a look underneath the mailboxes—then she moves to the side, so she's wedged right between the wall and the mailboxes. "Look! There's another way in."

We squeeze next to her to find a snowflake-shaped lock built into the side of the last mailbox. Each of the snowflakes has a dial on it, where we can flip from numbers one through seven.

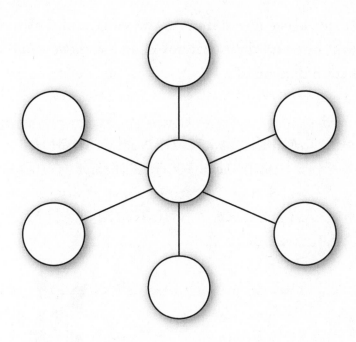

"We have to open this," I say. But how?

"I think . . . ," Eliza whispers. "Could it be? No. But maybe."

"Spit it out already!" Frank says.

"I think this might be a magic circle. All the numbers on each line have to add up to the same sum. We have to use the numbers one through seven, but we can only use each number once."

I scratch my head. I feel like I've done one of these before. It's like a distant memory.

"If we figure out which number goes in each circle

to make every line add up to the same sum, I'm sure it will open up these mailboxes, and then we can see what's hiding here."

ADD TWO HUNDRED TO THE SUM OF EACH LINE, AND TURN TO THAT PAGE.

⟵⟶

TO ASK ELIZA FOR A HINT, TURN TO PAGE 97.

"THE FLORAL ARRANGEMENT arrives at three o'clock," I say, setting the grandfather clock to three. Nothing happens.

"I think you have to pull this weight here," Mom says, reaching forward. The clock starts chiming, and on the third ring, the clock swings open. Completely, off the wall, to reveal a tiny pathway into the walls.

"Here we go!" Mom says. She looks giddy about this new discovery, and now I know where I get it from.

Mom files in first, then Frank, then Eliza, and I'm last. Every passageway we go through is narrow and full of cobwebs. There are no lights, but I didn't expect there to be any inside the walls.

Every so often, we hear voices through the walls. Fernando di Cannoli and Byron Bookbinder are having a discussion in the fire den. In the hallway, Harris is bellowing on the phone to Luther Covington. In the library, Reese and January are shouting about her future career, which seems a bit early, if you ask me. January is barely a teenager.

But we don't have time to linger and listen. I feel like we're racing toward the end—to the final piece of this long and haunted puzzle.

We don't know what we're looking for, but soon we find it: a set of staircases goes down into the dark. We shine our flashlights, but the dark seems to eat up all our beams. There's no telling what's down there.

Mom takes a step forward.

"Mom, no!"

She turns around and smiles widely. "You make me brave, hijo. The only way we're going to solve this is to keep moving forward. We can't let fear stand in the way of getting to the truth."

"If we get into trouble, we'll solve our way out," Eliza says. "One problem at a time."

"That's what we *always* do," Frank says, pulling on my sleeve.

A knot in my stomach loosens. I think I *have* been letting fear control me this whole case. Ever since Mom went missing on us the first night . . . I don't think I've taken a breath since—not even when we found her again.

I sigh deeply and let go of my anxiety—all the worst-case-scenario worries that are tripping over themselves for attention in my head.

And then I nod. And Mom nods. And Eliza nods. And Frank says, "NOD!"

The four of us go down into the dark.

At the bottom of the steps, there's an iron door. It almost looks like a dungeon down here. It must be some sort of cellar.

We open the door.

"Welcome," says a cool voice. "I was thinking you'd find our little spot."

I look frantically around for the source of the voice, but I can't find anyone. This tiny room is empty, and yet . . .

"Take a seat."

I know that voice.

"We prefer to stand," Mom says.

"Suit yourself. I think you'll be doing a lot of lying forevermore, so you can stand while you can."

Eliza and Frank are crawling around the room while Mom and I are straining to listen to the voice. Frank finds something and points, and we slowly and carefully walk over to him.

It's a speaker.

No one is down here.

"Yes, I'm afraid it's true," the voice says. "Sorry to say I couldn't join you. I have a previous engagement upstairs. Don't worry, the door locked behind you, so you'll have your privacy."

"I thought you lost your master key . . . *Sunny*," I say, finally recognizing the voice.

"What an easy lie," she says with a laugh. "Completely unverifiable. No one can prove I *didn't* lose my key. And while the storm is raging, Reese and Harris

405

couldn't call a locksmith to get the locks changed. It allowed me to very easily slip into your room."

"And Reese's room all those times?"

"Oh, I don't need a key for Reese's room. I have a spy on the inside."

Spy on the inside? What does that mean?

And why is she even doing this?

TO ASK WHY SHE'S DOING THIS,
TURN TO PAGE 132.

←——→

TO ASK WHAT SHE MEANS BY A SPY
ON THE INSIDE, TURN TO PAGE 214.

TIME TO TURN the tables on the ghost.

"Eliza, Frank—find the exit. Get Reese and the police!"

"Hey, that rhymes!" Frank says. Eliza grabs her brother by the hand, and the two of them run.

I am fully aware that Mom and I are the bait. We're the distraction for the ghost, just here to buy Eliza and Frank more time.

But that doesn't mean we're helpless. We have things in the basement that we can use. Like these millions of hanging cloths that are projecting these freaky ghost holograms . . . which we could use to tie up the ghost. But there's also that patch of mud, near the bottom of the slide. If we can lure the ghost over there, then maybe we'd get it stuck. Or at the very least, slippery and dirty.

TO TRAP THE GHOST IN THE HANGING CLOTHS,
TURN TO PAGE 467.

←——→

TO LURE THE GHOST INTO THE MUD,
TURN TO PAGE 26.

WE HAVE TO go search for Mom and Eliza. I could never forgive myself if something happened to them while Frank and I were just lying around on the hotel bed.

"Come on, Frank!"

"Where are we going?"

"Uh . . . sneaking! Crawling!"

He jumps up faster than I've ever seen him. "YES!"

We leave the room without being totally sure where we're going next. But the second the door clicks behind us, I pull Frank against the wall. The hallway is still and quiet. Too still.

I don't understand—sure, the sun is down, but it's not bedtime! There shouldn't be a haunting this early. But it definitely feels like the calm before the storm.

Goose bumps prickle on my arms.

Then we're flung into darkness.

I cling to Frank, and he hugs me back—which is the first time I've ever gotten a nonfidgety hug from him. *That's* how scared he is. I'm practically shaking, because I can faintly hear a hissing noise. Are ghost snakes a thing?

I'm starting to think we shouldn't have given Mom and Eliza our flashlights. I dig into my pocket and fumble with the key . . . and try to find the keyhole to go back inside our room. I can't see a thing—I'm running my hand all over the door.

And right when my fingers brush the keyhole, the hall lights come back on. At the end of the hallway, there's a girl standing in fog. I can't see her face, but she's got blond pigtails. She's wearing a blue dress, and her hands are red, like she's been finger painting with blood.

Nope, nope, nope.

"Come play," she says with a sickly sweet laugh.

"W-we're good here," I say, my voice shaky. I try to put the key into the door, and I drop it accidentally.

"Come play," she says between giggles.

"What games do you have?" Frank says. "Monopoly? Clue? Connect Four?"

Does he not notice her bloodstained hands? I wrap my arms around him protectively. Because I don't trust him not to walk over to her.

"Thank you for the offer, but it's a hard pass," I say.

"Come play," the girl says again, more demanding this time. The giggling is gone.

The lights are snuffed out again.

And then there's a terrible sound—the world's most terrible sound. Mom screaming from somewhere above us. The lights come back on.

"MOM!"

The girl at the end of the hallway darts around the corner. I sprint after her. I don't even have to make a choice here—my feet run of their own accord. I think we *must* be running toward the Dead Room. But to my surprise—and horror—in front of the Dead Room, there's an attic ladder that's been pulled down by its string.

I did *not* agree to creepy old attics when I took on this case.

But what choice do I have? The girl is halfway up the ladder. I climb behind her, and Frank is behind me.

When I get to the top of the ladder, I turn around and help Frank. It's freezing cold up here, and I can hear the winds smacking the house. The light is dim—enough to see, but not well.

I do not see Mom or Eliza.

"Hello?" I call. "Mom? Eliza?"

I hear Mom's shriek again. This time she says my name. *"Carlos!"*

"Mom!"

I run through the attic, between stacks of boxes taller than me, past old dusty cloths. The floor creaks beneath my feet—I'm fairly certain that the wood is rotted.

"Carlos!"

Now I *know* that came from my left. I barrel through some junk on the ground, kick my way past a fire extinguisher, and duck under an old moth-eaten drape.

"Carlos!"

The same exact inflection as before. I've hit the wall,

410

but Mom isn't here. Where is she?

Frank comes running behind me. "You're fast!"

"*Carlos!*"

That's when I see it: a speaker. So Mom isn't here. She isn't screaming. It's just a sound bite that they probably got off her when she was stuck in the Dead Room. It was all a trick, and I fell right into their trap.

We have to get out of here! I pull Frank back the way we came, but there is a ghost blocking my way to the ladder. A *different* ghost. Not the creepy little pig-tailed girl, but a ghastly green one that looks like it has boogers for skin.

Worst of all, the ladder is all folded up into the attic—a giant chain and lock are wrapped around the rungs. There's no way out.

"Carlos," Frank says, pointing at the ghost. No—he's pointing *behind* the ghost. All the way across the attic, there is a single window . . . and our only chance of escape.

But the ghost stands in our way.

TO KNOCK OVER THE BOXES ONTO THE GHOST,
TURN TO PAGE 170.

←—→

TO SPRAY THE GHOST WITH THE
FIRE EXTINGUISHER, TURN TO PAGE 497.

WE NEED TO get to the chimney. If we can crawl down it, then we'll be back in the house. We can shout for Mom and Eliza—the chimney puts us where we need to go.

"Come on!" I say, yanking Frank away from January. He screams—she was really holding his hair tightly. "Run!"

"Oh no you don't," Sunny says, moving to block us. But she doesn't know where we're going, and she runs the wrong way. Perfect!

I give Frank a leg up. He crawls into the chimney, and I follow.

"After them!" Sunny cries.

"I'm not crawling in there!" January says.

"Well, I'm too big!"

I can hear them arguing as we shimmy down the chimney. Only . . . it's getting narrower and narrower, and I don't think we're both going to fit.

"Frank, move your leg!" I glance over at him, and he's totally smushed against the wall. And so am I . . . there's nowhere for either of us to move. We are wedged in.

"We're Santa!" Frank says.

"No," I groan. "We're stuck!"

CASE CLOSED.

412

I EDGE CLOSER to the table and pick up a paper. I go to read it, only . . . it's a series of scribbled numbers. But how do I convert the numbers to letters?

968 46 843 56229, 63 46 843 4255.

9428 8463?

84733. 36 668 438 228448.

4 63837 36.

Go team kind

Minus the D, you mean

"Eliza, can you look at this weird number code?" I ask her, and she crosses the lair to come to my side.

She takes one look at the numbers and laughs. Then she pulls her phone out of her pocket.

"There's no cell reception right now because of the storm! That's not going to work."

"It's not for calling people. It's for this!" She shows me her screen.

"It's a phone code," she says. "The numbers translate to letters. The tricky thing is that each number could be three or four different possible letters. So I recommend starting with the small number sequences. Those should be easier. And work your way up to the big ones."

968 46 843 56229, 63 46 843 4255.

9428 8463?

84733. 36 668 438 228448.

4 63837 36.

414

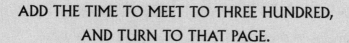

ADD THE TIME TO MEET TO THREE HUNDRED,
AND TURN TO THAT PAGE.

←→

TO ASK ELIZA FOR A HINT,
TURN TO PAGE 61.

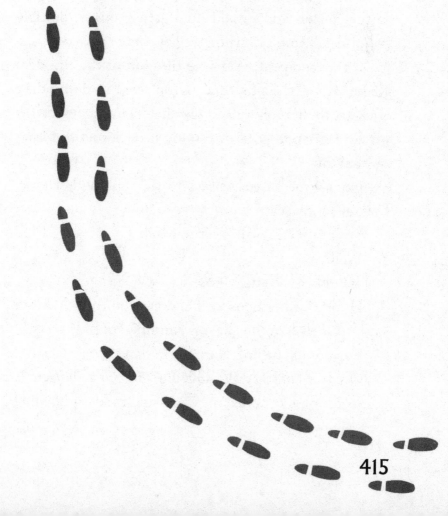

415

"WE HAVE TO warn Harris," I say as I stare at the translated message I've written on a sticky note.

GET OUT REESE
OR I AM COMING FOR YOUR HUSBAND TONIGHT

"You want to talk to Harris?" Eliza says, reaching down and touching some of the green jelly. "Because I want to talk to Fernando. Between the license, the Luther letter, and a food item as a prop in multiple hauntings, I think it's time we got some answers."

At that moment, everyone files out of the fire den. Reese, January, Sunny, and Byron seem to be heading back to their rooms. I notice that Harris goes to his office. Fernando goes to the kitchen. Something isn't quite right.

"Excuse me," Cricket says to us, rubbing her eyes. "You're in my seat."

We get up and walk over to Mom.

"Well?"

I hand her the sticky note.

"Hmm. Rather nonspecific, don't you think?" Mom says. "It feels like the ghost is running out of threats."

"So you don't think Harris is in danger?"

"On the contrary, I think he's in *more* danger. It seems to me like coded messages and random howling

416

noises don't work on Reese. I think the ghost is figuring out that the only thing that will *really* send a message to her is action. Action focused not on Reese herself, but on someone she loves."

"So . . . Harris is in trouble."

"Unless we stop the ghost—and fast," Mom says.

"Then let's go," I say, pulling Mom and Eliza toward the kitchen. "Fernando is our biggest lead. We have to confront him."

We head to the kitchen, where Fernando is standing at the kitchen island. Just staring at an empty bowl in front of him.

"Why didn't you go back to bed like everyone else?" I say. "Are you plotting with Luther again?"

Flustered, he drops the bowl he is holding.

"Oh a-my! Look at the time! I must go—"

"Not so fast," Mom says. Even though she's smaller than him, she has a really strong don't-mess-with-me-because-I-am-in-no-mood-for-nonsense presence. It stops Fernando cold.

"W-what do you want?"

"An explanation," Eliza says. "For this." She reaches into her backpack and pulls out the license we found in the safe.

"It's not mine!" Fernando says automatically. It's almost like a knee-jerk reaction.

"Then why is your picture on it . . . *Stefano*?" I say. Fernando di Cannoli begins to sweat. And his eyes dart to the door, like he's looking for an exit. "I . . . I . . ."

He tries to dash to the door, but Frank grabs hold of his legs. "Nice try, Ferdinand! If that really is your name!" Frank says.

"It's not. It's Fernando."

"No, it's Stefano," Eliza says.

"You're not leaving until we have some answers," Mom says.

"Answers?" Fernando says. "W-what are you talking about?"

Mom nods at me. I can't believe she trusts me to take over. I hope I make her proud!

TO ASK ABOUT THE DRIVER'S LICENSE,
TURN TO PAGE 127.

←——→

TO ASK ABOUT THE LETTER FROM LUTHER,
TURN TO PAGE 187.

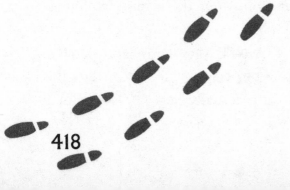

I MOVE CLOSER to the wall to look at the blood.

In the dark, it's glimmering and bright red. It spells out:

LEAVE THIS HOTEL, OR IT WILL BE YOUR TOMB

Doesn't take a genius to decipher that message.

"How can we leave the hotel if we've been locked in a room *in* the hotel?" Mom sighs. "Either this ghost has conflicting messages, or it's not very smart."

Frank moves closer and sniffs the message on the wall. Then he sticks his tongue right on the wall and takes one big lick.

"Don't!" Eliza cries, but it's too late. Frank is lapping up the blood like a dog.

"Look, I'm a vampire!" he says.

Eliza gags. "That is so gross, Frank."

"Is not! You eat it all the time!" Frank accuses.

"Eat what?"

"Ketchup! Here, have a taste!"

There's a pause.

"Wait—what?" I say.

"This is ketchup!"

We all touch the "blood" on the wall hesitantly, since Frank is the kind of person who would think it's hilarious to trick us into actually licking blood. But I

419

have to admit . . . it *does* smell a lot like ketchup.

And it tastes like ketchup too.

"He's right!" I say.

Frank grins. "And don't you forget it!"

"Gee," I say, "I wonder who has the greatest access to the kitchen."

"Anyone can get their hands on ketchup," Mom says. "Let's not jump to conclusions."

Frank jumps, and the wall rattles. Ketchup slides to the floor. We all glare at Frank. "What?" he says. "I'm not jumping to conclusions. I'm just jumping!"

"Great, now we're going to slip in it," Eliza says, pointing her flashlight down. She hums thoughtfully, then takes a knee. "This is weird, right? Look at the floor."

I kneel next to Eliza, take off my jacket, and wipe the ketchup away with it. There seems to be an inlay set into the floor.

"It's a compass rose!" Mom says.

"There's no rose!" Frank says. "There's no flowers at all!"

"It's just what a navigational key on a map is called," Mom says.

In the middle, there's an arrow. I can move it to face the north, east, south, or west. But which direction should I point the arrow to? If I pick the wrong one, it could spell disaster!

"We have to figure out which direction the last arrow in the pattern points," Eliza says.

"Is there a pattern?" I ask. "It looks very random to me."

"There has to be a pattern," Eliza says, running her fingers over the arrows at the beginning of the sequence. She mumbles to herself, "North, east, west, south, east . . . there just *has* to be."

TO TURN THE ARROW TO NORTH, TURN TO PAGE 35.

←——→

TO TURN THE ARROW TO EAST, TURN TO PAGE 158.

←——→

TO TURN THE ARROW TO SOUTH, TURN TO PAGE 256.

←——→

TO TURN THE ARROW TO WEST, TURN TO PAGE 334.

"WE'RE SORRY FOR disrupting your work," I say to Sunny. "You can get back to it now."

"Thank you," she says, and she rolls her cleaning cart down the hall.

"Why did you let her go so easily?" Eliza asks.

"I'm pacing myself. We'll have plenty of time for interviews, and she's not our only suspect. We have lots of people we could talk to."

I walk toward the staircase, and Eliza and Frank follow me. The interview with Sunny was shorter than I wanted, and I'm not sure if we gleaned anything important from it. But detectives have to try and try again. This is part of the job.

And eventually a suspect will crack. Someone has to give us a nugget of good information, or a lead, or a clue *sometime*. I need to have patience.

"So . . . does that mean you'd like to talk to Fernando di Cannoli now?" Eliza asks. "Since we chose Sunny over him last time?"

"Or Cricket," I say, pointing over the banister. Cricket is at the concierge desk, and I did want to follow up with her. After we asked her about Reese, her voice got high-pitched, so I'm almost certain she's hiding something.

TO INTERVIEW FERNANDO, TURN TO PAGE 180.

←——→

TO INTERVIEW CRICKET, TURN TO PAGE 124.

"CAN YOU TELL us about the first haunting, Mrs. Winters?" I ask. "How did this all begin?"

Reese puts her hand on her husband's arm. "When it started six weeks ago, it was just some normal howling. Some *oooooo*s in the night."

"OO*ooooooooooooo!*" Frank says, and Eliza elbows him.

"Where was it coming from?" Mom asks.

"The first time? Outside . . . the grounds. I remember because I was alone in my room, and I thought Harris might be outside, and I got frightened. The wails were coming from the firepit."

"How do you know it wasn't a wolf or coyote?" Mom says.

Reese frowns deeply. "There was something mystical about the voice. I know what a wolf sounds like. This voice sounded . . . human. Or human-esque. Like the cry of a banshee. I was going to check, but then the guests were stirring, and I had to reassure them that it was just the wind."

"Is there a chance it was actually the wind?" I ask.

Reese shakes her head. "I just told you—it sounded human. And the second night, the howling moved *inside* the lodge. What wind is inside?"

That's a loaded question when Frank is around. But luckily, he doesn't break any wind to illustrate the point.

"What happened after the howling?" Mom asks.

"This and that. Mad cackling in the night. A few

ghost sightings from guests—always in different locations. On the fifth or sixth day, the ghost hung the guests' underpants from this chandelier."

"Underpants." Frank giggles.

"After that, I noticed noise coming from the Dead Room—"

"The *what?*" Eliza chokes.

"There's a door on the second floor, in the staff hallway that's perpetually locked," Reese explains. "We don't have a key, and the hinges are too strong to break. We call it the Dead Room because it's dead space. Anyway, there was noise coming from the room . . . but it had previously been silent for four decades. As long as I can remember." She shudders.

"But sweets," Harris says. "The Dead Room isn't even the worst of it. Tell them about the other hauntings. Like that trouble with the mice—remember the mice? Or that horrible hair incident. Which do you think was scarier, January?" he says to his daughter.

January shrugs, clearly bored. She doesn't even look up from her music playlist.

TO ASK ABOUT THE MICE, TURN TO PAGE 76.

←——→

TO ASK ABOUT THE HAIR INCIDENT,
TURN TO PAGE 197.

"IT'S REALLY NICE of you to offer to help us, January. But I think we can handle it ourselves."

January bristles. "Fine! Be that way!" She pulls her headphones over her ears—like she didn't want to listen to us anyway—and storms across the lobby. When she reaches the foot of the stairs, she turns around and shouts, "By the way, you just made a *huge* mistake!"

Her words echo around the lobby long after she leaves. *Huge mistake. HUGE MISTAKE.*

I hope she's wrong about that.

"Now what?" Eliza says. "We did need her help to get Fernando out of the kitchen."

"We'll be fine," I say. "I know the perfect time to break into that wall safe."

"When?" Frank says. "Who? What? Where? Why? How?"

"Tonight," I say. "When Fernando is sleeping."

"AOOOOOOOOOOO!"

We set the alarm for three a.m., but this noise is not our alarm.

It's the sound of a howl. . . . I want to get up, but I can't move out from under the covers. It's so cold . . . the type of cold where I need to curl up.

"C-C-Carlos!" Eliza says between chattering teeth. "S-something's wrong."

I can hear her shuffling—and I don't understand how she has the energy to get out of bed, when all I can do is breathe hot air into my hands.

"The thermostat says it's f-forty-one degrees," Eliza says. "Dangerously cold. Get up, Carlos!" She puts her cold hand on my ankle and yanks. "We have to get out of here!"

"Aooooooooooo!"

"W-what's that?" I shiver.

"Let's go—"

She pulls me into a sitting position, and I roll out of bed. She pushes me into the hallway.

The warm air hits me in a rush, and it's like my brain suddenly wakes up.

"Eliza—what happened?"

"The temperature in our room dropped."

"Do you think it broke?"

She gives me a dark look.

"Someone wants us to freeze," I say. I knock on Mom and Frank's door for a solid thirty seconds, but there is no answer. I try the walkie-talkie.

"Come in, Mom!" I say. "Are you in your room? Over!"

"Carlos, I'm . . . *skirch* . . . Luther . . . snowstorm . . . you were here . . . *skirch*."

"You're cutting out, Mom!" I say. My heart is thudding. Are Mom and Frank in danger? I already felt so much pressure to prove myself as a junior detective; now I feel like *everything* is falling on my shoulders. "Mom!"

"Frank . . . *skirch*."

I look at Eliza. "The snowstorm must be messing with the radio signals," she says.

"*Aooooooooo!*" comes the howling again.

I ignore it as I look down at the walkie-talkie. "This thing sounds like a dying robot." I try to chuckle, but it comes out hollow. With Mom and Frank who knows where, it feels like our solid team of four is being whittled away. Maybe it's a coincidence that they've been separated from us, but it feels menacing.

"Hahahahahahahahahahahahahaha."

The sound echoes down the hallway.

"*What* is that?" I whisper. Even though I know exactly what that was: maniacal laughter.

Eliza takes a deep breath. "Okay, do we follow the sound of the laughter? Or the sound of the howling?"

"So much for checking out Fernando's wall safe."

I look to Eliza for guidance, and she grimaces.

"You pick between the laughter and the howling," she says. "Because honestly? I'm not optimistic about either one right now."

I feel frozen from the inside out—Mom and Frank might need me, and Eliza and I may be in trouble. Usually this is where my brain starts whirring. But for some reason, the only thing I feel now is fear.

"Carlos?"

"This ghost—it's ruining my detective skills! I have to prove to Mom that I'm worthy of being here, but right now, I have no gut instincts. I'm just scared."

Eliza grabs my hand. "I'm scared too, Carlos. But you are putting too much pressure on yourself. You can make this decision. I'm right here with you."

TO FOLLOW THE LAUGHTER, TURN TO PAGE 140.

←——→

TO FOLLOW THE HOWLING, TURN TO PAGE 254.

"**DO YOU HAVE** any ideas about where my mom could be?" I ask Byron.

I'm still not sure if I trust him, but I'm really worried about Mom.

"What do you mean?" he says.

"She went missing sometime around three in the morning. She was right behind us . . . and then she wasn't."

Byron gulps. "Have you . . . have you checked every door, every closet, every room in this lodge?"

"Why would she be in a room and not come to us?" I ask. "And why wouldn't she answer my walkie-talkie?"

"Are you sure you're on the right channel?"

"Positive," I say irritably. "Look, do you have any ideas or not?"

"She disappeared last night, you say?"

I nod.

"Well, if that's true, then I wouldn't have seen her. I wouldn't have known."

"Weren't you out and about last night?" Eliza says suspiciously. "Your stuff was just lying on the chair here."

Byron adjusts his glasses, clearly avoiding the question.

TO ASK WHERE HE WAS DURING THE HAUNTING, TURN TO PAGE 115.

I WANT TO check out that fenced garden.

"Very gothic," Eliza says. I'm not sure what that means. "It doesn't go with the vibe of the log cabin. It's too . . . spooky."

"A perfect hiding place for a ghost?" I say, holding the gate open for her and Frank.

There's a fountain in the middle of the garden, and at the four corners there are four statues: a bear, a moose, a horse, and a deer. I edge closer to the deer. Beneath the statue, a plaque reads:

A buck and a doe went forth down the slope
On a day that would seem unappealing.
The snow cascaded, and soon an avalanche
Left our poor deer both reeling.
All tangled in knots, they grumbled and griped
At their poor, unwise venture with feeling.

"That's a weird poem," I say. I look up at the deer's iron head. "So, do you think this is it? How do we open it?"

"Like this!" Frank says, crawling on top of the deer's back. "Giddyup!"

"That's not it," Eliza says.

Frank reaches forward and grabs one of the antlers. It twists. "Cool! A loose tooth!"

430

He pulls on them all, and they all wiggle.

Eliza leans in closer. She's facing it head-on. "Look closely, Carlos! The antlers have numbers on them . . . one through eight, from left to right."

"But which ones do we pull? And in what order?" I say, throwing my hands up in the air. I just want that key already!

"I wonder," Eliza says, "if we already have the answer . . . and don't even realize it yet."

"What do you mean?" I ask as I stare up into the deer antlers. I'm practically willing the deer head to open up so I can grab that key and rescue Mom and *why* is this taking so long?

"Look at the plaque," Eliza says. "I think that weird inscription is a clue."

"Okay?" I say. "But I don't see any numbers in there."

"You don't?" Eliza says. "I do!"

"Me too!" Frank says.

"You can't even read yet," I say.

Frank grins.

THE ORDER IN WHICH YOU PULL
THE ANTLERS IS YOUR NEXT PAGE.

←——→

TO ASK ELIZA FOR A HINT, TURN TO PAGE 192.

I DECIDE ELIZA is right: it *is* too dangerous to take the snowmobile.

"Come on—let's go on foot," I say.

"Aww, man!" Frank says, disappointed. "Why?"

But there's no time to explain it to him—we're far behind Sunny, and we need to catch up. We follow the footprints in the snow, sprinting through the harsh winds and the hard sleet. The more we walk, the harder it is to see.

Then, suddenly, the footprints disappear.

"How did this happen?" I say. "Where did she go?"

I turn around. The footprints behind us are gone too. The falling snow and the gusty wind must have filled in all the tracks.

Uh-oh. We have to find shelter . . . fast.

We wander through the woods, but I don't know where we're going—we're totally lost. With no way back to the lodge or the cave.

I'm getting colder and colder. My brain is all fuzzy, my energy zapped. . . .

I don't remember fainting, but I wake up with fifteen blankets over me, looking at a ceiling I don't recognize. "Uh . . . hello?"

"Oh, you're awake! Thank goodness!" says a woman I don't know, running into the room. "I found you and your friends on the mountain. Is there a parent or guardian I can call for you?" the woman asks.

Oh no . . . Mom! How disappointed will she be in us? In guilt, I sink deeper into the mattress.

"You really were totally frozen," the woman says, tucking the blanket around me. "Like human icicles."

Great. Instead of a nice end to this case, I got an ice end.

CASE CLOSED.

ELIZA'S RIGHT: WE need Fernando's alibi. And we're not going to get anywhere unless we push him on it.

"Mr. di Cannoli, what were you really doing at three in the morning?"

"Sleeping. As I said."

"LIAR!" Frank shouts.

Fernando frowns. "Okay. I'll show you what I was really doing. Follow me."

Eliza and I look at each other excitedly.

Fernando leads us to the door, and we head into the backyard of the lodge. "This way!" he says, gesturing into the wooded trees.

We follow him through a patch of evergreens, so deep into the glen that we can't see the lodge.

"There," he says, pointing into the mouth of a cave. "If you go in there, you'll see exactly what I was doing. You go first. I'll follow."

So we go in first. In the back of the cave are three hibernating bears, all curled up in each other's arms. I turn around, but Fernando di Cannoli is nowhere to be seen. He's ditched us!

"Lazy bears, will you get up, will you get up, will you get up? Lazy bears, will you get up, will you get up today?" Frank sings, and I put my hand over his mouth.

One of the bears stirs. Uh-oh.

435

"Run!" I mouth.

"No, climb!" Eliza whispers back.

We back away slowly and climb the nearest tree. We hide high in the branches, so that the bear doesn't see us.

Below, the angry bear roars, pacing between trees. There's no way we can get down from this branch until the bear goes back into hibernation.

This is unbearable!

CASE CLOSED.

"MULTIPLE SOURCES REPORT that you and January have been fighting lately," I say to Reese.

"Is that a question?"

"Yes. Why?"

Reese bites her lip. "You know . . . motherhood is very difficult. Children don't always cooperate! They like to think they know what's best for themselves, but *I* know what's best for her. You're telling me you don't fight with your parents?" she asks.

Screaming matches? No way.

I shake my head no. Eliza does a half shrug.

"Well, you're not even teenagers yet. You will." She swivels in her chair. "January is going to be fine. I've hired a special tutor for her, since she wants to learn video editing so badly. But I'm not sending her to public school. The closest one is a forty-five-minute drive from here, and Harris and I do not have the time. Besides . . . she has to be on the premises to learn about the hotel before she takes it over one day."

"Have the fights been worse than usual lately?" Eliza asks.

"Actually, in the past few weeks, the fights have almost stopped. It's a relief, honestly, since we've been screaming in each other's faces for over a year now."

"Is there a reason the fights stopped?"

"She grew up, I suppose."

Eliza and I exchange a look.

TO ASK WHY SHE DIDN'T WANT TO HIRE
DETECTIVES, TURN TO PAGE 394.

438

TIME TO GO to bed. But first we have to catch Mom up on the things we kinda maybe sorta learned.

We knock on the door to room 237, and Mom swings it open. "Welcome back," she says with a grin.

"Is the room bugged?" I ask.

"Clean, clear, and ready for private conversations!"

We file into the room. It's a standard hotel room, only rustic looking. The walls are wood, and there are wood beams across the ceiling. The two beds have plaid comforters. The armchair in the corner is made of logs, with mountain-print patterned cushions. And the pictures hanging up are all of evergreen trees and moose.

Frank follows my line of sight, sees the picture, and says, "Mooooooo!"

"That's not a cow, Frankie," Eliza says.

"I know that. It's a moose! Don't mooses moo?"

"No."

"Then they should! We should call cows mooses and mooses cows. That would make a lot more sense!"

"It's not mooses, anyway," Mom says. "The plural of moose is moose."

Frank scrunches his face and looks up as he thinks. "Two moose, two mooses, two moosen, two meece . . ." He's really mulling this one over. "I'm gonna go with meece."

"You don't get to choose grammar," Eliza whispers,

practically twitching in horror. "Grammar is a set of regimented, inflexible rules that you have to follow—"

"MEECE!" Frank shouts in her face.

Mom smiles at me and shakes her head. Then she pats the bed, and we all sit down around her. "Don't keep me in suspense! What did you find?"

We recap our conversations. I know we've only just started asking questions, but it seems like we have so much more to uncover. Like what Cricket's phone call was about, and why January and Sunny were fighting, and what Fernando di Cannoli is hiding, what the truth is about Byron's story, and how far Luther is willing to go to get what he wants.

"We still have a long way to go," I grumble as Eliza finishes recapping the last piece of our conversation with Byron Bookbinder.

"Patience, hijo. We arrived in the evening, so tomorrow we'll have a nice full day of investigation. And besides . . . there may even be a haunting before the night is over." She winks at me. "Now, Carlos and Eliza, you take this room. Frank, you're coming with me to the room next door. If you need something, kids, knock on the wall."

"Sleepover!" I say to Eliza, and we high-five.

"Awww," Frank says, frowning at my mom. "I wanna be part of the sleepover! I want Eliza! Or Carlos!"

440

Mom pretends to look hurt. "But whoever stays with me gets a chocolate bar."

"I WANT CHOCOLATE—I mean, Detecto-Mom!"

They leave, and then it's just Eliza and me. We brush our teeth, then bury ourselves in bed—she takes the bed next to the mountain-view window. I take the bed near the bathroom and door.

"I thought for sure the rooms would be split by family. You and your mom, me and Frank," Eliza says.

"Frank's a handful. He probably needs the most adult supervision." I yawn. It has been a long day of travel.

A silence stretches between us. It could be ten seconds or thirty, or a minute or five—one of those moments when you think you've fallen asleep, then someone says something to wake you up.

"Carlos?" Eliza says softly. "It just got really cold in here, don't you think?"

I try to answer her, but I'm too tired to lift my head.

"OOOOOOOOOOOOOOOOOOOO!"

I pop out of bed.

"Eliza, did you hear that?"

I click on the light. The clock on the wall reads 3:26 a.m. Eliza is awake, the covers pulled up just under her eyes.

"Eliza!" I shake her leg. "I thought you weren't scared of ghosts."

"I'm not," she whispers unconvincingly.

Thud. Thud-thud. Thump.

A loud banging noise. But it doesn't sound like footsteps.

"Eliza! Let's go!"

She grabs her backpack full of supplies and tools, and I open the door. In the next room, Mom and Frank's door is ajar. My heart drops to my stomach—why would their door be open? I slowly inch into their room. "Mom? Frank?"

"Back here!" Mom says, waving from the corner chair. She's putting on her slip-on shoes. Frank is yawning and rubbing his eyes. "Let's go!" she says, ushering

Frank and me into the hallway, where Eliza is waiting.

Thump. Thud-thud.

That sound again—like someone's banging on the walls from the inside. The hallway lights flicker. We're pitched into darkness.

Mom grabs my arm, and I jump.

"Look!" Frank says. "The footprint brick road!"

I can't see if he's pointing, but I know what he's looking at: glowing footprints stamped all across the carpet. They lead to the stairs. They're the only thing that's illuminated in this darkness.

"Ghost ectoplasm," I whisper.

"What? Carlos, *no*, I'm sure there's some logical explanation for the footprints," Eliza says. "Here—everyone take flashlights." She passes them out, and we each grab one.

We start down the hallway. Following the trail of footsteps, wherever they lead.

"Ooooooooooooooooooooo!"

I jump. The sound seems to be coming from all around us. It's loud and wailing.

We walk down the wooden staircase to the foyer. The front doors are ajar, which could explain why it feels like it's zero degrees in the lobby. Shadows dance on the walls.

Thud. Thump. Thud-thud-thud.

That noise! It's definitely coming from the fire den.

Screeeeeeeeeeee.

Suddenly one long, loud screech—like metal scraping on metal—echoes to our right, also from the fire den.

But the glowing footprints lead right out the front door of the hotel, into the snow. Into the cold and the darkness.

I don't know what's more terrifying: the hair-raising noises to our right, or the glowing footsteps straight ahead. I wish we could be in two places at once, but we can't. . . .

So do we follow the sound, or do we follow the sight?

TO FOLLOW THE NOISES IN THE WALLS, TURN TO PAGE 218.

←——→

TO FOLLOW THE GLOWING FOOTPRINTS, TURN TO PAGE 173.

"WHAT DO YOU know about the hauntings in the Sugarcrest Park Lodge?" I ask Luther.

"Besides the fact that they're fake?"

"What makes you say that?"

Luther laughs, but it isn't humorous. "*Obviously*, it's a publicity stunt gone terribly wrong. Karma is a—"

"But wait," I say. "Why would Reese haunt her own hotel? She said things were going very well for the lodge before the hauntings started."

"And," Eliza adds, "why would she *keep* haunting her hotel, if it's driving all her customers away?"

Luther frowns. He may be a good businessman, but he's not a good detective.

"Maybe it's a ploy or a distraction. Maybe she needs everyone to look one way while she searches for something. Who knows? All I know is that there are a few wicked people in that house. Live ones."

"What do you mean?"

Luther ignores the question. Instead, he picks up his phone and speed dials a number. "Hello, Miss McCoy—it's Luther Covington. Three detectives from the Sugarcrest case have lost their way and ended up down here. I need you to come collect them. Now." A long pause. "Perfect."

He hangs up the phone, and his lips curl in a wolfish smirk. "Cricket is sending your mother to fetch you.

445

Seeing as our time together has come to an end, I wanted to offer you a little . . . ah . . . *reward* for your services."

I have no idea what he's talking about, but Eliza frowns. "What are you asking us to do?" she says grimly, as Frank lets out a little snore from Eliza's lap. I think he's really fallen asleep!

"All you have to do is nudge Reese Winters in the right direction. You have her ear. She trusts you. Just tell her the hotel is too haunted to save. Encourage her to sell. When I buy the property, I'll give you three a nice cut of the money. I'll pay you more than they're paying you to solve the case."

There's a quiet, tense pause.

"That's unethical!" Eliza finally says, disgusted.

"Yeah! We can't do that—she hired us to find the ghost. We promised we would!"

"Don't be naive, children. I'm offering you a big incentive, for a small service."

"You're asking us to lie!" I can feel my cheeks getting red. I glare into Luther's cold, dark eyes.

He laughs humorlessly. "If I had a dollar for every time I've lied . . . oh, wait, I *do*. And I'm rich. Welcome to the real world, kids."

Mom runs into the lobby of the Super Hotel Express, relieved to see us. She escorts us right into the car, and

446

we begin the drive up the mountain to the Sugarcrest. It's a slow drive, because the snow is coming down so thick we can barely see out the front windshield.

Meanwhile, I can't stop thinking about what a corrupt, dishonest person Luther is. I can't believe he thought he could *bribe* us into quitting the case.

Eliza looks deep in thought, staring out her window. And Frank is in the middle seat, fast asleep on Eliza's shoulder.

"You kids are quiet," Mom says, looking into the rearview mirror. "Especially Frank. I didn't know it was possible for him to be this silent."

"He's sleeping," Eliza says.

"Mom, where were you? You were right behind us—then you were gone!"

She puts on her brights, then seems to think better of it. The glare from the snow is blinding. "I *was* actually right behind you. But as I crossed the lobby, someone grabbed me from behind and dragged me back. It was so fast, I couldn't even scream."

"Who was it?" Eliza asks.

"Was it a ghost?" I say.

"I don't know. I don't think so. Not unless ghosts are solid."

"They *can* solidify," I say. "That's what makes them so dangerous."

Eliza shoots me a skeptical look, and I roll my eyes back at her. I can't believe how ridiculous she's still being about ghosts!

"Ghost or not," Mom says, "it had a terrifying face. It didn't have any features at all . . . just a white face with empty sockets for eyes. It really was a split-second glance, though—I was wrestling it off me. The second I saw its face, it ran."

"Ran where?"

"Into the lobby, but that's the funny thing, niños— it vanished from the lobby by the time I ran after it, seconds later. It was too quick a disappearance for it to have climbed the stairs or ran into the fire den."

"See?" I say to Eliza. "Ghost!"

"Or," Eliza retorts, "a secret passageway in the hotel."

"We'll keep our eyes and ears open for either one," Mom says, trying to defuse our fight. "Anyway, I searched around the hotel, then I ventured out into the snow. I walkie-talkied you—"

"We forgot it," I say.

"It's my fault," Eliza adds. "I left it on the nightstand."

"Well, that can't happen again." She frowns. "I don't like how someone lured you out of the hotel, then locked you out. I thought getting grabbed from behind was scary, but . . . what the culprit did to you? That's truly dangerous! You could have frozen out there."

448

"Culprit? So you don't think it was a ghost, Mom?"

"The noises? Maybe. But the glowing footprints?" She snorts skeptically. "When have you heard of a ghost wearing shoes?"

She has a point there. And even if a ghost did wear shoes, it definitely wouldn't need to stomp on the carpet. It could float. And if the shoe prints don't belong to the ghost, we have our next direction.

"Whose shoe was it?" I say.

"There we go," Mom says, proudly beaming.

We get out of the car, and Mom has to carry Frank up the walkway into the lodge. The front doors are unlocked *now*, and it seems like there's no longer a haunting happening. All traces of the glowing footprints are gone, and no banging noises plague the halls.

To be honest, the normalcy of the hotel after all the commotion is unsettling in itself.

Cricket's sitting at the counter—no, *sleeping* at the counter.

As we walk up the stairs, Mom turns to me with a sour expression. "I'm really upset that you left the premises without alerting me," she says. "We'll talk about your punishment in the room."

Punishment? What? My stomach drops like a stone. Mom was so relieved at the Super Hotel Express, and so calm in the car—and now that we're back in the Sugarcrest, *now* she wants to punish us?

"Mom, you don't understand," I say, trailing behind her on the steps. "We didn't mean to leave. It was an acci—"

"Quiet!" she snaps. "I don't want to hear it. You constantly disobey me, and I'm sick and tired of it."

I shrink into my jacket. I feel like I could cry. Eliza squeezes my hand.

I march back to room 237 in silence, and all four of us go into the same room for Mom's I'm-disappointed-in-you lecture. She shuts the door behind her with extreme force. Did *my* mom—the most calm and even-keeled person ever—just slam the door? Her back is to us; she pauses at the door. She must be angrier than I've ever seen her in my life.

Then she turns around with a big grin.

"Great job! I think they bought it."

Okay, now I'm confused.

"Bought what?" I say. "Aren't you going to yell at me?"

"Me? Yell?"

Now I'm really *really* confused. "But on the stairs, you snapped."

Mom laughs. "It's called acting, Carlos. I don't know who was around, but we can't be too careful. I don't

450

want anyone to know the nature of our working relationship. If they realize we're equal partners . . . let's just say, I would rather the ghost come after me than you."

"A little late for that," I joke.

"That's what I'm afraid of," she replies seriously.

OUR ALARM GOES off at three in the afternoon. If I had it my way, we'd sleep all day to make up for being awake nearly all night. But we have lots to do.

Right now, I think Eliza and Mom are right: the glowing footprints *were* a trap to lure us out of the house. But . . . why? Did we stumble upon something important yesterday when talking to suspects? Or is someone trying to use our disappearance to scare Mom away from the case? Or is the ghost a vengeful spirit that has nothing to do with the people in the house?

All these questions and more, to be investigated today.

Eliza braids her hair in the mirror. "So," she says, pausing to yawn, "whose footprints did we see?"

"I don't know," I say. "It was big—clearly a man's shoe. Of the people who live in the Sugarcrest, we have three options: Harris Winters, Fernando di Cannoli, or Byron Bookbinder."

Mom comes into our room with her key. She looks a bit tired, but it's amazing what a long nap can do for Frank. He is talking so fast, he's practically buzzing.

452

"What do we do, where do we go—let's go crawl! Sneak! Do you think ghosts can be sucked up in vacuums? Do you think ghosts taste like whipped cream? Do you think—"

"Good afternoon to us," Eliza grumbles.

Mom smiles. "I think I'm going to start my day by talking to Sunny. Would you like to come with me, or do you have other ideas?"

"I think," I say, "we're going to try to make an ID match on the glowing shoe situation."

"That's right—why waste all four brains on the same suspect? We can fan out. But tell me, hijo, who will you interrogate first? Do you have any idea who owns the shoe that made the glowing prints?"

TO CONFRONT HARRIS WINTERS,
TURN TO PAGE 20.

←——→

TO CONFRONT FERNANDO DI CANNOLI,
TURN TO PAGE 249.

←——→

TO CONFRONT BYRON BOOKBINDER,
TURN TO PAGE 185.

"SO REESE IS really stressed out right now," I say to Harris. "What's on her plate? Can you give us more details about the main source of her stress?"

"Isn't that what *you're* supposed to be investigating?"

"So the ghost hauntings are really getting to her," Eliza says.

"It's been a nightmare—every evening, a new terror. The guests are leaving, the business is tanking, Luther Covington is breathing down her neck to sell. But she has to add the ghost to the regular problems of running a hotel. Like Cricket, who has been a disorganized, jittery mess lately. Sunny . . ." He drops his voice very low, even though we're the only ones in the hallway. "Who we can't get rid of, much as I want to. I can't believe she lost her master key last night—yet another thing Reese has to deal with. And then add the haunting issues and the hotel issues to the family drama! A hat trick of stressors."

"Family drama?" Eliza asks.

"January is starting her tween angst."

"I don't know what that means," I say.

"She's been fighting with her mom a lot lately. Screaming matches between the two of them."

"Why?" Eliza asks.

"Because she doesn't want to be homeschooled anymore. It's so much easier for us, though, to have her here. Especially since Reese is grooming her to

454

take over the family business one day. But I suspect January is lonely. I think she wants friends her own age. If you see her around, maybe you three could be her friends."

Of course Frank launches right into song. "Make new friends, but keep the old. One is silver, and the other's gold." He pauses. "I can never remember which one's silver and which one's gold. What's better—old friends or new friends?"

"They're both important," I say.

"Hmm," Frank thinks. "Then the song should say: one is gold, and the other's also gold."

"Yes, right, well, that's an important discussion *for later*," I say, with a pointed glare at Frank.

"I'm sorry, but I really do have to go now," Harris says. "Reese has me doing a lot of grunt work today. But thanks for coming to talk to me. With all this personal attention, I'm really starting to feel confident about Las Pistas."

"I'm so glad to hear that. We're very grateful that Mrs. Winters decided to hire us."

"No, Reese didn't hire you. *I* did. She definitely didn't want to hire you."

That stings, but I can't pretend like Mom doesn't have some stiff detective competition. "Oh. Well, I'm glad you were able to convince her to go with Las Pistas over our competitors."

455

Harris chuckles, a deep, low laugh. "It wasn't that. She said she didn't want *anyone* poking into her business. Didn't want any snoops here. She was livid when I hired you. But I don't know what she was so nervous about. I mean, we want these hauntings to stop, and we have nothing to hide, right?"

Eliza and I exchange a look. But Harris doesn't notice. He's in a better mood than I've ever seen him. Smiling so wide that his eyes crinkle, he marches down the hall, leaving us alone with antlers and wood walls and the Dead Room's red door, looking as intimidating as ever. I swear I see a shadow move under the door . . . but then it stops.

"Well, he was certainly in a better mood," Eliza says, paying no attention to the Dead Room door. "A complete one-eighty change from yesterday."

"Even bigger than that!" Frank says. "A three-sixty change!"

"Three-sixty is a complete circle," Eliza explains. "That would put Harris right back where he started."

"EXACTLY."

"So," I say. "What is Reese hiding?"

The Dead Room door rattles. Its hinges squeak and shudder.

And then the door stops.

Eliza and I are grabbing each other's hands tight.

The Dead Room has a definite pulse. I can feel it. Like its own sinister heartbeat, coming from behind the door. But there's one thing I don't understand: it's daytime. I thought that ghosts were only active at night.

Slowly, carefully, with my eyes still rooted to the door, I pull Byron's EMF reader out of Eliza's backpack. I turn it on, and the light blinks a few times. Green . . . and then the needle spikes, and the light glows red.

Paranormal activity. I want to run away, but I am glued to the spot.

"YAY, A GHOST!" Frank cries, and he runs toward the Dead Room.

Eliza and I break from our frozen state and chase after him. We stop in front of the door. I feel like I'm in a horror movie—the character who's too curious. The doorknob twists, and the door shakes again.

"There's someone locked in there!" Eliza says. The door stops moving.

"Yeah," I say. "A ghost. We have to leave—*now*." The door begins to tremble violently again.

"Can you hear us?" Eliza whispers. "Hello? Hello!"

There is silence. A shadow moves in the crack under the door, and the doorknob turns. But if something is howling or speaking, we can't hear it through the thick door.

Eliza sinks to her knees. "If you can hear us," she says to the crack under the door, "turn the doorknob once."

The doorknob slowly rotates.

"Cool!" Frank says. "A magic trick."

"It's not magic," I whisper. The EMF reader is going wild, and I try to rub out the goose bumps on my arm. "It's supernatural activity."

"Super *unnatural*," Frank says.

Eliza ignores us. "Turn the knob once for yes, and twice for no. Are you a ghost?"

Turn. Turn.

"Are you trapped in there?"

Turn.

"Do you know a way out?"

Turn.

"Where?" I ask.

Nothing.

"It's got to be a yes or no question, Carlos."

"Oh . . . right."

"Are you Ms. S?" Eliza says, and my heart nearly stops as I stare urgently at the doorknob.

Turn.

"Mom!" I shout, knocking on the door. I start turning the knob and pulling at the door myself, but it's totally useless—it's dead-bolted shut, and we don't have a key. "Mom! *Mom!* Is that really you?! How do we get to you?"

"Yes or no question, Carlos."

458

I bang the door in frustration.

Suddenly the doorknob starts twisting again.

Turn. Turn. Turn. Turn. Turn. Turn. Turn. Turn. Turn. Turn. Turn.

Stop.

"Eleven," Eliza says, writing the number down in her notebook. "That was eleven turns."

"And here's three!" Frank says, doing a few pirouettes on the rug.

"This is going to be tedious and time-consuming," she says seriously, "but there's no other way to communicate."

It takes *forever* to record the number of spins and stops. But when the doorknob stops for good, we're left with this series of numbers:

11-5-25-9-19-8-9-4-4-5-14-2-5-8-9-14-4-20-8-5-4-5-5-

18-8-5-1-4-2-21-20-1-14-20-12-5-18-19-8-1-22-5-1-16-1-

20-20-5-18-14-7-15-15-21-20-19-9-4-5-6-15-18-20-8-5-1-

14-19-23-5-18

"If we can crack it, we can help your mom," Eliza says. "I bet this code will tell us where to go, or what to do to get her unstuck."

"Or it will send us to a TRAP!" Frank shouts. "How do we know that's not a ghost in disguise? A lying ghost!"

"Is not!" Eliza says.

"Is too!"

"Is not!"

"Too, too, too!"

As they argue, I take the notebook from Eliza and start solving.

TO GO OUTSIDE, TURN TO PAGE 42.

TO GO TO THE ATTIC, TURN TO PAGE 195.

TO ASK ELIZA FOR A HINT,
TURN TO PAGE 378.

460

FRANK PULLS AWAY from January, screaming in pain. She ripped out whole clumps of his hair.

"This way!" I grab Frank's hand. We run to the edge of the roof. With the snow piled up so high, we only have a short way to fall, but this is *not* safe.

Neither are the culprits behind us who want to turn *us* into ghosts.

"Ready?" I say to Frank. "One . . . two . . ."

"THREE!" Frank cries, yanking me off the building.

For a split second, I think we've made a terrible mistake. My stomach jumps into my throat, and we are in free fall . . .

"AHHHHHHHHHHHHHHHH!" we scream.

Then we hit the soft and cushiony snow, and we slide right down the snowbank.

I look up. Are they going to follow us? Or was that stunt *just* stupid enough that they wouldn't dare attempt it?

They're leaning over the edge. Sunny is shaking her head, and I can hear January say, "Not a chance!"

Did we do it? Are we safe?

No . . . because Mom and Eliza are still who knows where in the house, and the culprits will just go after them next.

"Carlos—run?" Frank reminds me.

Oh, right. I dash into the house. We have to stop

461

them before they can get to Mom and Eliza. In the lobby, Cricket is sleeping at the concierge desk, and that's where I have a bit of inspiration.

"Cricket!" I shout.

"CHIRP CHIRP!" Frank says.

She rubs her eyes and yawns.

"No time for that! We need you to come to the roof. Mom! Eliza! Reese! Harris! Byron! Fernando! Help, help, help!"

Reese and Harris emerge from their rooms, where they were clearly getting ready for bed. I pull them toward the attic ladder, which is currently folded up.

"What's the meaning of this?" Reese says, annoyed.

"Just wait," I say. "In a minute, this ladder is going to come down, and our ghosts will be walking right into us."

It doesn't even take a minute. The ladder starts rolling down from the attic, and two people come scurrying down.

"I can't believe you let them get away!" Sunny snaps.

"Well, I was not going to jump off the roof after them!" January retorts. "It's not worth breaking my neck!"

They reach the bottom, turn around, and realize they're face-to-face with Reese, Harris, Cricket, Frank, and me.

"Uh-oh," January whispers.

462

"January? Sunny?" Reese says, falling to her knees. She bursts into tears.

January looks like she wants to go comfort her mom . . . but then thinks better of it. Sunny's face looks as hard as stone.

"What now?" January asks her aunt.

But it's Frank who bellows, "THE GIG IS UP!"

"This is a Class B felony," Harris says, rubbing Reese's back as she continues to sob. "I've been doing research. Criminal sabotage."

"Are you pressing charges?" Sunny says quietly.

Harris frowns. "It's up to my wife."

"Thank you, detectives," Reese says. "If there's anything I can do for you . . ."

"We do have one request. But not for you . . . for *them*." I turn to Sunny and January. "Tell us where to find the rest of our team. Now."

January ended up spilling the beans. Apparently Mom and Eliza were trapped in the walls of the hotel, and we found them easily once we knew where to look. When the blizzard cleared, Reese did have the police take Sunny away for criminal sabotage. January, it seemed, was on the verge of a major punishment. And Reese handed us a big fat check.

And then Mom, Eliza, Frank, and I drove home, and everything returned to normal. We're back where it's sunny and warm. Well, not *warm* exactly, but warmer than Sugarcrest Mountain (a low bar, I know). Eliza, Frank, and I had school, Mom had more cases, and there was always the promise of a future mystery for us as long as it fell over one of our school breaks.

"The only thing that stinks about taking faraway cases is that we don't get a debriefing with the clients," I complain to Mom two months after the case, as we're sitting at the kitchen table. I'm doing homework and she's working on a thievery case with her business partner, Cole. "I wish we could hear from Reese and Harris."

"That's funny!"

"What do you mean?"

She looks up from her casework. "Oh, well, you're just sitting here, passively waiting for news. I figured a detective like you would have, you know, done some detecting by now."

I grin and stand up. "I'm going to Eliza's—be back soon!"

"Good luck, hijo," she says, waving goodbye.

I run a few blocks to Eliza's house, where I know her parents have a computer. When I ring the doorbell, Eliza answers.

"Carlos? What are you doing here?"

"I need your parents' computer!" I say, pushing into her house.

464

Eliza and I sit in her parents' kitchen with the computer in front of us. Okay, so where would I go first for information on our case? First I google the Sugarcrest Park Lodge.

The two-star rating they had during the weeks of ghost hauntings has gone back up to three stars. Still not as good as their original four-star rating, but I'm sure it will get better soon.

And the reviews are *glowing* with praise about the hospitality of Reese and her husband, Harris. People loved the staff changes—the new housekeeper and the new concierge are gems. There was even a new chef who specialized in chicken nuggets.

Seemed like a lot of good changes were happening there. Guests mentioned that January played piano for them in the library and was a conscientious host as well. I don't know if she's putting on a fake act or not, but I'd like to think she's changed for the better.

Eliza clicks Reese's name, and Reese's most recent reviews pop up. And I gasp when I see the third one down.

LAS PISTAS DETECTIVE AGENCY
Review by Reese Winters
★★★★★
They saved my hotel, my livelihood, and quite possibly my life. Best agency around. Make sure

to request their three little detectives. Nothing
can get in their way.

I guess she was pleased with the outcome after all.
"Short but sweet," I say.

"Just like us!" Eliza adds.

Frank, who's standing in the kitchen doorway,
groans. "UGH, TOO MUSHY!"

Eliza turns around. "Frankie, don't scream in the
house!"

He perks up. "Scream? Do you think the ice-cream
truck is nearby?"

Do I have to break the bad news to him? "Frank, it's
February. There's no ice-cream truck."

"You scream, I scream, we all scream for ICE
CREAM!" And he runs away giggling.

He can scream all he wants, but I think my screaming days are behind me. I faced fears and came through
stronger. Now, like Reese said, nothing can get in my
way.

CASE CLOSED.

THESE CLOTHS GIVE us so much material to work with, and I'm going to trap the ghost in a web of its own making.

"Do you trust me, Mom?"

"Always."

She grabs the hand I'm holding out to her, and together we weave through the hanging cloths, keeping an eye on the shadowy figure that is *definitely* following us now. I don't know what it has planned, but it can't be good.

The hologram ghost kids are still screaming these shiver-inducing shrieks, but I can't listen. I have to get to the middle of the room.

I grab the edge of a cloth, and Mom grabs another.

The shadowy figure pauses. I think it's waiting for an opening to attack us.

So I give it one. I turn my back on it, and it lunges.

Mom and I dive out of the way and run in a circle around it. We pull tight as the ghost thrashes and flails, trying to get out of our tangled net.

"Let me out of here!" it snarls. A female voice. "Let me go!"

I grab a few more cloths and tie them around the ghost for good measure. Then I pull back the figure's hoodie, and the glow of the blue ghost kids reveals a woman with black hair tucked under her ears and a frowny, downturned mouth.

467

"Sunny? You're the ghost?"

She scowls.

"So . . . you didn't lose your master key after all! That's how you were able to plant a threat in our room!"

"And you're working with someone else," Mom says. "Who?"

She doesn't answer.

"We found a message that says 'team kin,'" I say. "You're working with a relative. But who are you related to? Reese?"

Silence.

"You might as well talk, Sunny," Mom says. "You're tied up. We've called for backup. So we'll try my son's question again. Are you related to Reese?"

"My sister," she grunts.

"So . . ." My head is spinning. "You and Reese were haunting the hotel together?"

Sunny snorts. "You think Reese would try to scare herself away?"

"So it's January, then," I say. "Byron said he overheard you two fighting."

Sunny gets very quiet.

"But *why*, Sunny?"

"Because the hotel was supposed to be *mine*. But Reese stole it from me. Then she made me work in housekeeping, when we both knew I was supposed to be the boss."

468

"You could have left," Mom says. "You didn't have to work here."

"This is my home!" Sunny cries. "This place should be my legacy. Reese made our parents change their will before they died—I don't know what she told them, but they listened. They took away my birthright. I want it back."

So Sunny was still haunted by the past. It followed her around as much as any ghost. And even though I was *technically* wrong in my paranormal argument with Eliza . . . in a way, I feel partially right.

The basement door bursts open. "Carlos!" Eliza shouts, climbing into the basement with lanterns. Following behind her are Frank, Reese, Harris, January, and Byron, who is clearly the fifth wheel of the group.

"Astonishing!" Byron marvels. "The exquisite detail in every phantom!"

"These are just holograms," Eliza says. "You can't put them in your nonfiction haunting book because they're fake."

"I would denote that these spectral discoveries are spurious, but—no, no, I see from the seething look on your face that this will not suffice."

"What is Byron doing here?" I ask.

"He was with Reese," Eliza grumbles. "He begged to come, and she wouldn't say no to the lodge's only guest."

"Where are the police?"

"It's a blizzard, remember? They can't get up here for a while."

"I didn't even know this place was down here," Reese whispers. "How did you find this?"

"Through the Dead Room," Eliza explains.

Harris chokes. "You were in that thing?"

"We just said that, Mr. Beard Chin," Frank says. "Clean your ears!"

"That's not very polite, Frank," Mom says.

Frank blows a raspberry.

"We'll give you the whole story later. But for now," I say to Reese, gesturing toward the human we have wrapped in the cloths, "here is your ghost."

"Sunny?" Reese says. "But it can't be. . . ."

Harris gasps. "Of course it can! It makes perfect sense! Sunny knows all your deepest fears—she understands exactly how to haunt you. She knows the hotel inside and out. She has a master key!"

"But who is Sunny working with?" Eliza asks. "She has a partner."

Sunny smiles at her niece. "Want to tell them, or should I?"

Reese and Harris both swivel toward their daughter, and Byron Bookbinder squeals, "Oh *ho*! Plot twist!"

There's a cold silence. "What is she talking about, sweetheart?" Reese says.

"I don't know!"

470

Sunny smirks. "Yes, you do, partner."

"You liar! You liar! She's a liar!" January says desperately.

"Fess up! We were in this together!"

"It was *her* idea!" January shrieks, pointing at Sunny. "She tricked me into it! It wasn't my fault, Mom—you have to believe me!"

"January makes sound mixes, right?" I say. "She's the one putting together all the audio and visual effects. She got these cloths for the holograms, which she animated herself. That six-foot-tall ghost that chased me and Frank down the slide—that was a hologram you made, right?"

"Holograms need some sort of screen or cloth to work," Eliza says. "Which explains the basement. And we found costumes in their lair, which meant they were alternating between holograms and dressing up to keep everyone on their toes."

"Reese is trying to groom you to become the next owner of the hotel," I say, "but you don't want to take over the hotel, do you, January?"

"They're lying! It wasn't me!" January insists.

"Oh, give it up!" Sunny snaps.

Reese frowns as she watches her sister and her daughter bicker. And all I can think is how betrayed Reese must feel, that her two closest blood relatives would turn on her like that.

Reese and Harris discuss what sort of punishment to inflict on Reese's sister (possibilities include calling the police, banishing her from the property, getting a restraining order), and their daughter (possibilities include grounding her, making her write apologies and morality essays, sending her to a camp for wayward youth next summer).

But while they're talking, Mom puts her arm on my shoulder. "You did good," she says quietly, under the sound of the Winters family's argument. "No . . . you did *great*."

"This case was the scariest thing I've ever done," I say. "I just wanted to prove myself to you so badly, and instead I was screaming my lungs out half the time."

Mom smiles. "Screaming or not, you *did* prove yourself. You know what that means, right?"

I shake my head.

She swoops to my level and plants a kiss on my forehead before saying, "It means I better make sure you stay at Las Pistas Detective Agency, because if you ever left, your competing business would wipe us out."

It must be a scary thought for her—one that may haunt her more than any ghost—but she should know that I'm *always* going to be on Team Las Pistas. Now and forevermore.

CASE CLOSED.

THE KEYS TO the snowmobile are in a pocket under the seat. I rev up the engine and hop on.

"YAY!" Frank cries, scooting behind me.

Eliza has a disapproving frown, but she slips behind Frank. Frank always has to be sandwiched between two responsible people, as a general rule.

"You had better be careful!" Eliza shouts.

I slam my foot on the gas, and we speed after Sunny, following the footprints. Visibility isn't great—there are a few times I nearly drive into a tree. The storm makes it impossible to see two feet in front of me, let alone ten.

I put Eliza and Frank on footprint duty, so I can concentrate on driving. Soon I hear Frank singing, "Left. Left. Left right left!" And Eliza's more precise, "Head to two o'clock. Now back toward eleven o'clock . . ."

"There!" Eliza shouts suddenly, and I slam on the brakes. But I lose control of the snowmobile. It spins in the snow.

"AHHHHHHHHHH!" Eliza, Frank, and I scream as the snowmobile narrowly misses Sunny and skids into a pile of fresh powder. Where it finally stops.

Sunny starts to run, but with the sleet and the wind in front of her, we catch her almost instantly and tackle her into the snow.

"Get! Off!"

It takes all three of us to keep Sunny from running.

And by the time we've restrained her—by tying her hands with my scarf and her legs with Eliza's—we've gotten snow inside our coats somehow, and freezing slush starts sliding uncomfortably down our backs.

We try to pull Sunny to the hotel, which I can see in the distance through the trees and a little ways up the mountain. But it is a difficult task, as she keeps trying to wriggle away. All the while, my gloveless, mittenless hands have this sharp pain.

"I wish I had earmuffs," Eliza shouts over the wind. "My ears are on fire."

"My fingers," I say.

"My little piggies!" Frank adds. When we look at him blankly, he explains, "Toes."

"Come on, Sunny!" I shout, tugging her toward the lodge. "Faster!"

It takes forever. When we finally get there, I can't feel my hands at all. I'm afraid to look at them—afraid to see how red they'll be. But to my surprise, they're totally white. And hard. I can't knock on the door like this. I use my elbow to ring the doorbell.

"Get Reese," I pant to Cricket as Eliza, Frank, and I collapse in the warm lodge. My numb hands start to throb—along with my ears and tip of my nose.

"We have one ghost," Eliza says, yanking the scarf, forcing Sunny into the lobby.

"And my mom has another," I add.

474

It turns out that being outside in a blizzard for a long time without gloves, earmuffs, a hat, or proper boots is not so great for your skin tissue or blood vessels. Who knew?

In the hospital later—in the sunrise hours of the morning—Mom sits on a chair while we huddle together on the patient table. Through the wall, I can hear Reese and Sunny arguing—and a nurse coming in to tell them to please be quiet.

"Think they'll work it out?" I ask.

"Reese and January, yes." Mom says. "Reese and Sunny?" We hear another shout. "Who knows? But we did our job, we saved Reese's hotel, and now I'm more concerned about you three at the moment." She looks at a spot just left of my eyes, and I realize she's looking at one of my ears.

Our ears, hands, and feet are wrapped in bandages. We're waiting for the doctor to come back with further instructions about how to treat our frostbite. Mom buries her face in her hands. I can practically see the guilt crushing her, even though it was our choice to leave the cave.

"We're fine, Mom," I say.

"You are not!" she cries. "You have frostbite!"

"Frost*nip*, technically," Eliza says. "And just one spot of superficial frostbite. It hurts, but the damage to our skin is reversible."

Mom crumples into her chair. "I recklessly let you wander outside in the cold. It's my responsibility to take care of you and make sure you're safe."

"Mom, as long as we're detectives, we have to be cool with a little danger."

"Cool," Eliza says. "I see what you did there."

"I don't!" Frank says.

I look Mom straight in the eye. "You're the one who told me to push through the fear. It's not fair for you to pull us off the next case—"

"Who said anything about pulling you off?" Mom says.

Eliza and I exchange an excited glance. Frank picks at a scabby blister.

"You three have a job at Las Pistas for as long as you want one. I'm not one to turn away talent."

I sigh in relief. "Good. Because the three of us are not planning on being left out in the cold."

Mom looks at my frostnipped hands and my wind-bitten ears, and her eyebrows rise. And I suddenly realize the humor in what I've just said.

"Well," I add, grinning, "at least not again."

CASE CLOSED.

THE DOGS DOWNSTAIRS are too dangerous to approach. I don't know what sort of danger lurks in the Dead Room, but maybe it won't be as bad as a pack of feral dogs.

"Carlos," Mom says again.

"Don't worry, Mom. I'm not going downstairs."

The dog behind me growls. It inches closer, forcing us toward the Dead Room. There's no choice; we're pirates walking the plank. I gulp as we reach the door; it's still ajar, icy air emanating from inside. I turn around, and the giant dog bares its ugly fangs.

"Okay, okay, we're going in," I grumble. I turn to Mom and Eliza. "Ladies first," I say, *not* to be chivalrous but because I'm scared out of my wits.

But Frank, brave soul that he is, shouts, "I CALL DIBS!" And he marches into the room. Eliza chases her brother. I follow Eliza, and Mom brings up the rear.

We're inside, in the darkness. We close the door behind us, but not all the way. Mom leaves it open a crack. I only hope those dogs will go away soon, so we can escape. I reach into Eliza's backpack and get a flashlight.

The light shows a small room—low wood ceilings, old and creaky wood floors. The walls are smeared with something red. It looks suspiciously like blood. There's a bit of it dripping to the floor repeatedly. *Drip. Drip. Drip.*

No light bulbs in the Dead Room. It doesn't feel like a room . . . it feels like a tomb. Or maybe I feel that way because at the edge of the room, in the corner, there is a full-sized coffin lying there.

The worst part is that there's *no* sign of January or the ghost monster. Maybe I made a mistake by running. Maybe I should have followed. . . . I should have trusted her yesterday.

There are so many different choices I could have made. But didn't. "I should have chosen differently—I should have chosen better."

"What are you talking about, hijo?"

It's a good thing we're locked in the Dead Room, because this is something I can only admit in the dark: "Mom, I'm losing my touch. The ghost is . . . my head is all cloudy. I mean . . . what kind of detective is afraid of his own case?"

"All of them," Mom says. "I get frightened every single case."

"You do?"

"Of course. I'm scared of the ghosts, kidnappers, death threats, thieves . . . and I'm scared of failure. Of what happens if I don't get the job done. Two different kind of fears, external and internal, all swirling around each other."

That's exactly—*exactly*—how I feel. "I just wanted you to be proud of me."

478

"Hijo, I am always proud of you."

I suddenly feel like crying. And for once, the pressure and the fear I've been carrying around with me loosen, just a little.

"We can talk more about this later," Mom says. "But first we have to get out of here. This is time-sensitive. So what have you two been up to?"

Eliza quickly explains what happened to us—and January—before we met up with her and Frank. "And where were you?" she finishes.

"Frank and I got a phone call to the room, saying that you two were down at Luther's."

"Why didn't you check our rooms? Knock on the door? You would have seen we were here!"

"Well," Mom says, "because it was your voice on the phone."

Eliza chokes.

"That's impossible!" I say.

"Oh, it's possible all right!" Frank says. "It happened, buster!"

"It must have been a recording of you, hijo. You didn't converse with me . . . I could hear you in the background. And I didn't have any reason to doubt what I heard with my own ears. So I woke Frank up, and the two of us drove down to Luther's."

"But," Frank says, "we were TRICKED. FOOLED. BUMBLEBUZZLED."

"Bamboozled?" Eliza corrects.

"Yes, bambleboozled!"

"When we got to Luther's, it was clear you two weren't there. That's when you walkie-talkied, but we were too far away for the transmission to work. It was *then* that I realized we were probably lured away from the hotel on purpose, and you were in trouble."

"And you were!" Frank said. "From a really cute, fuzzy-wuzzy killer puppy!"

I look to the exit. "Do you think we're safe from the dogs now?" I take a step toward the door, and suddenly it shuts. And clicks. Even before I reach the door handle, I know we're locked in.

"Oh no," Eliza whispers. "Oh no, oh *no*!"

I swivel around. I guess there's nothing to do now but examine the Dead Room. Maybe we can find a way out . . . that isn't the front door.

TO LOOK IN THE COFFIN, TURN TO PAGE 37.

←→

TO EXAMINE THE BLOOD MARKS,
TURN TO PAGE 419.

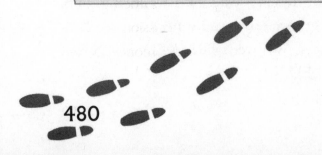

"LET'S READ THE letter to Cricket," I say, grabbing and opening the letter. A check for eight hundred dollars falls out.

"I'm rich!" Frank cries. "Rich, rich, RICH!"

"You know you can't deposit that unless your name is Cricket McCoy," Eliza says.

"So I'll change my name to Cricket McCoy!" Frank says. "Big whoop."

"Can I read the letter?" I gripe, and the two of them quiet down.

DEAR MISS McCOY,

ENCLOSED FIND YOUR LATEST COMMISSION, AS DISCUSSED. KEEP UP THE GOOD WORK. MORE CHECKS TO FOLLOW, SO LONG AS YOU CONTINUE.

CORDIALLY,
LUTHER COVINGTON

"Commission?" I say.

Eliza bites her lip thoughtfully. "Commission means she's getting paid based on a certain number of services rendered or products sold. It's, like, different from a salary. When you get a salary, you get the same payment every week, no matter what. But a commission can fluctuate. In good weeks, you could get a lot of money; on bad ones, you could get nothing."

"Is a concierge usually paid this way . . . with a commission?"

"Wrong question," Eliza says. "We should be asking why Luther is paying Cricket a commission when she's not his employee."

"Is she a spy?" Frank says. "A super secret agent spy?"

"Or," I say grimly, finally understanding what Eliza's getting at, "is Cricket getting paid by Luther to be our ghost?"

"It's the best theory we've got so far. Want to test it on Cricket?"

"What kind of test?" Frank says. "A math test? A spelling test? I can do a spelling test! I can spell cat! K-A-T."

"No," I say, "you can't."

"Can't? K-A-N-T." He grins at me, and I can't tell if he's pulling my leg.

"Frank . . ."

"Frank!" he says. "F-R-A-N-C."

We stare at each other for a moment. His smirk gets wider and wider. "Why are you like this?" I finally say.

And he chortles.

Eliza rolls her eyes. "Are we going to go see Cricket or not?"

"Not," Frank says.

"Yes, let's go," I say. "But get ready for her to get *really* defensive on us." I grab Eliza's backpack off the couch, hand it to her, and head to the door. Out in the hall, there's absolutely *no* indication that a haunting happened

482

last night or that someone left a threat in our bathroom. It looks like a perfectly normal lodge, minus the disturbing animal heads mounted on the walls.

We head to the lobby, where Cricket is smacking gum and swiveling in her desk chair.

"You!" I shout from across the lobby. "We know what you're up to. Time to come clean."

"I don't know what you're talking about," she says coolly.

"DON'T PLAY DUMB WITH US!" Frank shouts.

"I'm not playing."

"Then you're actually dumb?" Frank says.

"I am confused. And insulted."

I lay the letter from Luther Covington on her desk, and Eliza waves the eight-hundred-dollar check like a flag, just out of Cricket's reach.

She nearly chokes on her gum. It goes flying out of her mouth and lands on the floor of the lobby.

"Yum!" Frank says, picking it up.

"Where did you get that letter?" she says, her white face getting splotchy with an angry flush. "You stole that out of my mailbox!"

"You have a lot of explaining to do," I say. "You're the ghost."

"*What?* That's absurd!"

Eliza points to the letter. "It says right here, 'Keep up the good work.' Luther is paying you a commission to haunt this hotel."

"You've got it all wrong!"

"Oh?" I say. "He's *not* paying you a commission?"

"He is," she mumbles. "But not to haunt the place." She sighs deeply. "Mr. Covington doesn't have the time or patience to haunt this hotel for six weeks. He just asked me to refer guests to his hotel when they run out in the middle of the night. He's giving me a cut of every room, like a finder's fee."

"Isn't that a conflict of interest?" Eliza says.

"Of course it is, but you have no idea how little they're paying me here! I see how much money these rooms go for, and Mr. and Mrs. Winters pay me minimum wage!" Cricket cries. "I still have student loans to pay off, and I want to go to grad school without going bankrupt. And I wasn't convincing people to leave the Sugarcrest. It was only *after* they were storming off in a huff that I even mentioned the Super Hotel Express, so when you think about it, what I was doing was only slightly immoral and not at all illegal, and *please* don't get me fired!" She clasps her hands together. "Please—I really need to stay employed."

Eliza and I look at each other.

TO TATTLE ON CRICKET, TURN TO PAGE 23.

←——→

TO LET CRICKET BE THE ONE TO TELL REESE THE TRUTH, TURN TO PAGE 488.

"SO YOU SAW the ghost two nights ago?" I ask Fernando di Cannoli. "What did it look like? What did it do?"

He shudders.

"From my room, I heard pots and pans clanging. So I came down to see. But all the lights were out. Suddenly I could hear it. Scratching and moaning, coming from . . . *there*." He points to the dumbwaiter, which is like an elevator that kitchens use to send food up or down to different floors without someone having to carry it a whole flight of stairs. "Then I saw it in the dumbwaiter!"

"But if all the lights were out, *how* did you see the ghost?" Eliza asks skeptically.

"It was glowing!"

"What color?" Eliza demands.

"A ghostly color. I—I could sense it. It was here."

Something about Fernando's story isn't adding up. I mean, the details aren't great. But it's something Mom warned us with a case like this: when people are frightened, their hearts pump faster and their adrenaline runs. That makes it harder for suspects to remember things accurately.

We have to figure out who's misremembering something because they were scared . . . and who is lying.

I press Fernando di Cannoli for more details. "What did you do after you saw the ghost?"

485

"I ran! Certo!"

I groan. "You *ran?*"

"Well, I came back yesterday morning to find the kitchen in chaos. Everything—*everything*—was out of the drawers and on the floor. Pots, pans, spatulas, baking trays, serving utensils. Everything except . . ."

"Except?" Eliza whispers, her eyes wide.

"The knives."

I gulp. "Where were the knives?"

"Stuck in the wall in an X. Like a warning."

"A warning for who?" Eliza asks. "For you?"

"No, no. For . . . *them.*" He looks around again frantically.

"You think the ghost is after Reese, Harris, and January?"

"Shhhhh!" he says. "Don't say their names."

"What, are you afraid we'll summon them?" I joke.

But Fernando isn't joking. He seems *truly* afraid of Reese, Harris, and January. Like *they're* haunting *him.* I have to find out what is going on between Fernando and the Winters family. I don't know if it has to do with the ghosts in this lodge, but as a detective, any clue could be the key to the mystery, right?

Then again, maybe I should explore where the ghost was—in the dumbwaiter.

TO ASK FERNANDO ABOUT THE WINTERS FAMILY,
TURN TO PAGE 317.

←——→

TO CLIMB INTO THE DUMBWAITER,
TURN TO PAGE 271.

"OKAY, CRICKET," I say. "We won't tell Reese. But *you* have to tell her the truth about your arrangement with Luther."

She nods. "I will. I promise."

"So you have no idea who the ghost is?" Eliza says.

My best friend looks frustrated, and I bet I do too. If it isn't Cricket, then what did we hit upon that made the ghost destroy our bathroom? Was that just a random act of haunting?

"I'm super sorry, detectives, but I don't know anything about the hauntings. I'm petrified of ghosts. I try to stay as far away as possible. But if I were you, I'd talk to Mr. Winters."

"Why?"

"Just a hunch. He's always stomping around at three in the morning. It's, like, extremely bizarre. Or maybe Sunny. She has the attitude for it. She's always gloomier than a cloudy day. Although, now that she's lost her master key, she probably won't be sticking around here too much longer. I can say with certainty that the ghost isn't Mrs. Winters, though."

"How do you know that?" Eliza asks.

"Yeah! How!" Frank demands.

"Haven't you seen her reaction to the ghosts? She is seriously rattled."

"Thanks for the tips," I say. "And if you think of anything else . . ."

488

"I will find you, yes. Now I'm off to talk to Mrs. Winters. Thank you for letting me do it." She gets up from the chair and heads toward Reese's office.

From the concierge desk, I can see that Harris isn't in his office. And Sunny doesn't have an office. So where they are right now is beyond me. But they have to be somewhere in the lodge, now that we're snowed in, right?

"Who do we interview, Carlos?" Eliza asks.

"Whoever we find first."

I head back upstairs to the staff hallway, with every intention of knocking on Sunny's door and Harris's door—and maybe even Fernando di Cannoli's door. Any door that's going to give me answers and, more importantly, give me back my mom.

But I don't even have to knock. Because coming out of his suite is Harris himself.

"Mr. Winters!" I say. "Can we talk to you?"

"A little busy," he says.

"But we have important investigative questions to ask you."

Harris frowns. "I thought I was hiring your mother. She *is* still on the case, isn't she?"

Is she? I don't know—but I have a really squirmy feeling about it. Maybe she's fine . . . maybe she's in trouble . . . but we won't know unless we keep digging.

"Yes, she's on the case. But with Las Pistas Detective

Agency, you get four brains for the price of one."

"Braaaaaaaiiiiiiinnnnns!" Frank says like he's in a zombie movie, drooling a little.

Okay, *three* brains for the price of one.

"Don't worry," I say at the sight of Harris's skeptical glance. "He's very skilled."

"At what?"

"Uh . . ." I pause.

"Um . . ." Eliza hesitates.

"I can burp the alphabet! Wanna hear?" Frank says. "A—*urp*!"

"Okay, that's enough skills," I say loudly, over the sounds of his B-*urp* and C-*urp*.

"While I'd *love* to stay for the whole alphabet," Harris says, "I've got a lot of chores from Reese to complete. She needs all the help she can get right now."

TO ASK WHY HARRIS CONSTANTLY WANDERS THE HALLS IN THE MIDDLE OF THE NIGHT, TURN TO PAGE 333.

←—→

TO ASK WHY REESE IS SO STRESSED, TURN TO PAGE 454.

WE HAVE TO get back into the attic while the ghost is on the roof.

"This way, Frank," I whisper, and we walk closer to the edge. Which is really dangerous when I think about it, because it's *Frank* we're talking about. But he seems to be taking this seriously.

"The name's Bond. Frank Bond!" he says in a deep voice.

Okay, he's taking it semi-seriously.

"Look, Carlos!" he says, pointing over the edge. The grounds of the Sugarcrest Park Lodge are barely visible, but in the lamplight of the front entrance I *do* see this:

A spot on the grounds where the snow is piled up higher than everywhere else. It's nearly halfway up the side of the building—almost like a ramp from the second story to the ground. But we're on the third story.

"Come on," I say, pulling him back to the attic. We've looped around the chimney, so now the ghost is farther away from the attic window than we are. All we have to do is reach out, and—

There's a face in the window!

I jump back. The window opens, and the creepy girl ghost climbs onto the roof, blocking our only exit. We're surrounded.

"Don't move," she says. The mask on her face is peeling off, and I can see her shrewd dark eyes.

491

"There are two ghosts," I say with a groan. "Two cul-prits."

"And you call yourselves detectives," says the ghost in front of us, the one whose hands Frank slammed in the window.

One of them is Sunny. It *has* to be. I look at the one next to us . . . the creepy little girl ghost. I was right: the blond hair is a wig, for sure. But Frank was right too: you can't pretend to be smaller than you are, and the one next to us is definitely small. Smaller than an adult.

"Hi, January," I say quietly to the ghost next to us. "So . . . you're working for your aunt, are you?"

She pulls off her mask.

"Why?"

"You know why," she says.

I try to remember all the things we were told about January: she wants to go to public school and not live on this mountain, Harris said. And Byron told us that Reese and January were fighting. And I overheard the conversation where Reese wanted January to take over the hotel, but January saw her future in . . .

"Video editing and sound mixing," I say aloud. "So *that's* how you were able to fake so many hauntings."

"How?" Frank says, pulling on my sleeve.

"And of course Sunny wanted Reese gone, so she

could run the hotel that was rightfully hers. You two had different but overlapping goals, so you worked together."

Sunny walks closer to us. And if we don't want to be caught by them, Frank and I have two seconds to act. My eyes dart to the chimney. There's no smoke, so there's no fire burning. But I can't forget there's also the edge of the roof, where the snow was piled high. . . .

"GET OFF ME!" Frank screams as January wraps her fingers in his hair.

TO CRAWL DOWN THE CHIMNEY,
TURN TO PAGE 412.

←→

TO JUMP OFF THE ROOF, TURN TO PAGE 461.

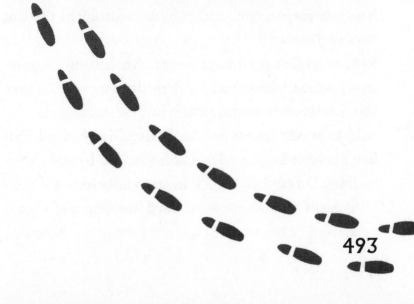

"CAN YOU TELL us about the recent hauntings?" I ask. "As many details as you remember."

"It's every night, a new thing," Reese says. "The windows rattle and break. There's ooze on the floor sometimes. There are . . . there are threatening messages."

"Messages?" I ask.

"Terrifying symbols on the walls—in blood. I wash it off, but it always comes back."

"And howling?" Mom asks, checking her precase notes.

Reese nods. "There is *always* howling. But I can never find the source of it."

Eliza scrunches her eyebrows together. "Is there a pattern to when you hear the sounds and see . . . well, what do you see?"

"We see a *ghost*," January says. She chips off some of the black polish on her nails. "The pattern is that it happens every night, and *only* at night, after the sun goes down."

"The recent hauntings have been getting progressively scarier," Reese adds. "The last one—two nights ago—took place in the kitchen. The noise woke the remaining six guests in the lodge, and they all fled like I had let loose a bucket of bedbugs. I'd rather have bedbugs, to be honest. At least I know how to eradicate bedbugs!" Reese rubs her brow like she's got a headache. "These hauntings are *ruining* my business.

494

The reviews online have been awful since this started. I used to be sold out. Now people are canceling their reservations. I've never had more vacancies."

"How many guests do you have left?"

"Just Byron Bookbinder," January answers.

"Thorn in my side," Reese mumbles. "He keeps asking to go into the Dead Room."

The Dead Room? My insides feel like lead. "Um . . . what's a Dead Room?"

The Winters exchange a dark glance. After a long pause, January says, "There's a room in the hotel that is locked. We can't get in."

"Try a key," Frank says. "Duhhhh."

"There is no key," January says, glaring at him. "We've tried to break down the door, we've tried to take it off its hinges. Mom even brought in a locksmith to make a custom key for it. It won't open."

Eliza looks at me eagerly. Her expression says, "We have to get into that room!" It's the exact opposite of what I'm thinking.

"Why call it the Dead Room?" I ask.

"Because it's a room we can't use. It's dead to us. What else would you like us to call it?" Harris asks.

"The empty room?" I say. "The extra room?"

"The vacant room, the hollow room, the unoccupied room," Eliza says.

"The unoccupied room. Because *that* rolls off the

tongue," January says sarcastically.

"This is all making me ill," Reese says.

"Ah, the nervous poops," Frank says sagely. "Eliza gets them before every test."

"Frank!" Eliza says. Her face turns lobster red.

But thankfully, the Winters aren't listening.

"Sweets," Harris says, turning to his wife, "these hauntings are causing too much stress. You haven't been sleeping. You've had migraines. These ghosts are scaring you to death! You need to step away from the lodge—"

"I can't step away, Harris. This place is my life."

January sighs heavily, like this is a fight she's heard many, many times.

"Reese, sweets, this place is unhealthy. A danger, even! Tell them about the hair incident, Reese! Tell them!"

"I'd rather tell them about the mice. That was much more terrifying."

"You must be joking," Harris says. "Nothing could be scarier than the hair."

TO ASK ABOUT THE MICE, TURN TO PAGE 76.

←→

TO ASK ABOUT THE HAIR INCIDENT,
TURN TO PAGE 197.

"FRANK," I WHISPER. "Slowly . . . grab the fire extinguisher by your right foot."

He bends over quickly, ignoring my advice to go slow. The second he lunges, the ghost runs toward us. With a wide, devilish grin, Frank pulls the pin and squeezes the handle. Thick white foam covers the ghost, and it starts coughing.

Ghosts don't breathe, so they don't cough, right?

We dart past the choking ghost, toward the window.

"Frank! Cover me!" I say.

"Got it," he says, waving the extinguisher around. "Want another taste of fire foam?" he taunts. "COME AT ME, GHOST."

"Don't egg it on!" I groan.

The window opens just as the ghost comes at Frank again. He lets the fire extinguisher loose, but it's clearly running out of foam.

"Come on!" I say, giving him a leg up through the window. There's a ledge just below—which would put us on the roof. I don't know where we're going to go from there, but we have to get out of here.

Frank crawls through, then reaches back for me. "Your turn, Carlos!" Somehow Frank is smiling as he holds out his hand. I wish I had even a tenth of Frank's bravery. I'm sure the expression on my face is one of complete terror.

I scramble headfirst toward the window. I'm halfway

outside, then I'm mostly out! Almost there! I can make it—

The ghost grabs my ankle. Cold hands, solid hands.

"HEY!" Frank says. "KEEP YOUR HANDS TO YOURSELF!" And he closes the window right on the ghost's wrists.

There's a howl of pain from the other side of the glass. But the hands let go of my ankles. Frank and I wobble across the roof, careful not to get too close to the edge. We have to get away from the attic's only window. But it's slippery up here, and with the snow and wind raging, it feels even more dangerous.

"It was Sunny, right?" I shiver. It *had* to be.

Frank shrugs.

"What, you don't think so?"

"BLOND," Frank says. "Ghost girl was blond. Sunny has black hair. How do you explain *that*, Mr. Explanations?"

"It was probably a wig," I say. "We never did see her face."

"But . . . ," Frank says thoughtfully. "She was SMALL. People can't just shrink."

"So who do you think it was?"

He pauses. "A ghost."

I gulp. "Yeah . . . that's what I'm afraid of."

For a second, I wish Eliza was here. I want someone

to convince me ghosts aren't real. "Think," I whisper. "How do we get down from here?"

"There's a window in an attic!" Frank says, like I didn't know about the window we *just* crawled through.

"Great idea, buddy, but let's keep brainstorming."

Across the roof, someone is crawling out of the attic window—the one we just came through. With the weather and the darkness, I can't see who it is from this distance. I hate to say it, but I think I'm going to have to get closer if I'm going to figure out this mystery.

Unless . . . maybe we can go back through the attic window while the ghost is out on the roof. It might be our only way to escape.

TO MOVE CLOSER TO THE GHOST,
TURN TO PAGE 134.

←——→

TO ESCAPE THROUGH THE ATTIC WINDOW,
TURN TO PAGE 491.

I LOOK AT January. "You're the ghost," I accuse her.

She doesn't say anything, which gives me my answer.

"You're not denying it!" I say.

"No," she agrees, "I'm not."

"Where are my mom, Eliza, and Frank? What happened to them?"

"Don't worry," January says. "You're about to find out."

Something clonks me over the head.

I wake up on a ski lift, next to the Las Pistas team. We're dangling a hundred feet—or more—above the ski slope, and the chairlift is *not* moving.

"What happened?" I groan.

Mom, sitting next to me, wraps her arm around me. "We got picked off one by one."

"Like boogers!" Frank explains.

"And now we're stuck up here," Eliza says, her teeth chattering loudly. "At least until the ski lift opens again."

I hate to admit it, but the trail went cold . . . literally.

CASE CLOSED.

500

I HAVE TO think quick on my feet, now that Frank messed us up with this Mr. Mouse business. And I think our best shot is trying to book a room.

"You don't have us in the system because we haven't checked in yet," I say. "We need to do that now."

"And do you have an adult with you, Misters and Miss *Mice?*" He smirks.

"How dare you!" Eliza says, in a very loud voice. Her cheeks are scarlet. "How dare you talk to us like that! Haven't you heard of the Mouse family, wealthy oil tycoons, number thirty-two on the Forbes list of the wealthiest people in the world? That's our parents. They are parking the car, but when they arrive with suitcases, they will be appalled to hear about the way you treated us. I demand to speak with your manager!"

The desk clerk's smile falters. "That won't be necessary—"

"I *demand* it," Eliza repeats.

"How about a free upgrade on your room?"

She leans over the desk. Her expression is intense— almost terrifying. "Get me your manager. Now."

"Yes, ma'am," the clerk squeaks, and he disappears into a back hallway. When he comes back, he's visibly sweating. "Follow me." He leads us down a hallway, all the while trying to apologize. "Very sorry again, ma'am. Very sorry, sirs. Here's the door. Please remember how very contrite I am." He bows as he backs away slowly.

"I REMEMBER NOTHING!" Frank shouts.

We turn into Luther's office. Luther Covington himself is sitting at a desk, rubbing his bald head. His dark eyes narrow at us as we come in.

"Miss Mouse, Mr. Mouse, Mr. Mouse, my apologies on behalf of my employee. Please take a seat." He gestures for us to sit down in the three chairs he's got across from his desk, and we obey.

"Actually, sir, we aren't the Mouse family."

"There *is* no Mouse family!" Frank cries.

Luther cocks one of his eyebrows.

"I'm Carlos Serrano, and this is Eliza and Frank Thompson. We're detectives hired by Reese Winters. We are investigating the ghost at the Sugarcrest. And we need to talk to you."

"So," Luther says with a cold smile, "she hired detectives, did she?" He squints at us. "Pint-sized detectives."

"Hey!" Frank says. "I'm *quart*-sized!"

"Not helping," Eliza whispers.

Luther smirks and leans back in his chair, like a mob boss. "Reese is scared. This is perfect! It's only a matter of time before she caves, and then the Sugarcrest Park Lodge is *mine*."

TO ASK LUTHER ABOUT HIS PLANS TO BUY THE
SUGARCREST, TURN TO PAGE 244.

←——→

TO ASK LUTHER WHY HE WAS AT
THE SUGARCREST JUST NOW,
TURN TO PAGE 183.